The Anniversary Killer

by

Stevie Shaw

Detective Constable Shelly King is young, and may have human failings; but she tries to be the best cop that she can be. When an allegation of rape comes to her ears, she has no idea of the full story which is about to emerge. Her investigations will take her to a dark place; maybe change her view of men along the way.

Starting in Greater Manchester, and soon leading to the Canary Isles, Shelly and her police colleagues find themselves on a mission. They think they have a plan that will work; to snare an offender, and keep an innocent person safely protected. However, things don't always go according to plan. It might be wise not to take anything for granted...

The Anniversary Killer

Chapter 1

July 2008.

Samantha slid open the glass doors of the hotel bedroom, and stepped out onto the cool stone floor of the balcony; closely followed by her new husband. Already eleven days into their marriage, and with a ten-day tan to show for it; they had lost themselves in the luxury of a Canarian hotel, but would soon be flying back from Fuerteventura to the UK.

In a couple of days, they would plough all their energies back into 'BeSecure', the company that they had worked so hard to develop. With her skills as a manager, administrator, and customer services face, and his as a locksmith and general engineer, their combined efforts had seen BeSecure established in York. They were becoming well-known in the area, and had plenty of orders on the books. It certainly hadn't come easy; long days, weekend call-outs, endless hours promoting their new enterprise, and chasing tardy payers. They both felt that they deserved this long-awaited honeymoon and downtime.

Leaning against the cool white wall of the balcony, which came almost up to her neck, for privacy; Samantha brushed back her long blonde hair, and murmured:

"Let's go to the *Cabra Brava*, tonight; I loved it there. It would be nice, for our last night."

Her groom nodded, and snuggled up behind her; wrapping his arms around her naked body, protectively.

"Just a real lazy day, today, I think." Continued Samantha. "By the pool. Hmm, it's almost brunch time already."

"That's fine." He agreed. "I'll take another walk over the dunes this afternoon, get my exercise; but you can relax in the sun all day. Top up that tan of yours... it's looking good."

He caressed Samantha's shoulders, and stroked softly down her arms, as they looked up to the cloudless sky. It certainly looked like there would be sun, all day; as there had been for most of their honeymoon.

Back in the bedroom, Samantha began to get dressed, slowly; watched admiringly by her attentive husband. He was sat on the bed, and stroked her legs gently, as she stood in front of him, in her underwear. She smiled down at him. Blissfully happy that, after their three-year engagement, they had finally tied the knot.

After brunch, and a short spell browsing around the hotel's shop to look at potential souvenirs, Samantha made for the pool. Her husband donned his walking boots, and set off; complete with sunglasses, sunhat, and a shoulder bag with a bottle of water, sun-cream, a camera, and a couple of other items.

The fringe of the dunes was barely a ten-minute walk away from the hotel; and would-be explorers soon lost themselves in the wild-ness of the scrubland. The clusters of dry bushes and rocky paths dotted with yellow lichen took the groom away from his bride, and the rest of civilisation.

A further five-minute stroll under the hot sun, and he became aware that he was not alone. A man, shaded by a tattered hat, was sat on a rock, as if waiting for company; and waved him over.

Chapter 2

Five months later.

"Are you in tomorrow, Adora?"

Adora looked up from the bar table that she was cleaning, on the edge of the terrace of *La Cabra Brava*, in the resort of Corralejo, at the northern tip of Fuerteventura. She mopped her brow,

"I'm always in. Well, it feels like it."

"Well, I'll see you tomorrow. Goodnight." With that, Marco picked up his jacket, and left.

"Goodnight, Marco."

Adora was just about finished; and took a few items of cutlery through to the kitchen, before gathering up her bag, and long, flowing scarf. She was short of stature, and the scarf was almost as long as her. She wore it most days; a present from her husband, Louis. A constant reminder of him.

Passing the printed, but slightly fading, picture of her husband which was sellotaped to the wall, she leaned in and gave him a faint kiss. With a resigned sigh, she opened her mouth to say something to him; but, changed her mind, stroked his face, and set off to walk home.

The lights of the main street were bright. Although the shops had now closed, and most of the restaurants, too; there was still the sound of plenty of activity coming from the street-side bars. Adora glanced in *Sixties*, and gave a friendly wave to a customer who had dined in *La Cabra Brava*, earlier that evening. He waved back, and stood up, placing his empty beer glass on the high shelf, just beside the unused pool table.

"All done?" He called, with a smile. "You work a long shift."

Adora paused, as he seemed to be coming over to speak with her. Her wave had been out of politeness to a customer, not particularly looking for a chat. She wanted to get home.

"Yes, I'm done, at last. Home time."

The man stepped down from the terrace of *Sixties*, and joined her on the pavement.

"You don't know where *El Toro Blanco* is, do you? I said I'd meet up with my wife there, but I'm not sure where it is?"

Adora knew *El Toro Blanco* bar well.

"Yes, of course." She was off duty, but happy to help. "It's just this way. I'm going that way, myself. I'll show you."

"Oh, thanks."

He fell in step, beside her, and the two of them walked off the main high street, round past a small hotel complex, and turned right towards what looked like a private, residential urbanisation.

Fifty metres further on, they came to a low black metal gate, which was open; despite the sign instructing people to keep it closed. Adora pointed across the road.

"Just over there."

"Oh, that's great. Thank you very much. See you again."

He turned, and crossed the road with a single glance backwards, as Adora entered her housing complex and pulled the gate shut after herself, with a clang. Low-level white floodlights, set on the ground, picked out the eerie shadows of plants and trees against the white walls of the first row of apartment buildings. She followed the uneven path across the rather dark, cactus-strewn garden; and out of sight around the back of some two-storey properties, close to the swimming pool, which was now empty and closed.

Pulling out her small leather purse, and extracting her door key, she waited for the motion-sensitive light over her front door to bathe the area in a flood of light. As it did so, she inserted the key, opened the door, and stepped inside; pulling the door closed behind her.

Adora flicked on the light, and saw the face of Louis, smiling down at her. Alas, it was only his picture; hanging on the wall in the hallway, to greet her as it always did. She looked at it sadly.

"Oh, my darling. Where are you?" She murmured.

Depositing her bag on the dining table, as she entered the open-plan lounge; Adora unwrapped the scarf from her neck, and draped it casually over a coat hook on the wall, as she always did. Then, she immediately pulled up her waitress' uniform-black top over her head, and cast it into the washing basket as she stepped into the bathroom. She pulled down her black pants, and dropped them into the washing pile, too. She was just reaching for the shower tap, when a noise at the door caught her attention. She had barely heard it, but it sounded like somebody knocking, quietly.

Unlikely to be her mum, thought Adora. Her daughter, Natalia, was staying with Grandma, tonight, just a few blocks away; as she often did when Adora worked a late shift. Or, perhaps it was. Sometimes, if Natalia couldn't settle, Grandma would bring her home; knowing that Adora would be home just about now.

Adora pulled a large and fluffy blue towel round herself, and stepped back to the front door, which she opened wide.

Crash! With a massive force, once opened, the door was thrust into Adora's face, sending her petite body sprawling backwards. Before she could even think about questioning, protesting, screaming… Adora felt the pain of a man, much bigger than her, shoving all of his weight on top of her, and jamming his hand tightly over her mouth.

Almost as fast, he used one hand to push himself up from the floor, dragging her up with him so that he could shut the door. It slammed, and she was alone with him, inside her flat.

8

There was silence, and time stood still. Nothing in Adora's world moved. The man pushed her against the wall, and stood there, holding her mouth; then slowly drew up his other hand in front of her face, to show her that he was brandishing a large, evil-looking, knife. With both trembling hands, she clasped the towel as tightly as she could, around her body.

She gasped.

"Please, don't hurt me."

Her terrified eyes looked into his face. Adora knew this man... knew that he was the British customer whom she had spoken with, walked along the street with, only minutes earlier.

He pushed his face up close against hers; his eyes piercing deep into her own.

"Ok, now in a moment I'm going to release your mouth. And, you're not going to scream, are you?"

He held the knife to her throat, to reinforce the wisdom of remaining quiet. The fingers of his other hand dug ferociously into her face, at the side of her mouth.

Adora shook her head, frantically.

"Let's go through there."

The man led her from the hallway, and into the lounge; then, turned back, and looked at the door of what might be a bedroom. He kicked it open, and ushered her firmly inside. His groping hand located the light switch, and flicked it on.

Adora was still clutching the towel, covering her modesty as best she could; but fearing what might follow.

"Now, before I let go of your mouth, I'll just explain something. I know you have a daughter. Natalia, isn't it?"

Too scared to speak, and unable to, anyway, because of his hand over her mouth, she nodded.

9

"Well, if you do everything that I tell you, like a good girl, no harm will come to Natalia. Got it?"

She nodded again.

"But, if you try anything ..."

He raised the knife again, and touched it lightly against her cheek, teasing the blade across her face, close to one of her eyes.

"It won't be just you who gets sliced up." He sniggered, as if he had just thought up the expression 'sliced up', and it amused him.

"No, if you give me any trouble, I'll do what I want to you, and then, later, I'll come back for little Natalia. Why, she's a pretty little thing." He added, seeing a picture of a very young, dark-haired girl, placed on a bedside table.

He looked more closely at the picture. The little girl was sat on a sofa, dressed up in her finest, as if at some party – perhaps her birthday. Next to her, and looking proudly on, was a man. No doubt, her father.

"She won't be seeing him again." He grunted, and made as if to spit at the picture. "Cowardly vermin that he was. Cried like a child, begged..."

Then, as if to bring himself back to the moment, he sought confirmation, again:

"I'm going to release your mouth, okay?"

Slowly, he drew his hand back; hesitantly, ready to grab her again, if she made a forbidden sound.

"Now, here's how it's going to be. I'm going to give you a lot of pleasure... you'll enjoy it more if you relax. It will be better than that filthy pervert ever gave you. We're going to have fun."

He smiled. Adora trembled.

"I may be with you for up to an hour. But, then, you'll never see me again. Well, you won't see me again so long as you stick to the promise that you're going to make."

Adora clutched the fluffy towel even more tightly around her body; wishing that she had not taken off her outer clothes as soon as she had entered her home.

"I'm going to film what we do... I like seeing a woman enjoy herself. Think of yourself as a movie star. You are going to show the camera that you are enjoying every second of it. You smile, you touch me lovingly, you beg me to keep on doing what I'm doing. Not a hint of looking unhappy. Got it?"

She said nothing, as he pulled a phone from his pocket, and proceeded to activate the camera.

"Or, if we don't get a good movie, we might have to try again, and keep trying, until we do. Get it now?"

She nodded, and mouthed almost silently, through quivering lips: "Yes."

"And, provided I go away happy with what I see, I won't be back. Neither of us will see each other again. Oh, that's such a shame, isn't it?"

He grinned, and tickled the knife gently across her face, once more.

"Of course, if you decide to report any of this, or tell a soul, remember that I will have evidence that you and I had consensual sex. You begged me for it. The whole world can watch the movie, and see. Why, with your husband gone, you must be gagging for it. And me, well... I'm only human."

Adora's body shook.

"And then there's Natalia." He continued. "Your little girl. I'm sure you wouldn't want any harm to come to her, would you?"

She shook her head.

"So, do we understand each other? You're going to do absolutely everything that I say, and you're going to do it with a smile on your face."

11

The man stood back against the bedroom door, which was now closed, and looked at Adora.

"Lose the towel." He said.

Still trembling, Adora relaxed her grip on her comforting blue towel, and allowed it to fall towards her waist.

"Stand up." He commanded.

Adora stood, still holding the towel. A gesture of his hand told her to cast the towel aside, which she did, shaking with terror. He admired her lean body; tanned, smooth, in the snug matching black bra and knickers. He stepped over to the dresser, close to the bedroom door, and brushed some items from the surface; watching them crash to the floor. Then, he rested his phone carefully against a small flower vase; taking care to position it so that the viewing range covered the whole length of Adora's bed.

"Okay, the filming starts now; so, from this moment, you need to smile. If you speak to me, you call me 'Darling'. Do you understand? I should write these instructions down. Must be simpler." He muttered to himself.

"First, you can do a strip, for me. Well, for the camera. For anybody who might one day see this film, if you speak out."

Under his direction, responding to his signals, Adora slowly unfastened her bra, turned her back to the camera, gradually rotated back into a frontal view, and let it fall to the ground. Out of sight of the camera, he mouthed his appreciation – she was doing a good job – but, remember to smile.

Then, she put her hands to her knickers, and – not too fast, he reminded her – allowed them to drop to the ground. Around, she twirled; before lying on her back on the bed, and softly stroking her breasts with her fingers.

Soon, her attacker came into the picture. Having stripped, he lay on top of her; reminding her, with constant whispers, to sustain the pretence of enjoyment.

"Natalia." He whispered, as his tongue licked Adora's ear.

12

For more than half an hour, Adora endured the pain, fear, anguish and humiliation. From behind, then on her back with her legs held over her head, then with Adora on top, then he forced her to perform oral sex, snatching at her tightly by her hair. There seemed no end to the depraved demands of this monster. Only when he was sexually satisfied, did the man cast her down, like the dirty scrap of rubbish that she now felt herself to be.

As he dressed, having examined his film and turned off the camera with a satisfied smirk; Adora whimpered to herself, with tears rolling down her cheeks.

"You can have your towel back, now." He said; offering it to her as if in a gesture of kindness.

She snatched it up, and pulled it around herself.

"So, you know what will happen if you try to report any of this."

The man had said it several times; but seemed to need to reassure himself, as much as to restate the threat to Adora.

"So, we won't be seeing each other again, will we? You don't come after me, and there's no need for anyone to see what a little tiger you are in bed." He smirked.

"And, of course, little Natalia should be safe. I wouldn't want to have to do to her what I did to you. Although ..."

He left the thought hanging in the air, just in case any further threat was necessary.

"Don't leave your home again, tonight. I'll be watching. Okay?"

Adora nodded.

Seconds later, she heard the click of the front door, as he shut it behind himself. She leaned over the edge of her bed, grasping onto the mattress for support; and violently vomited on the floor.

13

Chapter 3

Eight years later – Friday 12th August 2016.

Ping.

Shelly looked down from her computer screen at her phone, sat on her desk. She picked it up to read the text message that had just come.

"Shit." She muttered.

Above the rabble of working officers in a Greater Manchester Police investigation room, nobody heard, or cared.

Shelly King was a popular young officer. At twenty-seven, she seemed to have a good future ahead of herself in the force. Being a police officer was all she had ever wanted to do. There was no family history of policing. No ex-policeman father whose footsteps had to be followed in to make him proud. Shelly's father was a joiner; and he would have been proud of his daughter whatever she decided to do with her life.

Shelly was considered a rare breed among her colleagues. Naturally attractive, with quite short blonde hair, and a fit, wiry body. The less noble of the men regarded her as a lesbian. This was a common enough attribution in the force; for any attractive young female who didn't succumb to their irresistible charms, or give any indication of wanting to sleep their way up through the ranks.

In fact, Shelly didn't think of herself as a lesbian. She merely had no intention of letting sex get in the way of her devotion to her vocation. More than this, she did nothing to discourage or dispel the rumour. If it acted in some way to repel unwanted attention in the workplace, then that suited her just fine. She had once made a comment that she later regretted. It had seemed wittily flippant at the time, just casual banter. But the words she had used were:

'Of course, I'm not a lesbian. Exclusively.'

14

It had brought a laugh from her colleagues in that moment, down the pub. But, later, she wished she had never tried to counter any insinuations about her sexuality through the use of ill-chosen humour.

Shelly was simply determined to be the best police officer she could possibly be. Not ambitious for promotion, or glory, or recognition among her peers. Just because it was the right thing to do. And, because she believed that she was darned good at it.

It had been a long day for Shelly; the twelfth of August 2016. 'The glorious twelfth'. The day felt nothing like glorious. It was seven fifteen, and Shelly was approaching the end of a rather tedious shift; so, she would be glad to get out of the place and go home to relax. It was Friday, although Shelly's shift pattern didn't really recognise the concept of a 'weekend'.

Trawling through old files, looking for connections between known felons and 'dubious characters' could be fascinating; but there was a time to draw the line. Their recent investigation into a gang of heartless shits who had been targeting widows, to relieve them of the burden of their savings, was all but complete. Shelly's DI was already celebrating, and congratulating his team on a job well done. The CPS were happy with the fraud charges, and it was just about time to move onto the next project. Shelly had found more than enough in her research to tie together that loose cluster of undesirables. They would be doing serious prison time; of that there was little doubt. So, Shelly was ready enough to sign off for the night.

But, the reason for her complaint, upon spotting the text, was because it meant she would need to make one more house call, before going home.

Three weeks ago, she had visited and interviewed a woman called Mariana Navarro. It had been in connection with the frauds. Mariana had been duped by two women, and been on the point of losing a considerable sum to them. However, she had somehow managed to stop herself from taking that final step of commitment; smelling two rats, just in time. Her evidence had been important to Shelly, who had been greatly impressed by the woman's astuteness. However, useful and adequate though it had been, Shelly still had the feeling that Mariana was holding something back. Intuition told her that there was something more … something really important that she wanted to say, but couldn't quite bring herself to put into words.

15

Now, Mariana had sent Shelly a message, asking her to come and see her as soon as possible. Shelly sighed, and thought about her flat, and the bottle of cool white wine waiting in the fridge. But, she was a professional.

"Boss?" She called across to a nearby desk.

"Yes?" DI Lloyd Williams looked up from a file of papers that he was ordering into a folder.

"I'm going to get off. I just got a message from Mariana Navarro. The Spanish woman in Tyldesley? You remember speaking to her, with me? She wants to see me."

"Yes, course. What does she want?"

"Don't know. But I'll call and see her on the way home."

Lloyd nodded: "Ok. Want me to come along?"

Shelly shook her head: "No, it's fine."

She stopped short of adding that, if Mariana had something extra to add to her statement, the words might flow more freely if the conversation was just between the two women. Not that Lloyd Williams was threatening, hard, unable to encourage her ... but, he was, well ... a man.

"I'll let you know in the morning, if there's anything we need to add to the case file."

"Ok, well get straight onto it. I want this done and dusted tomorrow, if possible. Monday, at the latest."

Shelly logged off, picked up her bag, and slid her white jacket from the back of her chair. She slipped it on, over the snug black t-shirt.

"See you tomorrow, Boss."

She made for the door.

"I'll be here, unfortunately."

DI Williams waved her away, and resumed doing battle with his paperwork.

16

Chapter 4

Fifty minutes later, Shelly drew up outside the small block of flats where Mariana lived, and was glad to find a space right outside. Although it was still light, she could see Mariana's curtains at the first-floor window were drawn, and a light glowed dimly through a gap. She flicked the alarm on her car, and the beeping noise brought a movement from the curtains, as Mariana peered out.

Shelly waved, and Mariana acknowledged with a raised hand, as she pulled the curtains back into place. The front door of the block buzzed, as soon as Shelly approached it, and she was able to go straight up the dingy concrete staircase, to flat 2A. The door opened, and Mariana looked out.

"Come in. Thanks for coming."

"That's ok." Shelly replied.

She said nothing further yet, but she could see that Mariana had been crying. Police officers are not social workers. But, Shelly was by nature very kind and caring. She had quite taken to Mariana, on the three occasions that she had met her; and, knowing something of her background, was impressed by her strength and courage. She knew Mariana wasn't a woman to cry for nothing. Shelly chided herself momentarily, for not having taken a quick look back at the notes. However, she remembered the main points.

Mariana was a Spanish woman in her mid-forties, who had lived in the UK for many years. She had come here from Spain with her new husband, Vito, in 2005, and gone to live in North Yorkshire. They had worked hard, trying to create a good life for themselves. They had a daughter, Izzy, born in 2012; and everything looked good for them.

However, in 2014, Mariana's world fell apart. Her husband was found dead, in mysterious circumstances. Having disappeared suddenly, and then not been seen for over a week, his body was found in a lake, in Cumbria. Mariana, understandably, was shocked beyond measure, and totally distraught. The only thing that kept her going was their beautiful little daughter, Izzy.

The police 'did what they could'... but no murderer was ever found. In fact, based on the evidence, it could not even be concluded that Vito *had* been murdered. His death was officially 'unexplained'; much to the anger of Mariana. Any suggestions that perhaps Vito had been depressed, and taken his own life, were immediately dismissed by her. Mariana's opinion of the police became 'low', to say the least.

She continued to live in North Yorkshire, with her daughter, for almost a year afterwards. Then, suddenly, she pulled Izzy out of school, came to the north west, and found a property on the fringes of Greater Manchester.

"Please. Sit down." Mariana gestured to a chair.

Shelly sat, and Mariana put a cup of tea into her hands, which she had already prepared. Looking round, Shelly saw some birthday cards on display. Clearly, it had recently been Izzy's birthday, as announced by the pink number four on some of the cards. There was a tidy line of little plastic ponies – my little ponies – proudly standing to attention on the window sill, with two young and colourful princesses stood behind the string. On the coffee table in the centre of the room, stood a wine bottle and a glass. The glass had been used, but both were empty.

"You're upset, Mariana. What is it?" Shelly asked.

Mariana looked at the floor, then cast an anxious glance over to a door, which was her daughter's bedroom. She walked across to the door, looked in, then withdrew and closed the door to leave her daughter to sleep.

"I... I don't know who else to talk to."

Her voice was close to failing her. She sat down, and dabbed a tissue to her nose. A tear rolled down her cheek. She brushed back her hair from her face.

Shelly was a patient young woman, and waited, without interrupting. If Mariana needed time, she could have it. However, almost a minute passed, without a word; so Shelly felt bound to try and move things along.

18

"You want to tell me something, I think."

She leaned over, and put her hand gently on Mariana's arm.

"Whatever it is, I'll try and help. Is it about the fraudsters?"

Mariana instantly shook her head.

"No, it's nothing to do with that."

She looked Shelly fully in the face.

"You're a good person. When you came here and started asking me questions about the fraud, I knew I could trust you."

She sniffed.

"And that's not easy, I promise you. Not after my previous experience with the police."

Shelly knew that she was referring to the investigation into her husband's death. Sympathetically, she nodded.

"I know. You've had an awful time. I'm sorry we couldn't help more."

The term 'we' meant the police in general. Shelly had not had any involvement in the case of Vito's death; that had been a different force, altogether. But, she had listened to Mariana, who had poured out a lot of pent-up anger at the first of their meetings. She had even gone back to the office and looked up the case; although she had never mentioned this to Mariana, for fear of raking up old wounds even more.

Mariana composed herself.

"You were good enough to come here, at..." She glanced over at a clock on the wall, and was surprised at the time.

"Oh, I'm sorry; I expect you were on your way home. Friday night, too."

Shelly reassured her:

"That's ok. I told you that you could call me anytime. What is it that's upset you so much?"

19

Mariana took a deep breath, before attempting to explain.

"Ok. Well, you remember when you came to interview me, and I got upset because I … well, you know, I always thought the police should have done more to investigate what happened to Vito?"

She paused for breath.

"I remember, of course. You had every right to be upset."

"Hmm. Well, anyway, at the time, you and your boss, Mr … er … Williams? The Welsh man?"

Shelly nodded:

"Yes, DI Williams."

Mariana continued:

"Yes, DI Williams. Well, you both told me that the police can only investigate so much. There has to come a point where you have to record the facts as you have them, but then take a step back. You can't investigate everything to the ultimate degree. You remember?"

Shelly was puzzled, but she did remember that conversation.

"Yes, I remember us saying something like that."

"Well…" Continued Mariana: "I want to know whether it works the other way round. If I tell you something … If you are told something … but I don't want to press it further, don't want to press any charges … will you still look at what you're told?"

Shelly's wrinkled face showed that she didn't fully understand; but she tried to give Mariana a sensible answer anyway:

"Of course, we'll always listen to what we're told. But, even if we're told something in confidence, I can't promise you that it won't go further. In some circumstances, if a crime has been committed, or someone is about to commit a crime, or is in danger …"

Mariana waved a hand to stop her.

20

"Yes, I understand that. I know you can't promise to keep something to yourself. But what I mean is this: if I'm the … aggrieved party … if a crime has been committed against me … can you promise not to make it public if I tell you right now that I don't want to prosecute?"

Shelly was becoming confused, and anxious for Mariana.

"Mariana, if someone has hurt you, or threatened you, we'll do our best to protect you. If you're afraid of reprisals for giving evidence against someone …"

Mariana leaned back in her chair, and sighed. Finally, she plucked up the courage to go on. In a quiet voice; guilty, ashamed, she said:

"I was assaulted."

Shelly didn't interrupt, so Mariana continued:

"I was raped. Twenty-eighth of May, last year."

Shelly gasped. Quickly composing herself, she remembered the protocol.

"Ok Mariana. Maybe it's best if we go together to speak with colleagues of mine, who have experience at supporting women in this position. We can …"

Shelly got no further.

"No, there's no need for that. Not at the moment. It was fifteen months ago. I'm not going to give you a statement so that you can bring charges against him for what he did to me. That's not why I'm telling you."

She looked Shelly in the eye.

"Ok, I can't deny that I think about it every day, and maybe I am still traumatised by it, and maybe I should be counselled by a trained professional … but that's not what this is about. There's more than I've told you, a lot more. I've always distrusted the police, since … but I trust *you*, Shelly. If you'll listen, I'll tell you the whole story. Then, you can do what you want with the information. But, I'm not bringing charges against him for what he did to me."

Shelly nodded.

Mariana continued:

"And, before you ask, please don't record this conversation. Just listen to me. Please."

Shelly nodded again, and reluctantly confirmed:

"Ok, if that's what you want."

Mariana began an account, and Shelly listened carefully.

"Vito died in July 2014. They found his body at the end of July. They said he'd been dead about a week."

She paused, and wiped her eye.

"The police 'did what they could'; but, there wasn't enough evidence to launch a nationwide manhunt to find a killer, even though I knew in my heart that he was murdered."

Mariana took a sip of her tea, before resuming.

"But, you know all that, of course. You read it in the police files, and I went over it all again when you met me for the first time."

Shelly agreed: "Yes, that's pretty much as I recall it."

Mariana continued her tale.

"But, then something else happened to me. On the twenty-eighth of May, a man broke into my house during the night. He was wearing a balaclava mask. He had a knife."

Her eyes glazed over a little, as she recalled the fateful night.

"He knew that I was alone; that I'd been widowed. Knew I was Spanish, before I even said a word. He knew that Izzy was asleep in her bedroom. He made sure that I knew he was well aware of my little girl, not yet three, sleeping a few metres away."

Shelly tried hard not to show her shock.

22

"Go on, you're doing great." Shelly encouraged.

"Well, he was holding Izzy over me, like a threat. He said that, if I didn't do exactly as he said, he'd take Izzy instead of me. As well as me, in fact. He knew that I wouldn't sacrifice my little girl, to save myself."

At this point, Mariana's voice started to waver. Brave though she was, she needed a moment to compose herself. Then, she went on:

"He had a set of instructions, on a sheet of card. He told me to read them, very carefully. He knew exactly what he wanted me to do. And how to get me to do it. He kept on saying Izzy's name ... as if I was likely to forget."

Mariana sniffed back another tear, before carrying on:

"And, what's more, he filmed everything that he did to me. On his phone. He raped me, right there in my own bedroom. He said – his instructions said – that I had to make sure that on the movie I looked like I was enjoying myself. It had to look consensual, and enjoyable. I had to make sure that anyone who saw that sick movie would think that I was begging for it. It was his insurance policy. He knew I could never report him, or he'd post that movie on the internet for all to see. I'd be totally humiliated; and, in any case, a jury would think that I was loving it. All consensual. Nothing 'forced' about it."

By now, Shelly's hand was to her mouth, and she too felt tears in her eyes.

Mariana continued:

"And, he kept talking about Izzy. How, if I ever reported it, he would come for her. Humiliate me by posting extracts of that video online, and take Izzy, giving her the same treatment ..."

Mariana finally broke down, and she sobbed wildly. All the pain of the last two years flooded out, in Shelly's supportive arms.

"And, he would check the movie before he left, and if at any time I looked like I was resisting, or didn't want it ..."

She sobbed again, for a moment.

23

"But there's more, Shelly. There's something more that I haven't told you yet. And this is where you'll probably think I'm delusional – or paranoid – or ... I don't know what."

Shelly looked at her; hoping against hope that whatever it might be, it wouldn't be something that would undermine her capacity to believe Mariana.

Mariana continued: "It was him. I believe it was him. The man who raped me was the same man who killed Vito."

There was a silence. Then Mariana added one more thing:

"And ... He's done it before."

Shelly observed her closely, trying to take everything in. It was a moment before she spoke. Then, leaning forward, watching Mariana closely, she asked:

"So, you think that the man who raped you was responsible for your husband's death? Why do you think that?"

Mariana looked down, deflated.

"You don't believe me, do you?"

"I'm not saying that, Mariana; but what makes you think there's a connection?"

Mariana looked sullen.

"For a long time, I couldn't think straight. Although every day and every night the memory of what he did to me was in my head, I just couldn't understand. Then, finally, some of the things that he said started to make sense."

Shelly took hold of Mariana's hands, and squeezed them.

"Slow down, just a little, if you can. Let's go back to some things ... deal with them one at a time."

Mariana looked up, hopefully, and nodded her head.

"You said 'He's done it before'. What exactly did you mean by that? What has he done before?"

Mariana brushed back a strand of her long dark hair, that had fallen across her face, and explained what she meant.

"All of it. He's come after widows before, or at least women on their own with children. He knew exactly what he was doing. It was just like a film script. The instructions on the card … it was like they always have to be followed."

"What did the card say, can you remember?"

Mariana paused for only a second, before replying. The words were indelibly stamped in her memory, and she recounted exactly what she had seen:

"Be pro-active. Look happy at all times. Imagine I'm your Spanish husband. Love me passionately. Think of your little girl / boy. This will take one hour; then if you get it right, you'll never see me again. If you get it wrong, you may never see your child again, but the world will see you."

Shelly gasped. Then the two sat, in silence, for a few moments. Finally, Mariana spoke.

"Every word. I know every word. I read that card over and over again. While he was doing what he did to me, I focused entirely on that card. Want me to read it to you again?"

Shelly was almost too emotional to continue the conversation. However, she knew that she had to be strong. Strong for both of them.

"Mariana, what you've told me, is … I can't begin to understand how horrific it must have been for you."

"Still is." Said Mariana, absently.

"Yes, still is, of course." Shelly agreed. "But … you said at the start that you don't want to try and bring charges against this man."

Mariana shook her head:

"No, I'm not wanting you to go find him and charge him for what he did to me. I've survived this. Well, I am surviving it."

Shelly stroked her hand, and squeezed it again.

Gently, she asked: "What do you want me to do with what you've told me? You know I can't keep everything to myself, don't you?"

"Yes, I know that. But what I want is … that, maybe with the information I've given you, you can stop him doing this to anybody else. I don't know how. But, maybe it will help?"

Mariana's pleading eyes looked at the young detective hopefully, desperately.

Shelly planned her words carefully: "Ok Mariana, you know that I can't make any promises. But, we owe it to you to try and support you in whatever way we can. But, in order for us to be able to do that, you're going to need to give us a formal statement that we can work from. I know you wanted to speak with me first, and I'm glad that you did. So that I can take this forward, and maybe, just maybe, stop it happening to anybody else, I'll need you to give me something formal. Can you do that, Mariana?"

Mariana sighed.

"I was dreading telling anyone. For fifteen months, I've kept it inside. For most of that time, I thought it was all about me. That I deserved it."

She shook with emotion, and more tears trickled down her face. Shelly moved closer and gave her a strong, comforting hug.

"You didn't deserve it. You've done nothing wrong. All you've done is look after your daughter, without your husband. None of this is your fault."

When she released the embrace, Mariana looked up at her, and a steely determination had replaced the weak and tearful expression on her face.

"I *will* do it." She said. "I'll give a full statement. But, I want you to be there. Will you be there?"

"Yes, course I will." Promised Shelly.

Chapter 5

Sleep evaded Shelly. Throughout the restless night, tossing and turning alone in her bed, she could think of nothing but what Mariana had told her. Finally, around five, she got up and went to the window. Casting the curtains aside, and looking out from her third-floor window, she saw a milk float passing along the narrow side street that led to the back of the shopping precinct. She wondered whether Mariana was also looking out of her window; scared, dreading what she might see. Like she had probably done every day for the last fifteen months.

Shelly cast off her t-shirt, and went into the bathroom to take a shower. As the water flowed down her, she thought about how to give her boss the news that a major case may have just presented itself to her. Would she be allowed to work it? Or would he instruct her to hand it over to another team? She would do her best.

Arriving at work just before seven, Shelly set about her preparations. She had already written up the gist of the previous night's conversation with Mariana; whom she had promised to call this morning, to discuss arrangements for her statement.

The office wouldn't be fully staffed today, but she wasn't alone for long. Lloyd Williams was also in early, and greeted his young DC warmly, in the soft Welsh accent that she so liked to hear. There was something always reassuringly calm about the DI. Shelly respected him. He was invariably confident and in control, not one to panic. A man that she would always want on her side.

"Couldn't sleep, Shelly?"

Getting straight to business, Shelly joined her boss at his desk.

"Last night, I went to see Mariana Navarro."

"Yes, what did she have for you?"

"Hmm. Not what I was expecting."

Shelly's expression told Lloyd that it was serious. She launched into the tale, recounting what Mariana had said to her. Lloyd listened carefully, without interruption, until she had finished. Then, he leaned back in his chair, thoughtfully.

"And she's coming in to make a statement?"

"Yes, I'm going to call her in a bit, and go pick her up."

Shelly waited, hoping that he wouldn't tell her to hand this right over. To her relief, he didn't.

"Ok, get her in. Dawn can come in on it with you. Let's see what she's got to say, then I'll go speak to the DCI."

This was as good as Shelly could have reasonably hoped for. Dawn Pardell was a detective sergeant, and the team's most highly qualified interviewer. She was also a woman. Shelly understood why the boss wanted an experienced officer like Dawn to be in on this.

"Right, Boss. The fraud case stuff is done. I've just sent you the completed file."

"Ok. Good work, Shelly. Let's hope it stands up."

He looked over at Shelly, as she took a moment to tidy up her desk, and replace some stationery items that had become untidy. He liked his young protégé. She already had six years in the force, and two years in CID; but, by his standards, she was still a novice. Lloyd was forty-one, and had been in the force for nearly twenty years. There wasn't much that he hadn't seen, on the streets of Manchester. He was well-respected, and well-liked too, by his colleagues. He was divorced, now, as was not uncommon for police officers whose ambition dictates that they endure the stressful demands of the job, as well as the unsocial hours. He looked again at the figure of Shelly, from behind. As she turned around, he averted his gaze, and logged onto his computer.

Later that morning, Shelly, Dawn Pardell, and Mariana sat down in an interview room in the bowels of the police station. Dawn had been well-briefed by Shelly, and they had both studied the original police notes concerning Vito Navarro's disappearance and death. Mariana was

28

composed, and ready. She had waited a long time for this moment; though, in truth, she had been waiting only for herself. Waiting for the brave Mariana inside the frightened woman to say: 'I'm ready for this'.

Dawn took the lead, putting their guest at her ease, and reassuring her that *she* was in control. She was the victim here, and she could take a break, or stop the interview altogether, whenever she wished. Dawn began the formal part, by checking that she understood correctly the details about the death of Mariana's husband, confirming times and dates. The coroner had concluded that Vito died between the twenty-second and the twenty-fifth of July 2014. Then, they spoke about the months after that, when Mariana continued to live with her daughter in the town of Pickering, North Yorkshire.

Soon, they got to the date that Mariana had specifically told Shelly about, which was the twenty-eighth of May 2015.

"Talk me through that day, if you can, Mariana; starting with the moment you got up in the morning."

Dawn sat back, patiently.

Mariana glanced at Shelly, then looked directly back at Dawn, and began her account of the day.

"It was a Thursday. I took Izzy to nursery. It was just down the road. Chester Street Day Nursery. She went Tuesday, Wednesday and Thursday. While she was there, I worked a few hours in the shop. It was a little corner shop, only two minutes away from the nursery. Very handy. I did ten hours a week there."

Dawn asked for details of the address of the shop, and noted it down.

"Go on."

"Well, after I picked Izzy up, we went down to the precinct to pick up a couple of things, then we went home. Got in about half past four. Then, we had tea. Then, I did some housework, and watched television, and put Izzy to bed around a quarter to eight."

Dawn nodded, and Shelly smiled supportively.

"And did you see anyone else, neighbours perhaps; before you put Izzy to bed, or afterwards?"

Mariana shook her head.

"No. We weren't close to any of the neighbours. There was an elderly woman in the flat next door, she was nice. We had a ground-floor flat. But, she didn't come out much. I didn't see much of her."

"Ok. Izzy went to bed around seven forty-five. Was that the usual time."

"Yes."

Dawn paused, conscious that they were approaching the sensitive part of this account.

"And, what did you do for the rest of the evening?"

Mariana's voice faltered only slightly.

"I took a bath around half past eight, when I was sure Izzy had gone to sleep. Then, I watched television from nine until about half past ten. Then I went to bed."

"Ok."

The silence was waiting to be filled, as Mariana recalled the events later that night.

She had gone to sleep, as normal. The room had been dark, with just a faint sliver of light coming in through the gap in the curtains, which she always left just a few inches open.

Then, she had been awoken, abruptly, forcibly.

A figure was leaning over her, and had put his hand over her mouth. The room was dark, but as she came to consciousness she could make out that his face was covered by a mask. A hideous, all covering, balaclava mask; with just space for his mouth, and two slits for his eyes. His hand was inside a protective rubber glove.

He threw his weight right on to her, and pressed his face close to hers, peering into her eyes. She wanted to cry out; but, even if the dryness in her mouth and throat had enabled it, his hand firmly blocked the opportunity.

"Shh!" He whispered. "We don't want to wake Izzy. That would be really bad for her."

She stared into his eyes, her body tense and frozen; unable to move because of the weight of his body crushing hers, and the fear of what he would do if she tried.

Then, she saw the knife. It was a hideous looking, jagged blade. Like a dagger. Maybe eight to ten inches long. It looked like the sort of thing guerrillas and terrorists use. Perhaps she exaggerated the size, because it was up close to her face. It glinted in the light that crept in through the window. He slid it up against her throat, gently enough to leave no scar; firmly enough to show that it could slice through her neck in an instant.

"You don't need to worry." He said, still in a whisper. "Nobody else needs to die. You've already lost your husband. Filthy Spaniard that he was. But, you don't need to die. And, Izzy doesn't need to die. So long as you do as you're told, everything will be fine. Do you understand?"

She had no way of speaking, but managed to nod her head, frantically.

"She's so pretty, isn't she? I can see why Vito thought the world of her. Although, eventually, he would probably..."

He tailed off. The knife in his hand slithered along the curve of Mariana's neck, as he spoke.

Mariana didn't attempt to make any response.

She wanted to say 'Please, please don't hurt us. Take what you want, there's some money in the drawer. Please, just leave.'

But, the man's gloved left hand was still firmly across her mouth, so that she couldn't say anything at all.

"Now, I want to make sure that we understand each other."   He whispered.

"That way, Izzy is quite safe. She'll wake up in the morning, and never know anything happened."

He paused for a second, then added, with a smirking tone:

"She'll wake up in the morning. That should be enough."

He leaned his head even closer to Mariana's petrified face, and brought his eyes right up to hers; as if trying to pierce deep through into her soul.

"I'm going to let go of your mouth, soon. And when I do, you're not going to scream, are you?"

She shook her head, violently.

"You're not even going to say a word, are you?"

She shook her head again.

"Not a single sound. We don't want Izzy to be woken up, do we?"

Weakly, she shook her head again.

"Ok." He continued. "But, before I do, I want you to look at this."

Releasing her throat from the threat of the knife for a moment, his right hand stretched across and flicked on the switch of a bedside light.

"That's better! Now I can see you."

Mariana could see now that he was dressed in combat gear. Mostly dark green, flecked with black and brown. She couldn't see his shoes, or boots.

He brought up in front of her face a card, about the size of an A4 piece of paper.

"I want you to read this. It explains everything."

She dragged her terrified gaze away from his eyes, and tried to focus on the card, with a set of instructions printed on it.

'Be pro-active. Look happy at all times. Imagine I'm your Spanish husband. Love me passionately. Think of your little girl / boy. This will take one hour, then if you get it right, you'll never see me again. If you get it wrong, you may never see your child again, but the world will see you.'

He gave her a few moments to read it.

"You're going to have the best sex ever. Better than that Spanish rat could ever manage. I'll take you to places you only ever dreamed of. The only regret you'll have is that it is just this once. You're never going to see me again. Sorry about that. Is that ok?"

She was too terrified to nod, or shake her head, or even think which.

"So, I will take my hand away from your mouth. One sound, and it will be the last sound that Izzy hears from you. But it won't be the last sound that Izzy hears. You get my drift?"

Mariana nodded again.

Slowly, as if expecting a storm to rush through her lips, he loosened his hand, and gradually withdrew it from her mouth.

"Ok." He said, soothingly. "Just lie still for a moment, while I get set up. We want to be comfortable, don't we?"

She said nothing, but looked towards the bedroom door, which was closed. He had placed a bag in front of it, so that it wouldn't open in a hurry. In any case, he was at the side of the bed between her and the door. There was no escape route, even if she had thought about trying to dash away.

But, of course, she couldn't.

Izzy. The most precious thing in the world to her. Izzy was all she had. And she was all Izzy had.

Mariana was still lying in her bed, clutching the bedclothes to her chest, her hands shaking.

Having positioned his phone on the chest of drawers, pointing towards the bed, and switched on the camera to film everything in its line of sight, he seemed satisfied.

33

"There! All ready. Now, so that you don't make any mistakes, let's go through this one more time."

He lifted up the card of instructions, and held it in front of him.

"Read them out to me. Quietly."

In dismay, she looked at the card again. Her mouth moved, but no sound came out.

"Read them to me!" He ordered, sternly, but keeping his voice down.

Mariana swallowed, and in a wavering voice began to read:

"Be pro-active. Look happy at all times."

"That's right." He interrupted. "I'll be checking the movie before I leave. If I see anything on there, anything at all that says you're not having a good time, well … I shall have to go discuss it with Izzy. Go on."

Mariana read further:

"Imagine I'm your Spanish husband. Love me passionately. Think of your little girl / boy."

"Girl, in your case. Izzy. Pretty little Izzy." He interjected.

"Carry on."

Mariana continued, weakly.

"This will take one hour, then if you get it right, you'll never see me again. If you get it wrong, you may never see your child again, but the world will see you."

"All clear?" He asked, brightly.

She noticed that the knife was now in a holster, at his side.

"Well? You may speak quietly when I ask you a question, otherwise, say nothing. Understand?"

"Yes."

34

He placed the instruction card on the drawers, next to the camera, where she could see it if by any chance she should forget what was required of her.

"All right then. The camera is rolling, so start smiling."

Mariana attempted a weak smile.

He stepped close to the bed, and gently took hold of the bed-clothes. She released her grip on them, and he pulled them slowly back, to take a look at what Mariana was wearing.

She had gone to bed in a maroon coloured t-shirt, with a small flowery pattern and tiny red ribbon at the neck. His eyes moved down her body, and he looked at the black knickers that she was wearing.

Quietly, he issued her an instruction, reminding her yet again to obey it to the letter, and with a smile on her face.

Compliant, she got up off the bed, on the far side, well away from the door; and in full view of the camera. Then, slowly, she peeled up her t-shirt, and pulled it over head. He sat down on the bed, and admired her breasts.

"Stroke them." He whispered, flicking his eyes downward to them.

Slowly, she brought up her hands, and placed one on each breast; gently rubbing her hands across her nipples.

"Do a twirl."

She spun slowly round, completing three hundred and sixty degrees.

"Now, turn your back to the camera, and very slowly take off your knickers."

With her face away from the camera, Mariana briefly allowed her false smile to fade. Catching sight of him looking at the side of her face, she quickly reinstated it. With two hands, she slowly pulled her knickers down, and let them fall to the floor.

"Now, turn around."

She did as she was told, and responded to his non-verbal gesture, reminding her to put more effort into looking 'happy'.

"Now, there are so many positions, aren't there?" He mused.

"Which shall we try first?"

He lifted up his sweater, and cast it on the floor. He dropped his pants on the ground, too; and Mariana could see that he was erect, and ready for sex.

He looked at her, waiting.

"Well, what do you want to do first for the camera? Oral? Anal? Me on top? You on top? Front? Behind? What do you fancy?"

Without comment, but still managing to maintain the faintest of smiling expressions – though she didn't know how – she lay down slowly on the bed, on her back, and raised her arms up behind her head.

"You know what? First you can give me a blow job. Just to warm me up, and show that you're keen."

He pulled down his boxer shorts, and threw them across on top of his combat pants. All that he was now wearing was the fearsome balaclava mask, and the gloves.

"Don't forget Izzy." He whispered.

He clambered onto the bed, and straddled over her, pulling her up so that her face was close up against his throbbing penis. Then, he gently eased her forward, so that her mouth could close around it.

She did so, and after a gentle start, he was soon thrusting forcefully into her mouth, as deep as he could go. Tugging at her hair, to keep her in place, he made sure that she felt the strength and power of his erection.

As he pushed himself to the back of her throat, almost choking her on himself, he whispered gently to her.

"Vito was number six, you know. Would have been number seven, but 2009 was a busy year for me. Maybe I'll manage a double, one year, to catch up."

Mariana heard his words, and remembered every one; but they didn't make any sense to her, and were the lowest of her priorities at that moment.

Then, when the attacker had tired of the present position, he withdrew, and 'invited' Mariana to turn around, with her bottom towards the camera. If there could be any consolation at all in this moment of terror and subjugation, she was glad of the chance to bury her face temporarily in the pillow.

He entered her from behind, taking hold of both her arms behind her back, so that she couldn't move away. He amused himself in this way for a few minutes.

Next, he flicked Mariana round onto her back, and lifted up her legs, pulling them up to the side of her head. Then he entered her again, and forced into her with everything that he had.

"Keep smiling!" He mouthed, with his face away from the camera.

When the intruder had satisfied himself, climaxing with a blood-curdling roar, he withdrew; and quietly gave Mariana a further command.

"Lick me clean! Do it like you're loving it."

She did as she was told; now way beyond any thoughts of resistance or escape. Instead, in her head, she was counting down the time. The instructions said that this would take an hour. She wanted to look over at the clock on the wall; seeking reassurance from the slow, rhythmic ticking, which meant that everything comes to an end, eventually.

Finally, he had had enough. It looked like his sexual appetite was satiated. If only she could be sure that his desire for violence, cruelty, and humiliation were equally satisfied.

"Now, you can give me some kisses, and say thank you, and tell me how good it was, and how much you love me. Izzy!" He hissed, as a final reminder.

She wondered whether, for this final – she hoped – piece of artificiality, he was going to remove his mask. She hoped not. Prayed not. If he believed that she couldn't identify him, then, surely, that made her safer. Not that 'safe' would ever mean anything again, to her.

In front of the camera, Mariana kissed her attacker deeply, through his mask; long, slow kisses. She told him how much she loved him. Then she thanked him, for the best sex ever.

After what seemed forever, he released his grip on her – he had been holding her hair round the back of her head, out of the camera's view.

"Ok, you can get dressed again now, and go back to bed."

His whispered words had barely left his lips, when she picked up her knickers and pulled them on. She replaced her t-shirt, and sought sanctuary under the bed-clothes, as he pulled on his clothes.

With her face turned away, Mariana could see out of the corner of her eye as he went to the phone that had filmed everything, and picked it up. He stood looking at it for a few moments; evidently reviewing his work. He seemed pleased.

"Good job. You were pretty convincing. Why, anyone seeing that would be sure you had kinky tastes, and enjoyed your sex with a masked man. Thanks, Mariana."

She said nothing, for a few moments. Then:

"I did everything you asked. Please, go now. I'll never try to come after you. Just leave me and … leave me in peace."

After so many mentions of little Izzy's name, Mariana couldn't bring herself to speak of her again in this monster's presence.

"Oh, don't worry. You'll never see me again. So long as we both keep our word."

With that, he finished tying the buckle of his belt; and replaced the knife, which had been next to the phone on top of the drawers, in its scabbard. While there, he picked up a framed photograph which was displayed on top. Mariana and Vito were on a beach, just paddling in the sea. Behind them were crashing waves, and a blue sky.

"He wasn't much of a swimmer." Commented the man.

Then, he picked up the bag which blocked the doorway, and glanced round to make sure he had left nothing behind.

He opened the bedroom door, and was stepping through it; when he turned back for one last reminder. Mariana could see that he was smiling.

"Do not leave this room for five minutes, ok? Or I *will* be back. Just remember: movie, Izzy, silence."

And, with that, he closed the bedroom door behind him, and she heard his footsteps moving along the hall, towards the front door. There was a quiet click, as he pulled the front door shut behind him. He was gone.

DS Dawn Pardell and Shelly were sat, open-mouthed. Never had either of them heard such an horrific account. An assault so brutal and traumatising that it had taken Mariana well over a year to bring herself to recount it. Yet, she could remember every single detail.

And, there was so much in there. To Mariana, this was the most horrific thing that had ever happened to her; yet she had somehow managed to see that there were indications in here that this was not an isolated or random attack. It was not a one-off. She was not the only woman to have suffered at the hands of this monster.

After a minute of silence, Dawn spoke.

"He had a complete face mask. But, did you have any suspicion... even the slightest thought... that maybe you recognised him? Could he have been someone you had met, or seen, before?"

Mariana shook her head.

"No. I'm sure I've never met him before. Maybe he had seen me. Been watching me, even. But, I don't know him."

Dawn nodded, accepting this.

"I think we'll take a break there. Is that ok with you, Mariana?"

"Yes."

Chapter 6

Grim faced, Shelly followed Dawn along the corridor towards the team's principal investigation room. Pushing open the glass door, they saw DI Williams, just popping a laptop into its case. He looked up as they entered, and knew instantly from their shocked and deathly expressions that there must be something serious going on.

"What?" He asked, as they approached.

"Can we have a word, Boss?"

They stepped straight into his private office, which was used only for the most confidential of matters. Lloyd preferred to work in the main room, with his team, whenever possible. Shelly closed the door, behind them; as a few of their colleagues followed the trio with enquiring eyes.

Ten minutes later, they emerged. Lloyd picked up his jacket, and followed them back to where Mariana was being kept company by a very young-looking WPC.

"Thanks, Tina."

Dawn released the girl from her minding duties, and closed the door after her.

"You remember DI Williams?" Shelly asked, knowing the answer.

Mariana mustered a polite smile for him.

They all sat down, and Lloyd sensitively asked Dawn to take the lead.

"Ok, Mariana. We've had a brief chat with DI Williams. We're not going to ask you to go through all that you've told us again, today. Heaven only knows how painful it must have been for you. But, for now, we just want you to know that we take all this very seriously. There was such a lot in what you said … we need to have a think about how to take this forward."

Shelly interjected:

"Mariana, because there's so much, we will almost certainly need to ask you some more questions; just to clarify a few things. Will that be ok, if I keep in close contact with you?"

Mariana nodded.

It was DI Williams' turn. In a soft voice, he said:

"You did the right thing in coming forward. It was very brave of you. And, just because quite some time has elapsed, that doesn't mean we take things any less seriously. I promise you we'll investigate all this thoroughly. We'll keep you as fully informed as we can, right through this."

Both Dawn and Shelly glanced at their boss; impressed by such sensitivity.

He continued:

"Is there anything you'd like to ask us, now?"

Mariana had a question ready.

"Can you make sure no police in uniform come to my house? If he's watching me, I don't want to give him any reason ..."

She sighed.

Shelly took it upon herself to reply.

"Mariana, you moved away from the town where you lived. I'm sure he won't have a clue where you are."

Mariana looked back at her.

"But, he knew me, didn't he? He knew my name, knew all about Vito. Knew Izzy. What if he's someone who still knows me, even though I don't know him?"

Shelly bit her lip. Yes, Mariana was right. She realised that, if she was in this poor woman's position, she would probably feel every bit as insecure and anxious.

DI Williams intervened.

"How about we get someone along to fit some extra security for you? Just for reassurance, although I agree with DC King, there's almost certainly nothing to worry about. It might help you rest a little easier."

"Thank you, yes. I'd appreciate that."

Lloyd continued:

"Just before you go, can I ask a couple of basic things?"

Mariana nodded.

"You're Spanish, clearly. But your English is impeccable. How long have you lived here?"

She smiled.

"I was born in Spain, but my parents moved over here when I was four. I lived here until I was nearly thirteen, then we moved back to Spain. My English, then, was better than my Spanish. I came back here again after I got married."

"Ah, I see. And, do you have any family here in the UK?"

"No." She said. "I don't. Apart from Izzy."

Dawn picked up some papers from the table in front of her, with an air of finality.

"Ok. That's all. Let's leave it for today, shall we? You'll be wanting to pick your daughter up?"

"Yes, I must."

Chapter 7

An hour later, it was a sombre looking DI Williams who continued to look at his computer screen, as Shelly and Dawn entered his office. Shelly closed the door, and they sat down. Lloyd effected a final click, then swivelled back in his chair, to face his officers.

"Ok. Think text-book, Shelly. Think of this as a training exercise, to support your career development. If you were running the show, what would be your first step, here?"

Shelly was surprised. She knew, of course, that she wouldn't be 'running the show'. But, this was a good opportunity for her to show her professionalism, and a great way to focus the mind.

"What resources have I got?"

Her boss smiled slightly.

"Tell me what you plan to do, and I'll tell you whether you get the resources."

"Ok."

She thought for a moment, and glanced across at Dawn, before making her pitch.

"First, I'd thoroughly check the background. Hers, and her husband's, and his death."

"Yes?"

"And then, I'd get a psychologist in; to help analyse everything that Mariana's told us. There's such a lot in there. It's a stretch to take everything at face value."

She continued, almost apologetically:

"I like her. I want to believe her. But, she lost her husband in tragic circumstances. That much, we know. If we believe the basics of her report

44

of being raped, well … it's a stretch to believe all the details. Her husband's killer? He's done it before? She's traumatised. We need a professional opinion about how much, if any, of her statement is … emotionally compromised."

Lloyd nodded, approvingly.

"Go on."

"Then, we take into account his or her view, and we scrutinise every bit of what Mariana said. On the face of it, it's possible that we are looking at a serial rapist. So, we cross-check everything she's told us about him against the database. We look for cases with any similarity. And, despite what she believes, we don't rule out that this could be someone known to her."

"Very good. Anything else?"

Shelly sniffed.

"We look after her. We make sure that the police don't let her down."

Lloyd shifted his chair.

"Dawn. Your view of Mariana's statement, please."

Dawn pushed up her glasses from her eyes, to rest them on her blonde hair, that was now showing streaks of silver.

"Ok. A number of elements. One, she is certainly traumatised, as Shelly says. Whether that's through the alleged rape, or the loss of her husband, or our recent inquiries about the fraud that nearly caught her out, or something else … I don't know."

Lloyd nodded again.

"Two, we need to have a conversation with social services, about the child. She could be at risk in that home."

Dawn glanced down at her notes, before resuming.

"Three. If … if what she says is all true … then we could possibly be looking for a man who kills other men, then goes after their widows. On a regular basis. I find that doubtful, but can't rule it out."

"Ok."

Williams paused for a few moments, deep in thought.

"But, what's your gut feeling?"

Dawn looked at Shelly, then back at her boss.

"Something very bad."

Lloyd sat up straight, and told them how it was going to be.

"I've already spoken to the DCI, to let her know something has come in. I like the psychologist angle. But first, you two need to trawl through everything we have. When he's finished the fraud handover, you'll get DC Burnley to assist. Until then, you keep this case just between the three of us, got it? Then, we may need to bring in the psychologist."

"Right, Boss."

"Yes, Boss."

Lloyd sent them on their way:

"Get to it."

As they rose to leave the office, he added:

"Keep in very close touch with her, Shelly. And keep me informed of everything. Oh, and find out why she came to Tyldesley, from North Yorkshire."

"Will do."

Walking back to her desk, which was on the opposite side of the room from Shelly's base, Dawn suggested:

"Do you want to use this hot desk?"

There was an empty unit, next to hers.

"Yes, I will." Shelly agreed. It would be useful for them to work in close proximity, for now.

There were nine other desks in the room, occupied currently by six other regular members of DI Williams' team. If any of them thought anything odd about Shelly shifting her working base, nobody commented on it, at the time.

As the senior, Dawn gave Shelly a directive:

"I'll work through her statement, and you get digging on the background; then we'll compare notes before we get out of here tonight, ok?"

"Sure."

And they got to work.

Later in the day, Dave Perryman, a seasoned DC, leaned back comfortably in his swivel chair. With the hint of a grin, he made a remark to Shelly about her choice of close company. If it was designed to provoke her, or insinuate something about her preferring to be in close proximity to females, rather than males, she ignored it. Away from her eye contact, Dave smiled. He had been mischievous, certainly, in his teasing way. But, in reality, he liked Shelly; respecting her perhaps more than she realised.

By the time Dawn and Shelly were ready to share their afternoon's work with each other, everyone else had left the office. DI Williams had left for a meeting in Warrington; having reminded them to call him if anything urgent came to light.

"Ok, background?" Dawn invited Shelly to go first.

Shelly composed herself.

"Mariana Navarro, born Mariana Carmona, twenty-first of December 1970. She's forty-five. Born in Valencia, Spain. She came to England in 1975, with her parents, and two older sisters. They all moved back to Spain in 1983. She met Vito Navarro in Spain, and married him in 2006. They just had the one daughter, Izzy, born eighth of August 2012."

She paused, to consult something.

"They came over here in 2007. Vito was a joiner, by trade. Mariana spoke good English, of course, which probably helped. He worked for a few local companies, in Yorkshire. Then, in July 2014, Vito was reported missing. Mariana reported it, at Pickering nick. That was on the twenty-third. It wasn't until the thirtieth that his body was found, in a lake in Cumbria, close to Penrith. He had drowned. Suspicious, but the coroner could do no more than classify it as 'unexplained'. There were some injuries on the body, but these could have been caused by the rocks and shingle around the edge of the water."

Dawn nodded, thoughtfully.

Shelly continued:

"The police couldn't find any motive for foul play, and Mariana couldn't offer them one; although she was adamant that he hadn't been depressed or worried about anything, and wouldn't have taken his own life."

"And afterwards?" Dawn asked.

"Well, Mariana continued living in the family home, which was rented. Then, in 2015, she moved, with Izzy, from Pickering to Tyldesley. She rented a flat there, where she still lives today. We haven't checked yet, why she came to Tyldesley; but she said that she doesn't have much to do with the neighbours, and didn't mention any friends in the area. The alleged rape happened on the twenty-eighth of May 2015; and it was soon after that when she moved. Exact date not confirmed, yet. Also need to check her employment details. And, if we're going to have another look at Vito's death, we'll need to look again at his friends, colleagues, and acquaintances."

"Ok, that's fine, for now. We'll come back to it, later."

Dawn smiled; she was impressed. Although they had been on the same team for several months, they hadn't had occasion to work together, previously. Hopefully, they were going to hit it off.

"Good work, Shelly."

She opened a small notebook, and prepared to discuss the transcript of Mariana's interview.

"Before I start this, I know you would like to believe every word she says."

Shelly smarted.

"I'm not a trainee." She said, curtly.

"No, I know you're not. But, in your previous dealings with Mariana, she has been on our side, as an innocent victim. So, your natural inclination, now, is to assume that she's still 'innocent', and you have no reason to doubt her. But, given the accusations that she's making, we need to try and be objective."

"Yes, I know."

"Ok, let's go through the main points of what she's said. Pull me up if you disagree with any of these summary points."

She took a deep breath, and began.

"One. Mariana alleges that she was raped in her own home, on the twenty-eighth of May, last year. Two. She claims that the man who allegedly raped her is also responsible for the death of her husband, found over a hundred miles from her home, ten months earlier. According to Google, it's a hundred and seven miles from Pickering to Penrith."

Shelly nodded.

"Three. According to Mariana, this man has raped other women. He practically said as much. Four. According to Mariana, he comes after other widows, and rapes them. Five. Put the first four points together, and the insinuation is that we're looking at not just a serial rapist, but a serial killer who is also a serial rapist."

Dawn stopped. The two women gazed at each other, trying to take in the enormity of what was opening up before them.

Shelly broke the silence.

"Ok. Devil's advocate. Let's say Mariana was raped; but the trauma of everything has overwhelmed her. Confused her so much that she has imagined the details that point us towards a serial-killer-rapist."

Dawn nodded.

"I agree, that's possible. For that reason, I also think that your suggestion of a psychologist getting involved is a good one. What puzzles me, more than anything, is how she remembered all those details so precisely. Does it mean that she's been rehearsing them, all this time? Is she trying to provoke us to open up the investigation into Vito's death again?"

Shelly leaned over to look at Dawn's screen, where she had typed up Mariana's statement. She realised that she might be invading Dawn's personal space, and hastily drew back.

"Sorry." She said.

Dawn smiled broadly, and unconsciously stroked her wedding ring.

Noticing it, Shelly raised her eyebrows, and cocked her head to one side.

The two women laughed.

"I'm not a lesbian." Said Shelly, with a further chuckle.

"So I heard." Confirmed Dawn. "Not exclusively."

Chapter 8

The next day was Sunday, the fourteenth of August. Shelly called Mariana on the phone, just to keep in touch. Only a couple of minutes of small talk; but, Mariana appreciated it. Shelly arranged to go visit her the next day, which she did, bright and early on Monday morning, before coming into the office. She wanted to reassure her that they were looking seriously at everything Mariana had told them; make arrangements for a security advisor to call, and just check up on a couple of points.

For example, why had she chosen Tyldesley as her new home? Had she known anyone in the area? When did she move? Was she still in touch with anyone back in Pickering?

Tyldesley had been a very random choice. It was far enough away from the North Yorkshire market town of Pickering, and anonymous enough, for her to disappear from the home that she knew the attacker knew, and feel relatively safe. She hadn't known anyone in the area, but managed to find the flat as a private rental, through a property website. She moved at the end of June, last year. And, no, she had severed all contacts in Pickering.

Armed with this extra information, Shelly arrived at the office, to find DI Williams just seeing out DCI Floella York.

The DCI was, by most accounts, an acquired taste. She had a reputation for missing nothing, and remembering everything. From most of her colleagues, there was a grudging respect for her. She was known by a variety of nicknames, depending on whether she was regarded favourably, or otherwise. Ma'am, of course, was the official form of address, to her face. But, behind her back, she was 'Flossie', 'The Black Queen', or even, based on her initials the most disrespectful of all 'Fuck You'. But 'The DCI' was the safest bet.

Lloyd summoned in Shelly, and called across to Dawn, to come and join them in the office. Behind the closed door, Lloyd updated them.

"I've got the green light, provisionally, to pull in Dr Sheen."

Dr Marcus Sheen was a criminal psychologist, who had worked with them before. He wasn't the easiest to get along with; he could be temperamental, and sometimes seemed to drift into a reality of his own. But, he was insightful; good at his job.

Lloyd continued:

"But, first, convince me that it's worth it."

He sat back in his chair, and looked to Dawn to begin.

"There are some really interesting points in her account, Boss. I feel... Shelly and I feel that we could use a professional opinion about Mariana. I think we should start with his view of the statement, before we consider asking Mariana to meet with him."

"Definitely!" Chipped in Shelly.

"Which points, specifically?" Lloyd asked.

"Well, we accept that we have to be wary of taking things at face value; otherwise, it means we are going on a hunt for a serial-killer-rapist."

He nodded.

"Yes, that's my reading of it."

Dawn continued:

"But, there is something in the wording on the card of instructions that she says he made her read. It says: *'Think of your little girl / boy'*. If he had created instructions just for her, why would he say *'girl / boy'*? He knew she had a girl."

Shelly interjected:

"Yet, if we conclude from this that he had raped before, and had prepared a card that could be used more than once, how come it also says: *'Imagine I'm your Spanish husband'*?"

She went on:

"And, of course, she also says that he told her *'Vito was number six'*. Can that really mean what it infers: that Vito was his sixth victim? Murder victim, that is. And, could there be other rape victims out there?"

There was a silence, before Lloyd snatched up the phone.

"You two need to be checking the database for alleged sexual assaults or rapes with any similarities to this. I'm calling Sheen."

Chapter 9

During the next few days, Mariana was interviewed further, as Dawn and Shelly tried to fill in as many gaps as possible. They resisted trying to make the judgement about whether Mariana's story was completely true, or had been corrupted by time, memory and emotion. But, although their professional scepticism held them back, both officers felt that this was something extreme.

By Wednesday afternoon, after a couple more 'chats' to elicit a few further details, Dr Marcus Sheen, criminal psychologist, had been brought in. Sheen was in his sixties, with thinning silver hair; and had the air of a retired headmaster or slightly eccentric academic. He was wearing a light coloured sports jacket, and dark green corduroy pants. Some days, he sported a flamboyant bow-tie; but today his shirt was open at the neck. He wouldn't have looked out of place watching a test match, at Lords.

Arriving at the team room, he made straight for DI Williams' private office. Lloyd, already at his desk, called Shelly and Dawn to enter. DC Frank Burnley was pulled in too, and brought an extra chair with him.

Shaking Dr Sheen's hand, Lloyd said:

"Thanks for coming over, Marcus. You know DS Pardell. This is DC Shelly King, and DC Frank Burnley."

Turning to Burnley, he added:

"If you're not fully up to speed yet, Frank, just listen in, for now. You'll be working on this full time from now."

The doctor had already been sent a brief by Dawn, but hadn't yet had the chance to analyse the transcript of Mariana Navarro's interview. He was filled in by a combination of Dawn and Shelly. Frank hadn't yet been given more than the most basic outline of the case.

Looking over the transcripts, which had swelled thanks to further conversations in the last two days, Dr Sheen listened with interest. Finally, the account reached the point of a natural break, and the four officers looked to Marcus, waiting for a comment.

Dr Sheen sat, motionless, for a moment. He was looking upwards towards the ceiling. It wasn't clear whether he was fully attuned to the conversation; or so deep in his own thoughts that he had zoned out. Shelly shot a glance at DI Williams, who held his patience. Finally, Dr Sheen turned his head towards Dawn, and spoke:

"Well, you've met her, and I haven't. How does she come across?"

Shelly wanted to reply; but, out of courtesy to her seniors, held back.

Dawn replied:

"We think it's predominantly true. We find parts of it almost too much to believe. But, for now, we're treating it as substantially true."

DI Williams didn't contradict her, and returned his gaze to Dr Sheen.

"Anything hit you straightaway, Marcus? Anything we've missed, that shows this woman to be lying to us?"

Marcus rubbed his eye, and shook his head. After a moment, he spoke up:

"No. I'd like to meet her."

DI Williams looked at his junior officer.

"Is she ready for that, Shelly?"

Taking the bit between her teeth, Shelly confirmed:

"I'll get her ready, Boss."

Then, by way of explanation to Dr Sheen:

"She's very reluctant to push this in terms of trying to get a conviction for what he did to her. It's not what she wants. She simply hoped to give us some information... get it off her chest, perhaps... then walk away and leave us to it. She wouldn't be wanting to speak to a... no offence doctor."

Marcus grinned; a flash of his personality coming through.

"None taken. But that's interesting, in itself. So, she says that she doesn't want him to be brought to book for assaulting her? What about for murdering her husband, if indeed he did so?"

Lloyd interjected:

"That's why we need your help, Marcus. This is very complicated. Right, Shelly, how quickly can you get Mariana to meet Dr Sheen?"

"I'll speak to her this evening. See what I can do."

"Well, don't hang about."

With a sideways glance at Marcus:

"Psychologists don't come cheap."

If Dr Sheen recognised the remark, he ignored it.

Chapter 10

By Friday afternoon, the nineteenth of August, Shelly had persuaded Mariana to allow the psychologist to come along and meet her, at her home. Izzy would be away at an extra session of nursery care; ostensibly to help her prepare for school, which she would be starting the next month.

Arriving at her flat, with Dr Sheen, Shelly noticed that the extra security features had been fitted to Mariana's front door. A panic alarm had also been issued, courtesy of the crime prevention unit.

Mariana admitted her visitors.

"Mariana, this is Dr Sheen, that I told you about."

"How do you do?" Mariana greeted him politely, though warily.

After the greetings, niceties, and arrival of a cup of tea, Dr Sheen began to talk to Mariana, asking about the area, her daughter, her job; attempting to put her at her ease.

Eventually, the time came to speak of more sensitive matters.

Mariana retold a much briefer version of events, which Marcus assured was sufficient for the purpose of this first meeting. Implicit in that was the notion that there might well be further meetings.

However, there were a few specific points that he wanted to broach, in this first encounter; and, when the opportunity arose, he asked his questions.

"Mariana, there are some things that you've told the officers, which just need a bit more explanation, if you could. Can I ask you about them?"

"Yes, that's why you're here."

"Quite. Well, I know *what* you've told the police, and I know how difficult it must have been to tell them about such awful things. But I want to know how you came to decide to speak to Shelly, here. And how you managed to choose what to tell her, and why. That way, I'm not just coming at things from the same angle as the police."

Mariana didn't fully understand; but did her best to humour him. She was more than a little intrigued; and unused to speaking with 'a shrink'. Although she didn't know it, Marcus was trying to assess whether the key points of her account would remain constant, even when distracted by this confusing approach. Would her answers be emotionally charged, and would the sensitive triggers be what he expected them to be, in a person who was telling the truth? Beyond that, did she even know whether she was telling the truth, or not? Was her distress, real though it was to her, no more than the equivalent of a back pain which proves to be psychosomatic, and with no real physiological cause?

He asked her, subsequently, about her husband. Memories of him. Important dates... anniversaries. Anything remotely meaningful that she could find in the attacker's words: *'Vito was number six ...'*

As Marcus asked his questions, Shelly listened on; looking positive, trying to encourage Mariana to participate. At times, she wondered what the hell Dr Sheen was playing at. Where on Earth was he going with some of these random, offbeat questions? But, she managed to bite her tongue, and to look as eager for Mariana's responses as possible. This was so that the poor woman would think Shelly understood the reasoning for these lines of enquiry, and thus be more likely to engage.

The meeting lasted for around an hour; before Dr Sheen concluded that they had done enough, and he called it to a close. Leaving Mariana to her weekend, Dr Sheen paused, close to Shelly's car. His own car was waiting for him, just out of sight of Mariana's flat, around the corner.

His face was grim, and his expression slightly distant; as if fascinated by what he had heard, and still processing ideas and possibilities through his mind.

"Well? What are you thinking, Doctor?"

Shelly realised that maybe she should wait for him to disclose his thoughts, and possibly only through the route of DI Williams, but she couldn't resist.

Marcus stroked back his thin grey hair, and sighed wearily. He turned and looked into Shelly's eyes; holding his gaze for a little longer than she found comfortable.

"What am I thinking? I'm thinking that you better start looking for a serial-killer-rapist."

He continued to give Shelly a long, rather wise look; and added:

"And I know you'll want to catch him, yourself. You're a good cop. But, don't forget, you're part of a team."

His words surprised her. She nodded, without comment, and got in her car.

Chapter 11

DI Williams had clicked into highest gear, and assumed control; like a captain preparing his troops for a perilous upcoming mission. He issued strict instructions to Shelly and Dawn to take the full weekend off. From Monday, this inquiry would be full-on. The pressure of what they might encounter, in the coming days and weeks, might be enough to cause the hardiest of cops to double up and vomit, before collapsing, exhausted. He wanted them sharp, alert, fresh. And, besides, he wanted a little time to think through the strategy; as well as get to speak with the DCI, update her, and discuss resources and workload.

On Monday morning, at eight-thirty, Lloyd's whole team were instructed to move into the incident room, which adjoined their main office. Some of the officers had already caught a whisper of the seriousness and the nature of what they were about to be told.

In all, there were eleven people in the room, when the last to arrive, Dave Perryman, walked in, and closed the door behind him. Dave glanced around, nervously; wondering if he had just missed something, or ought to have read a briefing that he had somehow missed.

Sat on a desk close to the glass presentation wall, DI Williams nodded to Dave to sit down, and waited for everyone to settle. DCI York was stood, just concluding a hushed phone call, close to the external window.

Lloyd looked round. Dawn and Shelly were sat at a desk, just to his right. Frank Burnley was just behind them. On the other side of the room, the two youngest members of this CID team, DC Alice Hawley and DC Tom Appleby-Haigh, were sat together; looking apprehensive about what was to come. They had both joined DI Williams' unit in the previous six months; eager for action. They had struck up a bond; through common inexperience. DS Graeme French, one of the old guard, with over twenty years of experience, and one of Lloyd's most trusted lieutenants, hung his jacket on the back of his chair, and adjusted his tie. Dr Marcus Sheen was sat, uncomfortably and impatiently fingering his brief-case, in front of him. WPC Shirley Wolfenden, and Carol O'Toole who was a member of the civilian support staff team, made up the full complement.

60

"Ma'am?"

Lloyd's enquiry was a matter of courtesy; deferring to her, if she wished to lead this briefing.

"Go ahead." She instructed.

Lloyd stood up, looking serious, and placed his hands on his hips. His expression, without a word, told the team that they were going to hear something momentous, and they had better pay attention.

"Just over a week ago, we received information from a woman who alleged that she had been raped, on the twenty-eighth of May, last year ..."

He went on to explain the details. That this woman had been widowed, and that she believed her assailant had been responsible for her husband's death. That he was a serial offender.

Occasionally, members of the team appeared about to interrupt. Each time, a wave of his hand stopped them; and, each time, his continued explanation covered the queries that they had wanted to raise.

The generalised mood within the room shifted during the course of half an hour. It went from interest, to shock, to incredulity, to dismissal of something too far-fetched, to ... 'OMG this is real!'

At the conclusion of his summary, Lloyd asked Dr Sheen to say a few words. Just in case his team had any lingering doubts about the seriousness of what they could be dealing with.

Marcus, who had been listening to Williams, but observing everybody else, got up; and walked slowly to the front of the room.

"I've studied the transcripts of what Mariana said to DC King and DS Pardell. I've interviewed her myself."

He hesitated, and stroked back his thinning grey hair; eyeing his audience.

"Like most of you, perhaps I've been in this line of work too long, and I went into it cynically. Couldn't possibly be real. She must be a very sick and troubled woman. I tried to make her trauma fit with the production of a fantasy account. I couldn't."

61

He looked at DI Williams, with a shrug.

"Thank you, Dr Sheen."

The room was silent, apart from the sound of his footsteps, as Marcus returned to his chair and sat down.

DCI Floella York stepped forward.

"Needless to say, this is an investigation of the utmost sensitivity. Nothing you have heard is to be repeated outside this room. Does everyone understand?"

There was a general murmuring of 'Yes Ma'am'.

"DI Williams will be leading the investigation, and I will be supporting him."

She turned to Lloyd, and nodded curtly to him, before walking forward, past the team, and leaving the room. As the door closed behind her, Lloyd got straight to business.

"Dr Sheen will be leaving shortly. Dawn and Shelly will be briefing you all again in more detail, immediately after this session. You will all be allocated roles by Dawn, and I expect you to give her every support that you can. There's a lot of research going to be done, and I expect everyone to pitch in. It's a lot more than Shirley and Carol could handle on their own. We will meet again at five pm today. The DCI expects a daily progress report, and she's going to get one. Carry on Dawn."

Without waiting for any questions, he strode towards the door, followed by Dr Sheen, and they both left the room.

As soon as he had gone, a barrage of questions rose up from the floor.

How had this come to light? Why had Mariana Navarro come to Shelly? How come everybody had been kept in the dark?

With a raised hand, as if controlling the traffic, Dawn spoke assertively:

"Shelly and I are going to forward you everything we have, in the next few minutes. Read it carefully. We'll come back in here at eleven. Bring your ideas. Keep an open mind."

Immediately after the meeting had broken up, Shelly and Dawn set about forwarding all the relevant transcripts and notes. It was quite a package; made up of the interview notes, Dr Sheen's brief report, links to the background on Mariana, the case of Vito Navarro's unexplained death, and a few other items. The team members devoured it eagerly; still with a mixture of professional caution, downright disbelief, and guilty excitement.

Chapter 12

The next few days were frantically active. Gradually, each member of the team came to feel that they knew Mariana Navarro, and to a lesser extent her late husband. Shelly remained the main personal contact, visiting Mariana at home, to save her from the possible further trauma of feeling like a police exhibit. Dr Sheen also visited her again, and tactfully probed into what Marana could remember about her attacker.

Mariana had already managed to say that the man seemed to be a Northerner; or, at least, not a Southerner. Unfortunately, although she spoke excellent English; she was not adept at picking out local dialects.

She had managed to describe something about his physique. He was no more than average height, maybe five feet nine inches tall. And he was muscular; though not athletic. Strong, quite broad shoulders. How old was he? She found it difficult to say. His manner of speech was slow, more like an older man's. But, his voice sounded more like that of a younger person. The best she could do was 'somewhere between twenty-five and forty-five'.

He was white, and she hadn't seen any tattoos on his body. His breath didn't smell like that of a smoker. There was some particular scent about him; but she had never been able to figure out what it was. Nothing fancy, she had said, like perfume or after-shave. Something more down-to-Earth. Diesel, petrol, oil? She couldn't tell.

Sat at the desk next to Dawn, Shelly was poring over the transcript of what Mariana had told them was written on the attacker's card.

Still looking at the notes, she addressed Dawn:

"We already picked up on this possible disparity – it says 'girl / boy', despite him knowing that she had a girl. Yet it also says 'your Spanish husband', which would seem to imply that these instructions were specifically for her."

Dawn nodded, and had an answer:

"Just because Mariana was able to recite the whole set of instructions, word for word, it doesn't mean that she can't possibly have made a mistake. Maybe it didn't say 'Spanish'. But, because she read it as 'Spanish' the first time, she has convinced herself that it was, and she has repeated this all to herself so many times, she can't get rid of the word."

Shelly wasn't convinced.

"Hmm, maybe. That's one for Sheen."

At that moment, Frank Burnley stepped into the office, and walked briskly over to them. They both looked up, to greet him.

"Got something?" Asked Dawn.

Frank's specific task had been to find reports of rapes or sexual assaults that bore any similarities to this case; and, in particular, any alleged links between murders and subsequent assaults.

"Not sure. Probably not, but it's something I'm just going to check."

"Share, then." Said Shelly, looking hopeful. "Spill, Frank."

Frank sat down at his desk, and proceeded to log into his computer.

"Well, it's something I came across, almost by chance. I was looking for reported assaults on widows. Not just sexual assaults, because I figured that, if other victims were made to feel humiliated, and scared of reporting a sexual assault, like Mariana..."

He paused to concentrate on bringing up the details of a certain report.

"Can't multi-task." Mouthed Dawn, to Shelly.

He continued:

"So, maybe an assault that impacted elsewhere, such as a trip to hospital, or damage to property, or something … could find its way into the records."

"Go on." Shelly encouraged him, as he seemed to have come to a halt.

"And I found this." He went on.

65

"The key word was 'Spanish'.

He read some details from his screen:

"Spanish woman, Salome Mendez, took her own life 23.09.12, aged thirty. She was originally from mainland Spain, but lived in Fuerteventura, in the Canaries."

Shelly and Dawn glanced at each other.

"Go on." Dawn said.

"This was not long after the death of her daughter from leukaemia. Salome Mendez was a widow; her husband had allegedly been murdered in 2011. Killer never found. Nobody really picked up on this at the time; but, she left a note, saying that she had nothing left to live for, and nothing to fear any longer from the man who killed her husband and ended her life."

Neither Dawn nor Shelly spoke, as Frank scrolled down his screen, looking at more of the details.

"What do you think?" He asked.

Dawn resumed her own work, but commented:

"Have a proper look at it, Frank. I'd say it's unlikely, but no harm in checking it out properly."

Shelly was looking very thoughtful.

"You know, Frank might have something here. Even if this Salome Mendez has no connection, if one of the links is 'Spanish ethnicity', then maybe we should be scouring the Spanish police files. Something might come up."

By the next morning, Frank had studied the case of Salome Mendez as much as he could. Although he would have loved to discover a definite connection; the limited files that he was able to access left the connection 'inconclusive'. Enough, though, for him to persuade Dawn and Shelly that they should bring it to DI Williams' attention.

At their morning team meeting, Frank made his pitch.

"On the face of it, there are some similarities. But, without access to the local police investigation, and looking at her husband's death too, it's impossible to establish a real connection."

DI Williams was sufficiently interested to agree. Not least, because progress elsewhere was minimal.

"Ok, I'll make some calls … try and get us into their files."

By that afternoon, the contact had been made; and Frank was able to access the full report into the deaths of both Salome Mendez and her husband, Luca. By the time of their late day team meeting, Frank was able to outline the cases in some detail.

Luca Mendez was a fisherman; who made his living by providing fresh produce to the local restaurants in the resort of Corralejo, in the north of Fuerteventura, and close by. He lived at El Cotillo, a village just a few kilometres to the west of Corralejo. Luca was, by all accounts, an easy-going soul. No enemies, that anyone knew of, and happily married to Salome. On the twenty-third of July, 2011, he had gone out alone on the early tide in his boat, as usual; fully expecting to be home by the early afternoon. However, he had not arrived back with a catch for the diners that evening; much to the initial frustration of the restaurateurs, and subsequent concern of his wife.

It wasn't until the next morning, that Luca's boat was found; drifting in the shallows close to the rocky coves overlooked by the El Cotillo lighthouse, the *Faro del Toston*. Although accidents do happen at sea, it was immediately apparent that there may have been foul play. There was blood – lots of blood – found in the boat. After a night swirling around in the ocean, it was quite possible that even more blood had already been washed away. The police wondered whether Luca had been attacked, killed, and his body dumped at sea. There was an investigation, as thorough as could be. Though, in truth, without a single witness, there was very little that the police could do.

Salome, no doubt, was distraught. Yet, despite the trauma of being left to believe that her husband had died at another's hand, her suffering was far from over. A few months afterwards, her only daughter, Rosa, was diagnosed with leukaemia. A most pernicious and aggressive form.

67

Despite the best efforts of everyone, Salome lost her daughter on the second of August 2012.

Apparently – and in accordance with the note that she wrote – with 'nothing to live for', Salome ended her own life by slitting her wrists and bleeding out, on the twenty-third of September 2012.

When Frank Burnley had finished delivering this account to his colleagues, the team room was silent, and sombre.

"Of course, there's no proof that there's any connection, here."

DI Williams spelt it out.

"Similarities, yes. But, there's no evidence that she was assaulted, between losing her husband and taking her own life, is there?"

Frank flicked down to some further notes.

"Salome's mother – she was the one who found her daughter – reported that Salome had broken down and told her about an assault, some months earlier. It was after Luca died, but possibly at the time when the daughter, Rosa, was diagnosed."

Shelly, Dawn, and the rest of the team were looking on, horrified.

Frank continued:

"The reports are a bit sketchy. It seems that, because Rosa had just been taken ill, maybe her Mum didn't want to deal with any more grief, so didn't report it to the police, at the time. It really only came out afterwards; and, by then, perhaps it wasn't... well, wasn't perceived as a priority anymore."

Williams nodded.

"I can see how that might have played out."

Dawn Pardell raised a question:

"Frank, you said that there's this allegation that Salome Mendez was assaulted, based on what her mother said. Did anyone else corroborate this, at the time? And, are we saying it was a sexual assault?"

Frank sighed.

"Not clear, Sarge."

"Looks like she might have just confided in her mum, and maybe not even told her the full story. Told her to keep it to herself?"

The room was quiet, as several colleagues pondered. Finally, Shelly broke the silence.

"Frank, you said Luca Mendez died on the twenty-third of July, 2011."

"Yes." Frank confirmed.

She continued:

"What date did Vito Navarro die on?"

Dawn glanced at the information on her screen, and answered:

"Twenty-third of July, or thereabouts, 2014."

There was a brief pause, before Frank observed:

"Hmm, same date. Coincidence."

DI Williams scratched his head:

"Must be. Ok, I want you to dig into this a bit more, Frank. Find out if there's any suggestion that Salome Mendez might have been sexually assaulted. You'll need to contact the Spanish police. Do it asap."

"Right, Boss."

Chapter 13

The next day, Officers Rodriguez and Castillo, of the Cuerpo Nacional de Policia; were heading towards Lajares, a small town between Corralejo and El Cotillo, in the north of Fuerteventura. Millie Rodriguez was driving, and her partner, Martin Castillo, was relaxing in the passenger seat.

They had just concluded an interesting conversation – thanks to Skype – with a young British police officer, named Frank Burnley. Slightly puzzled, and somewhat dubious, they had, nevertheless, agreed to try and help this British enquiry; by making a visit to Lajares, in search of one Luciana Fuentes, mother of the late Salome Mendez.

Frank had not explained the full details of his interest; but, had requested them to speak with Senora Fuentes, to see whether she could add anything to what she had already told the police about Luca's death, and the events leading up to her daughter's death. This was, Frank had told them, in connection with a separate enquiry into a British murder case; which may, or may not be linked in some way. But, in order to be fair to them, he had mentioned that he wanted to establish the nature of the assault on Salome, if, indeed, there had been one. Also, the dates of those events; had there been anything significant about the dates?

Having already discussed this, and wondering whether they were wasting their time; Millie and Martin approached the sleepy town of Lajares, and turned along the lane that led towards the fishing village of Majanicho.

Within a few hundred metres, they came to a villa, with a slightly untidy wall, and shaded by overgrown bushes. Pulling up, Millie switched off the engine.

"This is the place."

They entered through the open gateway, and glanced around at the yard. An old dog kennel was set against the side wall, though no animal was inside it. A washing line was strung across the yard, but nothing hung on it, today.

Millie knocked smartly at the front door. Presently, the door opened, and an old woman greeted them. Showing their identification, the two officers were invited in; and Senora Luciana Fuentes led them through the house, and out to a covered patio at the rear, where she invited them to sit at a wooden picnic table.

Luciana was, perhaps, not quite as old as she looked. A widow, she had endured more, in the past few years, than many people have to see in a lifetime. The experiences had aged her; causing her thick dark hair to become grey before its time, and etching wrinkles across her forehead and deep into the sides of her face.

"Senora…" Began Millie. "We are sorry to bother you with this; but, we have been asked to come and speak with you again about some of the sad events of 2011 and 2012."

She looked around at her colleague, who took the cue:

"With the passage of time, sometimes it's worth revisiting what happened. Just to see if there's anything that's been missed."

Luciana looked sad, and not greatly interested.

"Nothing's going to bring them back, is it?"

"No. We can't bring them back." Officer Rodriguez smiled sympathetically. "But, what happened to Luca was never properly cleared up; so, it's still open to us to keep looking at things."

Luciana nodded.

"So, what did you want to ask me?"

Millie hesitated.

"Well, right now, we want to ask you about the time between Luca dying, and Salome taking her own life."

Luciana looked ashen-faced, and the hint of a tear came into her eye.

"It was a horrible time." She spoke almost in a whisper.

71

Millie Rodriguez persisted:

"When you were interviewed, following Salome's death, you were talking to one of the officers about the dreadful time that Salome had had. She lost her husband, and then your grand-daughter became ill. And, in amongst all that, you said that she had been assaulted, too."

Luciana's eyes were now glazing over, and she brought a tissue to her face.

"Salome didn't want to talk about it. She broke down, one day, and told me she'd been attacked. But, for some reason, she wouldn't report it. I think she just couldn't face one more thing. It was around the time that she had just found out Rosa was ill. She was fearing the worst. She was right to fear the worst."

Millie held back, allowing Senora Fuentes a moment, before she asked something more:

"This could be very important, Senora. What did she tell you about this attack?"

Luciana sniffed back a tear.

"She couldn't bring herself to say. It must have been bad. Really bad. But, she couldn't tell me."

Luciana looked up at the officers, as if needing to defend herself:

"I did ask. I did. I really tried to get her to tell me... but she wouldn't. Or couldn't."

Millie looked across at her colleague, knowing that she would have to ask what they were both thinking.

She took Luciana's hand, and asked, gently:

"Do you think it could have been a sexual assault?"

Luciana looked to the ground, and said nothing. After a few seconds, she nodded.

"Yes. I think it might have been."

Rodriguez and Castillo exchanged glances; before Castillo took up the questioning:

"Do you know roughly *when* the assault took place, Senora? When did she tell you?"

"I know when it was. It was on the eighteenth of February. It was soon after that, when she told me. I know it was the eighteenth, because it was while I was away in Lanzarote. She told me, soon after I came back."

Castillo persisted:

"And we know she didn't want to talk about it; but, did she say where it happened, and what time of day, perhaps?"

Luciana shook her head.

"I think it was during the day. She said something... I think Rosa was in school. I'm not sure. It was close to home, I think. Maybe it was in her own home. I don't know. She got all uptight, whenever I tried to raise it."

Castillo nodded.

"Ok, I understand."

Millie interjected, with a further question:

"This might be a strange thing to ask; but, did she ever make you think there was some link between her getting attacked, and her husband... apparently... getting attacked, too?"

Luciana looked up at her.

"I thought she *was* trying to tell me that. And, when she ... when she left us... she wrote a note saying that she wasn't afraid of the man who had killed Luca, and ended her life... It was vague. The police thought she meant that, by murdering her husband, someone had taken away all purpose from her life, too. But, I thought she was saying something else. Something that really linked the two things. But, nobody believed me at the time; and, eventually, I came to think I must have imagined it. I was very upset, confused."

73

"Of course. Anyone would be."

Millie stood up.

"We'll leave it at that, Senora. Thank you for speaking with us, it must be very painful."

Senora Fuentes rose from the table.

"Yes, it is painful. Each year, there always seems to be something that happens. Brings everything back. Three years ago, I went to Lanzarote, to visit my cousin. And, while I was there, another murder happened. The same day as poor Luca – the twenty-third of July. I was turning everything over in my mind, because of Luca's anniversary... then that murder happened, and everything came back again."

Senora Fuentes saw out the two officers; watching them from her doorstep, as they drove away.

"Well, that was interesting." Commented Martin Castillo. "I don't know what Senor Burnley will make of it; but, we can only pass it back."

An hour later, the two officers had reached their base, in Puerto del Rosario, and made a video call to Frank Burnley. Joining him at a quiet desk in an interview room, Dawn and Shelly sat in on the call.

"Thanks for doing this so quickly, we appreciate it." Dawn assured her Spanish counterparts.

"Did Senora Fuentes have anything to say... anything that caught your attention?" Asked Frank.

Millie Rodriguez answered for them:

"Well, she did say that she thought her daughter was trying to tell her something about being assaulted, but she never quite brought herself to explain much about it. It sounded to us like Salome wanted to tell her mum everything, but, couldn't. Perhaps she was ashamed, for some reason."

Martin Castillo joined the conversation:

74

"When we pressed her about whether the assault might have been sexually motivated, she said 'yes', it might."

Shelly spoke next:

"You asked her whether there was anything significant about the exact dates of Luca's death, the assault, Salome's suicide. Was there something about them, that meant anything to the family?"

Millie responded:

"No, the dates on which things happened didn't mean anything particular."

Almost as an afterthought, she added:

"In fact, her only comment about the dates was that, exactly two years after Luca's death, another murder, this time over the water in Lanzarote, brought it all back. She had gone there for a visit, probably trying to lose herself around the time of year that Luca died; and, of all things, there was another murder, right there on the island."

There was a silence at the British end.

Millie continued:

"The exact same date, two years later: twenty-third of July 2013."

"Hello?" Asked Martin. "Can you still hear us?"

He thought that a technical problem must have intervened. Although he could still see Frank Burnley, and Shelly, next to him; they were not uttering a sound.

Finally, Shelly responded.

"Yes, we've still got you. Er, you couldn't send us details of that death in Lanzarote, could you? July 2013."

Puzzled, but aware of a phone ringing elsewhere in the office, which was demanding his attention, Martin agreed.

"Of course. Is that it, for now?"

"Yes, thanks. We'll be back in touch, if... thanks for your help."

Frank killed the line; as Shelly and Dawn looked at each other, in disbelief.

Dawn was the first to speak:

"We should have asked them if they see many murders in Lanzarote."

"Rarer than hen's teeth, I should think." Grunted Frank.

"Same day, again. Wait until the boss hears this." Shelly whistled, through her teeth.

Impatiently, Frank refreshed his screen several times, awaiting the arrival of something from officer Castillo. Dawn had started to search for herself, and was narrowing down the search criteria, when Frank exclaimed:

"Bingo! Here it is."

The three of them crowded round the screen, as Frank opened up the information, and began to read out loud:

"Roberto Pastor – a local coach driver. Bludgeoned to death, not far from his home, in Playa Blanca. Twenty-third of July 2013."

"Any suspects? I assume nobody was convicted?" Dawn asked.

Frank shook his head:

"Nobody charged. A few people interviewed, but no charges were brought."

It was Shelly, who voiced what they were all wondering:

"Is there a widow? A Senora Pastor?"

Frank was already scrolling through the data that had been sent.

"Senora Aida Pastor. And, they had two children: Vanessa and Aimar. Roberto was only thirty-four, so I guess the children would have been young."

A morbid silence fell over the three of them, as they each inwardly pondered different questions.

Dawn was preparing to sketch out a spreadsheet which would list known victims; if this was, as it appeared to be, a pattern of events covering both Britain and the Canary Isles. She still couldn't believe that it was real.

Frank was wondering how he could go home that night, switch off from such a nightmare, and eat dinner with his wife, before tucking their little girl into bed.

Shelly was gazing at the calendar on the wall; noting that today was the twenty-third of August. She was fearful that, if a killer had really continued this devastating, evil sequence up to the present year; there might, somewhere, be a grieving widow in danger of being raped by a monster.

Dawn brought them back to attention:

"Let's find the boss."

Trooping back into the team room, the three walked across to DI Williams' glass-fronted office. They could see that he was sat at his desk, but on the phone.

Seeing their sombre expressions, he waved them in, and terminated his call.

"You've got something. Go on."

As the most senior of the three, Dawn recounted the basics of what they had learned, today. Frank chipped in, to clarify a few points gleaned from the notes of the Spanish police.

Williams listened, carefully. Immediately, decisively, the calm, firm voice with the Welsh accent instructed them:

"Get ready to set it all out for the team, in the incident room. I'm going to fetch the DCI in."

DI Williams snatched up his phone, and called his chief. Minutes later, the team had assembled in the incident room, and DCI Floella York walked in, and sat down.

"Dawn, an update, please." Instructed Williams.

Dawn recounted everything that had developed, today, thanks to the support of the Spanish police.   Periodically, she stepped to the glass demonstration wall, and added names, and details.

DCI York interjected:

"Some of these links are tenuous, Dawn."

"I know that, Ma'am.   But, given what we do know, that a number of incidents are on record, I suggest we can't rule out the connections, until we check them all."

DI Williams chipped in:

"Still early days.   But, we're going to have to move fast, here.   From now on, I want you to throw everything you can at the date.   Twenty-third of July.   If we take at face value what Mariana Navarro told us about her attacker, saying… 'Vito was number six… would have been seven, but he was busy in 2009…' scrutinise that date in the years since 2008."

The briefing continued, with colleagues asking questions, and contributing ideas.

"Why July twenty-third?"   Demanded Dave Perryman.

 "Maybe we can find something there to point us towards someone?"

DI Williams' frustration was starting to emerge:

"At the moment, we seem to be just hunting for victims.   We need to be examining each and every case, as soon as it comes to light, looking for connections.   Anything that might link victims together, and point towards where we should be looking for our perpetrator.   If it is one person."

Turning to DC Burnley, he continued:

"Frank, any connection between Luca and Salome Mendez and Vito Navarro, or Mariana Navarro?"

"I'm on it, Boss; but, I don't see anything yet."

Shelly said:

"At the moment, the only description we have is from Mariana Navarro. There's no description from Salome Mendez, and she can't give us one, now."

Dawn stepped in:

"So, as soon as we locate another death that could have been a victim of the same man; we need to get to the widow, if any, and try to find out if she was subsequently assaulted."

Williams nodded.

"Yes. That has to be the way in. If there are more, there must be connections. Of course, there is Senora Pastor, widow of Roberto Pastor. We need to find out whether she was ever assaulted, after Roberto died."

DCI York complimented the officers on the work they had done. As she left, she confirmed to DI Williams that the assistant commissioner would be getting an update the next day. The atmosphere, though professional, relaxed slightly, following her departure.

"We'll need more help from the Spanish." Observed Williams.

"We need to make contact with Aida Pastor. In fact, I think you two..." He looked at Dawn and Shelly... "Had better be packing your sunglasses."

Chapter 14

The next morning, a further call was made by Skype, to Millie Rodriguez, in connection with the widow, Aida Pastor.

"Good morning, Millie. Thanks for speaking with us again."

Shelly smiled. DI Williams had briefed her to try and gain Millie's cooperation, but he was reluctant for Shelly to reveal too much of their suspicions about the true depth and depravity of this case. Shelly felt slightly awkward. If a foreign cop had asked for her help in similar circumstances, she would have wanted to know the full story.

"Has our input helped you?" Millie asked.

"It has, very much. But it's prompted another question. I wonder if you would be able to help us out a bit more."

There was a hint of frustration in Millie's response:

"Well, if we knew exactly what it was you were trying to get at, maybe we could do more."

Shelly tried her best to empathise:

"Yes, I know. It's just that there are a lot of questions cropping up… a lot of possible links to a case we're working on… but I don't want to mislead you about it. I think Dawn and I might have to come over to Fuerteventura, or Lanzarote, quite soon. But, if you can establish a couple of things for us, you might save me the trip."

Cheerfully, she added:

"But if we need to come, anyway, I'll owe you a beer."

"What do you want?" Millie wasn't over-enthusiastic, but would help her British colleague if she could.

"Aida Pastor, the widow of Roberto Pastor; do you know anything about her?"

"Such as, what?"

"Well, after her husband's death, did she come to your attention again, for any reason?"

"Hang on."

Millie leaned across to a separate computer, to her right, and brought up the files. Shelly watched her, wondering what it was like for a young woman trying to make her way in the Spanish police. Was it a man's world over there, much as the police still was in the UK? Did Senora Rodriguez have to work twice as hard – be twice as good – as her male colleagues, just to be treated as something close to an equal?

Millie returned, to give Shelly her attention.

"There was a report, involving her, a few months after her husband's death. A neighbour reported a disturbance, at her house. Local officer paid a visit, but it turned out to be nothing."

Shelly nodded, with interest.

"And when was that?"

Millie checked:

"December thirtieth 2013. But, how can that be relevant to anything you're investigating."

"We're just looking at some patterns. Not sure whether it might involve a British traveller. Probably nothing at all. But, I think I might be coming to buy you that beer. If you drink, of course."

Millie huffed:

"I'm Spanish! Of course I drink."

Her next comment surprised Shelly:

"I'd be happy to share a beer with some female company. These losers here don't have much time for a little girl like me. We can compare notes."

Shelly chuckled:

"Actually, I was just wondering what it was like to be a female cop, over there."

Millie gave her a knowing look, and the wink of a confidante:

"I think maybe you can guess the answer to that one, my little coffee maid."

Having concluded the call, Shelly went to update Dawn and Frank. DI Williams was already with them, and gave Shelly an enquiring look.

"Possibly something. Apparently there was a reported disturbance at Senora Pastor's house, on the thirtieth of December 2013. Five months after the murder. But, when cops paid a call, she had nothing to tell them."

Williams looked resigned to the worst.

"Ok. Dawn, this afternoon I want you to lay out everything we've got, in date order. Put it all up on the board, and talk the whole team through it. Then, we decide where we go next."

"Will do, Boss."

At the team meeting, Dawn waited patiently for the rabble to settle down. She was looking tired and drawn. Already, as this case began to unravel before them, there were images and possibilities emerging that no cop liked to see. Especially, no female cop.

Dawn usually dressed brightly. Not overly flamboyant – she was now in her late forties – but colourful, and with style. She had been married for over twenty years, and at times felt worn down by policing, and... life. But, she was an attractive woman; and dressing accordingly sometimes helped her to remember there was life outside the police, and enabled her to keep the darker side of society in perspective. Today, she was in dark pants, and a silvery-grey top, with a quiet, discreet floral pattern. Serious. Business-like.

She took a deep breath, before she began to set out all that had been established, as colleagues listened quietly. It was a sombre account.

"Ok, these are the matters of interest. We can't be certain that they are all connected, of course, but this is what we currently have in our eye-line."

Williams interjected:

"We need to keep an open mind. None of these things may be connected. Or, all of them. Go on, Dawn."

She resumed:

"Twenty-third of July, 2011. Fact. Suspicious death of Luca Mendez, a fisherman; close to El Cotillo, a fishing village in Fuerteventura. His boat is found drifting, with lots of blood in it. Subsequent analysis showed it to be Luca's blood. He was an experienced boat man, and conditions were not extreme. Nobody charged with foul play – nobody saw anything."

Dawn paused to glance at her notes, before continuing:

"Fact. Luca's widow, Salome, took her own life on the twenty-third of September 2012. This was after the death of their daughter, Rosa, from leukaemia, on the second of August 2012. Salome's mother has told police that she believes Salome was assaulted, possibly sexually assaulted, on the eighteenth of February 2012."

"Poor family!" Muttered someone.

"Are we absolutely sure she *did* take her own life?" Chipped in Graeme French.

"Yes, I don't think there's any doubt about that." Confirmed Dawn.

She went on:

"Fact. Roberto Pastor, a thirty-four year old coach driver in Lanzarote; bludgeoned to death, on the twenty-third of July 2013. Nobody charged. He left a widow, Aida, and two young children, Vanessa and Aimar."

Dawn glanced across at a map that she had pinned up.

83

"For those of you who aren't geography majors, Lanzarote is just across the water from Fuerteventura, about thirty minutes by ferry. The local police have confirmed for us that, on the thirtieth of December 2013, there was a reported disturbance at the widow's house. But, when they visited, she sent them away, and there was no follow-up."

Dave Perryman opened his mouth to ask something, but changed his mind, and nodded to Dawn to continue.

"Fact. July 2014, around the twenty-third or twenty-fourth, according to the pathologist, Vito Navarro died. His body was found a week later, in a lake, in Cumbria. Cause of death: drowning. Fact, his widow, Mariana Navarro, alleges that she was attacked and raped in her own home on the twenty-eighth of May 2015. She claims that the attacker showed that he knew all about the death of her husband. He also held over Mariana the double threat of harming her only daughter, and exposing the sexual encounter online to humiliate her and confound any charges of non-consensual sex."

Dawn paused, and looked to DI Williams, who responded:

"Spell out the common factors, Dawn."

She resumed:

"So, common factors. One, the date. Twenty-third of July has cropped up three times. Two, Spanish ethnicity. All three murder victims were Spanish; two living in the Canary Islands, and one in the UK. We were drawn to the Spanish ethnicity by what Mariana Navarro told us; that her alleged attacker made numerous references to her husband being a Spaniard. Three, all murder victims were married with at least one young child. Four, possible assaults on each of the widows, some months after the husbands' deaths."

She stopped, and sat down.

DI Williams stood in front of the incident display board, deep in concentration.

"Thoughts?"

Dave Perryman was the first to step in:

"Have we checked for anything in 2015 and 2016?"

Frank Burnley replied:

"I've found a report of a Spanish man going missing in July 2015…"

He got no further, as both Dawn and Shelly began to demand why he hadn't said anything to them.

"Just today." He defended himself. "I was about to bring it to you. I just started to dig into it this morning."

"Where, Frank? In the UK?" Williams asked.

"North Manchester, near Rochdale. Esteban Rojo… reported missing on the twenty-seventh of July 2015. Nothing further… there's no report of him turning up. We'll have to check."

"Get on it, now!" DI Williams tone was more abrupt than usual.

"Will do, Boss." Frank interrogated his computer, looking for the details.

"And 2016? Has anybody vanished, or a body found? We're going to have to disclose everything to the Spanish."

Williams sighed.

"I don't like the idea of this getting out. But, if there's a pattern here, are we going to need to look for somebody who travels regularly between Britain and the Canaries? A Spaniard who comes here, or a Brit who goes there?"

"According to Mariana, he's British." Contributed Alice Hawley.

Shelly had remained quiet, but now spoke up.

"Boss. If there has been a murder this year, on or around July twenty-third, and if we're right in our suspicions… then it's quite possible that a woman could be in extreme danger of being assaulted. The usual pattern seems to be for him to pay a follow-up visit a few months after."

"Yes, I'm aware of that."

Williams glared at the ground.

"Frank, Esteban Rojo? Anything?"

Frank had been busily searching the files.

"Can't see anything about him turning up, Boss. I've got the address."

"Ok. Who reported him missing?"

Frank said quietly:

"His partner, Bev."

He continued, as if to answer the question that was in all their minds.

"They have a little girl, Talia."

Williams drew in a deep breath.

"You and Shelly get out there. See if you can get anything from Bev. But... be careful. You know what might have happened subsequently, but don't put the words into her mouth."

"Boss."

Shelly picked up her favourite white jacket, and the two of them made for the door.

"Whose car?" Asked Frank.

"You can drive." Replied Shelly. "A girl like me wouldn't get in just anybody's car, Frank; but, with you, I feel safe."

She was teasing as Frank knew.

"That doesn't sound like much of a compliment."

Chapter 15

Little more than an hour later, having negotiated the Greater Manchester traffic; Frank pulled up close to a tower block, where Esteban Rojo and his partner, Bev, were last reported living. Bernard Shay Tower looked tired and worn; having been battered by the northern winds and regular rain for too many years. The outward facing windows seemed to reflect only dark and grim interiors. The panelled surfaces which picked out a symmetrical pattern may once have gleamed a creamy matt finish; but now they looked shabby, and were streaked by the familiar route of biting rainfall.

On the square, around which three wings of the block were built, a group of youths were sat; with a couple of scruffy looking mongrel dogs. The boys were sharing rolled-up cigarettes, and drinking from cans of lager. Several empty tins rolled around on the ground, nearby. Care for the environment was not high on their list of priorities.

Frank groaned, as he looked up at the large sign which spelt out the name of the building – Bernard Shay Tower – in bold lettering, and a smaller one, not matching at all. It bore the initials BS and the symbol of a padlock alongside a telephone number; presumably to signify who to contact in the case of break-ins, boarding up, or other security issues.

He looked further upwards towards the seventh floor, muttering:

"What chance the lift works."

"Come on. The exercise will do you good."

Shelly was fit and agile; and the likely climb up seven flights of stairs did not daunt her in the slightest. However, to their surprise, the lift *did* work; although the smell inside was far from pleasant. By the time they reached the correct floor, they had agreed how they would approach this encounter. They made their way along the walkway, in search of number fifty-five.

Arriving at the door, they exchanged glances. The frosted-glass panel of the door had a crack in it, partly taped up. The kitchen window was partly covered by a grubby lace curtain, and on the sill inside there were some small plants. Shelly knocked at the door, and pulled out her warrant card, ready to introduce herself.

Presently, the shape of a figure became visible through the glass. A rattling noise told them that the door was being unlocked, and a security chain was being slid into place. The door opened, just enough for the occupant to look out.

"Bev Mitchell?" Shelly asked, holding up her identification.

The woman peered at the card, and then looked past Shelly, at Frank, who was hovering behind.

"I'm DC Shelly King, Greater Manchester Police. This is DC Frank Burnley. I wonder if we could come in and speak with you for a moment?"

The woman paused; then, reluctantly, slid aside the security bolt, and opened the door, revealing herself. She was slim, with a thin, bony face, and hair that was tightly combed back against her forehead, and tied back with a band. There was a hint of red, or maroon, covering part of it; apparently she had dyed it some bright colour a while back, and it had now mostly grown out or faded away. Bev Mitchell looked no older than thirty, and was wearing a yellow, faded t-shirt, over black leggings. She had a tattoo on her right arm; some flowery pattern, which may once have made a positive and artistic statement, but now looked worn and indistinct. From behind her, inside the flat, the noise of a television floated through; children's programmes, it sounded like.

"What's it about?" She asked, uncomfortably. She didn't seem to be in any hurry to invite them inside.

"It's about your partner, Esteban. Can we come in?"

Bev tilted her head to one side.

"Esteban?"

She stood back, and the two officers stepped inside her home. She closed the door after them, sliding on the security bolt, and followed them into her living room, where a small child was playing with toys, on the floor. The little girl didn't look up, as they entered. On a low table, there were the remains of her tea, and scattered over a sofa was a pile of washing. The room was untidy, but not smelly, apart from a faint smell of nicotine; and not the worst that either officer had seen.

"Sit down." Bev indicated the sofa and a tattered chair, but made no effort to clear away any seating space.

Frank remained standing, while Shelly sat on the edge of the sofa, facing Bev, who perched on a dining chair, that she swivelled round into place.

"Well, is there some news?" Bev seemed interested, but not excited.

"First of all, I need to check a few details with you."

Shelly began.

"You reported Esteban missing on the twenty-seventh of July, last year."

Bev nodded.

"And, have you heard anything from him, since then?"

Bev looked blank.

"No, of course not. I thought that was why you've come. I thought you'd found him."

Shelly looked over to Frank, who took up his part: "No, Bev. I'm afraid we haven't got any news for you. All we know is what you told the police at the time. He went out one morning … July twenty-third … and never came back. Is that correct?"

Bev nodded.

"So, why are you here?" There was an element of defiance, almost hostility, in her voice.

Ignoring her question, Frank continued: "Esteban didn't have a job, did he?"

Bev shook her head.

"Did he drive?"

89

She shook her head again, but added: "He could drive, but he didn't have a car when he went."

Shelly asked: "You told the police that none of his possessions were missing?"

"Nothing." Bev sighed. "But, just like you, they thought that he'd just had enough of me, and dumped me. And his child."

She looked down at the little girl, occupying herself in front of the television.

"What's her name?" Shelly was watching her play.

"Petra."

There was a tear in her eye, as she looked at her daughter. Frank asked, in a soft voice:

"How were things between the two of you, before he disappeared?"

Bev turned on him, sharply: "They were okay. We had our ups and downs. Doesn't everyone? But, I knew he hadn't left me, then … and I really know it now."

"What do you mean, 'you really know it'?" Shelly asked. "This is really important, Bev."

Bev turned away, and dabbed at her face.

"I just mean … I never believed he would do that to me. And, I still don't believe he would. But, if you haven't got any news, why are you here?"

There was a silence. Finally, Frank broached the subject of why they were calling on her now.

"Well, Bev, the truth is, we don't know whether Esteban is still alive, or not. We have no evidence that he's not, but... it's a mystery where he might be. And... we are looking at a number of cases where men disappeared, suddenly. And, we're looking for any similarities. So, the more we can learn about Esteban, about his life at the time he vanished, and..."

He paused, glancing over at Shelly.

"And, whether there's been anything happen subsequently, that you think could be relevant... anything else that you could tell us... anything at all..."

Bev had stood up, and walked over to her kitchenette, where she was filling a kettle.

"No. Nothing."

Shelly and Frank sat, in silence. Finally, Shelly had another go:

"What do *you* think happened, Bev? You've had over a year to think about it. What's your gut feeling?"

Bev didn't hesitate: "I think he was murdered. But, I don't think we... you... will ever find out who killed him. So, there's nothing I can do about it, is there?"

"We'll keep trying." Shelly replied. "But, we need you to work with us. If there's anything at all, that you can tell us..."

"I already said, nothing!"

Bev raised her voice, at which little Petra, playing on the floor, dropped her toy and looked round at her mother.

"So, if that's all?"

"Okay, that's it, for now. But, we may need to contact you again."

Shelly passed Bev her business card.

"When you've had a think, if anything comes up, call me."

Leaving Bev's flat, the two officers shared a suspicious glance back at the door, as it shut behind them.

"What do you think?" Asked Shelly.

Frank sighed:

"I think... I wouldn't be surprised if it's exactly the same story, again."

As Frank drove them back to base, Shelly looked sadly out of the car window. She was thinking about Bev, living alone in that flat; with just her little girl to care for and protect. Was that what she was trying to do, now? Had her partner been murdered; and, was she now refusing to say anything about a subsequent assault, for fear of endangering the innocent Petra? Shelly wondered what she herself would do, if she was in the same position.

"The boss said you and Dawn might be off to the Canaries?" Mused Frank. "Fancy a few days away with Dawn?"

Shelly ignored him. She knew he was teasing; but, right now, there didn't feel like much space in her mind for humour.

"Of course, if anyone can catch this guy, it will be you, Shelly."

She turned sharply to him, and he blushed slightly; unsure what had made him say that.

The next day, Thursday, DI Williams pulled Shelly into his office and took the report on the interview with Bev Mitchell.

"We couldn't get her to say that anything had happened to her, Boss; but, we both felt it. There's something she's not telling us."

Williams nodded.

"Have we found anything on Esteban's background? Or anything to link any of these victims, apart from the fact that they are all Spaniards?"

Shelly shook her head, as Dawn joined them.

"Okay, so I want you two to be ready to go over to Spain, at short notice. There's no point, yet. We might still find victims as far apart over in the Canaries as they are in the UK. So, we wouldn't know where to start. But, sometime soon, I want you linking up with our Spanish cousins, to try and make some connections."

Dawn agreed: "I've warned my Roy I might be going travelling without him. He wasn't too pleased."

"Nice to have someone to miss you." Commented Shelly, tongue in cheek.

"Boss!" Frank almost burst into the office. "I think we've got another one."

Within minutes, most of the team had gathered in the incident room, and DI Williams gave Frank the nod. He cleared his throat, and began to relate what he had just found.

"Twenty-eighth of July 2012. Tom Perez, aged twenty-four; found floating face down in a reservoir, about fifteen miles from his home, in Ripon, North Yorkshire. He left a partner, Maria, and a baby daughter."

The team listened, quietly, as Frank continued: "It didn't come up, at first, because we had it down as a suicide."

Dawn raised a point, which several of them were thinking: "Suicide, with a baby daughter? Why was it deemed to be a suicide?"

Frank explained:

"Well, at first, he was a missing person. But, when his body was found, there were some indications that he might have taken his own life. There wasn't a note, but it was in a place where there have been suicides before. He had money problems, gambling debts. He was a drug user. Nothing conclusive, but enough to suggest that it might not have been accidental, or foul play. The local police didn't spend time looking for anybody else."

"Hmm. Nice to know we always do a thorough job." DI Williams grunted. "And, Perez? He was Spanish?"

"Yes, he was." Confirmed Frank. "His widow, partner... has moved address, but I think I've tracked her down. It's an address in Leeds."

"Dawn, you and Shelly go see the widow. Frank, you keep digging. I hope you fail, but try and find me something from last month."

"Will do, Boss."

Chapter 16

Dawn drove her car towards Leeds, with Shelly in the passenger seat. Shelly gazed out.

"How long have you and Roy been married?"

Dawn raised an eyebrow.

"Twenty-one years."

Shelly nodded appreciatively.

"If he was a serial killer, you'd know, wouldn't you?"

Dawn paused.

"Well, I hope that, if he was a serial killer, I wouldn't have married him."

Shelly grinned.

"Yeah, of course. But, I mean, if it is one man who's carried out all these attacks... murders and rapes... wouldn't somebody know?"

Dawn kept her eyes on the road, but answered:

"There's no saying he has a wife. Or anyone at all. Maybe that's why he's so angry. Lonely. No sort of life."

Shelly pounced:

"So, shouldn't that make it easier for us? Don't we start by looking at men who live alone?"

Dawn sniffed.

"I wouldn't get too optimistic. Perhaps another point for the psychologist. Men, probably over thirty and under fifty, who may or may not live alone, and have probably travelled between the Canaries and Britain a few times? Doesn't narrow it down much."

"No." Shelly sighed.

As they reached the neighbourhood in which Frank had identified an address for Tom Perez' partner, Maria Mates, Shelly looked at the tidy row of houses; mostly bungalows, each with smart gardens.

"Nice properties."

They pulled up outside the target, which was fronted by an immaculate lawn, and expensive-looking drive, and got out. On the drive, in front of a closed double garage, with a white-painted metal door, was a white, sporty-looking Mercedes.

They walked towards the front door, and saw the figure of a woman, inside, passing the window to come to the front door. It opened, before they could touch the bell.

"Maria Mates?"

Dawn held up her warrant card.

"My name's Detective Sergeant Dawn Pardell, Greater Manchester Police. This is DC Shelly King."

The woman looked, politely, at the card.

She was stylishly dressed; in tight, dark pants, and a flowing, light blue top. Her jewellery looked expensive; sparkly ear-rings – noticeable, but not clumsy – matched a glassy necklace that hung against her chest. Her hair was blonde; long, and smooth; and her make-up had clearly been given daily attention.

"Yes, I'm Maria Mates. How can I help?"

"Could we come in for a moment?" Asked Dawn.

"Of course."

Maria stepped back, and invited them into her lounge; which looked as expensive and tastefully decorative as she did. A multi-faceted chandelier of dripping pearls dominated the room; and a large fluffy rug separated the huge wall-mounted television from a deep and comfortable-looking, ivory coloured, leather sofa.

Sitting down, as invited, Dawn began.

"We're here in connection with the death of Tom Perez, in 2012."

Maria drew in a breath.

"Oh."

Regaining composure which had been momentarily lost, she brushed back her hair, and looked enquiringly at the two officers.

"And?"

Dawn explained:

"We weren't involved in the case, at all. But, now, we're looking at it in some detail. It was recorded as 'unexplained', but the implication seemed to be that Tom had taken his own life. Is that how you saw it?"

Maria tilted her head to one side.

"Whatever I think, nothing's going to change, is it? Nothing will..."

She paused, seeming uncomfortable.

Shelly glanced around the house.

"Do you live here alone, Maria?"

Maria shook her head.

"No, I... well, the fact is, I've moved on. I have a new partner."

"That's good." Shelly smiled at her.

Maria seemed to be feeling guilty. However, there is no reason why a woman who has lost her partner shouldn't accept a second chance at a loving relationship. A lifetime as a grieving widow isn't for everyone. Shouldn't be for anyone. Briefly, Shelly thought about Bev Mitchell; the woman she had visited in the slightly squalid Rochdale flat, the previous day. If they had in common the terrible thing that she suspected, the hand that fate had dealt to this woman in the aftermath was altogether better.

And, after all, it was now over four years since she had found herself alone. Alone, apart from her little girl, remembered Shelly.

"You have a little girl."

Maria looked slightly surprised.

"Yes, Rosie. She's four and a half, now. She's at a day nursery."

Dawn took up the lead:

"Maria, as I said, Tom's death was officially 'unexplained'. There were some factors that pointed towards him maybe being suicidal. What did you think about that?"

"I... it was a shock, of course. I don't know what I thought. I couldn't think straight, at all."

"No, of course."

Dawn took her time.

"Tom was found on the twenty-eighth of July; but, you last saw him on the twenty-third of July. The pathologist judged that he probably died on the twenty-third or twenty-fourth."

"Yes, that's right." Maria agreed.

Dawn continued:

"And, what was his mood like, when you last saw him, that morning?"

Maria sighed; the frustrated sigh of someone who had answered all these questions many times before.

"Nothing out of the ordinary."

Dawn patiently and quietly persevered:

"It's more than four years since, now. What do you think, now? Would Tom have taken his own life?"

97

For the briefest second, Maria appeared to be stung to anger, and almost hissed the start of her reply. But, she soon became calm, once more.

"I don't know. But, nothing's going to bring him back. And, like I said, I've moved on. All I want is a good life for me and Rosie. I have a responsibility to her."

Dawn was aware that Shelly shot her a sideways glance.

"What made you say that, exactly? About having a responsibility to her?"

Maria looked away, then raised her face to look at a picture, hanging over the decorative fireplace. It was a professionally produced portrait of her, with a handsome, dark-haired man, with a neatly sculpted beard. He looked a little older than her; and had his arm protectively around her.

"That's Sean, my partner. He's good to me. He doesn't know everything about the past. I'd like to keep it that way. I just want to move forward."

"Maria, this is very important." Dawn persisted.

"Is there something that you can tell us, that you haven't told the police before? Did anything happen, after Tom died, that made you question how he came to die?"

Shelly wished that she had used skill such as that, when speaking with Bev Mitchell. Perhaps she could have prised out some useful response.

Maria opened her mouth, but closed it again, without saying anything. Significantly, thought both Dawn and Shelly, she didn't seem greatly surprised to be asked the question.

"Like I said. Moving forward."

She looked around. For just a moment, her gaze flickered towards a framed picture of a little girl, set in an alcove beside the window.

"As you can see, I've got a nice home here. A man that I can trust. He's gentle with me… patient. He looks after me. I'll never go back to Ripon, again. Too many bad memories."

She looked, almost tearfully, at the two women.

98

"Don't ask me any more questions. I've nothing more to say. I'm going to pick up Rosie, soon. And then, all I want to do is get on with my life, with Sean. So, please, just let me do that."

Shelly made a comment.

"Maria, we didn't want to upset you. But, if there's something else, something that frightens you, we can protect you. If there's something that threatens danger to you… it could mean danger to other women, too."

Maria stood up.

"I'd like you to go now, please."

"Okay, thank you. Take my card, in case you ever want to contact us."

Dawn put her card into Maria's unwilling hand.

"Goodbye, Maria."

The officers left. As they got into the car, neither spoke for a moment, but both wore grim faces. Finally, it was Shelly who broke the silence:

"Same again. I'd swear it's the same again. She thinks she's protecting Rosie. Doesn't want her new fella to know what happened. Definitely."

Dawn nodded.

"I agree."

Chapter 17

"What have you got, so far?" DCI Floella York was becoming impatient, as she faced the team for the Friday meeting.

"It seems that all you're digging up is a series of possibly linked deaths, but nothing at all to help locate a potential perpetrator. If these deaths were foul play, you need to get back out there and start searching for witnesses."

DI Williams looked thoughtfully at the display wall, as Dawn, Shelly, and Frank remained tight-lipped.

Williams summarised:

"He's clever. In every case, the death has been made to look like a probable suicide, or accidental. He's not leaving a signature... apart from a pattern of 'no signature'."

"Apart from the Lanzarote one, Roberto Pastor. Nothing accidental about that." Corrected Dawn.

DCI York asked:

"So, what is the connection, apart from the Spanish ethnicity? Nothing at all to connect any of these victims?"

DI Williams shook his head.

"Nothing apart from Spanish, and a bit of a pattern emerging around the north of England."

He stepped over to the map on the wall, and indicated locations:

"Tom Perez, from Ripon. Found in Gouthwaite reservoir, July 2012. Vito Navarro, lived at Pickering. Found over near Penrith, July 2014. Esteban Rojo, Rochdale. Disappeared July 2015. Never found."

Dawn spoke:

"Also, possibly, Luca Mendez; drowned off Fuerteventura, July 2011. And, Roberto Pastor, killed in Lanzarote; July 2013.

DCI York stood up, scrutinising the board.

"So, you have, possibly... a death in each year from 2011 to 2015."

"Yes Ma'am. But, if we believe that what Mariana Navarro told us is true, Vito was the sixth victim; killed in 2014. The implication was one killing a year, but not including 2009. He told her he was 'busy that year'."

DCI York quickly checked the maths, in her head.

"So, if it was 'one killing a year' as you put it, and the only gap year being 2009, then that would mean his first was in 2008."

"Yes Ma'am." Dawn confirmed.

York turned to Williams:

"Then you need to find a trigger that turned a man into a serial killer in 2008. Find witnesses in the areas at the times of these deaths. And get those women to talk. You believe they've been attacked. Get it out of them."

"Ma'am."

DI Williams looked at Shelly:

"You pay another visit to Bev Mitchell. You and Frank both suspected she was holding back. Dawn... go with Shelly. Have another go."

"Will do, Boss."

At the conclusion of the team meeting, Frank Burnley immersed himself into his search for any links between the victims. He was trying to avoid concentrating only on connections between probable murder victims, and keep in mind that the links – if any – could be between the women involved here.

He knew that they were all mums. But, none of them had attended the same maternity hospital. Nothing to link the children's nurseries or

101

schools. Some of the women were Spaniards, others British. The twenty-third of July… was that date significant in the lives of these people, rather than to the killer? He couldn't find anything there. Had some major event happened on July twenty-third, way back in history? Something with a Spanish connection? Frank racked his brains and explored every avenue that he could think of. Nothing.

What about the men's occupations… any common ground there? Nothing. The men were all Spanish in origin… did they visit Spain on a regular basis? Could any of them have met, either at an airport, or in Spain? This was something he would need more information about, from surviving partners. But it wasn't looking hopeful.

Was it about the children? Frank knew that the attacker seemed to have knowledge in each case about the name of a child of his rape victim. Did he know that already, or was it something that he dragged out of his murder victim, or subsequently researched?

The most demanding question of all, and Frank was getting nowhere with this too; was, did he already know his murder victims? Could each one of them have been random Spanish men, or had he already encountered them, perhaps through the course of his work? Could that be it? Was the killer also a Spaniard? No, Frank dismissed that – Mariana Navarro had confirmed that he was British. A well-practised linguist might fool someone with limited language skills; but Mariana, a Spanish woman herself, would undoubtedly know the difference between a Brit and a Spaniard speaking English.

That afternoon, Shelly arrived once more at Bernard Shay Tower; this time with Dawn as her partner.

Parking in an empty space, next to an old red Commer van that looked like it hadn't seen the open road for many a year, Shelly looked up towards the seventh floor. A rough-looking young man, with a shaven head, was leaning against the building. His dog sat on the ground next to him. Both of them glanced across at the two officers, with mild interest but no evidence of warmth.

"That's her place, up there." Shelly indicated.

Dawn looked up at the level, and watched two young mums walking together along the concourse, with buggies and shopping bags.

She considered.

"Well, if she was attacked at any point, perhaps somebody round here knows something. Maybe she has mates. Perhaps she told someone, thinking they would keep it to themselves. They don't go in much for talking to the police, around here, but she might have confided in a friend."

They went up in the lift, and soon emerged at Bev Mitchell's floor. As they approached her door, it opened, and a bony looking middle-aged woman, wearing grey jogger pants, stepped out.

"See you later, Love." She called, as she made to pull the door closed, after herself.

"Oh!" She was startled as she turned, to see the two smartly dressed women arriving at the door.

Something about her expression betrayed that perhaps she immediately recognised them as police officers, and didn't feel comfortable with that realisation. She paused from closing the door.

"I think you've got visitors, Bev."

Bev appeared, and barely suppressed a groan, as she recognised Shelly. She eyed the other woman, as Shelly began to explain:

"This is my colleague, DS Pardell."

"Do you want me to stay?" Muttered Bev's visitor, the bony woman who had been on the point of departing.

Bev nodded.

"Come in." She said to the officers, though with little warmth.

Shelly eyed the older woman.

"You're Bev's mum?"

103

The likeness was clear, and mum nodded.

As they entered Bev's main living room, Shelly looked around, to see whether little Petra was at home. There was no sign of her.

"Your daughter not here?"

"She's at a neighbour's." Grunted Bev.

Shelly got to the purpose of their visit:

"Does your mum know why we've made contact with you?"

Mum intervened to answer:

"She said you'd been to see her."

Dawn was pleased. This meant that perhaps her mum was someone that Bev confided in. Maybe told everything...

Shelly persisted; directing her question at Bev, but in a way that made it clear that her mum was invited to join in.

"You know we're looking again at Esteban's disappearance, Bev. And at whether anything might have happened since then, that could shed any light on it."

She looked from Bev to her mum, and back at Bev.

Silence.

Mum looked uncomfortable.

"What's your name?" Asked Dawn.

"Alice Mitchell."

Dawn turned to Shelly:

"We may need to ask around, speak to the neighbours. Somebody may have seen something relevant. There are eyes everywhere. You saw that guy downstairs? I bet he doesn't miss much."

Bev coloured a little, and frowned, exchanging looks with her mum. Finally, she spoke, in a quiet voice:

"What is it you're expecting to find?"

Dawn took a deep breath, and made the decision to disclose something.

"The thing is, Bev, we've been looking at other cases, similar to this one. Esteban isn't the only... person... to have gone missing in recent years. There have been others, with real similarities to your situation. Women left behind, not knowing if their partner was alive or dead."

She paused, trying to read any reaction. Bev remained tight-lipped.

Dawn continued:

"There have been instances where the women have been assaulted, just a few weeks or months after their partner's disappearance. For all sorts of reasons, they have been too scared to come forward and report it."

She stopped again. Surely this was enough to invite Bev to speak out, if there was anything to say.

Bev's mum was looking hard at her daughter; but Bev studiously straightened and folded a coat which had lain on the back of a chair, and avoided making eye contact.

Dawn nodded to Shelly, who took up the baton:

"If anything has happened to you, Bev, since Esteban went, it's not going to shock us. You are a victim here. We'll support you all we can, protect you..."

Alice's restraint finally snapped, and she burst in:

"Tell them Bev!"

"Shut up, Mum!"

Both police officers looked to Alice, and Shelly spoke for them:

"If you know something, Alice, you can tell us. We'd rather hear it from Bev, but..."

105

Alice stepped over to her daughter, and put her arm around her, speaking quietly:

"You can't go on like this, Bev. It's killing you. Eating away at you inside. Tell them."

Bev buried her face in her mum's chest, and her body started to throb, as the tears came. Tears that she had perhaps held in for too long. When she finally composed herself, she sat down, next to her mum, and faced the police officers.

"It was in January."

She stopped. Then began again:

"You mean I'm not the only one? He's done this to someone else?"

Refusing to be drawn, not wanting to compromise any evidence that Bev might be about to offer them, Dawn and Shelly held back.

Dawn replied:

"What happened, Bev?"

She sighed, and tried again to tell her story:

"It was January. Someone broke in... a man. He broke in, and attacked me."

"Go on." Urged Dawn. "Tell us everything."

Alice gave her daughter a comforting squeeze.

"Go on, love."

Bev began again:

"I was in the flat, one night, just watching TV. Petra was in bed. I was about to go to bed, myself. Then I heard a noise. It wasn't the door being forced... he had already got in, somehow. Like he just let himself in. I don't know how, because the door was locked."

She paused, to wipe her face.

106

"I got up, I was sat there." She pointed to where Shelly was sat.

"Before I could open that door…" She pointed at the door to the hall – "He was in, and he threw himself at me, knocked me down. He was on top of me…"

Bev started to sob. The other women understood, and waited patiently, until presently she resumed:

"He lay on top of me, with his hand over my mouth, so I couldn't call out. He was strong. He had a mask on, a balaclava, but he had his face pressed right up against mine. I could feel his body pressing right against me."

She looked at her mum, as if ashamed.

"I wanted to tell him, 'just take whatever money I have'… but I couldn't even speak."

Bev shuddered again, as the memories flooded back.

"Go on." Encouraged Dawn. "You're doing great."

Bev didn't feel anything approaching 'great', but continued, anyway:

"He started to tell me… it was as though he had got everything planned out, rehearsed. Like he knew exactly what was going to happen. Like a film script."

She sniffed back more tears.

"And that's exactly what it was. A film script."

"What do you mean by that Bev?" Asked Shelly, already fairly sure that she knew what the answer would be.

Bev cringed again, and squeezed tightly at her mum's hand.

"He made me have sex with him. He had a piece of card, with a set of instructions on. He held it up in front of my face, and made me read it. He pressed it so close to my eyes that I couldn't see it clearly. He had to move it back a few inches. And I had to read it."

Dawn and Shelly's attention was complete, as Dawn asked:

107

"What did the card say, Bev?"

Bev sighed, a disgusted sigh.

"It said I was going to have to pretend to enjoy it with him. Look happy. And, he kept speaking about Petra. He knew she was asleep in the next room. He kept making veiled threats… well, not veiled at all… threats about harming her if I didn't do what he wanted."

Shelly tried to offer a kindly, reassuring smile:

"You're being really brave, Bev. What happened next?"

Bev looked, briefly, as though she was going to throw up. She went on:

"He warned me not to scream, then he took his hand away from my mouth. He got up. For just a second, I thought I had a chance. His back was turned, and I scrambled up. I wanted to rush at him and knock him flying…"

She sniffed back tears.

"But I knew I wasn't strong enough."

They could see that she wasn't a physically strong person; who wouldn't have much chance in any sort of struggle with such a man.

"But I knew I wouldn't be able to… so I threw myself at the wall, there…"

She pointed over to her left.

"I banged on the wall and screamed as loud as I could, so that Jack next door might hear me…"

Shelly and Dawn were listening to every word.

"I only had a second, before he jumped back on me, and cracked me in the face. I banged against that table, and knocked it over, when I fell."

She sobbed.

"I wanted to run, but… I couldn't even get up for a moment, and he moved a chair against the door, so that I couldn't run out."

"That wasn't very clever." He said.

"Not clever at all. I could see that he was about to hit me again, and I put my hands up to protect my face. I said: 'I won't. I'll be quiet.' I didn't know what else I could do."

Out of the corner of her eye, Bev could see the tears running down her mum's face, and hear the soft sobs. She avoided looking directly at her mum.

"Then, he got out his phone, and put it on there."

She pointed at the fireplace, which housed a small electric fire.

"He filmed everything. He kept saying that everyone would see this, if I didn't do exactly what he wanted. I had to try and look like I was enjoying it. Like I was begging for it. But I knew that if I seemed to be enjoying it, he would be able to use it... the film... in his defence. Claim that I was willing... but I didn't..."

Bev finally stumbled to a halt, and broke off.

Dawn judged that it was nearly time to summarise, but needed her to confirm one more thing, in absolutely explicit terms:

"So, Bev, after he had set his phone up, to film everything, what happened? What did he do?"

Bev almost snorted with derision, and was about to demand 'What do you think?', but realised that she needed to spell it out.

"He raped me. Right there, on that sofa."

The four women sat silently together for a few moments, each with their own thoughts. Eventually, Bev continued:

"You're wondering why I didn't report it, aren't you?"

Shelly and Dawn looked as sympathetic as they could.

"Why did you feel you couldn't report it, Bev?" Asked Dawn.

"Because he threatened Petra. He threatened he would come back and harm Petra. And, he had that film. A film of me having sex with a strange man, while Esteban is gone…"

Alice let go of Bev's hand, and walked over to the kitchen area; where she proceeded to boil the kettle and make two cups of coffee. Dawn and Shelly declined the offer of a drink.

When she sat down again, complete with two cups, the officers got up.

"We won't be a moment, Bev." Murmured Dawn, as they stepped to the front door, for a quiet word together.

"We need to get her in to make a statement." Whispered Shelly.

"I know. I think she will. She's overcome the worst part, telling us."

Dawn made a brief phone call to DI Williams, to give him the news of what seemed to be a major breakthrough. He was pleased, shocked, disgusted.

"Get her in here, as fast as you can."

Chapter 18

There was no Saturday off for Dawn and Shelly. Although reluctant, Bev Mitchell arrived at their police station, just after ten in the morning. Her mum had made sure that she went, by going with her. A detailed interview conducted by Dawn and Shelly followed; with DI Williams and Dr Sheen out of sight, but watching through the one way glass.

Bev was anxious, perhaps prompted by her mum, to seek reassurance of her safety. She wanted to make sure he could never get to her again. That she was safe. That Petra was safe. Dawn promised they would be coming out to make her flat more secure. She would have a panic alarm, and extra locks on the door. The police would be looking out for her.

The poor woman was asked again about the circumstances of Esteban's disappearance, and subsequently recounted again the later events that she had told them about. It was established that the date of the assault on her was the twelfth of January.

The mode of attack was so similar to that alleged by Mariana Navarro, that the inescapable conclusion was that it was the same man. Bev's memory of the wording on the card of instructions that this man held in front of her was not as clear as Mariana's. The officers were careful not to plant any details in her mind, beyond those which she herself volunteered. But, they were in no doubt that the wording was substantially the same; and it was, in all probability, exactly the same card.

Bev's description of the attacker was similar to Mariana's. There was nothing significantly different; however, it was rather vague. When prompted about anything distinctive, such as a scent, Bev had been unable to recall anything. As for background and accent, she confirmed that he was white British, and felt he was probably a northerner.

DI Williams commented to Sheen, as they watched and listened:

"He plays on the threat to the little girl."

Sheen nodded, taking off his glasses to give them a wipe:

"There are a few things that women fear more than anything else. Rape, humiliation, and danger to their babies. He knows that, and plays on them all."

Back inside the interview room, Dawn was trying to elicit as much information as possible, while Bev was in the mood to tell all.

"You said that he made some comment about Esteban being Spanish. What did he say about that, Bev? Can you remember?"

Bev looked miserable, as she had done all morning, quite understandably.

"He said something about Spaniards. 'Filthy Spaniards' was the words he used. Like he hated Spaniards. I don't know why. Maybe he hates everyone who's not British. A racist. I don't know."

Shelly was curious about how the attacker gained entry to the flat.

"You said he managed to let himself in, but there was no sign of a forced entry?"

"Yes. It made me wonder whether he had a key. But I didn't know how. Then, later, I decided he couldn't possibly have got hold of a key. But mum had the lock changed for me, after I told her."

"When did you tell her?" Asked Dawn.

Bev sniffed:

"It was a few days after. I was too scared to tell anyone. But, she could tell. She knew."

When they had got as much information as they could, Dawn and Shelly prepared Bev for what might happen next. They would stay in touch, would certainly want to speak with her again. If anything else came to mind, she should call them. Then, they organised a lift home for her and her mum, who had waited in a side room, and Bev went on her way.

Later, DI Williams and Dr Sheen sat with Dawn and Shelly, to discuss her account.

Williams was increasingly frustrated:

"Have you dug into their background? Hers and Esteban's? There must be some link somewhere to the others. What are we not seeing?"

Shelly replied:

"Frank's been scouring everything he can lay his hands on. He can't find anything to link any of these couples with each other. There's no apparent connection between the men. They're not all from the same area. Not the same age or background. No suggestion that any of them had ever met each other."

Dawn agreed:

"That's right. And no connection between the women, either. Different areas of the north, different social classes. They don't seem to have anything in common apart from having a Spanish partner and being mother to a young child."

Dr Sheen was listening, and deep in thought. The others looked to him, sensing that he had something to say. He rubbed his chest, as though he felt a pain. Finally, he spoke:

"The accounts from Mariana Navarro and Bev Mitchell are irrefutably similar. Too similar to be a coincidence. If you had shown either of them the other woman's account, she would have recognised it instantly."

"Yes, that's for sure." DI Williams agreed.

"So, given the unlikely 'coincidence' of the disappearance of a Spanish man with a British wife or partner on exactly the same date – twenty-third of July – but in a different year, I'd say it was time to confront one of your other two likely witnesses with this information."

"Explain." DI Williams was pretty sure he knew what Sheen meant, but wanted to be sure.

"Well, if you were to have another go at..." He glanced in the file.

"Maria Mates, to see how she responds to hearing a story like this. She's refusing to play ball, so far. But, that's because she's scared of the humiliation... possibly rejection by her new partner. People disbelieving

113

her, maybe. Loss of her new, comfortable lifestyle. But, the trauma won't have left her. She'll still be feeling violated, angry. If she's part of this, of course… she'll come clean. There's a part of her that's itching to spill it all out."

He rubbed again at his chest, and winced, slightly.

There was a silence.

"We already tried, Boss." Shelly observed. "She didn't want to know us."

DI Williams considered for a moment:

"But that was before we had two stories so similar that we could present to her. I agree with Dr Sheen. It's worth a try. To see if she bites."

Sheen made an offer:

"How about I come with one of you two, to meet her? See if I can provoke a response?"

"Sure." Dawn was in agreement. "Shelly, you take Dr Sheen to meet her. She seemed to respond better to you."

Shelly nodded. Although she had no reason to comment on it, she felt rather flattered to think that Dawn, her senior, had recognised her people skills to such an extent.

"It's over in Leeds. Call her." Instructed the DI. "Try and arrange it for Monday."

Chapter 19

Monday August thirtieth was a Bank Holiday, which DI Williams hadn't considered. But, Maria Mates had, and had already made plans. So, on the Tuesday, Dr Sheen and Shelly drove to her house. Her agreement was grudging, far from keen. But, she had relented, and agreed to see them on that day; at a time when she knew that her partner Sean would be out at work.

As Shelly parked the car, Marcus eyed the properties.

"Nice place." He commented. "Orderly. Tidy. Affluent. Organised and stable."

Shelly didn't respond to his choice of descriptors, but recognised from his tone that he was commenting about the people who lived in this pleasant suburb, as much as about the properties themselves.

She picked up her white jacket from the back seat, and the two of them approached the house. Before they had reached the front door, Maria Mates opened it, and gestured to them to enter.

"This is Dr Sheen." Shelly introduced her colleague.

Maria forced a very brief and courteous smile.

"Not a GP, I'm guessing." She responded, curtly.

"No, I'm not." Sheen confirmed, continuing:

"I'm a psychologist. The reason I'm here with DC King is that we've reason to touch on some very sensitive matters. Some police business can be very upsetting. I work with the police to try and achieve the best outcomes for everyone, with minimum of grief."

He offered her a faint smile. Maria looked dubious, but invited them both to sit down in her comfortable lounge.

Shelly got straight to business; realising that she might only get one shot at catching Maria's interest.

"Maria, I'm about to tell you something that isn't in the public domain. It's not pleasant, and you may find it upsetting. I will also be asking that you don't disclose this information to anyone else, although I can't insist on that. Is it okay if I go ahead?"

Maria's face was impassive, and her body tense and still, as Dr Sheen observed her reactions to Shelly's approach.

"Go on." She said; trying to look not too interested.

"We're looking at a number of incidents that have happened over the course of several years, Maria. Some of these may be connected. The information that we've gathered so far makes us think that they *are* connected. So, if we can establish anything to prove that we've got that wrong, we need to know. Ruling things out is just as important as ruling things in... and we think that maybe you can help us there."

Sheen, barely in Maria's line of sight, nodded sagely in approval. He liked the tone that Shelly had adopted; but could already detect that Maria was becoming uncomfortable. She was avoiding eye contact, and giving undue attention to a stray blonde hair that had come adrift and attached itself to her sleeve. She really didn't want to hear what Shelly was about to say... that was obvious. It was also significant, he thought. Casually, he removed his glasses, and proceeded to give them a polish.

Maria didn't comment, so Shelly continued:

"Your Tom ... he died in 2012. July 2012."

"Yes." Maria muttered.

"One year earlier, in 2011, a young Spanish man went missing, presumed dead. Nobody was ever charged in connection with the matter. He left a wife and a little girl. We found out much later that his wife... widow... was later assaulted. We can't ask her about it now, because she took her own life."

Maria listened, with her head down.

"Three years ago, a year after you lost Tom, in the summer of 2013, a Spanish man was killed. He was battered to death. It wasn't in the UK... it

116

was in the Canary Islands. He left a wife, and two young children. The killer was never found. Nothing to console his widow at all. And then, to make matters even worse, we believe she was later assaulted by a man."

Maria looked mildly puzzled, and just for the briefest moment, Dr Sheen spotted that her eyes opened a little wider. She did not interrupt.

"Then, two years ago, in the summer of 2014, a Spanish gentleman living in the UK was found dead in suspicious circumstances. We found out much later, quite recently, in fact, that his widow was subsequently assaulted."

Shelly hesitated, and exchanged glances with Dr Sheen. She didn't want to give away any more details than were absolutely necessary. She realised that any carelessness now could potentially compromise a court case. It was important for Maria to confirm some things herself, without being led into this.

Maria showed no sign of engaging, and looked up at the clock on her wall, as if hoping that it was nearly time for her visitors to leave.

Sheen's hand moved to his chest, and he stroked it slightly, as if perhaps suffering from heartburn. He took up the tale.

"Last summer, July 2015, another Spanish man living in the UK suddenly disappeared. He's never been found. He had a partner, and a very young daughter. A lot to live for, yet he vanished."

He paused. To his – and Shelly's – frustration, Maria still didn't respond. So he went on:

"And we now know that his partner was later assaulted."

Maria finally showed some signs of emotion. She trembled, ever so slightly, and looked from Dr Sheen to Shelly, then back again.

Dr Sheen sensed that one final piece of information might unlock the door.

"The reason that these women didn't report the assaults at the time, was, they say, because they believed that the man who assaulted them was the same one who had murdered their partners. He had made certain threats to them about what would happen if they reported it."

117

Sheen stopped.

A single tear trickled down Maria's face.

Shelly interjected:

"So, Maria, you can see why we wanted to speak to you again, to see whether you can tell us anything that might link Tom's death to any of these other incidents that we're looking at."

Maria, with her guard demolished by the sheer horror of everything that had now been brought back from the reluctant depths of her memory, burst out:

"Are you saying it's the same man? He's done this lots of times? Done it to others, too?"

Shelly was quick to spot the important word.

"Too?"

Maria broke down in an uncontrollable flood of tears, and suddenly leapt up and rushed away to her downstairs bathroom. Sheen and Shelly simply looked at each other, with a mixture of emotions. Pleased that they seemed to have broken through Maria's defences, and hopeful that she might now give them what could be vital information. Sad that they had needed to cause her such upset; forcing her to relive the trauma that she had, until now, tried so hard to bury firmly in her past. They were both aware that there were some details that they had held back. They had not mentioned the nature of the assaults. No indication from them that they were sexual in nature. Also, neither of them had said anything about a card, with written instructions, or anything about the attacker, his clothing, a balaclava to hide his face, a camera phone, a fierce knife.

Presently, Maria reappeared, and sat down with them again.

"I was assaulted. Sean doesn't know. I don't want him to know."

"We'll do our best to keep Sean out of this, Maria." Shelly assured her; although quite why Maria was so determined not to tell her partner, she had no idea.

Maria continued:

"It was the second of December. The day after my birthday. It was a Sunday."

Maria's voice was quivering.

"I had been out with my sister. We went for a meal, in Ripon, and she dropped me off at home. And, when I came in, he must have already been hiding in the house; because he suddenly came into my bedroom and attacked me."

"Was your daughter with you?" Asked Shelly.

"No, my mum had her overnight, so I could go out with Elaine. But, he knew about Rosie. He kept talking about her. Said he was sorry he'd missed her, but he could always come back…"

She broke off, as her voice faltered.

"What happened, Maria, can you tell us?" Shelly was persistent, but patient.

"He… he… raped me!"

There was a silence, as Dr Sheen and Shelly held back; allowing Maria the time she needed to compose herself, before she went on:

"He made me do… the most disgusting things… and, he filmed it."

Sheen intervened: "Did you get a good look at him, Maria? Did you see his face?"

Maria shook her head.

"He was wearing a mask. One of those balaclava mask things. I couldn't see his face at all. That's one of the things that scares me most… that perhaps I might see him again one day, and not recognise him. Walking down the street. Not know that it was him."

"Did he speak to you, Maria? Did he say anything?" Again, Shelly was careful not to plant any particular ideas in Maria's head.

119

"Oh yes, he spoke. But as well as talking, he had written down everything he wanted from me. He had all his orders written down on a piece of cardboard. He made me read it. Read it out loud. He wanted to make sure I knew what I had to do."

"Can you remember what the instructions said?"

Maria looked at Dr Sheen.

"It said that I had to look like I was enjoying myself. Like I was getting a thrill from having sex, voluntarily, with a masked man. He told me that so long as I looked like I was enjoying every moment, I wouldn't be able to report it, because he'd produce the film to show that it was all consensual. He was right, wasn't he?"

Shelly nodded slightly, sympathetically, to show that she understood.

"And what else did he say to you, Maria? This is very important."

She wanted to ask whether the man had mentioned her partner, Tom, and indicated that he had played a part in his death; but managed not to put any words into Maria's mouth. She was rewarded for her patience, as Maria said:

"He said something about Tom. Called him a filthy Spaniard. Said he deserved to die. He seemed to know all about it."

Sheen looked sharply at Shelly, as if to warn her not to cross a line here. He knew how anxious and impatient DC King was to get to all the facts.

Maria resumed: "But it was more about Rosie. If I reported him, he was going to come back for Rosie."

Maria shuddered and wept. Through the sobs:

"I couldn't let that happen. I couldn't take that risk. He had a knife. He held it against my throat. He said if I didn't do what he wanted, he'd come back to meet Rosie. He said he was sorry he'd missed her."

Dr Sheen noted that Maria had already told them this. It was an expression that clearly remained firmly imprinted on her mind.

120

Maria went on, but this time with her tear-stained face down; thoroughly ashamed of what she was telling them.

"So, I tried to look like I was enjoying it. What else could I do? There was just one moment when he got distracted, and he put the knife down. I spotted it, and wondered whether I could reach it. But, he saw me look towards it, and he snatched it back."

She sighed, and swallowed hard.

"Could I have got it? I don't know. I don't know whether... what I was thinking. All I knew was, if I give him what he wants, he'll go away... and Rosie will be safe. I didn't even think about Tom. Didn't take it in, what he said about him. It was only afterwards, when I started to put together what he'd said... then I realised he had something to do with Tom dying. I couldn't believe it... I didn't think anyone else would believe it... I thought they would say I was crazy, that I'd made it all up..."

She collapsed into a heap of heaving shoulders and trickling tears; as Shelly offered a comforting arm around her neck, gently stroking back her hair.

Sheen watched the two women, and allowed them the moment, without interruption or comment. He reflected again on something he had said three days earlier, about what women fear most. His words to the team had been 'rape, humiliation, and danger to their babies'. The ever curious professional in him mused about whether this was some sort of continuum, a sliding scale of priorities. If so, what was it that determined which of these fears would be the greatest for any woman? Did it change, depending on the situation? Was the character of the woman a factor? Some sort of morality-based comment about them, if they had less anxiety about the safety of their babies than about their personal humiliation? He pushed such questions away.

"Maria, we'll need you to give us a statement to clarify all this. Can you do that?"

Shelly's question jolted Dr Sheen back from his lonely contemplation, and he nodded in agreement.

"Yes." Maria said, quietly. "But, I don't want Sean to know."

Chapter 20

By the Friday team meeting, Maria Mates had given a full statement. Her allegations appeared to confirm everything that the police had suspected; that she had been raped in her own home by the same man who had assaulted Mariana Navarro and Bev Mitchell. The methods he had used – a card of instructions, reference to her recently deceased Spanish partner, threats to her little girl, filming the act, wearing a balaclava, armed with a knife – there could be no doubt that this was the same perpetrator. And, if any further evidence were necessary, they were increasingly sure that these were assaults following targeted murders. Or, as one officer pointed out, perhaps 'targeted assaults following murders' – it could be that way round.

Hugely frustrating was the lack of a decent description of the man's appearance. The balaclava mask had done its job well. However, Maria had been slightly more forthcoming than the others about the man's accent. She felt that he had a Yorkshire slant, but possibly further north; heading up towards Durham or Middlesbrough. This wasn't a great deal to go on, but it was better than they had before, and the police were grateful.

In interview, which had been conducted by Dawn and Shelly, with Dr Sheen and DI Williams watching through the glass again, Maria had been asked why she was so desperate that her partner found out nothing about what had happened to her. She did her best to explain, and the psychologist went some way towards interpreting her reasons to the others. After the assault, Maria had been wracked with guilt; a shame that she had refused to share with anyone. Not uncommon in rape cases, assured Sheen. The thought processes were extremely complex. Somehow, she had come to blame herself for not fighting back, not doing more to prevent her attacker from now having this hold over her. The knowledge about her child, the film of her 'enjoying' sex with him. She had played her role too well. It would convince anyone that she was a willing partner. More than willing... eager... desperate.

When she had met Sean, a few months later, he had been hurting so badly following a painful break-up from a woman who had deceived him. As their relationship started to blossom, he had needed to hear her promise always to be honest with him. Never lie. And yet she wasn't in a place where she was ready to speak of her ordeal to anyone. So, she did just what he couldn't bear; she lied to him about her past. How she had come to move to Leeds. What she had been doing for the past few months of her life. Now, she couldn't bring herself to face him and admit that she had done the very thing that had hurt him so much before. The lack of trust would destroy their relationship, or so she believed. She wouldn't take the risk. She had long since gone past that window of opportunity during which she could have opened up to him. So, now, he must never know. DI Williams stressed this to the team, and they would do their best to respect her wishes.

"Marcus, does he know his victims?" Demanded Williams.

"I'd say unlikely." The psychologist replied. "He may have known his first victim; but, beyond that, the only trigger could be that the subsequent ones were Spanish. He might be killing them because they are all Spanish, just like the first one, whom he hated or felt wronged by."

DI Williams considered.

"But we don't know who his first victim was."

"Correct." The doctor confirmed. "You think it may have occurred in 2008, but so far you haven't found a victim."

"Frank?" Williams turned to Frank Burnley, who had been searching hard for a possible first victim.

Frank sighed sadly.

"Nothing, Boss. I can't find anything."

Suddenly Dawn chipped in: "What about the Spanish cops? Maybe we need them to search for us. It could have been over there."

There was a brief silence.

"Yep. Get onto it." DI Williams agreed.

Later that day, Dawn and Shelly tried again to reach officer Rodriguez, in Fuerteventura. Millie Rodriguez was away from the office, so they left a message indicating that they would call her again, later.

Just as they were about to make the call, DI Williams caught them, and pulled them into his office.

"I think it's time for your little trip. I want you to go over there, and work with the local cops. If there is something to be found from 2008, it could be vital. The information we could get from that, if it proves to be the killer's first victim, could unlock everything else. I don't want the Spanish trampling all over it. Plus, try and talk to Aida Pastor, widow of the one killed in Lanzarote."

"Roberto Pastor." Filled in Shelly.

"Right. Roy *will* be pleased." Added Dawn, in a sarcastic whisper to Shelly, as they tried to establish a video connection to the police in Fuerteventura.

"Hi again, Millie." Shelly greeted officer Rodriguez warmly.

"Shelly. You coming to visit us yet?"

Shelly blushed slightly, as Dawn gave her a quizzical glance.

"Actually, yes. We… Dawn and I… will be getting a flight in the next few days. Will you be able to assist us?"

Millie seemed pleased. Looking forward to the prospect of meeting Shelly in person.

"Yes, of course. Your boss will need to clear it with my chief, but I'm sure there won't be a problem."

"Thanks, Millie, we appreciate it."

"Anything you need me to do in advance?" Millie picked up a notepad, in case she needed to jot anything down.

"No, I think we better explain all the details in person, when we get there." Shelly said. "But you could get that beer chilled."

Chapter 21

Sat in the airport departure lounge at Manchester, early on Tuesday morning, the sixth of September, Shelly tucked her passport back into her travel bag after clearing security. She eyed Dawn, who had already settled down to glance through a newspaper.

"Have you ever been to the Canaries before?"

"Yes. Roy and I went to Fuerteventura a few years back, and Tenerife before that. You?"

Shelly shook her head.

"What's Fuerteventura like?"

Dawn put down her paper.

"Well, as I remember, at the southern end it was full of Germans. Lovely beaches, but if you don't speak German you can be a bit isolated. We took a day trip down there. I don't think we heard any English all day."

Shelly nodded, looking at a map of the island that she had picked up.

"We're going to the north, close to Lanzarote, aren't we?"

"Yes." Dawn confirmed. "The airport is in the middle of the island on the east coast. It's close to there that your mate Millie is based." She grinned. "At Puerto del Rosario. I expect she'll meet up with us."

Shelly protested weakly, with a half-smile.

"She's not my mate."

"Not yet." Muttered Dawn, mischievously. "In any case, we'll need to go north if we're to see where Luca Mendez died; although I don't think we'll learn anything from that. We may get to speak to the mother-in-law, but I'm not sure we'll get anything more from her. I don't think her daughter told her very much."

125

"Yeah, and we get the ferry from Corralejo in the north, to go over to Lanzarote?"

Dawn smiled and nodded.

"Corralejo is lovely. Very cosmopolitan. Laid back. That's where we stayed when we came. Just outside the town. Great beaches. You can lose yourself in the dunes, if you choose. Roy and I did, more than once." She added with a twinkle in her eyes.

Shelly laughed.

"That's too much information!"

She picked up her phone, which had just buzzed to announce a message.

"Oh, it's from Millie."

Dawn grinned broadly.

Ignoring any insinuation, Dawn read the message, and outlined the contents.

"She wants to know if we want a hire car arranging."

Dawn nodded.

"Good idea. Tell her yes. Unless you would prefer her to drive you around everywhere."

For Shelly, the teasing was starting to wear a little thin.

"I'll tell her yes." And she messaged back, accordingly.

An hour later, and the two officers were in the air, but not sat together. At the mercy of a late booking on a budget airline, they had to take whatever seats were allocated. Periodically, they managed to speak to each other, in the aisle. But, police business isn't something to be shared with a plane full of holidaymakers, so their conversation remained very bland.

Just before one pm, the Boeing started to bank to its right, still over water, and turn closer to the barren looking mountains to the south of

Fuerteventura. It soon landed at Puerto del Rosario airport, and the passengers quickly alighted.

Clearing customs, Shelly commented to Dawn, as they waited for their cases to appear on the carousel:

"It's a bit different from Manchester."

It certainly was; just a fraction of the size and bustle of Manchester. No lifts, conveyors, shuttle buses, or crowds. Making their way into the arrivals hall, which was large and airy, with a high roof, the two soon spotted the car hire desk that Millie had directed them to. After a brief wait for the particulars to be confirmed, they walked over to the car park, feeling the heat of the midday sun, and soon found their allocated Renault Clio.

As Dawn drove, Shelly read aloud some information from her phone:

"We can go straight to the hotel, and Millie will meet us there."

Half an hour later, and the two had reached the small, back street hotel, where a reservation had been made for them. It looked cheap and shabby, as they approached it from an oily street. However, once inside, they found it to be clean, and cool. Pleasant relief from the sun outside.

"Two single rooms." Confirmed Shelly, as she passed a registration form to Dawn.

She was ever so slightly relieved to find that there had been no misunderstanding, which could have so easily occurred during translation of certain words. The reference to Dawn as Shelly's 'partner' had not inadvertently led to the booking of one double room.

Around half past two, as they waited in the hotel reception, the automatic glass front door swept open. A figure whose face they recognised marched confidently in, and strode over to where they were sat.

She wore tight-fitting dark jeans, and a tight, light blue top; which made her appear quite muscular. Her short dark hair was neatly groomed, and her face glowed with a natural tan. She moved confidently, with purpose. Millie looked like she could hold her own against any woman. Or man.

127

She held out her hand to Shelly:

"Millie Rodriguez." She announced.

"Hi, I'm Shelly King, of course, and this is DS Dawn Pardell."

"Nice to meet you both. Did you have a good flight? You've collected your car?

"Yes, we got it, thanks."

Millie led them out onto the street.

"You might as well leave your car here, get in mine."

She opened up her small, rather tatty Opel, and invited them to get in.

"The office is not far away, but parking is tight at this time. It will be easier for you to walk back here, until you get your bearings."

Entering the police station with her two visitors in tow, Millie obtained temporary ID passes for them, and took them directly up the stairs to the first floor. They soon reached a busy, open-plan office, with several officers working away at their desks. It reminded Dawn and Shelly of their own base.

Millie leaned in through the open door of a side office, and spoke to her chief, who was sat inside. Inspector Hanst immediately got up, and came to greet the visitors.

"Ladies."

He shook their hands when introduced.

"Your chief, Ms York, asked us to give you all the support we can. Of course, I'll expect you to keep us informed. No secrets, eh?"

"Of course." Dawn confirmed. "We appreciate your help."

Having been taken through to a quieter room, Dawn and Shelly sat at a desk, facing Millie; who took the lead in what felt like a consultation.

"The more you tell me, the more I can help."

Dawn and Shelly exchanged a brief glance, before Dawn outlined their position.

"We appreciate it, Millie. You've obviously realised that this is a very serious business, and so far there's a lot of speculation on our part. We've been trying to rule out a lot of possible links to a series of deaths and assaults. But, up to now, the links seem to keep reasserting themselves."

"Go on." Millie's eyes drifted to Shelly, then back to Dawn, who continued:

"We suspect that a man has committed a series of murders; and, following each murder, he has come after the victim's widow, and sexually assaulted her."

Millie appeared shocked, as anyone would be. But, only for a second, and soon recovered her composure.

She replied:

"Based on what you told me on our calls, I couldn't help wondering about the dates. July twenty-third. What's that about?"

Dawn continued:

"Well, it seems that the perpetrator is making it his business to kill a man each year on July twenty-third. We have no idea why."

Millie narrowed her eyes:

"And why has this led you to Spain?"

Dawn explained:

"It seems that all his victims were of Spanish ethnicity. So far, we have... we think we have identified five victims. There are the two deaths that you know about: Luca Mendez in 2011, and Roberto Pastor in 2013. In addition, we have come across three cases in the UK of Spanish men going missing or being killed on or around July twenty-third: in 2012, 2014, and 2015. The case we're looking at from 2015, it's a man who went missing, and has never been located."

129

Shelly took up the story:

"The reason we believe that this case in 2015 is linked, is because the man's partner has alleged that she was raped, afterwards. The description that she has given us is unmistakeably the same as that given by the victims' widows in 2012 and 2014."

Millie considered for a moment.

"So that's why you were asking me about any subsequent incident reported, concerning Aida Pastor?"

"Yes. And, although we can't be sure, it sounded like Salome Mendez may have been assaulted, based on what her mother told you."

Millie whistled.

"Wow!"

She paused for a moment, taking all this in, then asked:

"2015... that's the latest?"

The Brits looked at each other, before Shelly explained:

"Well, so far. But, of course, we are keeping an open mind. If we find that there has been another one this year, around seven weeks ago, then there could be a woman out there in serious danger of being attacked."

Millie leaned back, and regarded Shelly.

"So, if you discover another likely murder victim, what are you going to tell his widow?"

"What do you mean?"

Millie explained:

"Well, she would certainly be in serious danger. But, she might also be your best chance of catching the bastard. And that's your dream, I'm sure. It would make your career, apart from anything else."

Chapter 22

Having passed the afternoon in a small office, trawling some of the Spanish police files not previously available to them, Dawn and Shelly were taking a break.

Dawn had spent the last two hours scouring everything she could find in connection with Roberto Pastor, his murder, and his widow, then the same for Luca Mendez.

Shelly had tried to find anything suspicious that could be involved, around July twenty-third in 2008, 2009, 2010, and 2016. These were what the team were starting to refer to as 'the missing years'. Although she knew that the killer had allegedly excused himself from any murderous activity in 2009, telling Mariana Navarro that he had been 'busy' that year, she would not ignore the possibility that he was lying.

"Found anything?" Dawn took a sip of coffee, looking hopefully at Shelly.

"Nothing yet. The Spanish recording system is... different from ours."

"Hmm, yes. So I see."

At that moment, Millie Rodriguez popped her head around the door, and Shelly was glad she hadn't been in the middle of saying anything less complimentary.

"How are you getting on?"

Shelly sighed:

"We're just finding our way around so far. But if there's something here, we'll find it."

Millie nodded.

"The chief has given me the go-ahead to run with you tomorrow. I can take you up north, if you want to go to Lanzarote and try to get hold of Aida Pastor?"

131

Millie looked from Dawn to Shelly.

Dawn replied:

"That would be helpful. Shelly, do you want to go, and I'll keep digging here?"

Shelly felt herself beginning to blush. She knew why, although she also knew there was no reason why she should. She was a cop, for Heaven's sake, a professional. 'Be your age!' She told herself.

"Sure." She said.

"Okay. Early start? We can get the eight o'clock ferry from Corralejo, but I'd leave here about six-thirty. That suit?"

Shelly suppressed a groan.

"Fine."

As Millie left them to their discussion, Dawn grinned.

"Chance to get to know the Spanish better." She remarked.

After another hour's work, the two of them decided to clock off; and were just signing out at the front desk, before the short walk back to their hotel.

Millie, and her regular partner Martin Castillo, were struggling through the reception area, trying to carry a number of boxes and folders.

"Want a hand?" Dawn asked.

"Thanks, yes. Just to Martin's car."

Dawn and Shelly each picked up a box, to lighten the shared load, and followed their Spanish counterparts through a side door, which led to the fenced-off police car park.

"You sampling the delights of the capital tonight?" Asked Martin, pleasantly, of Dawn.

"Probably just take a walk, and an early night. We've a lot to do."

132

Millie chipped in:

"Do that." Then, to Shelly:

"We'll get that beer tomorrow."

Later, having eaten dinner in the hotel, Dawn and Shelly took a walk down the streets of Puerto del Rosario, to look at the harbour. There was work in progress, and it looked like it would become a place that would give a good impression to the visiting cruise ships which occasionally docked here. They sat down on a low stone wall, which marked the boundary of a short promenade, and looked out at the shimmering blue water.

"How should I play it with Aida Pastor, if I get to speak with her?" Shelly wondered, aloud.

"Well, we can't put words into her mouth... but, maybe as with Maria Mates. Ask her to help us eliminate connections."

"Yes. I'll try that. It's a dangerous tactic, isn't it?"

"There's no easy way, Shelly. I think that's the least risky. And we won't get another chance. We'll only be here a few days. I don't think the boss would take kindly to us asking for a second trip to the sunshine."

As they wandered away from the harbour, and up the hill towards a street housing a series of offices, accountancy firms, and solicitors, which they knew led to their hotel, they discussed their strategy for the coming days. They were provisionally booked on a return flight to Manchester on Saturday, so they only had three more days to work the case. It was essential that they took back with them something useful. Something to unlock the door and find this monster.

Back at the hotel, they soon went their separate ways. Dawn rang the boss, and then her husband; both to receive updates appropriate to their station. Shelly went to the hotel bar, and made a couple of private calls of her own.

Chapter 23

The ringing alarm clock forced Shelly to let go of a lovely dream that she had been enjoying. It involved sunshine, sand, sea, and the company of someone her own age.

"Ohh!" She groaned, as she stretched, pushing out her arms above her head, as far as they would reach.

Acknowledging that it was six o'clock, and mindful that Millie would collect her at six-thirty, Shelly rolled out of bed, stepped to the window, and looked out at the street below. Just a street view, she thought. Still, it was a change from her usual bedroom view. Down below, a wagon was collecting rubbish from a cluster of wheelie-bins. On the other side of the street, a van was delivering produce to a small supermarket, ready for the day's trade. She turned away from the window, and observed her naked body in the full-length mirror. She went into the bathroom, and took a shower; before dressing in jeans and a light green top. She looked again at her clothes in the drawer, and picked up a pair of shorts. However, she put them back; she would stick with jeans.

By six-thirty, she was downstairs, stood on the hotel steps with just a shoulder bag; looking out for her driver, guide, and companion for the day. Millie soon arrived, and Shelly got into her car.

"Good morning. Did you sleep well? I hate staying in hotels. I never sleep well in a strange bed."

Shelly shrugged:

"I didn't do too bad. Quite a comfy bed."

Quickly leaving the capital, which, thought Shelly, slept in much later than Manchester, the two chatted. Millie pointed out a few sights along the way; at one point saying:

"I used to live over there." She pointed to a settlement raised up on a hill on the outskirts of the town.

134

"With my ex-partner." She added. Then:

"I checked up, and Aida Pastor has been working in a café close to where the ferry docks. So, if she's not at home, we may catch her there."

"Ah, good. I hope my visit doesn't upset her." Shelly commented.

Millie's response sounded slightly harsh:

"The woman lost her husband. Battered to death. What could upset her?"

Heading north, Shelly was soon admiring the beaches to her right, and barren hills, then rolling sand dunes to her left.

"Are you a beach person?" She asked.

"Of course." Millie grinned a cheeky smile. "You don't get a body tan like this by covering up and staying indoors."

"Maybe you'll get some sun on your body, if you get a few spare hours."

Shelly looked away towards the beach, and distant sea.

"Perhaps."

When they reached Corralejo, Millie got her car in line, ready to board the ferry; which was already loading for the short trip across the water. After they had driven aboard, they left their car, safely stowed, and went up on deck, to look back upon Corralejo, when the boat departed.

"Coffee?" Invited Shelly.

They bought their drinks, and wandered back to a place where they could sit down, and watch Corralejo fade into the distance. The sea wasn't particularly choppy, today; but there was a wind, that swirled and howled around the metal posts supporting the walkway above.

Millie cradled her drink.

"It's quite a case, this. Career-defining. Don't let anybody steal it away from you."

"I'll try not to."

Shelly recognised the voice of experience talking to her. Although Millie was only about the same age, she felt that this was someone with her wits about her, hardened by years in the job.

When they arrived and docked at Lanzarote, Millie manoeuvred her car past the lorries, and made a timely exit; flashing her police ID card at a marshal who tried to remonstrate with her for jumping the queue. Without comment, she took them away from the harbour, and started to head into the town. Pointing to her left, towards a jolly-looking bar:

"That's where Aida works. Have you had any breakfast yet?"

"No. It was too early for me."

"Let's get something here."

Millie pulled into a car park outside a tidy-looking cafe, within sight of the one where Aida Pastor apparently worked, and brought the car to a halt. They sat at a table on the outside terrace, and picked up a menu each. Millie chuckled:

"I expect you'll be needing the *'desayuno Ingles'* – English breakfast?"

"Why not?"

Within ten minutes they were both eating, though Millie opted for a lighter snack. Shelly watched the ferry on the other side of the harbour; which was already loading up again ready for the return trip to Corralejo. As she enjoyed her breakfast, Shelly was conscious that Millie was watching her, closely. She turned to face her, and for a brief second there was an uncomfortable meeting of eye contact, when neither spoke.

Millie soon filled the gap:

"Is it what you were expecting?

Shelly looked at her plate:

"The breakfast?"

"No." Millie laughed. "Police work."

136

"Oh. I've been doing it a few years. You get used to the rough times, don't you?"

Millie nodded:

"I expect you see more at the gritty end in Manchester than in a place like this."

"What are you saying about my Manchester?" Demanded Shelly, in jest. Then, with a grin: "It has its moments."

Millie finished off her pastry, and wiped her hands.

"And what about your colleagues? How do they treat a woman?"

Shelly took a sip of her coffee, before replying:

"The police have always been a sexist organisation... no secret about that. It's one of those places that was always a man's world. As much as the pits and the armed forces. But, it's changing. Technology helps. Brains are more important than brawn, now."

She grinned:

"And they can't manage without our brains."

Millie agreed:

"You got that right. Some of them can't tie their own shoelaces."

"That sounds like your opinion of men, generally, rather than police men."

Millie smiled, and looked Shelly in the eye:

"And what about you?"

Shelly felt the tension. She knew that she was being asked about her preference... Putting down her cutlery, after finishing off her *desayuno Ingles*, Shelly played it cool:

"I keep an open mind. I'm a cop, after all."

"Quite right." Millie approved.

137

Chapter 24

Shortly afterwards, the two women had reached the complex where Aida Pastor lived. It was smart, but modest; with traditional, white-painted houses, adorned by a blue trim. Just a fifteen minute walk for Aida, down to the harbour café where she worked.

Parking on the quiet road, Millie pointed across to a house where a window was open, and with a small white car parked on the driveway. That suggested somebody might be at home. They walked across to approach the door, and Millie knocked on it.

When it opened, a tall woman with light brown curly hair appeared. She was wearing dark grey jogger pants, under a loose-fitting light grey top. Very casual; she didn't seem to be heading off to work anytime soon. The smell of brewing coffee wafted out.

"Aida Pastor?" Millie held up her credentials.

The woman looked from Millie to Shelly.

"Yes."

"I'm officer Millie Rodriguez. This is officer Shelly King, from Greater Manchester police, in the UK."

Aida leaned back against her door post, obviously surprised by the visit. And curious.

"What can I do for you?"

"May we come in, Aida?"

As soon as she had said it, Millie hoped that she hadn't suddenly given Aida the impression that they had come to tell her they had found her husband's killer.

"Come in."

Inside the kitchen of Aida's small house, Shelly saw the signs of children. The fridge was covered in childish drawings and paintings. Colourful magnetic lettering spelt out a few short words, and two school photos were held in place by a fridge magnet in the shape of a volcano. Over the back of a chair, a child's jumper was folded. It was red, with some patterning in pink, so probably a girl's clothing. Underneath it was a mustard coloured jumper, and some dark blue pants. A small boy lived here too.

Millie leaned back against a dining chair.

"Aida, we're here in connection with your husband's death, in 2013. I know the police have spoken to you many times, but is it alright if we ask you some things?"

"You have no news then?" Aida couldn't hide her disappointment. "I thought maybe you had something to tell me."

"No, I'm afraid not. But, Shelly here is looking at things from a different angle; and we're hoping that you can help us clarify a few points."

Aida looked suspiciously at Shelly.

"Go on."

"Well, Aida..." Began Shelly: "We've found some similarities between what happened to Roberto, and another death. What we'd like to do is ask you to help us compare them, and rule out anything that's not relevant."

Aida sat down, and gestured to her visitors to do the same.

"What sort of similarities?"

Shelly knew that she was on delicate ground, here. On the one hand, she didn't want to upset this Spanish woman unnecessarily; and there was absolutely no proof that she was a part of this sickening pattern. On the other hand, the grounds for suspicion were clear; and Shelly did not intend to return to England still wondering.

"I can't tell you all the details of the other man's death, Aida. Another woman has suffered, as you have. I need to show her some respect."

139

Aida nodded, seemingly impressed:

"Of course."

Shelly continued:

"But, after her husband's death… a few months after… something else happened. Something that she was convinced was connected to it."

She paused. Millie and Shelly both observed Aida closely. She seemed to tense up. Did they imagine it, or did she begin to colour slightly, as if becoming uncomfortable.

Aida asked:

"This death… was it in the UK?"

Shelly thought quickly. She had been referring to the death of Luca Mendez, lost from his fishing boat off El Cotillo. But, if Aida had held back from reporting an assault through fear of reprisals, perhaps a similar incident in Britain would feel less threatening. Maybe she would start to think that her assailant was long gone, and would never come back.

"I'm based in Manchester. I've worked there for the last seven years." Shelly left Aida to draw her own conclusion.

There was almost a sigh of relief, from Aida, but she said nothing.

Millie stepped in:

"Aida, do you remember, a few months after Roberto died, the police were called here? It was New Year's Eve."

Aida avoided their eyes.

"I didn't call them."

"No." Confirmed Millie. "It was one of your neighbours, Senora Sollana. An elderly lady. You remember?"

Aida nodded, but changed the subject, turning to Shelly:

"What did you mean, 'similarities' to another death? What similarities?"

140

"Are you sure there was no reason to call the police, on December thirty-first, Aida?"

Aida scowled:

"What reason? And, what could it have to do with a case in the UK?"

Millie and Shelly exchanged looks. The bait on the hook seemed to be tempting Aida. She wanted to know, but was wary of giving away too much.

"Ok Aida." Said Shelly. "I'm going to tell you something that happened to another woman, and I need you to tell me whether this rings a bell. Will you do that?"

Aida nodded, putting her head down.

"Several months after a man was killed, his widow was assaulted, in her own home. The man who assaulted her said things about her husband. He knew all about the man's death, and about them having a daughter. The woman..."

Shelly got no further, as suddenly Aida threw her arms to her face, and burst into tears.

The officers held back for a moment, before Millie stepped forward and offered a comforting arm on her shoulder.

It was a couple of minutes, before Aida was able to begin telling them her story. On New Year's Eve, 2013, Aida had been at home, with her children. Despite encouragement from friends, she had refused to go out, or entertain any plans of celebrating or enjoying the end of year festivities. She was still grieving for her husband. Any thoughts of having fun at such a time, with Roberto so recently gone, made her feel sick to the pit of her stomach.

So, she had stayed home. Her children, being aged only four and two, were both in bed long before midnight; by around nine-thirty, in fact. Looking out of her window, she saw the young, newly-married couple next door, walking arm-in-arm along the lane. They were heading down to the

141

harbour, where the party was already in full swing. She felt a pang of envy; seeing two young people going out together, clearly in love.

She sighed, and drew the blind. There was a bottle of wine on the table, and an empty glass. Aida had planned to sip a quiet drink, and maybe listen to some music, before going to bed. She sat down on the sofa. Then, a knock came, at the back door. She was tempted to ignore it. She simply wasn't in the mood to accept the well-intentioned friendliness of old Senora Sollana, from next door. She was a good soul, and would genuinely want to offer Aida some company, to stop her missing Roberto. But, Aida absolutely didn't want it. However, there was little choice, without being rude. So, she got up from her sofa, and went to the door, which she opened, with a forced smile of politeness.

Crash! She was knocked off her feet, and felt a muscular masked figure pounce on top of her; pinning her to the ground, and smothering her mouth to prevent her from crying out.

The next thing she saw was the glinting blade of a horrendous knife – like a soldier's dagger – held close to her face. The attacker – clearly a Brit – quickly convinced her that she would not make any attempt to resist; as he held her hands behind her back, and frog-marched her into her own bedroom. There, he made her read a set of instructions from a card; telling her what to do, and warning her of the consequences if she should disappoint. Consequences not just for her, but for her little girl, or boy.

Aida did everything that he asked, and more besides; so determined was she that he would have no reason to resort to carrying out his threat to return and harm her babies. So ashamed was she, as soon as he had left.

The account that Aida gave was a familiar one, to Shelly; but it was the first time Millie had heard any woman recount such horrific treatment. She gasped, and barely contained her own emotions, as she heard about the camera, filming everything, about the multiple references to what would happen to Aida's children. She could barely face Aida, by the time this poor woman went on to talk about how the monster had taunted her over Roberto's 'pathetic crying', and 'begging for mercy'.

Why the next-door neighbour had felt it necessary to call the police, was not really clear. Given the time that the emergency call was made, the

142

attack would still have been in progress; although, unfortunately, it was some time later before two first responders reached the scene. Well after the assailant had done his work, and made good his escape. When they arrived, Aida had managed to convince them that there was nothing amiss, and sent them on their way. Possibly, with the busiest midnight of the year approaching, the two officers had not needed telling twice.

Perhaps Senora Sollana had seen the man lurking outside Aida's house, and heard the initial crash of his forced arrival. Her report had been somewhat confused; and, perhaps, further muddled by New Year's Eve drink. However, this would never now become clear. Senora Sollana had been old, and infirm; and died just a few months later.

At the conclusion of Aida's story, Shelly and Millie offered what sympathy and comfort they could. Aida wanted to know all about the other woman's ordeal; which, of course, Shelly couldn't reveal. She did, however, reassure Aida that she was certainly not alone in having suffered like this. Given the similarities in other accounts... yes, she confirmed, there was more than one other account... Aida should never fear being disbelieved.

As they left Aida's house, having made arrangements for a follow-up and further support; Millie and Shelly, grim-faced and silent, got into the car. Millie started the engine, but paused for a moment, before driving off.

"What were we saying about men, an hour ago?"

Chapter 25

Having taken a look at the location of Roberto Pastor's murder, and spoken with a former colleague of the man – who couldn't help them any further – Shelly and Millie left their car close to the ferry loading bay. Lots of tourists were drifting around the area, enjoying the sun which was now strong, and high in the sky. There was almost an hour before the next sailing, and the two stood on the quayside, looking across towards Fuerteventura.

"Ready for that beer, now? Asked Millie.

Shelly wasn't a daytime drinker; nor, in truth, a big drinker at any time – compared, at least, to most of her police colleagues. However, on this occasion, beer felt like the right thing. The two women had listened, together, to a most emotive account. Such experiences do bring people together in the strangest of ways. They were starting to enjoy being together... working together... brief though the experience would be. And, in any case, they had an hour to kill, and nothing else that they could profitably do.

"I'm in your hands. And... well, I suppose I'm buying. I did promise." Shelly grinned.

They sat on the upper terrace of a sports bar, watching the ferry, which was now approaching the harbour on its usual route.

"Salut!" Millie raised her glass and tapped it against Shelly's. "I take it everything she said corresponds with your other reports?" She took a sip from her beer.

Shelly tasted the amber nectar, and nodded.

"Exactly." She confirmed.

"So, what do you plan to do next?" Millie put her glass down. "You know I'll have to report it in to my chief."

Shelly knew that:

"Yeah, course. My thinking is that this is still a British investigation. We know he's a Brit... almost certainly living in England. But, we can't be sure he's not been on his travels again, this year."

She sighed.

"The description... it's so poor, again. Could be any one of a million men."

"Yes." Millie agreed: "Not particularly tall, quite muscular... no point expecting Aida to be able to help us much with British accents."

There was a silence, before Millie continued:

"So where exactly *are* you digging? You have to start somewhere, but the descriptions... they're not much help, are they?"

Shelly frowned, looking very sad.

"The truth is, as you pointed out yourself, the best chance of catching him might be to place a twenty-four hour watch on the widow of any Spanish man who dies in mysterious circumstances."

Millie looked thoughtful:

"Well, we've been checking out for any potential victim around July twenty-third, this year; and, nothing. Not in Fuerteventura or Lanzarote, anyway. Almost certainly not in the Canaries."

Shelly took up, perhaps what Millie was going to add:

"But, what about mainland Spain, or one of the other islands? Dawn's hunting, probably as we speak. A Spaniard dying in Spain? Well, it's not exactly going to stand out, is it?"

Millie continued:

"Then you'd better hope that, if he *has* already done it again, and that means there's nothing you can do to stop it... that he's committed the offence in the UK. Much better chance of getting to the widow before... before anything else."

Shelly grimaced.

145

"This job sucks, sometimes. Here am I, almost hoping that someone has been killed, so that we can set him a trap… because I don't have a clue what else to do to catch him."

Millie looked on sympathetically:

"You can't let it take you over. You're doing what you can. Maybe you need to switch off a bit. How do you switch off?"

Shelly looked hard at her:

"What do *you* do to switch off?"

There was a silence.

Finally, Millie replied:

"I go to the beach. I've done it ever since I started on the force, when I used to be in uniform. I figure that, on the beach, well… there's no uniforms there. I lose the clothes, and I lose the job. Just for a few hours. I switch right off, like I'm somebody else."

Shelly reflected, and nodded:

"Yes, I get that. No beaches in Manchester, unfortunately. Plenty of water, but no beach. So, I suppose I just watch TV, or get outside, go visit my dad. Go shopping. The usual stuff people do. "

She looked at Millie:

"You ever been to England?"

Millie shook her head.

"Nobody's ever asked me. By the way, Dawn… is she your 'partner'?"

Shelly smiled, and answered without facing Millie:

"Colleague. Partner in crime. I don't have a personal partner."

"Ah. Me neither."

Millie observed Shelly, hoping for some further comment. Finally, frustrated, she sighed:

"You Brits! You don't give much away, do you? You like to be difficult to read?"

Shelly laughed.

"You're asking me whether any partner of mine would be male or female. You touched on it before."

Millie grinned:

"Yes, that is what I was wondering."

"Well, as I said, I'm... er... easy going. I take people as I find them. If I'm attracted to someone, then that's fine."

Millie drained her glass of the final mouthful of beer.

"And, are you currently attracted to anyone?"

Shelly felt a warm tingle, as she smiled across at Millie.

"I might be."

Chapter 26

A couple of hours later, Millie and Shelly were back in Fuerteventura; and drove along the quayside, back through the resort of Corralejo. They had planned to take a detour across to El Cotillo, so that Shelly could see the area where Luca Mendez died, before driving south, back to the capital.

Shelly had telephoned Dawn, to let her know about Aida Pastor's story; and Dawn would relay this to the boss, back in Manchester. Whether this would now have to become a completely joint investigation, alongside the Spanish, was uncertain. For now, Shelly worked on the premise that DI Williams and DCI York were in charge. However, she realised that this might change. Millie, for her part, was more than happy to let Shelly act as senior investigator here; although she knew that she would have to report everything to her own chief, Marvin Hanst. She had the feeling that Hanst would be happy to let the British do as much legwork as possible.

Turning right as she approached the lazy village of El Cotillo, Millie took them past a number of apartments and seemingly almost empty hotels, and out of the village, keeping the distant sea on her left.

"It's quiet, here." Murmured Shelly.

The road became winding, and dusty; eventually starting to thread its way through dunes, as it continued away from the village. Eventually, they approached the red and white striped lighthouse, which had been in view for some time. Millie pulled up in the car park, and led Shelly towards the building.

"Out there." Millie pointed into the distance, over a patch of slippery-looking rocks that tailed away into the choppy sea.

"That's where Luca Mendez' boat was found. It had run aground on those rocks. He was never found, but there was a lot of blood in his boat. His blood."

Shelly looked out, and back inland.

"What did the police make of it at the time? Must have been suspicious, surely?"

Millie nodded:

"I'm sure they were. But, this old lighthouse is here for a reason. These are dangerous waters. There was no reason to think anybody wished Luca any harm. The most likely explanation, I suppose, was that he had injured himself, and bled to death before he could make it back to safety."

"Hmm. If that had happened, wouldn't he have secured himself in the boat, so as not to fall overboard?"

Millie shrugged:

"I can't disagree with that. With hindsight, it does seem puzzling. There's something else that I noticed from the file. There was no catch in the boat. No fish. So, it seems like maybe he met his fate before he had even gone out to sea."

"Hmm."

Millie added:

"You want to try the mother-in-law? Senora Fuentes?"

Shelly shook her head.

"I don't think there's anything else to ask her. You already got everything that she knows, I think."

"Yeah, I don't think she could tell us more."

They returned to Millie's car.

"You've worked with Dawn for long?"

Shelly replied:

"We're in the same team, but I haven't worked with her so much. She's good at what she does. She's a good woman, too. Well thought of. I wonder if she's managed to dig anything up, today."

149

Millie headed back through El Cotillo village, and away from the newer developments on the fringe of it. Soon, they were on the open road, and heading back towards Puerto del Rosario. Shelly looked up at the hills; barren, and dry, and admired the isolation of it all. Barely any traffic. A dead wilderness, but only minutes from civilisation.

As they got closer to the city, Shelly asked:

"You pointed out where you used to live, this morning. Where do you live now?"

"I have an apartment, just on the edge of town. Not very big, but it's quiet. Private. I can see the sea from my balcony. Plus, none of my neighbours know I'm a cop."

She added:

"I live on my own."

Having found a space in the crowded police car park, they went into the police station. Shelly signed in, again; and followed Millie up to their office, on the first floor.

Dawn, who had been given a desk in the side office, again, looked up as she heard them enter the main room. She waved her hand, through the window; and Millie led Shelly over to the small room.

Without delay, Dawn asked:

"She told it just the same as the others, then?"

"Yep, pretty much." Shelly confirmed.

"But, what was it that gave her permission to spill it out, after all this time? Has the fear of him coming back just receded, now?"

Millie intervened:

"I think it was the realisation that others have had the same thing happen to them. And that even more could be at risk. I think that... responsibility... has outweighed her desire to... play safe."

150

Shelly nodded:

"Yes, I agree with that. Well put." She smiled a warm, appreciative smile at her Spanish colleague; which Dawn noticed, but did not comment on.

"You've spoken to the boss?" Shelly turned to Dawn.

"Yes." Dawn hesitated slightly, before including Millie in her response:

"Our DCI, Floella York, will be speaking to your bosses, about who's going to head this up. It has to be a joint operation, now. But, as *we* are already fully engaged with it, I think we will expect to hang onto the reins."

Millie agreed:

"I think we all understand the priority, here. But, that's above my pay grade. Oh, by the way, have you found any new leads, today?"

Dawn shrugged, unsure:

"I've spent most of the day looking through anything I can find in July 2010, but there's nothing obvious. There are always missing persons, aren't there? I have a couple that might be worth following up."

"Who are they?" Millie showed an interest.

"Well, there's a Peter... Peter Manares."

"Where from?"

Dawn checked a note she had made:

"Ginina... Ginigin..."

Millie took over:

"Giniginamar?"

Dawn nodded, gratefully.

Millie was quick to make an astute observation:

"Well, that's a rather remote place. Not really on the usual tourist route. Doesn't fit the pattern if the killer comes here as a tourist and needs to take time staking a site out, and planning a follow-up visit."

Shelly pursed her lips, and nodded in approval:

"On the other hand, if it is connected, we could get lucky. Less traffic all round?"

"That's true. What are the circumstances?" Asked Millie.

Dawn filled in the gaps:

"Peter Manares apparently went missing on July twenty-fourth, 2010. Never seen again, according to the records. He was a married man, with three daughters."

Millie committed the details to memory:

"Ok, I'll arrange to follow that up. See whether he ever turned up. Giniginamar isn't a long drive."

Dawn turned back to her notes:

"There is another one: Jose Sebastian. Died in a car accident, July twenty-fifth 2010. In Morro Jable?"

Millie smiled. The pronunciation of the place was poor, but she knew exactly where Dawn meant.

"Anything look suspicious about it?"

"Only the date. He wasn't married... don't know whether he had a partner, or children."

"Ok." Millie nodded. "No harm in double-checking."

"Morro Jable's down south, isn't it?" Shelly asked.

"Yes, but it's only an hour away. Maybe a bit longer."

Shelly sighed:

"Nothing from any of the other gap years?"

"Certainly nothing from this year. Or, at least nothing has come to light yet. I'll be looking back to 2008 next."

Dawn leaned back, with a stretch.

"I think I'll take a break, soon. My eyes are aching."

She checked the time:

"I think I'll go back to the hotel for a while, then maybe come back and keep going this evening."

Shelly agreed:

"Yep. I'll come with you. We'll get something to eat, and come back in later."

Millie got up, to go report to her boss.

"Ok, see you in a while."

A couple of hours later, the two Brits returned to the task; having refreshed themselves at the hotel, and discussed the latest developments of the case over a light snack. Shelly had taken the opportunity for a quick shower, and a change of clothes; and was now wearing a distinctive dark green and silver, slightly Chinese-looking, silky top. It was expensive. Tasteful. Millie was already back in the office, when they came in, and immediately noticed the impressive garment; which she appreciated by an upward flick of her eyes.

However, she got to business:

"I've checked with the locals." She began. "They haven't any record of Peter Manares turning up. Could be worth a trip to check."

"How long would it take to get there?" Dawn glanced at the clock on the wall. It was just after seven.

Millie answered:

"An hour. We could go now; but if you want to take in Morro Jable as well, to check on any family of Jose Sebastian, better leave it until tomorrow."

"Yes, that makes sense." Dawn agreed. "But, are you still with us tomorrow?"

Millie cast an involuntary sideways glance towards chief Hanst's office; although she knew he wasn't in.

"I'm actually not on duty for the next two days. But, I'll take you down there; see what we can find. Although, from the reports into the road accident that saw off Jose Sebastian, I can't see that there's any way he's part of this. The other driver involved wasn't British; and, in any case, it does look like a genuine accident."

"Ah, well, let's leave him out of this, for now." Dawn was satisfied.

"Thanks for helping us again, if you're sure you have the time. You might as well go with Millie again, Shelly. You did a good job with Aida Pastor."

"Ok." Shelly cast a fleeting glance at Millie, then looked back to Dawn's computer screen, as Dawn got to the business of trying to locate anything suspicious that might be relevant from July 2008.

"I've already written it up, from Aida Pastor, and we can send the report through to the boss." Said Shelly. "So, if we're leaving Jose Sebastian to one side, and not going all the way to Morro Jable, maybe we could call on the Manares family this evening. Do you think?"

"Why not. Come on." And Millie picked up her jacket.

The traffic was sparse, and the light would soon be fading; what a pleasure it must be to drive on these roads, instead of the perennial, stress-inducing congestion of Greater Manchester, thought Shelly, as they cruised towards Giniginamar. It was getting dusky, by the time they passed a larger town, Gran Tarajal, as Millie filled her in on the place they were heading.

"It's not a big town. Not much happens here. Like I said, it doesn't seem to fit the location profile for this offender. But, who knows. If I could understand all the workings of a loser like this, I would be earning twice as much as a criminal psychologist."

154

Shelly thought, fleetingly, of Dr Marcus Sheen. She preferred the company of Millie Rodriguez.

Approaching the town, Shelly was greeted by a guard of honour; made up of two lines of chubby palm trees. Thanks to the breeze, they waved politely back at Shelly, as she looked at them. The road descended slightly, as it neared the harbour area. A sign indicated that the cultural centre was to the left.

Millie swung the car round to the right, and began to climb towards a bank of white dwellings which were built into the hillside, looking back down to the sea. They were either a collection of apartment buildings, or perhaps a hotel complex, thought Shelly. Millie slowed down, and looked over to her left.

"Down there, I think."

Shelly followed her eyes, and saw a separate cluster of white houses or two storey apartment blocks. Every house in town appeared to be white. The trim of green or blue was hard to make out, in the fading light. Although a tiny town, with but one road in and out, this was probably quite an exclusive area in which to live. A fine place, no doubt. So long as one sought a quiet life.

Pulling up outside a small block of apartments, which weren't old, but appeared rather tired and neglected; Millie looked across to the other side of the road.

"I think the address will be over there."

There was nobody about, as the two of them approached a door on the ground floor, number 4a, which was draped by natural leafy plants. They looked very dry, and barely alive. Millie knocked.

Presently, the door opened; to reveal a middle-aged woman, dressed in dark pants and top. She had a plastic basket containing a few items of clothing in one hand, and seemed to be in the process of sorting out her washing.

"Hello, Senora Manares?" Queried Millie.

The woman looked from one to the other.

"Yes, I'm Senora Manares. And you are?"

Millie held up her credentials:

"Officer Millie Rodriguez, Policia Nacional. This is officer King, from the UK. Martha Manares?"

Shelly proffered her own ID card.

Senora Manares looked anxious.

"Yes, I'm Martha. What do you want? Is there a problem? Is it my son?"

Millie had no wish to alarm her:

"We just want to speak with you about Peter Manares. Is Peter your husband?"

Senora Manares looked even more uncomfortable:

"Er... yes. Peter is my husband. Why do you ask?"

Millie and Shelly looked at each other. Police officers easily recognise the signs of someone who doesn't want to meet them. Millie continued:

"When did you last see Peter, Senora?"

There was a noise behind her, and a man's voice called out:

"Who is it, Martha?"

Martha Manares turned round, to face a gentleman, perhaps around the age of sixty, who came to the door. He was slightly stooped, and greying, with an unkempt whiskery beard, that didn't look like it had been shampooed, or even brushed, for some considerable time.

"What is it?" He asked again; not appearing to be a man who would welcome uninvited visitors.

"Police." Millie held up her card again, for the man to see.

"And you are?"

156

"Peter Manares." Said the man.

Millie and Shelly gasped, and looked from the man to his wife, and back at him, again.

Millie glared at Martha:

"According to our records, Peter Manares was reported missing, in July 2010. He is listed as a missing person. You, Martha Manares, reported him missing, yourself."

"Oh." She didn't seem overly upset. If anything, perhaps relieved that the police hadn't arrived at her door with bad news or some other trouble for her son.

She continued:

"Peter came back..."

Her husband interrupted her:

"I went away, it's true. That's not an offence is it? It was private. Family business."

"And you didn't think to notify the police that your husband turned up?" Demanded Millie, annoyed that this woman valued police time so little.

Peter answered for her:

"It's not as though you were actively looking for me, I'm sure, is it? I hadn't done anything wrong... committed no crime. It was just a private matter."

The officers were frustrated, but also relieved. Although this did not help them to get closer to finding their offender, at least it meant that Martha Manares had not suffered at his hands. After requesting some identification, which Peter Manares produced, and ticking off Martha for potentially wasting police resources, they left.

Millie slammed her car door shut, as she got behind the wheel.

"Ah, well, we should be grateful. No real harm done."

157

"Yeah." Commented Shelly, as she dispatched a brief text message, to let Dawn know the outcome of their visit.

"I guess that's it for today. You'll want to get home now?"

Millie drove off, without immediately replying. It was completely dark, now, and her headlights picked out the swaying palms at the side of the road, as they left the area of Giniginamar.

The two chatted as they travelled; Millie taking on the tourist guide role, as she imparted a few facts about Fuerteventura, although it was now too dark to see much. They reached the fringe of Puerto del Rosario in what seemed like no time; at which point Millie indicated:

"My place is over that way... but I can take you back into town. Unless you fancy a drink at mine?"

Shelly thought for a moment. Dawn wouldn't be expecting her back at the police station. The work was done, for today; and Dawn would almost certainly have gone back to their hotel for the night.

"Yeah, ok. Let's have a drink."

Millie changed lanes, and took a left at the roundabout that they had just approached, instead of following the route into the town centre. A minute later, they pulled up on a side street, and exited the car. Shelly looked around at a group of young men, who had just crossed over the road, with bags of shopping. A supermarket was just a little further down the street.

"This way."

Millie led them round the corner, and up a few steps to a secure door. She keyed a number into the pad on the wall, and, with a buzz, the door released to her touch. Shelly followed her along a short corridor, and up a flight of stairs to the first floor. Millie approached the second door, unlocked it, and stepped inside.

"Come in."

Chapter 27

The next morning, Dawn wandered down the street, and across a pretty square; glancing at four splashing fountains in full flow, which poured their contents against a shiny metallic splashback. Entering the police station alone, she signed in at the desk. She would meet Shelly in the upper office. At some point. No doubt.

The previous evening, just before she had needed to leave, a report had caught her eye. It was about a local man who had seemingly vanished, in July 2008. For a host of reasons – chiefly being that there was some suspicion the man may have been seeing another woman – his disappearance had not been filed as in any way suspicious. It seemed that nobody had looked at the file for at least four years. Dawn intended to make it her first task this morning; a thorough check on all the details.

It was eight forty-five; and, although several officers were already at their desks, and an animated discussion was in progress about something, there was no sign of Shelly. Dawn picked up her phone to call or text her; but then decided against it. She would allow her a little longer. After all, Shelly had gone off to visit that speculative lead down in Giniginamar last night; and may have got back quite late. There was no sign, either, of Millie. However, as Dawn remembered, Millie had mentioned that she was 'officially' off duty for the next couple of days.

She set about her task, and brought back up the details of the missing man who had caught her eye, the previous evening. His name was Louis Cranda; and he had lived in Corralejo, with his wife, Adora. She had originally reported him missing on the twenty-fourth of July 2008.

The more Dawn studied the details, the harder she found it to understand why the Spanish police had apparently been so disinterested. Perhaps her perception of such a report was now clouded; coming at it with such suspicious eyes, simply because of the date of the alleged event. Twenty-third of July, or thereabouts, had never previously been a significant trigger to set off alarm bells. Hindsight, she reasoned, was a wonderful thing. It could also cause people to jump to conclusions; so she would be thorough, and make no unwarranted assumptions.

159

Louis Cranda had been a waiter at a restaurant in Corralejo, where his wife also worked. The report of his sudden disappearance had been checked out by a local officer, and his details filed away. He was officially a missing person. But, subsequently, the case seemed to have been forgotten. The passing of time, and the less than prominent or logical organisation of Spanish police files eight years ago... Dawn tutted. Could this be a relevant case? She would certainly discuss it with Millie... arrange to follow it up. Or, perhaps she and Shelly would look into it themselves... where was Shelly?

Dawn picked up her phone and called her colleague. After a few rings, Shelly picked up.

"Hi, Dawn." She sounded sleepy.

"Morning. You joining me?" Dawn was not impressed.

True, it was not particularly late, and theirs was never a nine-to-five job. But, this was not a holiday. Men had died. Women had been raped. Every minute that passed without the detection of this monster possibly increased the risk that somebody else was about to be violated.

There was a pause, then Shelly responded:

"Sorry, I'm on my way." The line went dead.

Half an hour later, Dawn looked up, as Shelly breezed into the office. She looked tired, like she had had a long night. Dawn gave her a long look; especially taking in that she was still wearing the dark green, oriental top, but said nothing.

"You found something?" Shelly enquired, avoiding Dawn's eye.

Dawn shifted her gaze back to the computer screen:

"A man who was reported missing on July twenty-fourth, 2008. Up in Corralejo. No reports of him turning up. It could be a wild goose chase, like you had yesterday. But worth checking out."

"Uh huh." Dawn read from the screen:

"Is there a widow? A child?"

160

Dawn nodded:

"Yes. A young widow; well, if he's dead. And a little girl. Louis Cranda... he was twenty-seven at the time."

Shelly now seemed to be fully engaged:

"We need to look into it. Shall we go up to Corralejo... see if we can find the... wife?"

Dawn continued to examine her screen.

"Is Millie still available to help us today? It will make things a lot easier if we can use her?"

Shelly hesitated:

"Er... I think she is. She said so."

Dawn scrolled down on the screen, and made a couple of notes. Without looking up, she observed:

"We better make the most of our relationship with our Spanish colleagues. So far they have been very cooperative. We need to keep them sweet. Millie has been a treasure, hasn't she?"

Shelly didn't reply, but blushed slightly.

Dawn continued:

"It seems to be a good partnership; you and Millie. Why don't you see if she can go with you to Corralejo?"

"Ok."

Shelly knew that there was an undercurrent, here. Dawn's tone was a mixture of teasing, and chastisement. So long as Shelly managed to 'get on well' with Millie, and work effectively with her, then everything was sweet. But, this was a serious job; a matter of life and death. They were not here to have fun on a holiday.

Her partner continued:

161

"You do get that, don't you? This is important."

Shelly understood that she was being ticked off, as well as positively mentored.

"Yes."

She picked up her phone, and strolled over to the water dispenser, as she called a number. Out of earshot, she was speaking to Millie. Moments later, she came back with a drink, and sat down.

"She'll be here in about an hour."

"Right. And, you'll go to Corralejo?" Dawn asked.

"Yeah, but she said she'll look up the file first; see if anything's been added."

"Ok."

By eleven o'clock, Shelly and Millie were cruising up the coast road, towards Corralejo, in Millie's car. Conversation was limited. There seemed to be a tension in the air.

"Do you know the area where Louis Cranda's wife lives?"

Millie nodded:

"It's not far out of town."

There was a prolonged silence, before Millie spoke again:

"Eight years, it's been. Eight years since something happened. That poor kid... she won't even remember her father."

Shelly thought momentarily about her own father. He had recently retired, after working for thirty years in the building trade, mostly as a joiner. She should call him more often, Shelly told herself.

Millie continued:

"According to the file, she... Adora, his wife... was adamant that something must have happened to him, when she reported him missing. But, when

162

she was spoken to again, a few months later, she seemed less sure. She couldn't rule out the possibility that he had abandoned her."

Shelly raised an eyebrow:

"That's interesting. I wonder what could have changed her mind."

Millie muttered:

"Or who!"

"Indeed." Agreed Shelly. "That's the angle we've got to take, I think. Did someone say, or do, something, to cause her to change her story between July 2008 and the day she was spoken to again?"

Reaching the fringe of Corralejo, the road swept inland, past the skeleton of an unfinished hotel building. Millie continued along a straight road, until a range of buildings appeared on both sides. To the right, there was an accommodation block, with smart looking apartments. On the left, there were a few shop units, though not all seemed to be occupied. There was a bar with a cluster of chairs and tables, spilling out across the wide pavement, with a couple of men sat, drinking beer. Shelly noticed the sign above the bar: *'Clarkies'*. Among other clues, the sign advertising *Guinness* told the visitor that this was an Irish run bar.

They approached a roundabout, and Millie continued straight ahead, and up a hill. Further on, they came to another roundabout, where Millie turned right. A few minutes later, they pulled up outside a complex that Millie had identified as Adora Cranda's last known address.

They stepped through a black metal gate, which revealed buildings that were a sandy, almost terracotta shade. The surrounding communal gardens were dry and dusty, with deep-rooted cactus plants that looked like they had been there even longer than the houses.

Millie knocked at the door that she believed was Adora's. There was starting to become a familiar feeling about these visits. There was no answer. Shelly stepped to the side, and peered towards a window, which was closed. The rustling of pebbles and gravel betrayed that someone was coming towards them, from around the side of the property. Millie and Shelly both looked in that direction, as a tall man appeared. He was probably in his fifties; and had floppy grey hair, sunglasses, a flowery shirt, and khaki coloured shorts.

"You looking for Adora?" He asked.

Millie nodded.

"She's at work." Advised the man. "Won't be back before seven, at the earliest."

"Ah, ok. Could you tell us where she works?"

The man looked dubious; so, Millie held up her ID card.

"We're with the police."

"Oh!" The poor chap seemed even more worried. Perhaps he thought he might get his neighbour into trouble.

"It's nothing major." Said Millie. "But we've just driven up from Puerto, so we'd like to catch a word with her, if possible."

"Oh, yes. She works at *La Cabra Brava*, in town; near the top of the main street. She'll be there, for sure."

The man seemed to have accepted that he should assist where possible, and proceeded to explain where her place of work was.

"Thanks, Senor."

Millie led Shelly back to the car, and they drove off. It was only five minutes away, but another five minutes to find somewhere to park. Having done so, they approached *La Cabra Brava*, from which the sound of pop music was drifting.

"Let's get a coffee." Suggested Millie, and they sat at a table.

Presently, a waiter appeared, and greeted them with a flashing grin. Perhaps one that he reserved for all young female customers.

"Hi ladies. What can I get you?"

Millie requested two coffees; and, before the waiter departed, asked him whether Adora Cranda was here. She was, he told them; and would bring them their drinks. A couple of minutes later, a nervous-looking waitress headed their way, carrying two cups of coffee.

"Hi?" She eyed them, curiously. "I'm Adora."

"Thanks, Adora." Millie accepted her coffee.

"Can you join us for a moment; we're with the police." Both officers flashed their ID cards.

"This is officer Shelly King, from the UK."

"Oh." Adora was startled.

She looked across to the bar, and gestured to her colleague that she was going to sit with them.

Shelly took the lead:

"Adora, we're here in connection with your husband, Louis."

Adora was shocked, and put her hand to her mouth. Shelly continued swiftly, before Adora could read too much – almost certainly incorrectly – into the details of their visit.

"The thing is, Adora, first of all we need to ask you: have you had any news of Louis, since you reported him missing on the twenty-fourth of July, 2008?"

Adora's puzzled face flicked from Shelly to Millie, and back again.

"No. I assumed you were bringing me some news."

Shelly paused, before continuing with the questions that she wanted to ask; without allowing Adora too much time to consider her answers.

"When you reported him missing, you told the police you were sure something had happened to him."

"Yes, I..." She faltered.

"But, when you were interviewed again, a few months later, you seemed to have a different view. Like you had come to think that he might have deliberately left you. Even that perhaps there was no point the police continuing to search for him. Why was that, Adora?"

There was a long pause, before Louis' wife answered:

"I realised that he wasn't ever coming back. One way or another, I had to come to terms with it... I was never going to see him again."

She looked tense, and close to tears.

Millie interjected:

"But, what was it that changed your view, Adora? The police file shows that you were begging us to search everywhere for him, in July 2008; but, by January 2009, you didn't seem to want us to keep looking. Why was that?"

Adora just shook her head, as if having no proper answer. None that she wanted to share.

Millie glanced at Shelly, before pushing further:

"Some might find it suspicious, Adora. A man's wife doesn't want the police to look too closely into where he is... why he's disappeared. Can you see why that might look odd, Adora?"

The poor woman shifted in her chair, and looked, helplessly, at the two of them, before dropping her head. Shelly felt deeply sorry for her. Although she understood why Millie was taking this line of inquiry, as a tool to prise some meaningful response, it seemed terribly hard. If, as was quite possible, Adora's husband had been killed by the perpetrator that they were chasing... and, if she had subsequently been raped... Shelly glared briefly at Millie for being so cruel, then looked to the ground.

"How old is your daughter, Adora?" Asked Millie.

Adora looked up sharply. Shocked by this question, although she had been thinking, in that very moment, about her daughter, Natalia.

"Why do you ask about her?" Asked Adora.

166

"Natalia, isn't it? How old will she be, now?"

Adora mumbled:

"Ten. She'll be eleven, this year."

Millie softened her expression, and smiled gently at her.

"You'd do anything to protect her, wouldn't you, Adora? Any mother would do the same. She must be very precious to you."

Adora narrowed her eyes; conscious that these officers seemed to know something more than they had so far said. Or, suspected something, at least. Millie knew too, that there were things so far unsaid; elephants in the room. She pressed home for the truth.

"Adora, it's eight years since Louis went. Whatever happened back then, nothing can hurt you now. It's time to tell us everything."

Adora dropped her head into her hands, and burst into tears. The officers gave her time, before Shelly spoke:

"Is there somewhere more private that we can go, Adora?"

Adora nodded, through the tears, and got up. The officers followed her over to the bar, where she indicated to her colleagues that she needed to speak with the women around the back of the bar. She stepped past the kitchen, and opened a door, which led out to a private yard. They both followed her, and sat at a picnic table, next to pile of barrels and bottle crates.

"You know, don't you? How do you know?" Adora was sure that they were already aware of what had happened to her; although she had no idea how this could be.

"Who told you?"

"Whatever happened, you need to tell us, Adora."

Shelly tried to sound kind. Millie had been tough. It felt a bit like 'good cop – bad cop'. Boy, had she been tough. Shelly hadn't enjoyed what she had seen.

"It was a few months after Louis was... after he disappeared. I was still grieving. I couldn't believe he would leave me. But the police couldn't find him. Couldn't find anything. Then, one night..."

She paused, put a tissue to her face, and blew her nose. They waited, patiently.

"I had been working. There was a man. A British man. He followed me home, and... attacked me."

"Go on." Encouraged Shelly, putting her hand on Adora's arm.

"I had just gone into my house, and he came and knocked at the door. I answered it. I thought it was probably my mum, with Natalia. But, as soon as I opened the door, he smashed me backwards and..."

She paused for a sniffle.

"He overpowered me. There was nothing I could do. He raped me. He knew all about Louis. He said things... like he knew that Louis was dead. But, worst of all, he knew about Natalia. Kept making threats about what he would do to her... if I ever spoke up. He had a knife. A huge knife."

"It's ok." Millie reassured her. "You're safe, now, Adora. With your help, we're going to catch this man."

Shelly gave her a glance. One thing that she had learned, early in her policing career, was never to make promises that she couldn't be absolutely certain of keeping.

Adora sighed:

"I've had to keep this in for eight years. Not just losing my husband, but being raped... humiliated. He filmed everything, on his phone. He told me that, if I reported it, he would deny that it was rape, because he had a film that showed I was enjoying the sex. He forced me to smile... to look like I was enjoying it. But I wasn't..."

She let out a cry, and began to sob, again.

"And, Natalia. He threatened to come for her. Harm her. God knows what he would have done to her! So, I couldn't report it. Don't you see?

By the time I made sense of what had happened… that he had almost certainly killed Louis himself… I couldn't take the risk of saying anything."

Shelly patted her arm:

"And, is that why you didn't press the police to keep digging into what happened, when they spoke to you in January 2009?"

Ashamed, she nodded:

"Yes. I knew nothing was going to bring Louis back. To make the accusation would only put Natalia… and me… at risk of something even worse."

She looked beseechingly at them:

"I couldn't risk it. I didn't dare. You understand that, don't you?"

The women both nodded, sympathetically; and the three of them sat quietly for a few moments.

Shelly was replaying, in her mind, the account that Adora had given; when, suddenly, something came to mind about what she had said about the man. Or, rather, something that she had not said. Adora had not mentioned a mask.

Barely daring to hope, she asked:

"Did you get a good look at him?"

Adora looked into the distance, as though recalling what she had seen on that horrific evening:

"Oh, yes. I got a good look at him. I see his face in my mind every day. I can't get rid of it."

Chapter 28

Dawn looked at her phone, which buzzed on the desk, and saw that it was Shelly. She picked it up.

"Hello."

"Dawn, you'll never believe this. She was assaulted, December 2008, and guess what! She saw his face! He didn't wear a mask!"

Dawn almost dropped the coffee cup that was in her left hand.

"What!? Can you get her in here, to do a proper interview?"

Shelly replied:

"We're going to get as much as we can by way of a description, now. Millie's talking to her, as we speak. When we've made sure of getting the basics, we'll talk to her about coming in to go through everything. Millie says we can use an office at the station in Corralejo, if Adora prefers that."

"That's great. Well done! Call me back as soon as you've got a description that we can work with."

Dawn paused:

"You are sure that this is the same pattern, aren't you?"

"Definitely. Her husband went missing on July twenty-third, and she alleges that she was raped in her own home on the twenty-ninth of December, by a British man who had been dining in her restaurant earlier that evening. He threatened her with a knife, knew all about her husband, knew about the daughter, filmed the sexual assault on his phone..."

There was no reply.

"It has to be him, Dawn."

Dawn was thinking fast:

"Shelly, we need to process this as fast as we can. Every day that passes... well, you know."

"I know. I'll call you in a while."

Shelly returned to the yard, where Millie was still speaking with Adora; who was curious:

"You didn't tell me how you knew. How did you know something had happened to me? It's like you're not even surprised."

Millie looked at Shelly, who gave her the nod:

"We think this man may have done the same thing to other women. That's why we need everything you can tell us. It's vital, so that we can stop any harm coming to anyone else."

Adora raised her eyes in surprise:

"But, it's years ago! You don't mean he's still..."

She put her hand to her mouth.

"Then, he's still out there. He could come back!" Her voice had begun to tremble.

"No." Shelly reassured her. "There's no reason to think you're in any danger from him. But, we need the best description that you can give us, and now."

Millie had been making a phone call of her own, but now put down the phone.

"Adora, will you come with us to the local police station, so that we can just record a few things? It really is very important that we do this straight away. I can speak to your boss, if you like? Just let him know that we need to interview you about something... I won't tell him anything more."

Adora wasn't keen, but nodded: "Ok."

Barely half an hour later, Adora was sat with the two officers in a private room in the police station in Corralejo. She was made as comfortable as

171

possible. Although impatient to get to the business of the interview, Shelly and Millie knew that Adora had to be put at her ease. What followed would likely be traumatic for her. They also knew that Adora would want to talk about her husband's disappearance. Yes, there might be something relevant there; it would certainly be worth going over that again. But, for now, and for reasons that they hoped they would not need to explain to her, it was vital to get to whatever she could tell them about the attacker. Fast.

They began the formal interview with clarification of the basics. Adora confirmed her identity, and the details of her family. Then they got to speak about the fateful day of the alleged assault.

Adora had worked a full day shift at *La Cabra Brava*, where she was still working today. She had served a British man with a meal, during the afternoon. Nothing fancy... she couldn't remember what he had eaten; but he had certainly had a couple of beers with it. Then, he had left. She hadn't seen him again until the point at which she was finishing work, which was around eleven o'clock at night. He had been drinking at the bar next door: *'Classics'*. As Adora had left work, and started to walk home, he had caught her eye. He had asked her for directions to another bar, and she had offered to walk with him, as it was on her way home. Then, reaching her own apartment complex, she had pointed him in the right direction, and said goodnight. A few minutes later, he had come to her door; taken her by surprise, and forced himself upon her.

Shelly guided the interview, and did her best not to put any words into Adora's mouth. But, there were some details that she was determined Adora would clarify. Sure enough, one by one, all the points that Shelly expected to hear came out. The man was British. He carried a savage looking knife, and seemed prepared to use it. He knew all about Adora's husband, and appeared scornful of him. He knew the name of their little girl, Natalia; and gleefully held over Adora the threat of what he would do to the child, if he should feel the need to come back. That would be, he said, if Adora told anyone about what happened. He recorded all the sordid details of the assault with the camera on his phone, and insisted that Adora put on the pretence of being a willing and happy partner. That was his 'insurance policy', was the way that she described it.

172

However, two significant points were contained in Adora's account; two things that made it different from the story that Shelly had heard from other victims. Firstly, the man had no mask; so, Adora was going to be able to give them some sort of description of him. Shelly almost rubbed her hands together with glee, as she anticipated hearing Adora's best attempt at describing his appearance. Secondly, the man did not use a card with printed instructions; but he did refer to such a thing. He commented to Adora that he 'ought to write it down'. Although this proved nothing, it did reinforce in Shelly the belief that this perhaps was the first in this man's string of assaults. She hoped that it was.

Eventually, they reached the point where Adora felt ready to describe the man. Shelly and Millie's attention was absolute.

"He was British." Adora said. "English, I think. But, I'm not good at picking out Scottish, or Irish."

Shelly felt no need to point out that she had omitted 'Welsh', but bore it in mind.

"He was bigger than me, but not massively tall. He was strong, though. Muscly. Big shoulders."

Shelly nodded, noting it down.

"What sort of age?"

Adora narrowed her eyes, as if looking at him again, right there in front of her.

"Maybe thirty. Hard to say."

Millie observed her; feeling sorry for this poor woman. Everything that she heard made her hate men.

Shelly continued: "Did he seem to have a tan?"

Millie looked at her, rather puzzled. Shelly explained:

"Could tie in with whether he had just come to the island, or been here for some time. Even live here."

Millie acknowledged the point:

"True."

They both looked to Adora:

"He did have a bit of a suntan. Like the holidaymakers I see every day. He hadn't just arrived. But, I hadn't seen him in my bar before. Well, I hadn't noticed him."

"What about his hair?" Shelly suggested.

Adora thought.

"Dark hair. Not long. Going a bit thin."

How tall? What about his clothes? Any jewellery, tattoos, body art? Any scars or other injuries? Did he smell of anything? What about his voice? Was he well-spoken? Educated? Were there any particular expressions that struck you?

There were so many questions and prompts, which Shelly, assisted by Millie, used to try and prise out the best possible pen-picture of this man. By the end of their session, Adora was exhausted. In a quiet moment, while Millie and Shelly together made a call to Dawn, leaving Adora to her thoughts, she felt empty, hollow, alone. Louis was never coming back. She knew that. But, the constant questions about Adora's own suffering seemed to forget all about poor Louis, who was surely dead. He deserved better.

Shelly returned to sit with Adora, and pulled a computer screen round, into the best viewing position.

"Adora, would you be ok looking at some pictures? I've been sent some pictures of known offenders. If you will look at them, it's possible that you could pick him out."

Back in the UK, Frank Burnley had been busy. Although there was absolutely no evidence to implicate anyone in particular, there was no harm collating mugshots of known sex offenders. It was a long shot. But,

174

no harm in trying; so he had sent Dawn a sizeable package of shots, which she had now forwarded to Shelly.

"Ok."

Adora took a deep breath, before easing herself into position to study the screen. Shelly flicked onto the first of a series of pictures, each accompanied by a coded reference number. They soon continued as an automated slideshow; which would only pause if Adora directed it. At the sight of some of these men, Adora recoiled in disgust. They seemed hideous, brutal. But, perhaps that was because she had just been told that these were known, violent, sex offenders. In her mind, every one of these was as evil and savage as the beast who had murdered her husband and violated her. Some of these men were too old, or too young. Frank had not had the information about the suspected age of Adora's attacker; so had not filtered any out.

As she continued to look at the images, Shelly spoke, out of her earshot, to Millie.

"I want to speak to our psychologist. I'll get Dawn to contact him. There are a couple of things I want to ask him."

"Such as?" Millie asked.

"Well, for one, if Adora was his very first victim... is it likely, or at least possible, that he already knew her and Louis? Is there something different about the first victim... the trigger that sets off a serial offender on what follows?"

"Hmm. You may be right. But, in this case, she seems pretty certain that he's a visiting tourist. And, we know that neither she nor Louis ever visited the UK; so I'd say it's unlikely."

Shelly had to agree.

"The other thing I wanted to ask him..." She paused, to glance over at Adora, who was still studying the mugshots.

175

"As he's so meticulous, about the ethnicity of his victim, a wife, a child, and even the exact date each year; does that mean that he's too clever to have been caught up for any other sexual offence?"

Millie looked at Adora, and nodded: "So we could be wasting her time, looking at offenders. Maybe the key lies somewhere else."

Adora was having no luck at picking out a familiar face, and sighed with frustration as she continued: "Do you think a photo-fit session with a police artist might be any use?" Suggested Millie.

"Possibly. But, after so long… remember he'll be eight years older now. It could end up misleading people."

Eventually, Adora got to the end of the less than charming selection of men's faces.

"No." She declared, not for the first time. "None of them."

After a short break, they went over everything contained in Adora's statement one more time. Then, to her relief, they agreed to end the interview, and make arrangements to continue this another day. The officers gathered everything up, thanked their hosts at Corralejo police station, and took Adora home.

"Your daughter… she's with your mother?" Shelly realised that they had almost forgotten about Natalia, and it was now after seven in the evening.

"Yes. Mama will be looking after her."

"You've done really well, Adora." Shelly reassured her. "We'll be in touch soon." And they left her at her door.

Driving back to Puerto del Rosario, the officers had plenty to contemplate. They now had a reasonable description of their wanted man; although based on an encounter eight years ago. Just after eight, they reached Puerto.

"Will Dawn still be in the office?" Millie asked. She had heard Shelly in conversation with her by phone, during the drive south.

176

"Yes, I think so. I better check in with her." She added, in case there was any doubt.

"Sure." Agreed Millie, and made for the police station; where she pulled into the car park. Dawn was indeed still at work, and looked up from her phone conversation as Shelly walked in.

"Boss, Shelly's just got back."

The sound of DI Williams speaking at the other end was just about audible; then Dawn passed the phone to Shelly.

"Boss."

Shelly updated her DI with a professional summary of the day that she had just spent, interviewing Adora Cranda. She mentioned the points that she felt might warrant a view from the psychologist, and Williams agreed to raise them with him, the next day.

"Ok, good work Shelly. Get some rest, and we'll conference call with the team at nine in the morning. Well done."

"Thanks, Boss." Shelly returned the phone to Dawn, who was closing down her computer.

"You ready for something to eat?" Dawn asked.

"Er..." Shelly glanced at Millie, who was leaning against the door.

Dawn felt that there was a hint to be taken; and, without further reference to food, continued: "I'm going back to the hotel. I'll see you here at eight-thirty in the morning, if not before."

"Ok."

Shelly began to gather up her own things, as Dawn passed her, and left the office. Millie stretched; stiff after the driving.

"Pizza?"

Shelly shrugged: "Why not?"

Chapter 29

At ten pm, Shelly jumped, at the sound of her phone summoning her. She had been lying restfully on a soft bed, gazing at the ceiling. She was naked, warm, relaxed; enjoying a moment of peace amidst the turbulence of the last couple of days.

She frowned, and tutted; but dutifully picked up the phone anyway.

"Hi." She saw that it was Dawn calling.

"I've had the boss on." Began Dawn. "The assistant commissioner is on his back. Are you in your room?"

"Er, no. I came out for a bit."

There was a silence.

"Oh."

"Shall I come back? I can come back, if…"

"No." Dawn was decisive. "No, there's no need. But we need to talk in the morning, before the conference call. Just to be sure we're both on the same page with this. I'll explain then. Be in as early as you can, yes?"

Shelly agreed:

"Will do. I'll be there for eight."

Dawn terminated the call. Shelly cast her phone down, and lay back on the bed, again.

"Problem?" Asked Millie, who had just emerged from her en-suite shower, with a towel around the lower half of her body, and came to sit at Shelly's side.

"I don't know. Dawn didn't explain; but she needs to talk to me early tomorrow."

"Ah." Millie seemed to have a knowing look on her face. "I think I could hazard a guess as to what that's about."

Shelly was puzzled:

"What?"

"Well, think about it. This case is yours, a British matter; but does it become ours, now? There are people who would love to politicise this. You lot voted for Brexit. Wouldn't certain politicians love to stir up a debate about the lines of communication and cooperation becoming blurred, when you leave the EU? Isn't that the sort of fear-mongering some people thrive on?"

Shelly was surprised, but had to concede that the insightful Millie might have a point.

"Maybe." She paused. "Then I better not get caught sleeping with the enemy."

Millie grinned, and stroked Shelly's arm.

"I'll try not to let you sleep."

Shelly sat up, and looked Millie squarely in the face:

"I feel a bit guilty doing this. I'm here because men have been murdered and women have been raped. That's why we met."

Millie stood up, folded her towel across a chair, and stood, naked, in front of her.

"I understand that. But whether you go and sleep alone in your hotel room, or I massage your shoulders, back, thighs... and try and take you to the heights that drove you wild last night, isn't going to change any of that. Life goes on. But, I do understand. If you want to go, it's not a problem."

Shelly looked down, then slapped the bed frame with her hand.

"I fucking hate this job, sometimes. It screws with my mind. I feel so helpless. All I want to do is the right thing. Dawn probably thinks I'm... I

179

don't know what she thinks of me. But, she knows. She knows I'm with you. And, there's no reason I shouldn't be... It's just..."

Millie stepped closer, and pulled Shelly's face gently into her breast, cradling her head with a gentle touch. She stroked Shelly's fair hair; as the two shared a quiet, tender moment, before Shelly recovered her poise, lifted her head, and kissed Millie passionately on the lips.

Chapter 30

The next morning, Friday, Dawn took her time, walking from the hotel to the police station. It was another warm and sunny morning. She had just made a call to her husband, Roy; who had been complaining about the rain and grey skies of Manchester. In an attempt to make him feel better, she had played down how lovely the climate was in Fuerteventura; conceding only that it was dry today, and 'pleasant enough'.

She walked in, just as Shelly was taking off her jacket and hanging it over her chair. Dawn glanced around, to check whether Millie was with her. Without formalities, she began:

"Come in here Shelly."

She led Shelly into the side room that had become their recent home, and closed the door behind them. Shelly shuffled, uncomfortably; half expecting, from Dawn's manner, that she was about to be told off for some indiscretion.

"The boss called, last night. The assistant commissioner is all over this, now. He reckons that with what we have, now, any reasonable person would assume that a murder may well have been committed on July twenty-third, this year. That being the case, if we don't either make an arrest or at least locate the murder victim and warn his widow, we're going to get slaughtered for putting her at risk, and not protecting her."

"Oh!" Shelly gasped.

It wasn't quite what she had been expecting.

Dawn continued:

"Naturally, he wants the arrest and conviction. What he's not prepared to admit, is that, if we make a big noise about this, so as to make it easier to find the recent victim and his widow, we'll very likely scare the killer off, and possibly never find him."

Shelly sat down, as Dawn continued:

181

"So, when we talk to the boss in a few minutes, we need to be absolutely on task with this. Do you hear what I'm saying?"

Shelly nodded. Dawn looked across to the main office, where she could see that Millie had just arrived.

"There's bound to be some talk about whether we keep hold of this, now. We now believe that three of the couples targeted have been over here; two in Fuerteventura and one in Lanzarote. This could start to get very political."

Shelly thought back to what Millie had suggested: political mischief-making, in the light of the recent and controversial Brexit vote.

Dawn went on:

"So, we've got to be a hundred per cent together on this. We don't want any gaps in what we say. Right?"

Shelly nodded, again.

"We'll probably be asked about the cooperation that we've been getting. What do you feel about that?"

Shelly, completely honest, replied:

"It's been a hundred per cent. We couldn't have asked for more. Millie's been available to guide us through the files, take us to where we want to be, act as interpreter when needed, get us into the right places."

"Hmm. And, do you think she's shared everything with us, or kept anything back."

Shelly glanced through the internal window.

"So far, she's given me everything."

Shelly wished she had chosen a different expression.

"But I think that might have to change. She'll be reporting the Cranda case to her boss... probably as we speak. He might want to try and take it away

182

from us. Especially if he accepts the links to the Roberto Pastor murder, and Luca Mendez. I don't know."

Dawn had thought all this through. She had turned it over in her mind, all night.

"Well, from now on, be careful what you give her."

Dawn, too, wished that *she* had chosen a slightly different expression.

A few minutes later, Millie knocked, opened the door, and put her head round it.

"Do you want me in for your conference call?" She asked.

"No, thanks. And, we'll take it in here. Thanks, anyway." Dawn was clear enough.

Presently, the video call came through, and Dawn placed her laptop on the table, at a suitable angle.

"Morning, Dawn." DI Williams' voice came through first, then the pictures appeared.

Assembled at the Manchester end, most of the familiar team announced themselves, so that Dawn and Shelly knew who was part of the call. Frank Burnley, Carol O'Toole, and Dave Perryman briefly came into view, as DI Williams panned the camera around the room. As he placed it on the table, DCI York's stern face appeared. Sat next to her was Dr Marcus Sheen, and DI Williams took the seat next to him.

"Anybody else there with you?" Asked Williams.

"No, it's just me and Shelly."

"Ok. Start by confirming whether we have anything more on the Luca Mendez case."

Dawn had nothing much to add to that one.

"Now, just run us through what you established with the widow of Roberto Pastor."

Dawn deferred to Shelly, who reported on her visit to Aida Pastor. There were a few questions; but, it was largely accepted without query.

Then they moved onto the case of Louis Cranda. Again, Shelly gave her account of meeting with the widow, and hearing almost exactly the same story again. The key difference with this one, though, was that the man had not hidden his identity; Adora had been able to get a good look at his face. True, it was nearly eight years ago. But, given the situation, it was something Adora would probably not forget. Her description was along the lines of: male, aged around thirty, quite muscular, height around 175 centimetres, perhaps 180. His hair was short, dark, slightly receding; and he had no moustache or beard. The man didn't have any tattoos that she could see, nor any jewellery or piercings. He spoke confidently, as if he was reasonably well-educated; and Adora had assumed that he was a British tourist. She couldn't say whether his eyes were blue or brown.

As the team took in Shelly's account, she took it upon herself to ask Dr Sheen a question of her own.

"Dr Sheen, do you think he knew Louis Cranda?"

Sheen hesitated, and brushed back his wavy silver hair.

"Possible. Sometimes the manner of killing tells us something; but, as we don't have a body, it's not possible to comment on anything that differentiates it from the others."

Shelly had been thinking hard about this.

"Of the others, Roberto Pastor is the only one that was immediately obvious as a murder. He was battered to death, and his body wasn't even hidden from view. But, with the others: a possible accident for Luca Mendez, maybe accidental drowning for Tom Perez, no body even found for Esteban Rojo. He wasn't making a statement with the revelation of their bodies."

Sheen was nodding:

"That's very true. If anything, it makes me wonder whether Roberto Pastor was known to him."

184

There was a silence.   Then, DCI York, who had been listening and observing, spoke up:

"How has the cooperation been, from the Spanish?"

Without looking at Shelly, Dawn took it upon herself to answer for them:

"First class. They've given us every assistance, but not interfered. We get the feeling, though, that with the latest findings, they might be interested in stepping in."

"Hmm. The assistant commissioner called me in to see him, yesterday. He made it very plain to me that, given our suspicions, if we allow a woman to suffer a sexual assault, heads will roll. We can't let anything get in the way of our investigation."

Neither Dawn nor Shelly commented.

DI Williams intervened:

"Well, for now, we've had cooperation. You're flying back, tomorrow. Just make sure that, while you're there, you get everything you possibly can. Make full use of their files. Try to keep your heads down; but, if anybody tries to restrict you, or you feel that you're not getting the help, get back to me."

"Yes, Boss."

The conference call continued, with DI Williams stressing to Dawn that it was vital to make sure they had a way of staying in touch with Adora Cranda. If, at any time in the future, a suspect emerged; they would need Adora to look at him, and, hopefully, confirm an identification.

Three other points were discussed; firstly, the Spanish police's efforts to find witnesses and evidence in relation to Roberto Pastor's murder. No doubt they had done everything that they reasonably could; but... in the light of new evidence, could they make fresh efforts to find something? Secondly, the whereabouts of Louis Cranda. He had been recorded as a missing person, eight years ago. If, as was now suspected, he had been killed, could they reopen the investigation; try to find witnesses, and clarify his last known movements? Thirdly, now that Adora Cranda had alleged that she had been assaulted by a man that she perceived to be a British tourist, could they make efforts to identify any possible suspects who were on the island at that time? This could be a test of diplomacy; York and Williams knew what they wanted; but, telling the Spanish how to do their job would not be easy.

The team were not optimistic; realising that it would be impossible to locate and identify every British male, then between the ages of twenty-five and thirty-five, who was present in Fuerteventura in July 2008. It might be the case that only if a suspect was found, could his travel records be checked, with the aid of border control; to confirm whether at that time he had recently left Britain and entered Spanish territory.

Dawn and Shelly had one more day, before they were due to fly back to the UK. It was agreed that Shelly would revisit Adora Cranda, this time accompanied by Dawn. If any additional information could be elicited from Adora, then a skilled interviewer like Dawn was the person to get at it.

An hour later, Shelly had gone to fetch their car, while Dawn was gathering up her things, and fastening the shoulder bag, into which she had placed some files. She looked up.

Inspector Hanst stood at the door. He was a tall, solidly built man, and seemed to be blocking it. Nobody would be leaving that room unless he moved. As Dawn caught his eye, he smiled politely, and nodded, by way of acknowledging her.

"Rodriguez has filled me in. It looks like we have multiple homicides, a serial killer, and a serial rapist, too."

Dawn couldn't deny his conclusion.

"That's certainly the way it seems."

Hanst frowned.

"When were you planning on sharing the extent of your investigation with us?"

Dawn wavered. She didn't want to cause any trouble for Millie; but, they hadn't hidden anything.

186

"We have been sharing, as we've gone on. This started as a British problem; but, there's no doubt it's grown into an international one."

Hanst's polite smile had now faded.

"I hope we've given you every assistance while you've been our guests on Spanish soil. Now, you'll be passing us all the information you have, before you leave?"

Dawn smiled.

"I know my DI will be talking to you. We all want the same outcome here, of course."

She moved to the door. Slowly, Hanst stepped aside, and she walked past him. Joining Shelly, who was waiting outside the car in the police yard; Dawn opened the door to get into the car, just as Millie appeared, and walked across to them.

"You don't need me today?" She asked, looking at Shelly.

Shelly sounded nervous.

"Dawn's going to lead on this, today. She wants to meet Adora, for herself. I suppose it doesn't need all three of us."

Millie gave her a lingering look.

"No. Course it doesn't. Just don't let Hanst know you are going interviewing people on your own. You're well outside your own jurisdiction."

And, with the faintest wink, she turned and walked back into the building. Shelly opened her mouth to call after her, but decided against it.

"She's right, of course." Commented Dawn.

Shelly got into the car, buckled up, and the two of them set off for Corralejo.

Chapter 31

A passenger today, Dawn wound down the window, and enjoyed the feel of the breeze through her hair, as she looked over the white sand towards the sea. The beaches were quiet at this time of the morning; although she could see people making their way across from the parking lay-by, carrying bags, towels, surfboards, and kites.

"You really hit it off with Millie, didn't you?"

Shelly kept her eyes on the road:

"We worked well together. She's been very helpful."

Dawn turned to look at her:

"That's not what I mean, and you know it."

Shelly grinned.

"Fair enough."

Changing the subject, Shelly asked:

"What do you think the plan is, for when we get back? Is the boss planning to go public with everything we've got?"

Dawn grimaced.

"I don't see how he can. I don't think the assistant commissioner would welcome mass panic on the streets, do you?"

Shelly considered:

"Well, I don't think there would be a mass panic. Why would there be?"

Dawn responded:

"If we don't make an arrest, what do you think it would be like as we approach July twenty-third, next year?"

"Hmm. Fair point."

"On the other hand…" Dawn continued: "If we don't manage to find any report of a Spaniard going missing, or worse, in the very near future, what else can we do? The AC's right, we have to do whatever we can to protect some as yet unidentified woman from possible harm."

When they reached Corralejo, they went directly to *La Cabra Brava*. They had already called ahead, and got Adora's agreement to come from work during her break, and sit with them somewhere private close by. Adora spotted them crossing over the road to approach the restaurant, and motioned to her boss to let him know she was taking her break.

"Hi Adora. This is my colleague, Dawn." Shelly made the introduction.

"Hi." Adora responded, with limited enthusiasm.

"We'll go sit over here." Adora continued; leading them over to a small open-plan seating area, which surrounded a trickling fountain.

Having clarified a few points, and reminded Adora that they would be returning to England the next day, Shelly and Dawn brought her attention to the description of her assailant, that she had given the previous day. They went over everything again, and tried to tease out any extra details. Then, they moved on to ask her about anything that she could tell them about Louis' last known movements.

It was eight years ago, but Adora remembered everything about the day on which she had seen Louis for the last time. Although they worked at the same restaurant, they often worked different shifts. On that day, Adora had been due to work early, and had taken her daughter, Natalia, to her mother, before arriving at *La Cabra Brava*. She had arrived in work at nine-thirty, and gone about her daily tasks the same as any other day; fully expecting that Louis would arrive to join her on duty, three hours later. However, to her surprise, he never arrived.

An annoyed boss demanded to know where Louis was; they were short-staffed, now. Adora tried to call him on his phone, but got no reply. Very strange! Louis was normally pretty reliable. He liked a drink, but not in the morning; just later in the day, and in the evening, after his day's work. So, Adora discounted the possibility that he had got carried away with a drinking session. That just wasn't Louis.

189

To appease the boss, Adora stayed on for an extra three hours, to make up for her husband's absence. So it was, that at nine-thirty in the evening, rather than six-thirty, a tired and puzzled Adora made her way home. Her mother was already at their house, with Natalia; but had not seen or heard anything of Louis.

Adora went to a neighbour, Lizzie; a Danish woman in her thirties, who lived alone. Had she seen Louis? From her house, it was possible that she had caught sight of him from her window, if he had passed by that way. Lizzie saw most of what went on outside, from her airy front room, with double doors that were usually open to the garden. No, Lizzie had been home most of the day, but said that she hadn't seen anything of him.

Leaving Lizzie's house, Adora had spotted Tom; an old man who lived in the corner apartment. Had he seen anything of Louis? Yes. Earlier that day, not long after Adora had left for work, Tom had seen Louis outside. Nothing memorable or significant about that; but, yes, Louis had been there, walking away from his home, at around nine-forty-five. Tom remembered looking up at the sound of Louis' voice, as he had spoken to someone upon leaving his house. Adora had pressed Tom; what was Louis wearing? Apparently the usual clothes that he always wore when heading off to work, complete with his hat to keep off the sun; although he was a couple of hours early, so he was perhaps going somewhere else, first.

Beyond that, there were no reported sightings of Louis. He was well known in town, but none of the other shopkeepers or bar staff recalled seeing him walking past. That may have indicated that the route he took was away from town, up to the quieter estates, or across towards the dunes. Or, possibly not. Adora was unable to conclude that her husband had taken any particular route.

Having listened to all the details, and taken them in, Dawn asked:

"After you were assaulted, which cast a new light on his disappearance, did that give you any new thoughts about which way he might have gone? Or where he might have met up with anyone?"

Adora thought hard.

"Well, I just thought that, if he was taken forcibly by… him, it must have been away from town. Away from view. And, that could only be towards the dunes. But, I don't know. Louis could look after himself. I can't see that man being able to force him to go anywhere. Although, with that knife…" She shuddered.

Shelly intervened:

"The police… they never came up with any leads, so far as you know, about where Louis might have gone?"

She already knew the answer to the question.

Adora shook her head:

"They never really looked, did they?"

Dawn cut in:

"If they had started a search, where would you have told them to look first?"

Adora was adamant:

"The dunes. If I had known then what I'm sure of now, I'd have said he'd been killed and buried somewhere out there. There's so much space, so much soft sand. It seems obvious now, doesn't it?"

Shelly and Dawn looked at each other. It hadn't seemed obvious to either of them, but… perhaps Adora was right.

Leaving her, and promising to stay in touch, the officers returned to their car. Instead of driving back towards the main road out of town, they drove slowly in the opposite direction; up the hill, until they could take a left turn along what was clearly a dead end, approaching the very edge of the dunes. Pulling up, they got out, and stood there; marvelling at the wild beauty of the shrubby, plant-strewn, wilderness which sprawled out into the distance as far as the eye could see heading south, and eastwards until it reached the Atlantic Ocean.

"Do you think she has a point?" Shelly wondered, out loud.

191

"Buried in the dunes? It's quite possible, isn't it?" Dawn agreed. "But, what's the chances of finding him, now, if he was properly buried? I know the sands shift in the wind; but, if he has been there for eight years, I can't imagine him being unearthed now."

Shelly looked east, towards the sea, muttering:

"If I wanted to hide a body, that's where I would put it."

Driving back to Puerto del Rosario, they discussed their exit strategy. They would be going to the airport the next morning; so, wouldn't have much more chance to explore any of the Spanish police files, or get more face-to-face help from their European colleagues.

Dawn made an observation:

"You know how important it is that we maintain a good relationship with the Spanish, don't you? We may be asking them for a few more favours, yet."

"Yep."

"So, it might be a good idea to try and make sure that Millie's door is open to us, if necessary."

"Hmm."

There was an awkward silence. Dawn hoped that Shelly might suggest a way of keeping the contact warm; but she said nothing. Eventually, Dawn suggested:

"I better have a last hunt through those old files, in case I've missed anything. Maybe you could catch her this afternoon, if she's around? Buy her a 'thank you' drink?"

Shelly didn't respond. Dawn continued:

"Just in the line of duty, of course."

Shelly's expressionless face finally lapsed into a smile.

"Ok. If you say so."

Chapter 32

They arrived back at the capital's police station at four-thirty; in time to see officer Castillo driving out of the yard. He raised his hand in acknowledgement, as they drove in. Millie's car was still there; so, Dawn parked in the free space, next to it.

As they entered the building, and went up to the usual office, they saw inspector Hanst, deep in conversation with two other, senior-looking men, that they hadn't seen before. Millie was stood with them, paying attention to their conversation. Hanst appeared to scowl, when he caught sight of Dawn and Shelly. He shifted his position, so that his face was turned away from them, as he continued to speak to his colleagues. Presently, they were done; and the two strangers left the room with Hanst. Soon, Millie came over to where Shelly was checking her phone, and Dawn had started to interrogate her computer.

"You're off tomorrow." She observed, dryly. "Get everything you wanted?"

Dawn allowed Shelly to answer for them.

"We were just talking about it... how best to stay in touch. We're sure to need to confer as this investigation goes on. Probably on a regular basis."

"Sure to." Millie said.

Putting on a far more friendly smile, and leading Millie to one side, where their conversation might be more private, Shelly added:

"Can we get a drink, tonight? We wanted to thank you for everything you've done for us. Without your help, we would never have made the progress that we've done."

Millie hesitated; averting her eyes, and glancing briefly across at Dawn.

"Just us two, I mean." Shelly clarified, with a slight blush.

Millie wheeled round, and picked up her bag, which she had put on the desk. Without any discernible emotion:

"Sure."

Shelly smiled, relieved.

"Do you want to meet me at the hotel, about seven?"

"Yep. I'll show you a couple of bars, in town. Proper bars."

Dawn got on with the task of trawling through everything that she could find in connection with all the cases. In theory, she should be able to access any of the information again, later. But, there was no substitute for plucking it directly from the Spanish records, herself, without the need to ask for support.

As Shelly left for the day, Dawn said:

"Make sure you part on good terms. We need Millie on our side."

Two hours later, Shelly had showered, and changed; and was completing her packing as best she could, ready for the homeward journey tomorrow. They would be leaving for the airport around eight the next morning; and she wasn't sure whether this might be a late night.

Her phone bleeped; and she looked at it, to see a message from Millie. She was waiting downstairs, in the foyer. Shelly picked up her white jacket, and headed off to meet her.

As Shelly skipped down the stairs, she saw Millie, stood by the large windows, looking out towards the street. She was talking quietly on her phone, and turned away, briefly, as Shelly approached. She very quickly ended the call, and slipped her phone into the pocket of her jeans; turning back to smile at Shelly.

"Come on. We'll take a walk by the harbour; then a snack and a few beers?"

"Sounds good." Shelly agreed, following her out into the street.

The evening was warm, and bright. They enjoyed each other's company; but, each seemed nervous. As if there was something, perhaps more than one thing, that neither of them wanted to raise. There was certainly chemistry between the two of them; however, that seemed to be threatened, perhaps tainted, by the uneasy tension felt by them both. Each harboured a faint suspicion that the other might be using them to gain information. Eventually, after the small talk that accompanied their stroll around the harbour, they sat quietly at a pavement bar, each with a cold bottled-beer.

"Cheers!" Said Shelly, raising her bottle.

Millie clinked against it.

"Salut!"

She took a swig, then sat back, relaxed.

"What's the plan, when you get back to the UK, then? Are you going public with these cases?"

Shelly wished Millie hadn't asked. Although she knew they had to cooperate, she had an underlying suspicion that it was now going to be difficult. She didn't want to divulge too much, in case the Spanish police took it upon themselves to take some different course of action. Nor did she want to be accused by her bosses of passing on anything more than she should. So, it was with some relief, that she was able to say, with absolute honesty:

"We haven't been told yet."

She took a sip.

"No doubt they'll tell us in due course."

Millie eyed her:

"What's your gut feeling about how to go about it? Go public with what you have?"

"Hmm. Maybe there's something British about keeping our cards close to our chest. Protecting the public. The nanny state. Who knows?"

Millie sighed:

"Well, I wouldn't expect too much discretion from our end. I know Hanst is itching to make some noise about this. From his point of view, it looks like some foreigner has come to Spain, committed atrocities, and fled back to the safety of his home country. Where nothing much has been done to catch him."

Shelly smarted:

"That's hardly fair!"

Holding her hands up in a defensive gesture, Millie pointed out:

"I'm just telling you how he sees it. Not everybody trusts the British to share all the information they have. Some cops have long memories about British crooks fleeing your country, coming here, causing problems…"

Shelly was clear, and raised her voice just a little:

"Well, I can assure you we'll be doing everything we can to get to him. We've learnt a lot in the last few days. Especially from Adora Cranda. With her evidence we're much closer to catching him."

Millie put a calming hand on Shelly's arm.

"I understand. I'm with you. Just… don't expect to walk all over him. You'll need to keep him on side, Hanst; if you expect to keep the element of surprise back home, and only put out as much as you want to."

Shelly nodded.

"Ok."

She took Millie's hand, and squeezed it.

"Got any beers at your place?"

Millie grinned:

"Come on. Let's go."

Chapter 33

Millie opened her window, to let in the evening breeze. Lifting two bottles of *San Miguel* out of the fridge, she passed one to Shelly, who was stood beside her, looking out at the blue sky.

"Thanks."

Millie put down her own beer, and stepped up behind Shelly, placing her hands softly on her hips. She traced them upwards, and around to her stomach; then stepped in closer, leaning her own body against Shelly's back, and smelling the scent of her hair. Shelly arched her back a little, and stretched her neck; lifting her head up towards the ceiling. She made no effort to resist, or move away, as Millie's hands gently cupped her breasts, and stroked, through her clothes.

Eventually, Shelly turned around, and put her beer bottle down on the window sill. With two hands now free, she gripped Millie tightly, drawing her closer into an embrace. The two kissed, frantically, for a few moments. Then, both stepping back slightly, to look at each other, they released their grip.

"Shower?" Asked Millie.

Shelly nodded.

"Excellent idea."

Millie set the shower running, then began to take off her clothes, as Shelly watched her undress.

"You're very fit... toned."

Shelly admired her shoulders, and the muscular arms. Millie was certainly no stranger to the gym.

Unfastening her jeans, Millie slipped them down, and sat on a chair to remove them completely; now only wearing her black underwear. She continued; aroused by the sensation of having the fully-clothed Shelly watch and appreciate her. Slowly, she unfastened her bra, and placed it

197

with her other clothes; then took down her knickers, which she added to the pile. She stood, naked, in front of Shelly.

"Like what you see, girl?"

Shelly murmured:

"Undress me."

Millie did so, slowly; lingering over each garment, until Shelly was as naked as her. Softly, she stroked her breasts; thrilling to Shelly's visible response of arousal, as she half closed her eyes at the feel of Millie's fingers on her erect nipples.

They stepped into the shower; taking pleasure at soaping up each other's bodies with a scented lather, and then gently washing away all the bubbles. They took their time, but, finally, emerged; each wrapped in a soft white towel. Dabbing themselves dry, they finished off their beers; before Millie led Shelly away, and into the bedroom.

Shelly lay on her back, with Millie at her side, propped up on one arm, observing her. Neither spoke for a few moments; both in their own thoughts. Finally, Millie broke the silence:

"You're still on duty, aren't you?" As she ran her fingers up Shelly's leg, coming to rest on the inside of her thigh.

"What do you mean?"

"You're still thinking about the women, and what they suffered."

Shelly sighed.

"Actually, I was thinking something else. I was feeling quite guilty. What about the men? They've died. Probably a painful death; maybe even tortured before they died, some of them. Yet, we seem to think just about the women. You know what I mean?"

Millie nodded:

"True. It may have been horrible for the women, but they do still have a life."

Shelly rolled over to her, and hugged Millie tight; before scrambling on top of her, taking hold of her wrists as if to restrain them against the pillow, and looking down at this Spanish cop's superb body.

She began to rub her own body against Millie's skin. Then, she released her wrists; and used her hands to stroke Millie's breasts, with a gentle circular motion, pausing to attend to the hardening nipples. She leaned down, and flicked her tongue here and there; starting with the breasts, then creeping lower, until she was brushing her face against Millie's bushy pubic hair.

Shelly slowly slid her right hand down, and began to play between her legs, which Millie obligingly spread apart, to encourage Shelly's eager fingers to explore more deeply. Licking her fingers to moisten them, Shelly proceeded to tease their way inside; tugging gently at the hairs, tickling at the pink skin, flicking mischievously at Millie's involuntary yet inviting genitalia.

The Brit went even lower; while the Spaniard, beginning to writhe with pleasure, put her hands gently onto the top of Shelly's head. Tracing her fingers through her hair, playfully tickling at her ears; she gripped ever more firmly at Shelly's scalp, encouraging her to press firmly with her tongue.

"Keep going." She murmured. "Yes. Keep going."

Chapter 34

The next morning, Dawn glanced up from her coffee in the hotel dining room, as Shelly joined her. Dawn's breakfast was finished, and she was nearly ready to leave the room.

"Morning." Shelly greeted her with a bright smile.

"Hi. Good evening?"

Shelly grinned at her; a dazzling smile that suggested her evening, and the night that followed, had been a pleasant time.

She sat down, and a waitress appeared, to pour her a cup of coffee.

"Senora?" Asked the waitress; holding out the coffee pot to Dawn, too.

"Yes, please." Dawn pushed forward her cup, for a refill.

Shelly eyed the buffet counter, but decided against having anything.

"I'll stick to coffee." She said.

As they drank, Shelly reassured her partner that Millie was still very much on their side, and would try to give them further help, if she could. However, there was no guarantee that inspector Hanst could be relied on to present the same approach to this case that their own bosses might prefer. That, they both agreed, was a challenge that would have to be dealt with by DI Williams and DCI York.

"So, you parted on good terms?"

Dawn suppressed a chuckle.

"The best." Shelly smiled.

Less than an hour later, the two were heading for the airport. Returning their hire car, they walked over to the main airport building. Unsurprisingly, negotiating security was an easier business than was usually the case at Manchester; and they were soon comfortable in the departure lounge.

"You think we'll be back?" Asked Shelly.

"It's quite possible. After all, you have friends here."

Shelly blushed.

This time, the two were sat together on the plane; and quietly discussed everything they had. The DI was expecting them to check in at the office that afternoon; and they wanted to be fully prepared. Shelly, especially, didn't want to allow any suggestion that she had failed to do her duty; this had been a working trip, not a 'jolly'. She knew that Dawn wouldn't gossip about her leisure time with Millie; but, still, she felt that she had to be absolutely on top of everything.

They got into the office just after five; having endured the comparatively abysmal traffic of the Greater Manchester motorway network, after being spoiled by the quiet roads of Fuerteventura.

"Hi, ladies." Frank Burnley greeted them.

"Thelma and Louise are back." Quipped Dave Perryman.

"Show us your tan, Shelly." He added, with a leer.

Shelly, although tempted to retort that *he* would never be inspecting her tan, ignored his childishness; and spoke directly to DI Williams, who had just emerged from his private office.

"Briefing, now?" She asked.

He nodded, slipped on his jacket, and joined his team in the main room. In addition to Frank and Dave, Shirley Wolfenden was present.

DCI York appeared, as if from nowhere, and perched on a desk at the back of the room; listening in to the report which was delivered by Dawn, with occasional contributions from her junior partner.

The key point of difference, now, compared to where they were at before the two had visited Fuerteventura, was that they had an eye witness. One who had actually seen the man's face. Adora Cranda was now accepted to be a part of this pattern of crimes; her account had been too similar to the others for the truth to be anything else. She had confirmed that the

201

perpetrator was, apparently, a British man. He had been 'about thirty', give or take a few years, when she had been assaulted in 2008. This meant that he would now be around thirty-eight, also give or take a few years.

"Did the Spanish show any interest in reopening the case of Roberto Pastor's murder, to try and find eye witnesses?" Demanded DCI York.

Dawn shook her head.

"To tell you the truth, Ma'am, it was difficult to push the Spanish to investigate old cases; without, first, giving them every bit of information that we had, and second, telling them how to do their job."

She looked at Shelly.

"We did strike up a good relationship with a junior officer, there. But, she was duty bound to take what she was told to her own bosses. So, it was a bit tricky. We had to be cautious."

Shelly agreed.

"We were wondering how this is going to be played out for the public, and the media, here. We didn't ask, so we couldn't share."

York confirmed:

"That's why we didn't tell."

She looked at DI Williams, and stood up.

"Ok, this is what's going to happen. Lloyd and I have discussed this, and the assistant commissioner has given the go-ahead. On Monday, we'll be holding a press conference. We haven't finalised the wording; but, we'll be appealing for help to identify any recent victim. Male victim. We need to speak with Sheen, first, Lloyd.

That was twice that she had addressed him as 'Lloyd', noticed Dawn. Unusual for her to do that in front of the team. Perhaps the pressure of the case was effecting a higher level of bonding.

DI Williams nodded:

"He's coming in first thing, Monday."

DCI York continued:

"So, if you have a view on how to put this across; to find any male victim, bring us into contact with his widow so that we can protect her, and avoid scaring off the perpetrator, let DI Williams know by Monday."

"Ma'am." There was a general murmur.

DCI York left the group.

Williams spoke up:

"Ok, guys. Monday's going to be tricky. Put your minds to it; but, otherwise, try and get a break from this, tomorrow. Big week, next week. The clock's ticking."

"Yes, Boss." Shelly muttered.

She wasn't the only one who hoped, prayed, that for some poor woman, the clock hadn't already 'ticked'.

Chapter 35

The local and national press jostled for position, in the media room at one of the Greater Manchester police's shiny modern stations.

Having been briefed sufficiently to arouse their interest; the thirty or so assembled hacks had, nevertheless, been kept in the dark about what it was that DCI York was about to say. Cameras perched on tripods, and a multitude of microphones and recording devices poked forward like the trees in a forest, battling for supremacy, in front of the prepared desk.

At two minutes to eleven, a side door opened; and a line of officials trooped in, to take their places behind the appropriate name cards, set out on the top table.

Taking centre stage, was DCI York. She was flanked by DI Williams and assistant commissioner Farding. Next to Williams was Dr Sheen, and, in the end chair, Dawn Pardell.

Being the senior person present, assistant commissioner Farding cleared his throat, and spoke first:

"Ladies and gentlemen, thank you for your time, today. We'll be asking for your support and cooperation in connection with a very serious and sensitive matter. For operational reasons, there are certain details that we cannot go into, today; and I would appreciate your patience and understanding, in this regard."

He cleared his throat, again. Although a high ranking officer, with many years of experience in the force, he wasn't a natural, or comfortable, public speaker.

"I'd like to introduce my colleagues: DCI Floella York, DI Williams, DS Pardell, and Doctor Marcus Sheen."

He looked at them, one by one.

"And, now, I'm going to hand over to DCI York; who will explain why we've invited you here, today."

With barely disguised relief, he pushed away the table-mounted microphone that had been invading his personal space, and looked to Floella York, to continue.

"Thank you, Sir."

DCI York blinked, as a camera flashed in her face. With a brief, stern look at the photographer, she commenced reading from her prepared script.

"My team have been working closely with another force, in recent days, in connection with more than one unexplained death, which have happened in the north of England and elsewhere, over a long period of time."

She flashed a quick glance at the assembly.

"We have been given information that leads us to conclude that a crime of violence may have been committed against a male, somewhere in the north, within the last two months. Based on information received, we believe that the male victim of this crime may well be of Spanish ethnicity. I'm not at liberty to explain why, but we have good reason to believe that this may have happened on or around the twenty-third of July."

She paused, and took a sip of water, from the glass that was in front of her. Cameras flashed again.

"Excuse me."

Then, she returned to her script:

"We have further reason to believe that, unless we apprehend the perpetrator swiftly, another person will be at specific risk of violence, in the very near future."

She paused for a moment, glancing up at the sea of enthralled men and women of the press and media.

"I can understand that you will want to ask me about the sources of the information that has led to this investigation. I will have to ask that you respect that I am not in a position to reveal any more at this time. My only concern, at this moment, is to identify the man who may have suffered harm on or around the twenty-third of July. This will enable us to directly

205

identify another person at risk, and put protective measures in place, for their safety. Therefore I want to appeal for anyone who may know of a man who has gone missing, or come to some harm, to contact us at the number being displayed, or through any police station."

DCI York put down her notes, and sat back in her chair.

There were further clicks and flashes from the photographers, and the hustle and buzz of journalists eager to raise questions. Assistant commissioner Farding raised a weary arm, to silence the barrage.

"As DCI York has indicated, we're not going to get into a dialogue, here. We have good reason to believe our fears are correct; and we need your help to identify this man. Although we can't explain why, this really is a matter of extreme urgency. The safety of at least one other person is at great risk. If and when we are able to give you any more information, we will do so. Thank you, gentlemen. Er, thank you, ladies and gentlemen."

Farding stood up, and walked briskly out of the room, followed by his colleagues; leaving a puzzled but fascinated rabble of media personnel with a host of unanswered questions.

Chapter 36

In a large, traditional house, in Cheshire, the master bedroom's en-suite bathroom window was wide open. The morning was fresh, and bright. Having had a late night, the lady of the house had lain in bed late, before finally emerging and snacking on toast for breakfast. Now, after the semi-revitalisation of a rich coffee; the sound of running water immersed and cosseted her, as she allowed it to cascade over her body, enjoying a prolonged shower.

Meredith was gradually coming back to life. The empty wine bottle on the bathroom floor attested to the fact that, on the previous evening, she had relaxed in the bath in what had become her favourite way, in recent days. Red wine for company. It never answered back, always soothed and agreed with her; and touched her only in the places she wanted it to touch her.

She reached up, and turned the tap to halt the flow of warm water; then stretched over to take a soft towel from the heated handrail, which she wrapped around herself in comfort and luxury. It was at such moments that Meredith always recalled the days, not too long past, when the cold splash of water from a bucket or makeshift barrel, channelled over her in a yard or behind a tin bunker, had been the only relief, and relative luxury, to a soldier posted overseas in some God-forsaken middle-eastern country.

From the adjoining bedroom, familiar music announced that the lunchtime news on TV was giving way to the regional bulletin. She rubbed her eyes, and smothered her hair; stepping out of the shower and drifting into her bedroom, where she sat naked on her bed.

The words 'Spanish ethnicity' caught her ears, and she lowered the towel, slightly, to pay attention. It looked like a press conference. Had there been another shooting, or knifing? There seemed to have been a spate of them in the northern cities, as well as in London, in recent weeks; though nothing usually to do with the Spanish. Meredith picked up the remote, and wound the channel back a minute, to attend to the feature from the start.

207

She listened to the introduction from the senior police officer, who then gave way to his woman on the ground; she seemed to have operational control over whatever this was. Meredith's attention was soon complete, and she allowed the towel to drop to the bed. She stood up, staring at the television; as though such an attentive pose would make the information more detailed.

"Oh, shit!" She mouthed.

As the feature finished, and the news bulletin moved on to other items, she fingered the remote control, and wound it back, to listen to the whole thing, again.

Key points: Spanish, missing, July twenty-third. She swallowed hard, and sat down on the bed, almost in disbelief.

Meredith resumed drying her body, and stepped over to her dresser, about to pick out some clothes, when her phone rang. She picked it up from the bedside table.

"Hello?"

It was her father, retired Colonel Harry Wilde.

"Meredith. Have you been watching the TV news, this morning?"

Meredith frowned; wishing that he hadn't called. Or, that she hadn't bothered to answer it. Yes, she had been watching, and knew very well to what he was referring; but, why couldn't he mind his own damn business?

"Yes, I've just seen it."

Her father paused, then:

"And, what do you make of it?"

"I don't know." She snapped. "I've only just woken up. Give me chance to get my head round it."

Colonel Wilde remained calm, as officers do.

"Well, it looks to me like you need to contact the police. You never did tell them, before, did you?"

Meredith breathed heavily, but did not answer.

"So, you'll call them? They need to know. If only to rule him out."

Then, he added, almost menacingly:

"If you don't call them, someone else will."

"Ok, ok. I'll call them."

"Good girl." Her father approved. "I'll call you later, see what they said."

The call ended, leaving Meredith cursing; both at the TV news, and her father's intervention.

An hour later, Meredith reluctantly made the call to the number that had been on screen; and spoke to a police support officer, named Carol. Taking the basic details of what had prompted her to call in, Carol had been calm, but very interested; detached, but showing appropriate professional concern. Within minutes, Meredith had received a call back from officer Shelly King, who arranged to come and visit her at home, that afternoon.

Meredith didn't particularly want visitors; but Shelly had been insistent. Consequently, the householder had quickly tidied up those things that made her lounge look most untidy; empty bottles, unwashed glasses, discarded clothes, and the remains of yesterday's dinner, which had merged into supper for one.

She looked out of her front lounge window, and saw the old gardener, Reggie, closing the doors to the shed. Reggie Bailey was West Indian, and had looked after the Wilde's garden ("Wildlands" – he called it) for more years than Meredith cared to remember. He had already spent the morning, tidying the lawns and weeding the flower-beds. Meredith had forgotten that he was due, and hadn't even noticed him, today, nor acknowledged his presence. She usually had the decency, at least, to offer Reggie a cup of tea; although, perhaps knowing that he couldn't always rely on her to provide, he usually brought his own flask. Besides, it allowed

209

him to harbour the occasional tot of his favourite Caribbean rum, for those cooler outside days.

Meredith's car was parked on the drive, outside the double garage. It was a silver Range Rover. High specification, but it could do with a clean. She made a mental note to have it valeted, soon.

She looked at the calendar on her wall, on which she kept a note of whatever was due. Today, Monday, her employee, Susan was running the shop, and Meredith would have no need to go in. It was a florist's; and Meredith was lucky to have staff that she could trust. Tomorrow, her car was due for a service; of course, she would get it valeted then, too. Wednesday, she had a couple of appointments pencilled in; the accountant would meet her at the shop; and in the evening the house alarm was due for its biennial service. Thursday, she had a builder coming; to give her an estimate for some brickwork repairs that needed doing, and a landscaping job that she had in mind for the rear garden.

She sighed. At least the police officer's visit should not interfere with her week.

Chapter 37

Approaching Meredith Wilde's address, in leafy Cheshire, Dawn and Shelly were impressed with the size and quality of the neighbouring properties. Not, round here, the ever-pressing development of new homes. The gardens were extensive, the trees established. It was settled, pretty, and distinctly affluent.

Dawn whistled:

"There's some serious money, around here. Do we know where Meredith Wilde's resources come from?"

Shelly shook her head:

"Apparently she owns a florist's shop in Lymm; but Frank hadn't got any further than that."

"Flowers never come cheap." Observed Dawn.

Shelly drew up outside an exceptionally grand looking place, and looked at the sign on the open gate.

"*Freelands.*"

She pulled onto the gravelly drive, and approached the house, coming to rest close to the Range Rover.

"Barely room to park." She muttered, sarcastically.

There was, in fact, space for about eight cars; and, as likely as not, further room around the rear of the house. They admired the building. It was clearly an old, probably Victorian property. It had the air of one which might have been built to overlook a quiet country lane; which had later been planted with a spreading orchard, now mature, and populated with further, though slightly less impressive houses, for company. Although some of the older properties around here were showing neglect, the cost of their upkeep having outstripped the owners' means to provide; this one was well-maintained. Whatever the source of the original owner's wealth, the house's current owner apparently had significant means, too.

211

Walking to the front door, up two wide steps which gave access to a sheltered doorway, adorned by two traditional lamp-posts, Dawn rang the bell. There was the slightest buzz, audible from the outside; then, a voice came through the intercom, which was housed in a covered box, just to the visitor's right. Dawn looked up, to see that there was a discreetly placed camera watching her.

"Yes?"

"Police. We're here to see Meredith Wilde."

"Just a moment."

Dawn and Shelly eyed the heavy-looking door, expecting it to be automatically released; or, perhaps even to creak open as in some Gothic horror hall. It did neither; but, a few moments later, was opened from the inside, by Meredith. The officers held up their ID cards, which she looked at, without suspicion.

"I'm Meredith Wilde. Come in."

She drew back the door, and invited them into a broad reception hall. Closing it, after them, she led them through a wide vestibule, past a window with heavy turquoise curtains almost completely closing it off, and across to her front lounge.

"This way, please."

Looking around at the ornate decorations as they went – a mixture of traditional and modern, that betrayed a young person living in a house that had been built by the riches of a figure from the past – they admired the pictures and light-fittings on the walls; which blended into the smooth, but dimly-lit, texture of the hallway. A delicate floral scent hung gently in the air. Entering the lounge, they were invited to sit down, on a luxurious leather sofa.

"Coffee?"

"No, thank you." Dawn declined, on behalf of them both.

"Thank you for calling in, this morning, Meredith. We've already had a number of responses, but we felt we should come and see you as soon as possible, to hear what you can tell us."

Dawn glanced at her note pad. Shelly said nothing; but, as far as she was aware, there hadn't been any other responses which looked anywhere near as relevant as Meredith's.

"So, if you could talk us through why you called, from the beginning?"

Dawn sat back, and smiled at Meredith, encouragingly. Shelly studied this strikingly confident looking woman; curious about her life, her background, what made her tick...

Meredith began:

"Well, it was my then boyfriend, Gabriel... Gabriel Tevitez. He had been staying with me for a while; but, on the twenty-third of July, he left. I wasn't particularly shocked... he had only been here a few months; and, well, to be honest, things weren't really working out."

Shelly nodded, showing great interest.

"Go on."

"Well, he had come from Spain. I met him when I was posted in Gibraltar. I used to be in the army, until recently. I was deployed there, late 2013 into 2014. We met there."

Dawn interjected: "Was he in the forces?"

"No." Meredith shook her head. "He was a civilian; but, we met through my work."

"You left Gibraltar in 2014?"

"Yes. But we kept in touch. I think he always wanted to find a way to visit England."

Shelly asked:

"And, when did you leave the army, Meredith?"

Meredith's face darkened:

"September, last year."

There were several questions that both officers wanted to ask about leaving the army; but, that would keep. For now, Dawn focused on what seemed to be the most relevant and pressing line of inquiry:

"Tell us about the day that Gabriel left."

"Well, I wasn't actually here. I had stayed over at a friend's house, the night before. Gabriel told me he was going on a training course... a residential course, for a few days, down in Sussex. It was part of the final selection procedure; an assessment centre, for a job that he'd applied for. Then, when I came back, later that day, he'd gone; which I expected him to have done. So I thought nothing of it."

Shelly asked, rather surprised:

"So, was there any contact with Gabriel after that? In the next few days?"

"No. I texted him a few times, but he didn't reply. I thought 'Oh, he's just a bit fed up with me'. The truth is, things hadn't been going so well, and I thought he was punishing me."

"Ah."

"It was a Saturday, the twenty-third. But, he was due back the following Wednesday, or Thursday. I wasn't sure. But, he didn't come back."

There was a silence. Finally, Dawn broke it:

"So, when he didn't come back by the following Thursday, or Friday... weren't you worried?"

Meredith blushed slightly.

"Well... he wasn't answering any of my texts. I tried to call him, twice, during the week; but his phone was switched off. Gradually, I got more and more angry with him. I thought, well if that's how he wants to be, two can play at that game."

214

She faltered. A glimpse of the insecurity of a little girl inside the soldier betrayed that she had assumed she had been dumped, and wasn't shocked. Perhaps, at the time, she felt that was all she was worth. That she deserved no better.

She rubbed her eye, before continuing:

"Then, when it started to dawn on me that maybe he'd left me, I went and checked his things. He hadn't left much... but, he didn't really have much. He travelled very light. So, I figured that, yes, he had probably taken whatever was important to him, and gone."

"Did you have any thoughts about where he might have gone?"

"At first, no. But, then, I decided that he had probably gone back to Spain."

Shelly glanced at Dawn.

"Do you have an address where he might be in Spain? We could check it out."

Meredith shrugged: "No. He had come out of a bad relationship, when I knew him. He was only in temporary digs, in Gibraltar. There was nothing for him to go back to, there. The only place I thought he might have gone would be back to Seville, where his daughter lived, with his ex-partner."

Dawn and Shelly exchanged interested looks.

"He has a daughter, in Spain?"

"Yes. She's only about four, maybe five. I think he really missed her. Maybe that's why he went back, because of her. Or, maybe it was because of me. I don't know."

A sad, guilty looking shadow flickered over her face, as she avoided their eye contact. The opportunity to ask a question, that was in the mind of both officers, now presented itself to Dawn:

"Do *you* have any children, Meredith?"

Meredith looked to the ground.

"No. The army saw to that. Motherhood and cracking heads don't mix."

Inadvertently, she glanced at a framed picture, on a shelf. It was a picture of an impressively decorated, senior officer, with pips on his shoulder; proudly standing to attention alongside a junior-looking woman in uniform, who appeared to be Meredith. But, several years younger.

Dawn followed her eyes:

"Family footsteps?"

Meredith nodded: "My father."

Although not commenting on it, the same point struck both Dawn and Shelly. This woman had no children. So, if there was a connection to their case... if Gabriel Tevitez had been the victim of their serial killer, this was different from the others. In every other case that they had come across, the victim's wife, or partner, had been the mother of a child. That had been one of the key weapons that the monster had used as a means of threatening and controlling them.

"And, I take it there's been no form of contact from Gabriel, since July?"

Dawn was jotting down a brief note.

"No, nothing."

Shelly felt that she had to ask the question:

"Did you not think, at any point, to report him missing; in case something might have happened to him?"

Meredith shook her head:

"No, like I said, I assumed he had got fed up of me, and gone back home. To Spain, I mean. If something has happened to him, then... I'm sorry, of course. But, like I said, our relationship had just about broken down. It didn't really shock me that he'd gone. My father told me to report it... but, I didn't."

"Ok." Dawn suppressed a sigh.

"Well, if you can give us all the details that you can about Gabriel, so that we can make inquiries through the Spanish authorities, with the passport office, and so on? Do you know his date of birth?"

Meredith thought for a moment.

"His birthday was the fourteenth of November. Same as Prince Charles, I remember us saying. Er, it would be 1986 or 1987... I'm not sure."

"Ok, thanks. Meredith, could you excuse us a moment, while we make a couple of calls? We need to speak with our inspector. We'll go outside."

"Sure." Muttered Meredith, as the two got up, went to the front door, then out into the garden, to talk privately. Outside, and out of earshot, Shelly faced Dawn.

"What are you thinking? Seems to tick all the boxes, except for one, doesn't it?"

"No children." Dawn agreed.

"And, since the twenty-third of July... you don't think anything's happened to her, that she's not telling us about?"

Dawn was as certain as could be:

"No, I'm sure not. Just the way she's told it. Getting in touch within an hour of the press conference... No, if this is part of the pattern, he hasn't got to her, yet. And, we need to make sure that he never does."

"So, do we take her in, for a full statement?"

"I think that's best."

They returned to Meredith's lounge, where she was sat, alone. Shelly noticed, on a glass-topped table, another picture that interested her. In a smart silver frame, it was what seemed to be a very old black and white photo. An elderly man, wearing a straw hat, and with a bushy moustache, was shaking hands with a taller, smartly dressed gentleman. The tall man was looking at him admiringly, as if he had just achieved something to be proud of. Between them was a lifebelt, with the word *'Fleur'* clearly visible upon it. Meredith noticed Shelly's interest, and picked up the picture.

217

"This one was my grandfather." She said, indicating the tall man.

"And this…" She pointed to the other man:

"This is Monsieur Johannes LeVelle. If it wasn't for him, I probably wouldn't be here."

Shelly raised an eyebrow, waiting for Meredith's explanation.

"Grandfather was at Dunkirk. He was a captain, stranded on the beach in France, with what was left of his squad of soldiers. Johannes LeVelle was a fisherman, on the south coast. He had what everyone needed, that day: a seaworthy boat, *Fleur*. He saved grandfather and his men. Got them back home to *Blighty*."

"Ah." Shelly looked at the two men.

Meredith continued: "On that day, it must have been chaotic, of course. But, after the war, grandfather went to find Johannes Levelle; to thank him properly, for saving his life, and the lives of his men. He found him, in Sussex. That's where this photo was taken."

She paused, and stroked this sentimental picture, lovingly.

"He made Johannes a promise, that day. That if ever he or his family needed help, they should come to us. We – our family – would never forget what we owed him, and would do whatever we could to help."

Dawn, who was listening with interest, commented:

"That's quite a commitment. Very honourable."

Meredith replaced the picture on the table.

"That's always been drummed into us, in our family. We take our responsibilities very seriously. You used the word 'honourable'. Yes, honour is important in this family. We look after ourselves and each other. We always pay people back. We don't sit back and wait for someone else to pay our dues for us."

There was a slightly awkward silence, which Shelly broke by clearing her throat and picking up her jacket, ready to leave.

Chapter 38

Later that day, a reluctant Meredith gave a full statement to Dawn, who was accompanied in the room at the police station by Dr Sheen. Going over the circumstances of Gabriel's departure, she reiterated her feeling that their relationship had all but run its course.

During a break, Dr Sheen shared his view with Dawn, that there was something of a defence mechanism at work here. Certainly, Meredith was feeling guilty; perhaps there was more that she should tell them, which she had so far kept to herself. But, if guilt was influencing her statement, this was almost certainly guilt at not reporting him missing, earlier... guilt about not caring... rather than anything sinister to do with the man's disappearance.

Part of Dr Sheen's brief, and a main reason why he was party to Meredith's statement, was to get a feel for her state of mind. Her mental toughness. At some stage, and probably very soon, a decision would have to be made about how much to tell her about what they suspected; and about the extremely dangerous situation of which she was quite possibly a part.

Dawn and the doctor joined DI Williams, who had been watching and listening through the one-way mirror.

"Bottom line, Marcus. We have to decide how to tell her. Will she freak out?"

Marcus brushed his hand, thoughtfully, through his locks.

"What do you see when you look at her, DI Williams? A florist, or a soldier? There's a big difference."

"You can say that again. Why would anyone move from a career as a soldier, to... something like that?"

"Something so girly." Observed Dawn, with a wry smile.

"You know what I mean, Dawn."

"Yep, I do. So, if she's confronted with what we think happened, and what we fear could happen next, will she react as a fighter or a flower girl?"

They both looked to Dr Sheen, for the answer.

"I think you have to tell her... warn her. Leave the reaction to her. The way she responds may tell you all you need to know."

"Hmm."

Dr Sheen continued:

"If she's clearly frightened, and wants you to protect her, you need to get her well away from that house, and fast. He could strike at any time."

They pondered, and Sheen went on:

"However, if she wants to help you to try and catch him... if, because of her guilty feelings, she allows herself to believe that she owes it to Gabriel to try and catch his killer, then..."

Williams took over:

"We need to brief her, set up high level security, give her panic alarms, get the house under discreet surveillance, and wait for something to happen."

The three considered, before Williams, having made a decision, went on:

"I'm going to speak with the DCI; then, I want to tell her."

Shortly afterwards, DI Williams was in the incident room with his team; discussing a series of phone calls that had come in, as a response to the press conference. Although some seemed interesting, and should be followed up; none struck him in the same way as Meredith Wilde's contact. His gut feeling was that this was the important one. Frank Burnley had already scoured international records, to see whether there was any trace of Gabriel in Spain. His passport details had been traced, and a check completed to see whether he had recently left the UK. There was no sign that he had. To Williams' satisfaction, Gabriel was a victim, who must be found. Meredith was a potential victim, who must be protected.

When DCI York joined them, and was brought up to speed, she agreed that Meredith was 'the one'. The next challenge was, how best to tell her? However difficult and challenging that might be, one thing was clear; time was of the essence. If she was to be told, she would be told today.

Minutes later, Dawn returned to Meredith in the interview room.

"Meredith, I'm going to bring my boss in, detective inspector Williams. Doctor Sheen will be with us, too. There's something we need to tell you about."

Meredith shifted, uncomfortably.

"Ok."

DI Williams and Sheen entered the room, and Dawn introduced her boss. Williams shook her hand, and immediately placed his chair a couple of feet back from the table, so as to avoid crowding her.

"It's good to meet you, Meredith."

He nodded to Dawn; who, it had been agreed, would start to explain the situation.

"Meredith, you've had a shock, today. Coming out of the blue, the press conference… "

"Yes. It has taken me by surprise. But, nobody has told me yet what you think might have happened to Gabriel. I'm assuming you have no idea where he is; but, you said, on TV, that you were sure something had happened to him. How can that be, when I didn't even know it, myself?"

Despite her words, she didn't seem overly upset, or greatly worried about Gabriel's welfare. From the perspective of the police, perhaps that could be a good thing.

Williams took over:

"Ok, Meredith, what we're about to tell you, is not in the public arena. Only a small number of police officers know this; and, we'd like to keep it that way. It's crucial that we contain this. Do you understand?"

221

Meredith was puzzled, but desperately curious.

"Ok."

DI Williams took a deep breath:

"Gabriel was last seen on July twenty-second. He had gone by the twenty-third. The very day that we mentioned in the TV appeal. We have come across several other cases of Spanish men either going missing, or... meeting a violent death, on that very same date in recent years. We are currently examining cases which happened around the twenty-third of July in 2015, 2014, 2013, 2012, 2011, and 2008."

Williams stopped, to observe Meredith's reaction. Sheen and Dawn were also watching her, keenly; for any sign of surprise, shock... any other emotion. For a few seconds, it appeared that, perhaps, she hadn't grasped the significance of what she had just been told. Then, her eyes opened wide.

She let out a gasp:

"You mean..." She didn't know what to say, so stopped.

Williams continued:

"We believe that a single man may be responsible for the deaths of at least six men. The similarities between the cases that we're looking at are undeniable."

Meredith, almost incredulous:

"You mean you have a suspect? You've caught him, and you think he may have... done something to Gabriel, too?"

With an expression that conveyed his disappointment, Williams continued to explain:

"No, Meredith. We don't have a suspect. That's why we put out the appeal. That's why we need your help to catch him."

"Oh." She looked from DI Williams to Dawn, and also glanced briefly at the psychologist.

222

Meredith's head was in a whirl. She was still puzzled, baffled about so many things, that didn't seem to add up. Why did the police seem so sure that Gabriel, her Gabriel, had been murdered? If they didn't have a suspect, then... Trying to get her head round it, she asked:

"So, what are you doing to find him? Whoever did this? And, where's Gabriel?"

Williams explained:

"Now that we have the report of Gabriel as a missing person, and at the moment he is just that, a missing person; we'll do everything we can to establish his last known movements."

He looked at Dr Sheen, who nodded in agreement.

"The thing is, Meredith, there's more to tell you. You might be wondering what links these cases together."

It wasn't a question, but Meredith was nodding, curious:

"Yes."

"What I'm going to tell you now, Meredith, may be even more upsetting for you than what I've already said."

She paid attention, with baited breath.

"We believe that, in each of the cases I referred to, that's six deaths on or around the twenty-third of July in those other years... the wife or partner of the murdered man has subsequently been assaulted."

He paused, to allow Meredith to take in what he had said; then, went on:

"It is only very recently that this pattern of events has come to our notice. Until now, we weren't aware of this series of deaths... nobody had made any connection between them."

"Assaulted? How come? What do you mean?"

"We believe that the killer has revisited the victim's home, and assaulted his widow."

223

Aware of the need to try and reassure her, Williams pushed on:

"As we weren't aware of any connection, we weren't able to put in place any measures to protect the partners of the victims. This time, it's different. Now, thanks to you coming forward, we can protect you. We *will* protect you."

Having gone through a range of emotions in recent minutes, Meredith now wore a strange expression; one that fascinated and puzzled Dr Sheen. After the confusion and shock, then perhaps anger, she seemed to have composed herself. There was now a steely glint in her eyes.

Finally, she spoke; in slow, measured tones. It was as if the shroud of a mystery had suddenly been lifted from her.

"So, Gabriel... he didn't walk out on me. Someone..."

"We don't think he did. But, if you can help us build up a picture of his last known movements... Although you weren't here... anybody he might have seen, spoken to..."

Meredith thought for a moment.

"It was a Saturday. So, the gardener wouldn't have come. Gabriel didn't know any of the neighbours."

Dawn chipped in:

"Did he drive, Meredith?"

"No. Well, not in the UK."

Williams asked:

"Can you tell us anything about the company he was going to see, for the training course?"

"No. Well, there was a phone number, written on a scrap of paper. I tried it, when he didn't turn up. But, the woman who answered it said she didn't know anything about it."

She pulled a face.

224

"At the time, I wondered if she had something to do with it. I mean, had he found another woman? Probably not. I put it out of my mind afterwards; but, at the time, I just wondered."

Williams stepped in with a further question:

"Where did you stay on the Friday night, Meredith? You said you were with a friend."

Meredith blushed; clearly embarrassed, and hoping that this question might not come up.

"I went out with a friend, Lewis. We went for a few drinks in Manchester. I went back to his place in town, so I didn't have to drive home."

She avoided their gaze.

"We'll need an address for Lewis."

Meredith turned on Williams, sharply.

"I need an alibi, now?" She demanded.

DI Williams remained calm:

"It's important that we investigate everything properly. Nobody's suggesting anything suspicious at all; but, we owe it to Gabriel to check everything out. Did Lewis know Gabriel, at all?"

Meredith shrugged, almost sulkily:

"He knew he existed. Never met him."

"What was your relationship with Lewis?"

Meredith rolled her eyes:

"I met him in town, a couple of weeks earlier. We got on. Went out a couple of times."

Sheen interjected:

"Did Gabriel know you were going out for the evening with Lewis?"

225

She scowled.

"Not exactly. But, he knew I was going out... socially. Like I said, we hadn't been getting on so well. There was a bit of a communications breakdown."

After a few more questions to clarify the full name and address of Meredith's acquaintance, Lewis Heckel, they moved on to discuss plans for the future.

Williams raised the matter that was in all their minds:

"Meredith, as I said, we have reason to believe that, if Gabriel has been killed by our suspect, then there's every chance he will try to come and assault you. It's a very familiar pattern."

He was well aware that, so far, he hadn't told her anything about the nature of the previous 'assaults'. That point was in Meredith's mind, too.

"You said they have been 'assaulted'. The other women. In what way do you mean 'assaulted'?"

Williams looked to Dr Sheen, who took on the task of explaining:

"Meredith, in each case, the partner or wife of the victim has been subjected to a sexual assault. So, together, we need to come up with a plan to make sure that doesn't happen again. To you, or anybody else."

He sat back in his chair, and rubbed his chest, as if in some discomfort. There was a silence. Then, Williams resumed:

"We have to assume that he knows where Gabriel lived. Where you live. So, we need to decide, together, whether the safest plan is for you to leave your home, at least for now. We don't want you to be at risk."

Meredith's eyes burned:

"Leave my home?"

"Is there somewhere you could stay, while we make further inquiries, Meredith?" Dawn tried to sound supportive.

Meredith's expression seemed to flicker from afraid, to angry, to confused and insecure. She shrugged.

Williams said:

"In the short term, until you decide what you want to do, we'll put your house under surveillance. If he comes, we'll be there. We can give you a panic alarm, and a direct line to our emergency team."

She nodded.

"You said they were assaulted 'subsequently'. Has that always been on the same date, like the twenty-third?"

Williams shook his head:

"No, there's really been no discernible pattern to it. Sometimes a few weeks, sometimes months."

"Ah. Then, I'm a prisoner, or a fugitive, indefinitely?"

Williams replied:

"The most important thing, Meredith, is that we keep you safe. None of the other victims had the advantage of being forewarned. None of them had police protection. It's a lot to get your head round. For now, the police presence around your home will be discreet. Nobody else will know we are there, keeping an eye on you."

Meredith looked surprised.

"Discreet? Why? I thought you wanted to warn him off? Wouldn't it be better..."

She tailed off.

"Oh." A different realisation had suddenly struck her.

"You don't want him to see you, do you? You want him to come, so that you can catch him in the act. You want me to act as bait, don't you? Don't you?"

She had raised her voice.

"Maybe I should leave my door open, and a map to my bedroom?"

Dawn spoke out, in defence of their position:

"The most important thing is your safety, Meredith. As we speak, a surveillance team is being deployed, within view of your house. This is just to give us, and you, time to think through what we're going to do. If you want to get away from your house, and stay away, we'll help you to find somewhere. If you want high-level, visible security, we'll work with you on that, too. The most pressing thing at this moment is to keep you safe."

Meredith looked her in the eye; and, although still dubious, relented a little:

"Hmm. Ok."

Chapter 39

Meredith did not return home, that day. Instead, she went to a budget-priced motel, on the outskirts of Manchester. Just for one night, she assured the police. Just to clear her head; think things through. The police were more than happy with this.

In the meantime, Dawn and Shelly paid a visit to the city centre apartment of Lewis Heckel. Although Meredith had explained to them that she no longer had a relationship with him; they wished to confirm that she had spent the night of July twenty-second at his place, and find out what, if anything, he knew about Gabriel Tevitez.

It was seven o'clock in the evening, when they arrived; Lewis Heckel had just got home from work, at his job in a city centre accountancy firm.

"Lewis Heckel?" Dawn Pardell presented her card.

The man confirmed his identity, and invited them in. Although it was in a high quality apartment block, and comfortably equipped; his home felt very much the bachelor pad, and could have benefitted from the light touch of a woman.

"Meredith!" He exclaimed, when the officers outlined why they were calling on him.

He reached for a wine bottle, which stood on the kitchen worktop, then left it in place. Chiding himself; as if the mere mention of Meredith's name had evoked an involuntary reaction of reaching for alcohol.

"Yes, Meredith and I were seeing each other, around that time. It was never going to last."

He sneaked a somewhat lecherous glance at Shelly.

"Why was that?" She asked.

"Hmph. She, er… she's got issues."

"What do you mean by that?"

Lewis leaned back against the worktop, and eyed his visitors.

"Meredith's been through a lot. She's ex-army, you know? I think she's seen some stuff in there, that's left her... fragile, damaged. She's not easy to live with. Not the sort of woman for me."

Dawn was listening carefully:

"Can you be more specific?"

He sighed, and reached again for the wine bottle. This time, he picked it up, and proceeded to pour himself a glass. He watched it splash into the gleaming crystal.

"She has very violent outbursts. Like she forgets where she is. I didn't want her bringing Afghanistan, or wherever, into my lounge."

"Ah. But, she was with you, here, on the night of July twenty-second?" Dawn was determined to focus on what was relevant.

Lewis pulled a face.

"Hang on."

He stepped across to a calendar that hung on the wall, and flicked it back over a couple of sheets, then studied some entries on July's page.

"July twenty-second. I came back from Belfast on the twenty-first... yes, it was the day after that. Friday. We went out in town, and she came back here. Yes, she was here."

"Thanks, for that. And, what time did she leave, the next morning?" Dawn made a note.

He took a sip of his wine, and thought:

"About twelve, I think. Maybe one."

"One other thing..." Continued Dawn.

"Did you know that Meredith had a partner, at the time you were seeing her?"

230

"The Spaniard?" Lewis snorted.

"I think that had fizzled out even before I was seeing her. Maybe he got as fed up of her moods as I did."

"Did you ever meet him?"

"No." Lewis shook his head. "Meredith barely mentioned him, and I didn't ask."

The two officers had concluded their questions.

"Ok, well, that's all for now. Thank you for your help."

Leaving Lewis Heckel, a thought came to Shelly.

"Dawn! You know something we haven't really considered? Meredith doesn't have any children, but Gabriel does, in Spain. We need to check on his partner. She could be at risk, more than Meredith."

Dawn looked at her.

"You're right. She could be the target."

Chapter 40

As the team were being briefed on Tuesday morning, and were discussing Shelly's idea about Gabriel's ex-partner; a call came in from Meredith Wilde, which Dawn answered. After speaking in low tones for a while, Dawn put down the phone, and turned to her colleagues, who were still listening to Shelly's update.

"That was Meredith. She wants to see us. Boss?"

DI Williams gave her the nod:

"Go now. See what she's thinking. I'll make some calls about Gabriel's ex; see if we can locate her in Spain."

Shelly opened her mouth to suggest that she could call Millie, but closed it again. Williams was the boss; and more than capable of making the decision. Instead, she followed Dawn out of the office, and they went to the car park. They drove out to the motel where Meredith had stayed the night, and met her in the dining room, where she was drinking from a glass of fresh orange.

"Meredith."

Shelly smiled.

"How did you sleep?"

"Ok." She answered, brightly. "I've been thinking."

"You've had plenty to think about." Commented Dawn.

"And, I've made a decision." Meredith continued.

"It may be what you were hoping I'd say anyway, but, whatever. I'm going to stay at the house. Keep the surveillance low profile; and then, if this man comes for me, you can arrest him."

Dawn and Shelly struggled to control their emotions. On the one hand, this was, of course, the most likely way that they could catch their suspect.

And, yes, of course they had privately considered it as a plan. On the other hand, they had both listened to horrific accounts from women; savaged and terrorised by the beast. They didn't want … couldn't allow… that to happen to Meredith.

Dawn put a hand on Meredith's arm: "Our advice would be to forget it, Meredith. Nobody would blame you for getting out of there, and going somewhere that he could never find you."

Meredith smiled, thinly.

"I appreciate that. Thank you. But, in the last twenty-four hours, I've just found out that the man who I thought had dumped me did no such thing. He was stolen from me. So, I owe it to him to do whatever I can to help you catch his killer."

She paused, and picked up her glass of juice.

"Plus, I'm not prepared to run away and hide from anyone. I'm not being driven out of my home by some low-life. When you've seen the things I've seen… gone through what I've been through in the army… I'm not afraid of him. Bring it on!"

Shelly and Dawn regarded her, for a few moments.

"You're very brave, Meredith." Noted Dawn.

"We'll speak to our boss, and see what he says."

"Do it!" She replied. "Either way, I'm not going anywhere."

An hour later, DI Williams, Dawn, Shelly, and Dr Sheen, were in conference; discussing what Meredith had said.

"If anything should go wrong, Boss…" Began Dawn.

DI Williams was far from happy; but, realised that this could be the chance that they needed. A real opportunity to catch the perpetrator.

"She's a soldier, Dawn. If any woman could potentially carry off something like this, can you suggest a better one? And, being realistic, what alternative do we have?"

233

Sheen was listening, quietly; with a serious frown on his face. Sensing that he had an input to share, Williams turned to him.

"Marcus?"

He scratched his chin: "She may well have been a soldier, Lloyd. But, I worry about her state of mind. We know she left the army under something of a cloud."

The team had done quick checks on Meredith; and had already ascertained that, after fifteen years of exemplary service, her standards of performance had, apparently, slipped. She had achieved the rank of staff sergeant, and earned a glowing reputation. Then, for some reason, she had got into a physical fight with another soldier. After what had been a fierce brawl, the other party had ended up in hospital, with a broken arm, as well as severe bruising. The other soldier had been a male. No explanation had ever been forthcoming from either party; but, Meredith's record had been tarnished, and her career progression almost certainly hampered.

Subsequently, there had been more incidents of aggression; resulting in further disciplinary action. Meredith had received fair warning, that, if this persisted, the route that she was on could lead her to a dishonourable discharge. Seemingly, she had taken the hint; deciding that continued service was not for her. She had left the army of her own accord, after seventeen years of service.

"What state of mind would you expect, in a woman who has just been told that the man that she thought had dumped her has almost certainly been murdered, and that she is now the target for a vicious rapist?"

Sheen remained calm, as Dawn and Shelly held their breath. They weren't used to seeing their boss challenging the psychologist, like this.

"If we are to keep control of this situation, we need to be sure that she'll work with us, listen to us, not go maverick. I don't have that confidence, right now."

Williams nodded:

"Fair point. But, I guess we work with what we've got."

"Agreed." Sheen nodded. "Just, tread carefully with her. She's not the most stable. We heard that, from Lewis Heckel. And, until now, she seemed to accept that she'd driven Gabriel away. She's delicate. Perhaps the flower shop is better for her than the army."

Later that day, Meredith arrived back at her house. Then, under cover of a plain van, and handled by police staff in plain clothes, a range of equipment was delivered to her house. There were security cameras, panic alarms, and walkie-talkies. Two additional mobile phones were brought in, pre-loaded with specific features to enable direct contact with an emergency back-up team.

At the end of the lane, a workman's tarpaulin tent was set up; on the pretext of effecting repairs to a tiny overgrown sub-station, disused for years, which was tucked away just out of sight. This could accommodate and conceal two people, if staffed surveillance from that point was felt appropriate. In any case, a camera would be set up, close by; to monitor comings and goings.

Although they did not believe that their suspect was in the area, watching Meredith's house; it was possible. Consequently, the police tried to ensure that they visited as inconspicuously as they could. There would be no uniformed police to approach the property; and they would keep to as few visits as possible. Anyone attending should make sure they were as casual as could be, both in manner and dress.

Meredith was tutored in the use of the security equipment, and appeared confident in how to employ it; both to keep in regular touch with her support team, and to summon urgent help if necessary. Years of working in signalling and communications in the British army now stood her in good stead.

As DI Williams vacated his office for the evening, having left Frank Burnley as 'gold commander' in charge of the surveillance detail, one thing bothered him. He wanted to upscale the search for Gabriel Tevitez. Somewhere, he feared, a man lay dead. He might be buried. He might have drowned, like Tom Perez. However, to elevate the search might risk alerting the killer that the police knew more than he previously thought they did. For now, wrong though it felt, Gabriel's whereabouts might have to remain a mystery.

Chapter 41

The next morning, Meredith checked in as agreed; both to confirm that she was well, and that all the technology was operating correctly. However, while lying in her bed last night, she had had an idea, which she wanted to discuss with DI Williams.

When they spoke on the phone, she outlined what she had in mind:

"A panic room, or a safe room, as I would prefer to call it. There's plenty of space to fit one in. I've scoped it out, and adjoining the study, there's a space that's pretty much redundant. It could easily be made into a totally secure space, just in case I need to get to safety. I'd feel much safer."

"Sounds like a good idea." He agreed.

"I'll pay for it, myself." She added.

He couldn't visualise the room, having not yet visited Meredith's house, personally. But, in principle, it sounded sensible.

Thus it was that, during the next few days, a team of workers arrived to carry out modifications to Meredith's property. From the main road, it looked for all the world as if a small extension, with complementary landscaping, was being carried out. Inside the house, and planned specifically by Meredith herself, the work team got stuck into the solid structure of this large Victorian house, to create a room into which Meredith could disappear, at a second's notice.

In the meantime, the police team worked to a careful rota; to ensure that permanent, but discreet, surveillance was maintained. Nobody would come near the property, without being seen and monitored. Car registrations were checked; movements of local people were noted. The pattern of everyday life in this pleasant slice of Cheshire suburbia became ever more familiar to the team.

Fortunately, Meredith's employee at her floristry business, Susan, was more than willing to take on additional responsibilities; and virtually ran the shop on her own. Meredith had occasional visits from her father, which she didn't request or enjoy. Otherwise, her social contact diminished to very little. She was free to go out, wherever she wished, of course. But, to DI Williams' gratitude, she was extremely cooperative; and never went anywhere without their agreement, and discreet accompaniment.

As well as keeping a careful eye on Meredith, the team continued to carry out their other research. Nothing had emerged about Gabriel's last known movements. They fared no better in their investigation into the relevant days of the other victims. In truth, although they were looking, they were looking quietly. The last thing that they wanted to do was alert the killer that they might be getting close. They hoped and prayed that the very press conference hadn't done that. They had set the trap; and, they wanted him to bite. Consideration was given to putting out a subsequent statement, falsely intimating that no leads had been forthcoming. However, the decision was made to hold back on that, for now.

Inquiries into the whereabouts of Gabriel's ex-partner, who was called Savanna, concluded that she had moved house several times in recent years. She no longer lived at her last known address in Seville, and no forwarding address existed. The Spanish police didn't know where she was; so it was concluded that it was highly unlikely that a British traveller would be likely to find her. Slightly nervously, but on the balance of probabilities, the decision was made by DCI York and DI Williams that this line of inquiry was a dead end, and would not be pursued.

By Monday the nineteenth of September, Meredith's panic room... safe room... was completed. From the window of her study, which was reinforced with an extra-strong shuttered frame, she had a panoramic view of her rear garden, as she sat at her desk.

Two metres away, a reinforced metal door, on smooth and expensive runners, gave way to an inner room. If activated by the handset, which she had around her neck at all times while in the study, she could be secure, with the door closed and doubly-locked, within ten seconds. The inner room was equipped with monitors, from which she could see anything, or anyone, in the study. Nothing, she was sure, could penetrate that door. Although not very large, the room had a fold-down bed, a chemical toilet, and a wash basin. There was a small work-surface; on top was a kettle,

237

and underneath fitted a small fridge, into which she had packed a store of soft drinks and snacks. She had a phone, and a two-way radio, as back-up. At her direction, the safe room had been sound-proofed, too. She had a supply of oxygen installed, and the seals on the door were watertight and absolute; she could not be smoked out by anyone.

Aesthetically elegant, the room wasn't; but, lined with a fire-resistant coating, and with its own emergency power generator and LED lighting, it provided all the comfort and security that a potential prisoner in her own home could ever wish for. If a life was ever at stake, this was the extravagantly high-tech bunker that could conceal and preserve it.

Several times, Meredith carried out emergency drills. Fleeing from various parts of her home, to test out how quickly she could reach the sanctuary of her little cell. By the time DI Williams made a discreet visit to her, on the Monday evening, she was able to demonstrate, confidently, that she felt absolutely secure in her home. If the killer, or rapist, wanted to try and come for her, then let him do his worst.

So proud was she, of the safe spot that she had created, that she was organising an additional storage area, just outside the study. Here, she would place a range of containers; so that additional supplies of essential items could be kept close at hand. Then, if ever she was trapped inside the cell for a long period, she would be able to pick her moment when the coast was clear; to sneak out for anything that she might need. Such was the beauty of a large old house, with high ceilings, and obliging alcoves. Williams was impressed. No expense had been spared; to the surprise of the police, Meredith had insisted on organising and paying for all the work, herself. By way of explanation, she had said:

"This is my life that's at stake, here. I can afford to pay for it. It's what my grandmother would have wanted."

She had gone on to answer a question that had puzzled the police; the source of her apparent affluence. The house, she explained, had been left to her by her wealthy grandmother, as part of a substantial inheritance.

Although he didn't comment on it, Williams couldn't help but wonder whether Meredith's military experiences had caused her to get slightly carried away with the construction work. True, she should be safer thanks to this than she ever could without it; but, it seemed... well, excessive. Perhaps it was a further indication that she had been affected by her army history even more than anyone had recognised.

While he was with her, Meredith asked Williams about the ongoing investigation. Although she knew that no sign had been found of Gabriel, he must be somewhere. Even if he was dead; he had to be somewhere. Also, what about the other victims, in the recent past? She had been told that similar offences had been committed in each of the past five years; and, naturally, was curious about them. Surely there had been clues left, leads to follow up?

DI Williams knew better than to betray confidences. There was some very sensitive information here; and he would not be the one to share it too freely. However, this was a unique situation. Meredith Wilde, he felt, was being extremely cooperative; despite the turmoil that she must be going through. Perhaps he owed it to her to share, just a little.

"The string of offences that we're investigating... they haven't all been in England. This has become an international investigation. We've got the Spanish police working with us, looking into the cases that didn't happen in Britain."

"Right." Meredith acknowledged that this was a huge undertaking.

"And, how many of these have been here, in Britain?"

Williams considered, for a moment. Probably no harm in giving her a little more.

"We believe we're looking at three in the UK, and three overseas. There could be more."

"I see. So, are you looking for a Spanish killer?"

Williams was less comfortable, now. However, Meredith could one day find herself looking out for a murderer... trying to keep herself safe from a man in a crowd. Maybe she had a right to know.

"No, our suspect is British."

"And, surely after all these assaults, you have a description? Can't you tell me who I should be looking out for?"

Williams baulked at saying too much more.

"The descriptions, they're not helpful; because, in every case but one, he wore a mask. The woman who saw him without a mask, saw him several years ago. She's only recently had to try and describe him. So, the best thing we can do is to take every sensible precaution; keep in very close touch, stick to the script, and keep you safe."

Meredith nodded.

"If anybody tries to get to you in your house, we'll nail him."

Detailed plans had also been made to cover every movement of Meredith's when she was out and about. She wouldn't have a visible escort with her; that would be too obvious, and warn any attacker off. Instead, she would carry a specially adapted mobile device that would put her in immediate touch with the support team. They would never be more than a few minutes away; and, most of the time, she would be in their direct sight. For now, she wouldn't be spending much time staffing her shop. As the police already knew, her employee, Susan, was more than happy to become a full-time worker. Thankfully, Meredith seemed to be able to afford this change, without any stress.

DI Williams looked her in the eye:

"Do you feel safe?"

She smiled:

"Never safer."

Before DI Williams departed, Meredith allowed him to stroll around the grounds of the house, to familiarise himself with every possible access point. The front gardens, shrouded by trees, had a driveway that was open to the lane. Mature conifers, thick prickly hedges, and picket fences bordered the gardens for most of the boundary between '*Freelands*' and the adjoining homestead.

Walking around the back of the house, Williams drifted through a small orchard, which sloped away; descending to a private, walled garden, that was becoming overgrown. From here, he could hear the soft sound of slowly flowing water. Through a gap between trees and bushes, he could just see the glimmer of a stream, which trickled past the house. He looked up at a solid wooden post, about ten metres high; upon which was positioned a discreet camera, to monitor the area. Meredith had already shown him, on her phone, the range covered by this device. If anybody should try to gain access by this route, they would be in clear view; allowing Meredith plenty of time to access her place of safety, before he got close to the house.

Williams was impressed. Meredith certainly knew what she was doing; demonstrating this by the precise locating of cameras, alarms, and sensors, both outside and inside the property. She had taken full charge of her own security; and could transmit chosen images directly to the computer screen of her attentive support team, should she wish them to see, or check, any possible or potential intrusion.

Before he left, Meredith summoned DI Williams back inside, and led him to the monitor that was set up in her study. The screen was sub-divided into four separate images; sourced by four cameras, strategically placed inside and outside the house. Confidently, she flicked the controls on a key pad; to demonstrate both her range of cover, and her dexterity at managing the surveillance.

One of the images looked down from the main staircase, towards the front door. Despite the lighting being low, the quality was good; he could even make out the time indicated by the ornate grandmother clock, which stood to attention, close to the imposing entrance door.

Williams was able to leave with confidence. He would always retain a level of anxiety, and impatience. He just wanted his suspect to appear, and walk into their trap. If he should come... when he would come... they would have him.

Having reached the point in their investigation where they had identified a likely murder victim, who had perished on or around the twenty-third of July, this year; there was a strange feeling of limbo for the police team. It would be wrong to suggest that there was nothing to be done; far from it.

241

Precious resources were being ploughed into their mission to keep Meredith safe, and checks were still being made into the circumstances surrounding the final known days and hours of Gabriel and the other past victims. Contact was maintained with the other women; Bev Mitchell, Mariana Navarro, and the reticent Maria Mates. However, there was a real reluctance to make too much noise, which might scare the killer to ground. Questions were being asked, and, where possible, CCTV footage was being checked; but the team tried hard to keep their work as low profile as possible.

Uncomfortable meetings with the assistant commissioner had to be endured. He wanted progress; and was not satisfied with a policy of 'watching and waiting', which was how it seemed to be. DCI York and DI Williams were left in no doubt where the axe would fall, if this policy failed to bring the right result.

Chapter 42

In Fuerteventura, Millie Rodriguez kept in touch with Adora Cranda. Under the direction of inspector Hanst, she tried to dig up whatever she could about the last known movements of the men suspected of having been murdered. But, in truth, there was very little to be found. If anything of use could be uncovered, it seemed that it would come from Adora.

As the final week of September arrived, Hanst and Millie arranged a call; and conferred by video messenger with the British team. To Millie's disappointment, this proved to be Dawn and DI Williams; she had been hoping to see Shelly's face.

Neither team had anything particularly useful to report. The call was something of a routine courtesy; designed to reassure both sides that they were still working. Still committed. Still sharing. Millie had been looking again at the murder of Roberto Pastor, in Lanzarote. She had spoken to the local man who had been first to the scene of the murder; a taxi driver who had found Roberto, close to the coach parking area. He remembered the day well, as was to be expected. But, as he had told the police at the time, he saw nobody else in the vicinity, and was unable to give much help.

An unresolved point that frustrated both teams was, how did the killer locate and choose his victims? If it was at random, and limited by little more than their ethnicity, plenty of Spaniards could be found in Fuerteventura and Lanzarote; there was no doubt about that. But, finding Spanish men, with wives and children, living in England? That was less easy.

On Wednesday the twenty-eighth, Millie made a call from her phone. Sat alone at her dinner table, in her own apartment, Shelly picked up the phone, and accepted the video messenger call.

"Hi there, how are you?"

"I'm good. You? Good to see you."

Shelly put down her glass, and placed the phone at a comfortable angle against a bottle.

"Getting nowhere with this. That's what it feels like. It's my shift outside Meredith Wilde's house tonight. But nothing's happening."

Shelly hesitated, before adding, without conviction:

"I suppose that's a good thing, really."

"What's she like, Meredith?" Millie asked.

Shelly looked thoughtful:

"She's a strange woman, really. Former soldier, and a tough one, by all accounts. Then, she leaves the army, and goes into business running a flower shop. A bit different."

Millie agreed:

"Very different."

"Our psychologist, Sheen, reckons she's damaged, vulnerable. Maybe suffering, emotionally; after serving in Afghanistan."

Millie observed:

"Flaky."

Shelly felt embarrassed:

"I wouldn't call it that. It's just that, if we do get a visit from our suspect, I'm not sure how she's going to react. She's had years of training, seen combat zones, but... it could really freak her out."

Millie understood:

"But her house has been made super-safe, hasn't it?"

"Yes. There's no way he could get to her. Not so long as we monitor the place. But... we can't keep surveillance like this going on for ever."

Later that day, Shelly drove to the usual location that the team had started to use as a base, a short distance from Meredith's house. It was the back room of a former convenience store, still displaying the name 'Crawley'; which was no longer trading. Ideally placed, it would enable them to get to

244

Meredith's house in less than two minutes, by car. Being slightly to the east of her, it was also on one of just two routes that provided vehicular access to her home.

The other route, which was a continuation of the same road, winding away in a south-westerly direction, had a convenient junction just three hundred yards past her house. The team had installed a camera here, and had the means to effect a road block at this spot, within a matter of minutes, should it be needed.

Dave Perryman's car was already parked, at the side of Crawley's. He had done the early shift, and waved to Shelly from the window, as she pulled her vehicle in. He unlatched the door, and allowed it to swing open, as she approached the building.

"All quiet, Dave?"

Shelly knew what the answer would be.

"As the grave. I don't know how people can live like they do round here."

Dave was a city boy; feeling nothing but boredom when forced to spend his time in such rural surroundings. He debriefed Shelly about the few comings and goings, that had all been logged in their book; and corresponded with the camera captures that had been shared with them, thanks to Meredith's technology.

Meredith had received two visitors, that day. The first had been fully expected, and in line with an appointment made; the alarm engineer, to carry out a service that had been deferred a couple of weeks ago. The content of the service was less than in previous years; thanks to Meredith's own security upgrade. However, he had been required to check the sensors, and make sure the alarm bell functioned as it should. His red van with the company logo on the side had been seen; arriving, parking in the usual spot at eight forty-five, and departing less than two hours later.

The other visitor, also expected, had been the gardener. He had arrived just after nine, but had gone by ten. Just a flying visit for him, today. Perhaps the grass was too wet for him to mow, after an overnight shower.

Shelly glanced at the screen, which currently showed a view from the interior camera, looking towards the front door, which was closed.

"She's not going out today?"

"No plans to. So you'll have a quiet evening. I hope you brought a library book."

"OK. Thanks, Dave. You get going."

Dave didn't need telling twice. He was glad to get away, for an early finish. Shelly saw him off, clicked the latch on the inside of the door, and settled down to read through the recent notes that had been added to the surveillance log, since her last duty shift, a couple of days ago.

In the last few days, there were noticeably fewer items being recorded than previously. Perhaps a few points were becoming so mundane that each duty officer had got out of the habit of noting them down. Long-term surveillance was a tedious task. It was certainly true that Meredith had become a creature of habit, and the team had got accustomed to what happened every day around here. Therefore, certain visits, phone calls, movements in the area, were only worthy of mention by exception.

Shelly made herself a cup of tea, with the kettle that had been placed on the little kitchenette. She was just beginning to drink it, when the monitoring screen made a bleep, and a live picture came into view, with a green light blinking in the corner of it.

It was Meredith.

"Hi, just checking in, and seeing who's there tonight."

"Hi Meredith, it's me."

By the time she answered, Shelly could see that the video messaging call had clicked into gear, and her own image was visible to Meredith.

"Ah. How are you, Shelly?"

"I'm good, thanks. All cool at your end?"

Meredith frowned, slightly.

"I guess so. I'm just getting a bit fed up of this. I'm a prisoner in my own home. And, I feel like I'm being watched all the time. Which I am, of course." She added, with a grin.

Shelly nodded sympathetically.

Meredith continued:

"I'm always on the lookout for anything at all out of the ordinary. I've even started to keep an eye on old Reggie. My gardener. Getting paranoid, I suppose."

Shelly was about to comment, but Meredith went on:

"It's a bit unnerving, not knowing who's at the other end of this line, watching me. There are certain places in my own home that I can't set foot in, without being seen by... your colleagues. You know what I mean?"

"Yes. I understand that. But, you have started to switch some of them off, for privacy, haven't you?"

Shelly was aware that, at times, sections of her monitor screen went off air; and realised that this was Meredith exercising her control over what was visible to her 'watchers'.

Meredith nodded:

"Yes, I do. I've got the hang of this, now; so I switch some of them off. I don't want your mates watching me wandering round the house when I step out the shower."

She laughed.

"Quite." Shelly agreed. "I don't blame you."

Meredith suggested something:

"In fact, just to humour me, can I try something?"

She looked down from the camera, and adjusted some controls. Two of the quarter-size images that Shelly could see swapped places, and Meredith appeared to be making some adjustment.

"How good is the picture quality? The lighting's off, but, you can see the hallway clearly?"

Shelly studied it.

"I can see the hallway, and just about make out the time on the clock."

She glanced at her own phone to check the time; adding with a chuckle:

"You're five minutes slow."

"So, this live feed is still clear enough?" Asked Meredith, as she pressed a button which rotated the angle of the camera very slightly; almost taking the grandmother clock out of view.

"Oh yes, it's doing its job."

"That's good. Thanks, Shelly."

They both fell silent, for a few moments; before Shelly suggested:

"Shall I check in with you later? About ten?"

"Yes. Thanks."

And, rather abruptly, Meredith cut the line to end the call.

Shelly picked up her cup, and resumed drinking her tea. She saw nothing of Meredith on her split screen, for the rest of the evening. There was nothing unusual about that; Meredith had merely stayed in a part of the house that was not currently being covered by the range of any camera. At ten o'clock, Shelly pressed the call button, to make contact with her, as arranged.

The buzzing was audible, as the technology summoned Meredith to the phone; but, there was no answer.

Shelly looked at all four images on the screen. The top left image looked towards the front door, from the inside. Top right was looking out over the rear garden, from an elevated position on the eaves of the house. The two lower images looked at the outside of the front door, from the garage; and down the full length of Meredith's conservatory, which was in darkness, apart from the slight glow of a light which penetrated into it from the lounge.

Shelly's charge was not to be seen on any of them. She wondered if Meredith had decided to have an early night. Almost certainly that was what she had done. Perhaps she had relaxed a little too much with a bottle of wine. No problem with that. It was Meredith's home. She needed to wind down, and relax. But...

Having asked whether Meredith wanted her to check in again later, and been told 'yes'... she really wanted to do that. Shelly buzzed the call button, again; holding it for a few seconds. She waited. Nothing.

"Hmm..." She muttered to herself.

She picked up her phone; wondering whether to send her a text message, just saying 'goodnight'. Changing her mind, she wished that she could just take a walk over to the house. Just stroll around it... check that there was nothing amiss. But, that would leave the control point at Crawley's unattended. Not a good idea.

A little worried, although telling herself there was surely nothing to worry about, she decided to press the call button, one more time.

Hopefully, she muttered:

"Come on, Meredith. Just say..."

Bleep! The large central screen sprang to life, and Meredith appeared in her view. She was draped in a towel, and her hair was wet. She had obviously stepped out of the shower.

"Hi, Shelly. I lost track of the time."

Quickly realising that she must not convey her own feelings of anxiety, for fear of making Meredith uneasy, Shelly simply smiled, casually.

"No worries. Sorry if I disturbed you."

Meredith smiled back. It was a warm, genuine smile. One that touched Shelly; took her by surprise.

249

"You're doing your job. I appreciate it."

She lifted a glass to the camera, and toasted Shelly's devotion to duty with a rich ruby red glass of wine.

"You're determined to catch this man, aren't you? I mean *you*, Shelly. I can see it in your eyes. He's *your* catch, isn't he?"

Shelly hesitated:

"We all want to catch him. We *will* catch him."

Meredith smiled.

"I wish you could join me. I could do with some company."

Shelly averted her eyes briefly. Then:

"We need to keep a low profile. Otherwise..."

Meredith understood.

"Of course. Maybe another time. I'll say goodnight, then."

"Goodnight, Meredith."

Chapter 43

By Friday the seventh of October, ten days later, nothing had changed. Meredith seemed to be handling her semi-voluntary 'house arrest', as she referred to it, remarkably well. Yet again, it was apparent that the years of training and military experience were standing her in good stead.

During a team meeting, it was decided that one member of the police team should try to get to know Meredith more closely. Try to really get inside her head. Shelly was the obvious candidate. She was single, just a few years younger than Meredith; and, somehow, seemed to have already developed a degree of affinity with her. Meredith was not explicitly told about the decision. It was felt that, by assigning Shelly to liaison duty on a regular basis, and affording her the licence to leave the monitoring point to spend time in direct company with Meredith, the relationship of trust might develop naturally.

In order to facilitate this, double staffing shifts were planned in; so that Shelly might pay discreet visits to the house, leaving a colleague in charge of the visual monitoring. Or, at times, Shelly would make a call to the office to let them know that watching the screens would be done remotely by them. She would never be away from Crawley's for more than two hours; and, for most of that time, she would be in Meredith's company. Only the few minutes of travel time between *Freelands* and the old shop, and back again, were the moments of concern.

So it was that on Friday the seventh of October, Shelly dropped in on Meredith. To any outside watcher – not that there appeared to be one – Shelly was just some casual visitor. She had passed observation of the monitoring screen to Frank Burnley, who was sat at his desk in the police station. In the unlikely event of any emergency arising in those few minutes, the team knew what the contingency plan was.

Shelly rang the bell, and looked up at the camera, close to the front door.

"Hello? Just a moment."

Meredith greeted Shelly; she was expected, recognised, and acknowledged. The door soon opened, and Meredith welcomed her visitor.

"Come in, Shelly."

Shelly hadn't seen Meredith that day; and was surprised to see that she was clad only in a short, light blue, dressing gown. It was just after three in the afternoon.

"Just had a workout." Explained Meredith.

She had a mini gym; with a treadmill, exercise mat, and a few weights, in a small room, upstairs.

"You could have joined me."

Meredith led the way along the hall, through the lounge, and into her kitchen. Shelly, following her, noticed that the grandmother clock seemed to have been adjusted. The grand old lady was managing to keep up with time, again.

"Juice?" Meredith opened the fridge.

"Yes, please."

Shelly accepted a glass of fresh orange; and Meredith poured one for herself, before perching on a bar stool, to face her visitor.

"Any news?"

Shelly frowned:

"Not really. We're still back-checking on the last known movements of the men. But, it's not easy to find anything, so long ago."

She glanced out of the window, at the mature trees outside. Autumn was marching on, and leaves were golden brown, losing their grip on the branches.

"No cause for alarm for you, though. No unexpected calls or visits?"

Shelly already knew the answer; having checked the log, less than an hour ago.

"Nothing to see here." Meredith grinned.

Shelly sipped her juice, and leaned back to regard her.

"You're dealing with this brilliantly, Meredith. I can only imagine how difficult it must be for you."

Meredith gazed into the distance, with a blank look on her face.

She shrugged: "Just a bit lonely, that's all."

Shelly thought how, if circumstances were different, she might see this as an invitation... a temptation. Meredith was an attractive woman. She had really looked after herself. Perhaps the army should get some credit for that. Shelly thought, for a second, about Millie. She never used to think only about women...

Meredith continued:

"This is not the time to try and build a relationship, is it? There hasn't been anybody since Lewis. I don't think there's much chance for me, at the moment, is there?"

"Not ideal." Agreed Shelly.

Meredith downed the rest of her juice, and asked: "And what about you, Shelly?"

There seemed to be the hint of a twinkle in her eye, as she looked at this detective constable, who was detailed to keep her safe. Shelly fumbled, momentarily; unsure quite what she was being asked. Then, assuming that she was probably just being asked, politely, whether she had a relationship of her own, replied:

"Oh, the job, you know... It makes things difficult. I'm not with anyone. Not right now."

She looked back directly at Meredith; who was still wearing just a soft bathrobe, and showing no sign of getting dressed. Meredith matched her

253

eye contact, and the two just looked at each other, for a few seconds. Finally, Meredith was the first to turn away; as she slid from the bar stool, and stood up.

"I suppose I better get dressed. Don't want to upset your mates, if they're on surveillance duty, today."

Then, she added: "Actually, I turned off the internal ones. It's nice to have a little privacy. Don't you think? Come."

She led the way back to the lounge, looked out, over the garden, and sat down in an easy chair; straightening her robe, and stretching out her long legs. She reached over, and picked up a calendar, as Shelly sat down, on the sofa. Examining it, she commented:

"Oh, the alarm company are coming back on Monday. Something to do with the backup battery on the rear bell box."

She chuckled: "Little do they know; my covert security system makes their humble alarm look like something out of the dark ages. The guy asked about the cameras. I told him they were all dummies."

Shelly smiled.

"Yep. It's like Fort Knox, here."

Meredith added: "Susan's coming tomorrow, to go through some things. I've told her to give some hours to her daughter, in the shop. She's worked as a Saturday girl for me, before."

Shelly nodded.

"You must be out of pocket, with all this."

Meredith grunted: "It's certainly not making me any money."

And, then, as if to negate the comment she had just made, she went on:

"I might take a holiday, in the near future. Would that be a problem?"

Shelly shook her head: "No, if you want to get away for a bit, why not? Where were you thinking of?"

254

Meredith smiled at Shelly, and her eyes twinkled:

"Somewhere warm. I wonder if your boss will offer me a police escort. Fancy coming somewhere, just to keep me safe?"

Shelly blushed.

"Er…"

"Just kidding!" Meredith assured her, breaking into a chuckle. "I wouldn't expect the police budget to run to that."

Shelly laughed; as Meredith continued: "Oh, and on Sunday I've got a guy coming to price up some brickwork, down at the bottom of the garden, there. I'm thinking of putting a little pond in."

She pointed out of the window; towards the orchard, and the smaller patch of garden beyond it.

Shelly's attention was drawn: "Do you know him? Have we done a check?"

"No, but he was recommended by the guys that did the safe room. He hasn't found *me*, I sought *him*."

Shelly was reassured: "Ok. But, let's check him out, anyway. Just to be sure."

Meredith nodded.

"This man… if you catch him… when you catch him… what do *you* think should happen to him?"

Shelly was surprised. As an officer of the law, she could only give one answer. However, maybe she owed it to Meredith to be as honest as her badge would allow.

"Who are you asking? A police officer, or a woman?"

Meredith smiled.

"I think that answers my question."

Chapter 44

The weekend passed without incident. Shelly took a couple of days away from duty, while Dawn stepped up as 'lead supervisor'. Meredith's visitors came and went; unaware that their movements were observed and routinely recorded.

Monday morning saw a team meeting, at which there were a few things to report. In the Canaries, investigations had been continuing in a less subtle manner than DI Williams would have liked.

Separate appeals had been launched for information about the deaths of Roberto Pastor and Luca Mendez, and officers had been searching for anything that could relate to the whereabouts of Louis Cranda. Williams was grateful for the fact that, at least, there was no public suggestion that the three deaths might be in any way linked.

In the UK, Dr Sheen and DI Williams had been party to an interesting conversation, which Sheen would report to the team.

"We were contacted by Meredith's father, Colonel Harry Wilde, retired. He knows everything that's going on; Meredith confided in him. Or, having met him, it might be more accurate to say that he extracted the information from her."

Some members of the team groaned.

DI Williams took over:

"He's not going to go public; he understands the sensitivity of this. But, his concern is his daughter's wellbeing."

"That's understandable." Commented Frank Burnley.

"He wants to make sure she's properly protected from him, I suppose."

Williams explained:

"Not just that, Frank. He has concerns about her state of mind. He told us some interesting things about her time in the army."

The team members all took notice, as Dr Sheen began to explain what the colonel had told them about Meredith:

"He was clearly upset when she left the army. He must have been hoping she would have a long and distinguished military career, just like he did. So, when she started to get into trouble, I imagine relations became very strained between the two of them. He wasn't happy when he found out that she had acquired a nickname: 'Savage'. No doubt partly inspired by her surname, 'Wilde'. But, it seemed to have come about because of her temper, rather than her family name."

Williams chipped in:

"He didn't quite say as much, but we think there was probably quite a rift between them. They seem to be on reasonable terms, now; which is why he came to us to raise his concerns. He believes she's very fragile; more than she allows people to see."

Dawn looked up from a note that she was taking:

"Fragile. That's the word that Lewis Heckel used."

Shelly nodded in agreement.

Dr Sheen continued with his contribution:

"Colonel Wilde worries how she could react; if, after her past experiences, she finds herself in a situation of extreme danger. To be fair, with his experience and position, he knows what he's talking about. He fears she could 'self-destruct'. His term, not mine."

Frank Burnley murmured:

"It would certainly explain why she chose to spend a fortune on the most elaborate security set-up we've ever seen."

Dr Sheen cleared his throat, and patted his chest, before resuming:

"The difficulty I have, from a psychological perspective, is that she isn't displaying either 'fight' or 'flight' tendencies, which you're all familiar with. She had the chance to flee away, and put herself completely out of harm's way, and she chose not to. She doesn't say things that suggest wanting to

257

stand up to him, either. She keeps the route to her sanctuary, her safe room, close by. It's not quite what I would expect. Doesn't quite fit."

He shook his head, puzzled; and brushed his hand through his hair.

"What's your view, Shelly? You've got to know her better than any of us?"

Shelly thought for a second.

"It's hard to tell. She's very… deep. All those years in the army. When does a soldier stop being a soldier? She's never shown any signs of breaking down. Not to me. She seems to have taken everything in her stride. But, maybe that's just a front."

She looked at Marcus Sheen.

"I agree with Dr Sheen. We need to keep a very close eye on her."

DS Graeme French commented that he had been liaising with other forces; monitoring any reports of assaults, missing persons… anything involving people of Spanish ethnicity, or with a Spanish connection.

Meantime, at her affluent home, Meredith was towelling dry her hair after a shower; stood at the open bathroom window, looking across at the trees of early Autumn. She was about to pull the window shut, when a sound startled her. It was a man's voice:

"Yep. Done that. But, why am I wiring it like that?"

There was a pause.

Meredith froze. How come a man's voice was audible, so close? It couldn't be more than five metres away.

Then, she realised. It was the alarm engineer; almost certainly at the top of a ladder, and speaking to someone by phone, as he attended to the alarm box, which was fixed to the wall, just a few metres away from the bathroom window.

She leaned forward, without making a sound, and saw that the man was, indeed, balancing on a ladder. He attempted to make some adjustment to

258

the box, while listening to a communication through headphones, that led to an upper pocket of his overalls.

She breathed a sigh of relief. No cause for alarm.

"But, if I connect it that way…" The engineer's voice tailed off, and there was a long pause.

Presumably, he was listening to directions coming to him down the phone line, that Meredith couldn't hear.

"Oh, so you'll override it at your end?"

Pause.

"I didn't know we could do that."

Pause.

"But, why?"

Pause.

"Ok. You're the boss."

Pause.

"Yep, holiday starts in one hour, and I'll see you in a couple of weeks."

He laughed; apparently, now in a better humour, at the thought of his upcoming holiday.

Pause.

"Ok, see you then. Cheers."

Meredith could hear no more conversation, but sensed a disgruntled muttering. He would do what he was told; but didn't seem to think that his instructions made sense.

Within a couple of minutes, he had finished his task, and put the bell-box back together. Then, he descended down his ladder, picked it up, and carried it back to his van; unaware that Meredith was watching him, from above.

Shortly afterwards, Shelly was back on surveillance duty, in the back room of Crawley's, having taken over from Dave Perryman. Meredith had invited her to drop in for a chat, later; so she planned to call in around six, before handing over night duty to Dave, again.

She checked through the log of weekend activities. A check had been done on the man who had visited, at Meredith's request, in connection with establishing a pond and building a surrounding wall, which she had mentioned. He was an Irish worker, going by the name of Brian Flannery. His address had been noted, and his car registration recorded. There was nothing remotely suspicious about him.

Meredith's other visitors over the weekend had been Susan, and her daughter, Naomi. Their vehicle details were also recorded, and the times of their visit logged down. Shelly approved; despite several different colleagues having a hand in matters, the procedure of monitoring and recording appeared to be operating well.

Today, just less than an hour ago, Meredith's alarm company had called, true to their appointment. Rewinding and checking the video surveillance, Shelly watched the arrival of the company van. It was a red Mercedes, just smaller than a transit van; with a metal ladder secured to the roof, and the security firm's logo on the side. The logo looked vaguely familiar to Shelly; who assumed she had seen the company's vehicles elsewhere. She looked at the live feed, which currently looked out from the garage; and saw that the van was still parked on the drive, next to Meredith's Range Rover.

The screen in front of Shelly emitted a bleep, and the central image flickered into life. Meredith's face appeared, and she heard her voice:

"Hi Shelly. Are you popping over? Now would be a good time, if that's ok?"

"Oh." Shelly checked the time. It was much earlier than they had arranged.

"Sure, if that's best."

"Ok. See you in five minutes?"

And, with that, Meredith clicked the live feed off.

Shelly made a quick call to Frank, who was at his desk in the office:

"I'm popping over to Meredith. Be back in an hour. Ok Frank?"

"No worries."

Frank had other things to occupy himself, but would keep an eye on the live camera feed, that was patched directly to their office.

Shelly drove over to *Freelands*, and parked in the empty space behind the Range Rover. Getting out of the car, she called Meredith from her phone, instead of ringing the bell.

"Just coming." Said Meredith.

The door opened within seconds, and Meredith welcomed Shelly in:

"Hi, warden."

It was a term she had come to use, occasionally; as a teasing swipe to the duty officer's role as her 'jailer'. Shelly grinned, ruefully. Then, as she was about to step inside, she stopped and looked back at the two cars on the drive. Two cars, but no red van.

"Oh, has your alarm engineer gone?"

Meredith followed her eyes to the parking area.

"Oh! Er, yes. He's gone!"

There seemed to be an awkward silence. Shelly didn't understand why.

"He's just gone? I saw his van on screen when I was leaving Crawley's."

Meredith nodded: "Yes he just left. A few minutes ago. Come in. Coffee? Or juice?"

Shelly followed her in. The door to the lounge was closed, and Meredith led her through the hall and directly to the kitchen. The sound of the

261

grandmother clock chiming behind her attracted Shelly's attention. Five times it rang out, announcing the hour.

"Juice, please."

Shelly joined her hostess in the kitchen, and accepted a glass of orange juice. Meredith didn't get herself a drink. Instead, she stepped towards the interior kitchen door, which led to the rear stairs.

"Can you come up to the safe room with me, Shelly?"

Meredith wasn't displaying any level of alarm, but seemed to want Shelly's attention to something.

"Oh. Yes, of course."

Shelly put her drink down, and followed her as she bustled quickly through the rear hall, and swivelled to take the stairs. She seemed to be in something of a hurry. At the very least, her gait might be described as 'business-like'. Curious as to the rush, Shelly went up the stairs, after her.

"Is everything all right, Meredith?"

Meredith paused, and turned back:

"Yes, everything's fine. I just wanted you to check something, for me. Call it a quality assurance test."

She smiled.

"I paid a lot of money for that safe room. I just want to check how good it is."

Still a little puzzled, Shelly followed Meredith along the landing, past the closed door of a bedroom, and into the study.

"It's the soundproofing that I want to test." Explained Meredith.

"I told them I wanted it to be soundproof, both ways. I want you to help me test that. If I go inside, or, better still, if you go inside, and make some noise, I'll find out whether I can hear you."

262

Meredith's eyes seemed to have a glint, showing that she was determined, excited. To Shelly, it seemed odd.

"So… you want to lock me in, and see whether you can hear me from the other side?" She asked, nervously.

"Yes. Oh, well, if that's alright. I don't want you to feel trapped."

She looked Shelly in the eye. The officer looked back. After a moment, Shelly, breathing heavily, responded:

"No, that's fine. I'll go inside."

She didn't feel comfortable about this. She wasn't at all claustrophobic… it wasn't that. She didn't seriously suspect that she was about to be locked in, and kept prisoner against her will. That would never happen. Shelly's unease came more from the fact that she couldn't understand Meredith's train of thought. There was something just… strange about this. But, she was here to support Meredith. To gain her trust. To give her what she needed, to keep her strong. She would go inside, and trust Meredith to let her out, as soon as she asked to be let out.

"Ok." Began Meredith, almost gleefully.

"After I close the door, I want you to shout. Bang a few things about. See if I can hear you. For about thirty seconds. Then, I'll open the door, and you come out, I'll go in. Tell me if you can hear the noise that I make."

Shelly nodded.

"Thirty seconds? That sounds fine. Don't leave it longer. I'll feel nervous. I don't like confined spaces."

Normally that would have been a lie. But, at the present moment, this was a confined space that Shelly was not looking forward to experiencing.

"No. I won't leave it any longer."

The door to the sanctuary was already in the open position. Shelly stepped inside. Meredith immediately pressed a button on the control panel, and the precisely engineered door glided smoothly and quietly into place. The two women maintained eye contact, until they disappeared from each other's view. With a click, and a slight hiss from the pressure of the airtight seal, the door locked itself securely.

Shelly looked around. Stacked neatly in place were the supplies that Meredith had prepared. A set of six plastic storage boxes stood, one on top of another, at one side of the room. Each bore a label, detailing what was inside. Four of them contained food items, while the other two held drinks. The emergency lighting had come on, as soon as the door closed. A gauge on the wall showed the temperature, as well as the oxygen and humidity levels.

At the other side of the room, a chemical toilet was fitted against the wall, alongside a wash basin. Next to that was a small fridge, and a microwave oven, placed on a small shelf. There was, thought Shelly, everything a person could wish for, if they were trapped inside; trying to survive a nuclear winter, in the aftermath of a nuclear weapon detonation. She tutted; chiding herself for watching too much post-apocalyptic science fiction.

Shelly picked up a pair of metal pliers, that were lying on the shelf; and proceeded to bang these against the stainless steel taps on the sink. Gently, at first, then more robustly; so that the level of noise gradually increased. She turned towards the door, behind which she assumed Meredith was still stood, and began to call out.

"Meredith? Meredith? Can you hear me?"

She continued to shout, and to bang metal on metal; creating a din that would ordinarily be heard with ease by anyone in the adjoining room, or even much further away, in a house like this. She wondered whether Meredith, on the other side, was also making noise. Periodically, she ceased her own racket, and listened. However, she heard nothing.

There was a click, and a hiss. The door began to slide open; perfectly smooth, on its runners. Meredith was stood on the other side.

"All quiet. You were making noise?"

"Oh yes. Plenty."

Shelly tried hard not to show how relieved she was that Meredith had opened the door to release her, exactly as promised. Especially, she did not want to imply doubt. Didn't want Meredith to feel distrusted.

"Out you come!"

Meredith indicated the control panel.

"Press this one to lock the door, and this one to open it."

Without further ado, she entered the room; as soon as Shelly had taken up her position alongside the controls.

"Go on!"

Meredith seemed eager. Impatient to try out her new toy. Shelly pressed the first button, and the door slid shut. Somewhat half-heartedly, she called out, and banged on the desk, stamped her feet. But, mostly, she listened. She could barely hear a sound coming from the other side of the door. Perhaps, when she listened intently, there was the faintest sound of shouting. But, unless fully briefed about this unusual house, nobody would ever recognise that somebody, just a couple of metres away, was trying to attract attention.

After what she judged was about thirty seconds, Shelly pressed firmly on the second button, and the secure door opened.

"I'd say you have yourself a sound-proof room!"

Shelly smiled. Meredith smiled back. She seemed pleased, perhaps relieved. The money she had invested in her own safety seemed to have been well-spent, indeed.

"Come." She said, and led Shelly back downstairs to the kitchen.

"You feel reassured, now?" Shelly asked.

"Oh, yes. I think that will do the job."

As soon as Shelly had finished drinking her juice, Meredith appeared keen to wash the glass, wipe the worktop, tidy the kitchen. She opened the fridge door, and looked inside; as if considering what to make for her

265

evening meal. She closed the door again, without comment. Conversation seemed to have dried up, and Shelly began to sense that, although she had been an invited visitor, perhaps Meredith had now decided that she wanted her privacy back.

Feeling a little unwelcome, Shelly said:

"Ok. I'll get back to Crawley's, unless you wanted anything else."

"No, I'm fine. Thanks for coming over."

Before she could leave, Shelly's phone rang out. She answered it, with an apologetic nod to Meredith. The speaker was turned up, as she had previously been using the phone in her car.

"Hi Dawn. What's up?"

"Call from Mariana Navarro. She wants one of us to call and see her. Preferably, you. You got time in the morning?"

Shelly paused: "Er, yes, ok."

Dawn explained that Mariana was feeling anxious, and just wanted reassurance that things were being done. Had there been any progress? She was missing Vito so much... Shelly knew she had promised to give Mariana whatever support she could; and, if this meant listening to her getting emotional over the memory of Vito, then she would do it. She made tentative arrangements with Dawn for the next day, and ended the call.

"Sorry about that." She smiled at Meredith. "Right, I'll go."

She now felt distinctly awkward, with Meredith seeming keen to see the back of her; as though she had just been unmasked as the gate-crasher of a party.

"Shall I ask Dave to check in with you around ten?"

Meredith shook her head: "No, there's no need, thanks. I'm going to have an early night. I'll probably be in bed before then. Tell him I'll check in tomorrow morning."

"Ok. See you, Meredith."

"Bye."

Meredith stood at her open doorway, and watched Shelly go to her car, turn it round, and drive off the property. Then, having had a good look all round at whatever was in view from the front door, she stepped back inside, and closed it.

Chapter 45

As Shelly arrived at her desk the next morning, Dave was scratching his head, frowning at the screen in front of him.

"I can't weigh her up." He grunted. "At times, she's as good as gold. Then, sometimes, you'd think we were her enemy. She's a weird one!"

Shelly looked enquiringly at him.

"Meredith. I checked in with her a few minutes ago, and she couldn't wait to get rid of me."

Dawn, who had also just arrived, and was taking off her coat, nodded; and, with a wink:

"Who wouldn't want to get rid of you, Dave?"

He stuck his tongue out at her, and grinned.

More serious, Dawn continued:

"I think the whole situation's getting to her. Eh, Shelly?"

Shelly had to agree:

"She has been acting a bit strange. Understandable, I suppose. How would you behave, Dave, if you were waiting for someone to take a pot-shot at you? That's what it must be like for her."

"Hmm." He dismissed it, and turned to deal with some message awaiting him on his screen.

Dawn said:

"Speak to her, later, Shelly. She responds best to you."

"Will do."

Before going to the surveillance of Meredith, Shelly went to Tyldesley, to visit Mariana Navarro. Mariana was quite apologetic, when she arrived.

Yesterday had been a bad day for her. Something seemed to have upset her... brought back some of the memories that she was trying to live without. But, as Shelly had made the trip, and made the time for her, she happily chatted.

She was curious as to whether the televised appeal, and the consequent step up in profile, had achieved anything. Shelly was unable to tell her much; but, she did manage to reassure her that, following the detection of an incident likely linked to the pattern, a woman was now being carefully protected.

"I think we're closer to catching him than we've ever been, Mariana."

Later, Shelly arrived at Crawley's, to take over from Alice Hawley, who had been on early watch. Seeing Shelly arrive, Alice opened the door, and admitted her colleague.

"Anything doing?"

"All quiet since first thing." Responded Alice. "I've barely seen anything of her, since early on. She was chatty, talking about the situation. Asking me about the case. About the other victims. Then, she seemed to switch right off. And, she switched some of the cameras off again this morning, too. She doesn't like to think she's being watched, does she?"

Shelly agreed:

"No. Still, so long as the approaches and all the outside areas are covered, that should be fine. She showed me her safe room again, yesterday. Tested for sound-proofing. That's the most high-tech bit of security I've ever seen. She's safe, there."

Alice nodded:

"Yep. She knows you're on, this afternoon. I expect she'll say hello at some point."

Meredith didn't say hello. All afternoon, Shelly observed the camera feeds, patiently. Some of them had been switched off by Meredith. From the outside, one live camera looked over the garden; and, from the inside, one looked down the stairs, at the inside of the front door. At no time did Shelly catch sight of her charge.

Finally, feeling frustrated, rather than anxious, she decided to call Meredith; just so that she would be able to pass on to the next duty officer that she had made contact. The next person on duty was Dawn; who arrived as Shelly was trying to establish a connection, through the video link. Shelly looked up, as Dawn entered the room.

"Just checking on her." Shelly said. "Haven't seen her, all…"

She broke off, as the screen came to life, and Meredith's face appeared.

"Hi, Shelly."

She appeared slightly breathless, as though she had been interrupted in the course of some physical exertion.

"Been in your gym?" Enquired Shelly.

"Yes. The gym."

Meredith said no more.

"I wanted to check all's well. We haven't seen much of you today."

Meredith seemed distracted; not interested in making conversation. After a couple of seconds, she replied:

"Yep, that's good. I'm fine."

Then, seeming to relax a little, she smiled:

"I've had a lazy day, today. Slobbed about all morning; then I decided I owe it to my body to have a workout. So, I've been on the treadmill. You can probably smell the perspiration from there. Who's taking over from you, tonight?"

"It's Dawn."

"Hi, Meredith." Chipped in Dawn, leaning into view.

"Ok. Well, thanks for checking. I'll see you in the morning. Bye."

And, the central screen went blank; leaving only the internal view of the front door, and that vista of the garden.

"Short and sweet." Murmured Dawn, to Shelly.

"Hmm."

Meredith leaned back in her chair, after switching off the connection to her surveillance team. She looked at her screen, and the two remaining images that were on view. Then with a few presses of the controls, she switched some cameras on, some off; checking which were showing current, live pictures, and which were locked with a still picture, frozen from earlier that day. Soon, she was sure that only the front door and the garden were live, and nodded with satisfaction.

She was just about to get up from her seat, when her phone rang. She picked it up, looking at the unknown number, curiously.

"Hello?"

"Oh, hi there. Is that Miss Wilde?" It was a woman's voice.

Meredith paused, before answering. She hated calls from people that she didn't know, and frequently ignored the phone when this was the case.

"Speaking."

"Hi, Miss Wilde. My name's Samantha Dann. I'm calling from BS, the alarm company. Our chap, Trevor, called to do a refit on your alarm bell, yesterday."

"Oh, yes."

Was this a courtesy call, following up to check that the engineer had done his job properly? Such calls irritated Meredith; but, today she listened.

"I just need to check whether our manager followed up after the site visit. I think Trevor left you around one pm, didn't he?"

"Yes, about that." Confirmed Meredith.

"And, did our manager visit you, later in the day?"

271

"No. Nobody else came. Just the guy who attended to the bell-box."

There was a pause. Then:

"Oh. Ok."

Perhaps Meredith was becoming impatient. She maybe had other things on her mind, than time management issues at an alarm maintenance company.

"Is that everything?"

"Er, yes, thank you. I'm sorry to have bothered you. Goodbye."

Chapter 46

Sat in Crawley's, Dawn whiled away the time by studying recent video footage and snapshots taken by Meredith's cameras. At one point, just as it was getting dark, she glanced out of the window, as a taxi swept past and headed along the lane in the direction of *Freelands*. The taxi's lights were on, as the light was fading fast. She was unable to see how many people were in the car.

She turned to the screen which showed the approach to Meredith's drive. But, the image from the camera seemed unusually bright. Like TV cameras which can portray a cricket match being played in good light, when the reality is that the arena has become quite dark. There was no sign of the taxi pulling in. It must have gone to one of the other houses on the lane. Presently, Dawn saw it driving back towards her vantage point; and straight past, back in the direction of Lymm. Dutifully, she made a note of the registration, and logged it on the daily record.

She looked at the screen again. The image seemed to have got much darker, now. That was a sudden deterioration, thought Dawn. Perhaps the quality of the camera could only handle a modest degree of light adjustment, to sustain a clear image. A light was on, now, at one of Meredith's upstairs windows.

There was a bleep; and the central image on her screen sprang to action.

"Hello Dawn. Just letting you know all is well."

Meredith was wearing a dark, leathery-looking jacket.

"That's good."

Dawn had noticed the jacket, so added: "Are you going out?"

"Oh, no. I just stepped into the garden. It's chilly in the evening, now, isn't it?"

Meredith slipped off the jacket.

"Time for a hot drink." She added. "Ok, I'll leave you to it. Goodnight."

And she flicked off the live feed. Dawn continued to look at the screen, thoughtfully. One of the cameras that was on display had been covering the rear garden; but, she had seen no sign of Meredith.

She looked again at the image of the house, looking in from the front. Quite dark, now; and the light of the window shone brightly. She thought back to the days that she and Shelly had spent in Fuerteventura; and how they had both noticed the speed with which it fell dark in the evening. Very noticeable. Quite different from the way that dusk falls in England. Far more gradual, here, she thought. Yet, tonight, the advent of the dark seemed to have taken her by surprise.

She watched the screen, as a figure appeared at the lit window. It was Meredith, although Dawn could barely make her out, at that range. The curtains were slowly pulled across, and the night shut out.

Was Meredith's behaviour showing a change, or did she imagine it? Probably the pressure of the situation was taking its toll. Dawn looked down again, at the log; scrolling back over recent days. Was there something that didn't quite add up? Something that she should be taking notice of, that she was missing?

She decided to cross-check Meredith's visitors over the weekend. An alarm technician was listed, and his vehicle had been recorded. Meredith's staff team, Susan and her daughter, had also called, as expected. They had stayed a couple of hours. Their departure had been logged. Meredith must have been glad of a little company, she thought. The poor woman's life had become very isolated.

Meredith had found a local builder, thanks to a recommendation: Brian Flannery. His credentials had been checked; and the car that he had arrived and departed in was correctly found to be in his own name. Dawn expected that he might well be calling again in the future; Meredith was apparently keen to employ him to do some work in the rear garden. The process of recording all these comings and goings still seemed to be tidy and efficient.

She was about to close the log, when she paused. The alarm technician... His vehicle had been recorded as arriving, as expected. But, how long had he stayed? Dawn didn't remember seeing an entry for his departure. She checked back, and looked again.

Dave had been on duty. Although he had some flippant attitudes, and could be a bit 'old-fashioned' at times, Dave was a good cop. He knew the importance of doing this right. It wasn't like him to make a mistake; but, it was possible. Or, had the technician not left until Shelly's duty shift?

Dawn picked up the phone, and called Shelly, to check whether she could clear this up.

Shelly thought for a moment.

"Oh, yes, I remember. He had left just before I went over to speak to Meredith. I remember mentioning it to her. I saw his van on the screen before I set out; but his van had gone by the time I got there."

"Right. But you didn't pass him on the road?"

Shelly considered: "No. I didn't think about it at the time; but, I assume he went the other way, not coming past Crawley's."

Dawn listened, and understood.

"Hmm. Yes, I suppose he must have. So, the reason his departure time wasn't recorded... It's just because he left at the moment you were heading over there."

Shelly could feel herself blushing; although, of course, Dawn couldn't see this on the phone.

Shelly said: "I should have logged it. Sorry."

"Ok. The system's working pretty well. We're keeping it tidy. Thanks, Shelly."

She ended the call; satisfied, almost, with the answer.

Just then, she saw a silvery-grey car trundle past her window. It was a large car, but old. A Volvo, by the look of it. Impressive, in its day; but rather the product of its own time, back in the seventies. Dawn made a note of the registration, and turned to look at the screen, in front of her.

Sure enough, within a couple of minutes, the still view that she was looking at, covering the front of Meredith's drive, was invaded by a grey Volvo. Dawn watched it roll up behind the Range Rover, and picked up her phone. She waited. After a few moments, Meredith's front door opened, at which time the driver's door of the Volvo swung open, and silver-haired elderly man climbed out.

"Ah!"

Dawn exclaimed, as she recognised the visitor. It was Meredith's father, Colonel Harry Wilde. No cause for alarm; although Meredith had not mentioned he was coming. Perhaps she didn't know, and this was a surprise parental visit. Or maybe she had forgotten to say. Possibly, she was becoming less cooperative with the police.

The arrival was duly logged.

Meredith didn't take her father indoors. Instead, she pulled the front door shut, after herself; and strolled with him around the outside of the house, and out of Dawn's sight, towards the back garden. Dawn looked at the other, smaller images, but none of them currently revealed the back of the house; although one looked out towards the orchard. Presently, Meredith and Colonel Wilde came into view; walking together down towards the lower garden. Presumably, Meredith was showing him her plans to do some development, and to install a pond on the lower level.

They sat, for a few minutes, on an old bench that was just on the perimeter of the camera's view. Then, with what seemed to be some agitated gesturing, Colonel Wilde stood up, and the two walked back towards the house; going out of Dawn's sight, temporarily. When they appeared within range of the front camera, Meredith made for her front door. Her father did not follow her, whether invited or not; returning instead to his trusty old car, which he started up, turned round, and drove away. Meredith watched him until the car had gone from her view; then, went back inside her house.

Dawn made a note of the time, logged it, and presently saw the Volvo drive past her window at Crawley's.

Chapter 47

The next day was Wednesday the twelfth of October, and Shelly was on surveillance duty, when her phone rang.

"Good morning, Meredith. All ok?"

With minimal formality, Meredith replied:

"I've decided I'm going out, today. Just for a ride, really. Get some air. I think I'm going stir-crazy, here."

"Hmm. Yes, I understand that. Where were you thinking of heading?"

Meredith seemed to have given this some thought, already.

"There's that garden centre, over Leigh way, Brent's. People go from miles around to see it. I think I'll take a drive over there, have a wander round. Maybe get a spot of lunch, then straight back here."

"Ok, no problem. Do you want company?"

Shelly didn't feel comfortable asking that question. She was doing her best to stay on good terms with Meredith; and she did understand that Meredith must be feeling cramped. And, to be fair, Meredith was freely sharing her plans. But, whenever Meredith was out of their view, Shelly couldn't help feeling a tad nervous. So, she was a little disappointed, when Meredith said, decisively:

"No. I'll go on my own. I'll keep my phone on me. Stay in public places. Nobody knows I'm going there. If you just make sure my house stays safe while I'm away, that will be fine."

There was a slightly uncomfortable silence.

"Ok, if you're sure."

"I am." Confirmed Meredith.

"I'll let you know when I'm ready to leave… probably about eleven."

"Ok, thanks Meredith. Speak to you soon."

Shelly frowned. Having ended the call, she immediately called Dawn, who answered promptly.

"Meredith's going out. She doesn't want company. She's going over to a garden centre, at Leigh. It's about twenty miles away."

"Hmm, ok. Well, we can't stop her. I'll let the boss know."

Shelly had an idea what Dawn was thinking, and said:

"I don't think it would be a good idea to follow her. If she spots us, it could really knock the trust we've gained. But, maybe if one of us gets there first, just to keep a discreet eye out for her..."

"I agree."

She paused, and glanced around to see who else was in the office.

Then:

"I'll get Tom to nip over. She won't know him by sight. He can just look out for her car, and let us know when she sets off back. Leave it with me."

Dawn put down her phone, and turned to Tom Appleby-Haigh, who was looking bored at his screen. A half-eaten sandwich sat in a plastic container on the desk in front of him, between a banana and a bag of crisps. Tom always seemed to be eating; though, to the irritation of some of his less fortunate colleagues, he never seemed to gain an ounce.

"Job for you, Tom. And you get coffee and a cake out of it."

His eyes lit up, and in due course, he set off to follow the East Lancashire Road to the celebrated garden centre. Known for its fine and artistic floral displays, even at this late time of the year when thoughts would be turning towards the business of Christmas, it would be a pleasure to visit.

Two and a half hours later, he sat in the café; drinking his third cup of coffee, and manfully resisting a second home-made scone. There had been no sign of Meredith. Periodically, he glimpsed cars similar to hers entering the car park, and paid special attention. But, he never saw her

278

coming through the front door of the store. To his frustration, it was a huge place, and he had to accept that he could have missed her; as she might have parked at the other end of the car park, and made her way in through one of the concessions in the food hall, or the pet area, or the children's playground.

Eventually, he made a call.

"Hi, Dawn. No sign of her here. But, it's busy, and there are several entrances. I'll have a walk outside, see if I can spot her car. But, it's a big place."

"Ok. Well, no worries Tom. Stay there another half hour. If you haven't spotted her by then, you may as well come back."

"Ok, Dawn. Will do."

He wandered off, heading for one end of the car park. After zig-zagging the rows of cars at the front of the main building, he continued round the side. He groaned when he saw how far the parking area extended. Dutifully, he continued, looking for Meredith's Range Rover. There was no sign. By now, he felt that she must have come and gone; and that there was little point continuing with this abortive mission. Finally, he gave up, and went back to his own car. He called in again; and, with Dawn's agreement, headed back to base.

"Well... waste of time that was." He grunted to himself, as he drove off.

It was after three-thirty when he entered the team's office; and both Dawn and Shelly looked up.

"No sign of her. But, like I said, it's a massive place."

Dawn looked pensive.

"I'll feel better when we know she's home safe."

She looked at the surveillance screen in front of her, which had been patched through from the base at Crawley's, that was currently unattended. A few moments later, she exclaimed, relieved:

"Ah! She's back."

279

She and Shelly watched the Range Rover sweep into the drive of *Freelands*, and Meredith step out.

"Is Dave on his way back to Crawley's?" Asked Shelly.

"Yep. He'll be there by four. Breathe a sigh of relief!"

They looked at each other; both wondering if they were taking this job too much to heart. Then, both remembering what was at stake; they told themselves that they weren't taking anything too seriously, at all.

They allowed Meredith time to settle, before Shelly called her on the phone.

"Hi, Meredith. Good day?"

Meredith hesitated, as if distracted, then appeared to give Shelly her full attention.

"Yes, thanks. Just had a wander round the garden centre. And a cup of coffee. I didn't buy anything."

"Uh huh."

Shelly glanced across at Tom, who was sat nearby. Strange that he hadn't seen her.

"Was it busy?"

"It's always busy there. Popular place."

Shelly knew that it was.

"Ok, I'll leave you alone. Give me a call if you want a chat."

"Will do." And Meredith put down the phone.

Dawn was observing Shelly, and taking note of the call.

"What are you thinking?"

Shelly shrugged:

"I was just wondering if she even went to Brent's at all. I don't know why she would lie to us… unless she feels she has the right to keep us guessing. Keep some control. I don't know. What do you think?"

She looked over in Tom's direction again:

"She had a coffee there, Tom. Did you have your eyes closed?"

Tom grunted:

"I don't see how I could have missed her. Although there are two separate sections to the café. And, there's a separate little pets' café… a café for owners with their pets. That's over in the mall, near the food stalls."

"Oh, well…" Continued Shelly. "No harm done."

Chapter 48

The weekend was quiet, uneventful. Meredith received a brief visit from her father. He stayed less than an hour, on the Saturday morning. Other than that, Meredith's appeared to be a solitary existence. Twice, Shelly offered to call in and spend some time with her. Twice, Meredith politely declined.

Marcus Sheen shook his head, and sighed a worried sigh, when approached by DI Williams about Meredith's current state of mind.

"She's withdrawing, into herself." He commented.

"How much of it stems from her military training, which tells her to isolate herself to stay out of danger, I don't know. What is she thinking about, hour after hour, alone in that house? I wish I knew."

On Monday morning, Dawn put the phone down, with a frown, as she concluded a call from Meredith. DI Williams and Shelly both looked enquiringly at her.

"She's going out again. Off to spend another hour at Brent's. She's leaving about eleven."

There was a brief silence, before the inspector spoke.

"We're going to keep eyes on her, this time."

Turning in the direction of Graeme French:

"Graeme, she doesn't know you, or your car. Get yourself to the end of her road, and follow her to the A6."

He turned round to where Tom Appleby-Haigh was sat.

"Tom, liaise with Graeme. Take over on the East Lancs road, all the way to Brent's. Go into Brent's, and park within sight of her car. If you think she's spotted you, abort. I don't want her spooked. If she thinks someone's following her, she might get scared. Plus, if she suspects it's us, we'll lose her trust. Ok?"

"Yes, Boss."

Graeme and Tom hastily set off to get their cars, and drive into position.

"Something's not right with this." Muttered Williams.

Dawn and Shelly exchanged looks.

"Boss..." Began Dawn. "I'll go over to the watch-point at Crawley's, and keep on top of things there."

DI Williams nodded, without looking up.

"Keep in touch with me, Tom!" He shouted after Tom, who was disappearing out the door.

Turning to Dr Sheen, he asked again what was on all of their minds:

"What's going on here, Marcus? We're supposed to be protecting her; yet it feels like we're starting to distrust her."

Sheen simply shrugged; then winced, and rubbed at his chest.

"Are you alright, Marcus? You've looked a bit... for a few days, now."

He waved away Williams concern, and attempted a smile:

"Just a spot of heartburn. I eat too late, and drink too early."

An hour later, Meredith's Range Rover pulled smoothly out of the grounds of *Freelands*. Dawn, who had taken over duty at Crawley's, watched her drive past. At the end of the lane, Graeme French started up his car; and prepared to follow her as she headed for the main road. A few moments later, she drove past him, and he pulled out to track her. He kept a polite and discreet distance; anxious not to let her suspect that she was being tailed.

By the time Meredith joined the main road, additional traffic, although light, made it easier for him to follow the same route while remaining inconspicuous. He followed carefully, speaking into his hands-free phone to let DI Williams know his position. As she approached the M6 motorway, he pulled back, and spoke directly to Tom, who was listening in.

"She's just joining the M6, now. She's all yours."

"I've got her." Confirmed Tom, who was watching from the motorway bridge.

He accelerated away, swept round the roundabout, down the slip-road, and off in pursuit of the Range Rover. He soon got it in his sights, and relaxed back in lane to follow her from well behind. When, finally, she pulled off the motorway to join the East Lancashire road, he remained at a safe distance, watching her go. Lucky with the traffic lights, he managed to sneak through, still a good distance behind her. Along they went, past Leigh; towards the roundabout junction that would take her right, towards Brent's.

"We're nearly at the Brent's roundabout."

Tom said to his phone, for his team's benefit; as he watched her pull into the outside lane, ready to turn.

The single car between him and Meredith suddenly adjusted its course, and pulled into the nearside lane; leaving him immediately behind the Range Rover. Pausing to check for traffic coming from the right, Meredith glanced in her mirror. For a second, Tom thought that she was looking directly at him. Recognising him. Taking notice. Then, her eyes went back to the road in front, and she made her manoeuvre; guiding her car rather slowly round towards the third exit – the right turn. Nothing else approached to Tom's right, so he too pulled out, and followed Meredith smoothly round, preparing to head towards Brent's, which was only a couple of hundred metres along this road.

Then, suddenly, to his surprise, Meredith's Range Rover swung round more sharply, following the round curve of the roundabout, instead of taking the third exit. Her indicators were still flashing right.

"Shit!" He exclaimed.

"She's not turning towards Brent's. She's going right round the roundabout."

"Don't let her see you!" Shouted DI Williams.

With only a second to make his decision, Tom followed the course that he had originally expected, and left the roundabout. To have done otherwise, following in Meredith's tracks, would have given away that he was following her.

"I've left the roundabout. But I'm going to lose her now!"

Tom cursed Meredith's manoeuvre; as, in his rear view mirror, he caught a last glimpse of the Range Rover completing another circuit of the roundabout, before it headed down the East Lancashire road, towards Manchester.

Why she had gone full circle around it, before continuing in the easterly direction, he couldn't understand. Had she done it deliberately, to check that she wasn't being followed? Tom was left to wonder.

"What do you want me to do Boss? If I go after her now, she may well clock me."

Williams was already on his radio, talking to another officer; trying to arrange for a traffic cop to look out for her, further down the road. He broke off from his call:

"Go to Brent's, Tom. Wait in the café, and let me know if you see her come in. Maybe she just went for petrol, or something."

"Ok, Boss. But, she's not gone for fuel; there's a petrol station just here on this side of the roundabout."

Chapter 49

An hour and a half later, Tom strolled, for the umpteenth time, back out through the front door of Brent's, to hover in the foyer area. He was still cross with himself, for losing Meredith. He felt that he had let down his boss. Let down his team. However, he knew it wasn't really his fault. The more that he thought about it, the more he became convinced that Meredith had deliberately adjusted that manoeuvre on the roundabout. Presumably, this was to make sure nobody could follow her without her knowing about it. Why she was so suspicious, he didn't know. Or, had her years of training kicked in; causing her to take her own additional precautions, in case a potential assailant was on her trail? Although Tom had to admit to himself that she had been justified. 'She was being followed, wasn't she?' He thought to himself. Perhaps he had underestimated her. But, why was she doing this? She was under their protection, and supposed to be working with them.

Having glanced, without any optimism, at cars in the car park; Tom turned to go back inside, and sat down, yet again, at a chair on the edge of the café. Several shoppers and browsers were wheeling their trolleys; transporting garden tools, floral displays, and late season bargains. He watched them, with no interest.

Then, suddenly, his attention was caught. Meredith came walking briskly in through the front door, and straight past him, to the first floral display. Tom turned his face away from her. She looked at the artificial flower arrangements in a range of wicker baskets, and almost immediately made her choice; picking one up and heading straight for the tills.

Tom picked up his phone, and called DI Williams.

"Boss? She's just showed up."

He related what he was seeing; and that Meredith was now heading out of the building.

"I don't think she recognised me. She's barely ever seen me."

"Ok. Well, you might as well follow her at a distance. Let us know whether she's heading home."

"Will do, Boss."

Tom followed her outside, and saw where her Range Rover was parked, not far from the shop. She put her purchase on the back seat, glanced around nervously, got in, and drove away. Tom hurried to his car, and drove after her; seeing her head back towards the East Lancashire road. At the roundabout, just five hundred metres along, he stayed well back. He had no intention of being caught out again. She turned left, heading back towards the M6 motorway. Perhaps she was now going home; though where she had been for the last couple of hours, only she knew.

Sure enough, an hour later, Meredith arrived at *Freelands*, and parked on her drive. She lifted out her flower arrangement, partially wrapped in a Brent's bag, and carried it inside. Watching her on the monitor at Crawley's, Shelly frowned. She had just arrived, to join Dawn on duty. Looking thoughtful, she said:

"Why would a florist go to a garden centre and buy a flower arrangement, at their prices?"

Dawn nodded, appreciating the irony.

"Just so that we can see she's been to Brent's, in case we doubted it." She commented.

"I wonder where she went in that missing hour and a half. The boss said the traffic guys didn't pick her up further down the East Lancs." Mused Dawn, adding:

"Which reminds me – the boss was trying to reach you, earlier. Your phone was off."

Shelly continued to look at the screen.

"Flat battery." She muttered.

Turning her attention back to Meredith's actions, and her missing hour and a half, Dawn tutted.

287

"If we ask her, she'll know we've been tracking her."

She picked up her phone, and brought up Google maps; trying to figure out where Meredith could have gone to and returned from, within that timeframe. She scanned the nearby towns: Atherton, Tyldesley, Swinton, possibly Bolton. Assuming that she perhaps wanted some time at her chosen location, rather than simply driving all the time, she couldn't have gone too much further than these.

That evening, Meredith stayed inside. She responded briefly to a call from Shelly; but showed no inclination to chat. The next morning, DI Williams pulled his team together.

"Meredith went AWOL yesterday. If we challenge her about it, she'll know we've been tailing her. I don't want that. Whatever trust we've built up, will be gone."

He looked at his team, and sighed.

"Several questions. First of all, *why* did she give us the run-around yesterday? Second, did she know she was being followed? Third, if she knew, or suspected it, did she realise it was us? Is she in touch with someone that we don't know about? Where did she go? Did she meet up with someone?"

Dr Sheen, who had just arrived, contributed, as he took off his coat:

"Something to bear in mind... whatever's going on with her, may have nothing at all to do with the case. She's a young woman, arguably with a delicate mental state following her military experiences. She's virtually a prisoner in her own home. Never at peace, because she's always looking out in case she gets a visit from some murderous rapist. What she's made of the loss of her partner, Gabriel; I don't know. Perhaps she just needed to get away from the situation for a couple of hours. Went and sat on her own somewhere. Had a good cry."

Williams looked at him. 'You look pale'. He thought.

There was a silence. Finally, Williams spoke: "That may be true. But, we need to eliminate as many possibilities as we can. So... thoughts?"

288

He looked around, hopefully.

Tom Appleby-Haigh commented:

"I don't think she knew for sure that I was there. I think it was her training that kicked in. Make sure you're not followed. She took no chances."

DI Williams nodded.

Dawn spoke up:

"Based on the time she was missing, and where she chose to deviate from her expected route, and that the traffic cops didn't pick her up further on, there are a few places she could have gone."

She looked at a map on her phone.

"Atherton, Tyldesley, Walkden, Swinton, Bolton... anywhere round there. Depends how long she wanted to spend in any particular place. Which ties in with whether she met up with anyone."

Shelly interrupted:

"Does she have any contacts that we know of, in that area?"

Frank, who was the research specialist, commented: "Her social network is surprisingly limited. She's a solitary soul, isn't she?"

DI Williams clapped his hands together, as if to announce a summary of his thinking:

"Ok. For now, let's give her the benefit of the doubt; in so much as there's no real connection between her giving us the slip and our hunt for the killer."

He turned to Shelly:

"You keep talking to her, as much as she'll let you. See if you can draw her out by sympathising with her claustrophobic situation. Like we could understand it if she felt the need to escape, temporarily. After all, she herself said she wanted to take a holiday, didn't she? Maybe something will come out."

At that moment, Graeme French, who had been quietly taking a phone call, swivelled round in his chair, and addressed Dawn.

"Dawn, have you got a minute?"

She turned to him. Graeme was looking thoughtfully at his screen, having been monitoring recent missing person reports.

"Sure, Graeme. What is it?"

Dawn and Graeme had worked together for a long time. Once, when they had been younger, much younger... there had been the flickerings of a romance between them. But that was in the distant past; and both of them knew better than ever to think about rekindling those feelings. For at least ten years, they had shown nothing but mutual respect and professionalism to each other. They got on well; as colleagues, and friends, but nothing more.

"I'm just seeing a 'misper' that's come in at York nick.

"Yeah? What's the interest?"

Graeme spun round from his screen, to face Dawn.

"A guy reported missing by his wife. Lee Dann, aged thirty-five. Lives in the York area, and runs a security company. He was on site visits over this way, a couple of days ago. Didn't arrive home on Monday night. Hasn't been in touch, since."

Dawn didn't immediately see the relevance. Shelly, who was listening in as she logged off her computer, looked up.

Graeme continued: "What was the name of the security company that came to service Meredith's alarm, last week?"

Shelly replied:

"BS alarms, wasn't it?"

Graeme sat up straight:

"That's the company he's with."

There was a pause, before Dawn called out to DI Williams, who was just leaving the room:

"Boss! A moment?"

He returned, and perched on the edge of Shelly's desk, as Dawn began to fill him in:

"Graeme's just come across a missing person, from York. He was last seen working on burglar alarm servicing, in this area. We think it's the same company as came to Meredith's last week."

Before Williams could say anything, Graeme began tapping vigorously at his keyboard, and brought up all the important details.

He read out:

"Lee Dann. Boss of a security company, BS Alarms, based in York. His wife, who also works for the company, expected him home on Monday the eleventh. He had been working in the Cheshire area. He sometimes stays over this way when he's working; but she was concerned when she hadn't heard from him by Tuesday evening. She reported it to York on Wednesday morning, the thirteenth. I don't think they've done much with it, yet."

"Get onto York. See who's dealing with it." Williams paused. "Probably nothing, but…"

Dawn interjected: "Graeme, find out if Meredith's address is on their books, and if she was scheduled for a visit from them last week."

"I'm on it." Confirmed Graeme.

"Do you want me to ask Meredith?" Shelly suggested.

DI Williams rubbed his chin.

"Ask her. But we'll ask the company too."

Within the hour, Shelly had contacted Meredith, and told her that she needed to come and speak with her about something. Meredith showed no enthusiasm whatsoever.

"Will it take long?" She had demanded.

The friendliness with which she had previously engaged with Shelly seemed to have dissipated completely in recent days. Shelly was puzzled. Not offended – she was too professional to be offended – but she couldn't understand why that hint of warmth and good humour had vanished. She attributed it to Meredith seemingly becoming worn down by the pressure of the dismal situation in which she found herself.

"It won't take long, but it's important." Said Shelly. "I'll be with you in an hour."

In due course, she arrived at *Freelands*; to find Meredith pottering with a large and tired-looking pot plant, close to her front door. Looking up, but apparently busy, and determined to continue with her gardening duties, Meredith greeted Shelly.

"Hi, Shelly. What was it that you wanted?"

There was no invitation to step inside; as Meredith clipped away at dry and crispy leaves, which needed to be pruned.

"It's about your burglar alarm, Meredith. You had it serviced, recently. Last Monday?"

"Yes, that's right." She continued to clip away at leaves.

"And, the man who came, I believe he was called Trevor Neesley?"

Shelly had been given this information by Graeme, following a further chat with the police at York.

"I've no idea. I didn't ask his name. He came and did something to the bell box. I think he replaced a faulty part."

Meredith proceeded to tidy the plant, and empty a few cuttings into a plastic bag. Finally, reluctantly, she looked up and gave Shelly her attention.

"Why, what's the problem?"

The tone of her voice was cool, almost surly. It put Shelly in mind of an obstinate teenager, who had no interest in courteous communication. Responding with a similar tone, Shelly explained:

"We're just looking into something. So, the engineer came, did his job, and left? You haven't spoken to him since?"

"No." Meredith confirmed.

"And, he was alone, when he came here?"

Meredith seemed a little surprised.

"Yes, I'm pretty sure he was alone. Yes, definitely. I saw him drive off. He was on his own."

Shelly looked at Meredith. There was surely no reason for her to tell her anything but the truth. No reason at all. Yet, she seemed... twitchy. Uncomfortable. Something was on her mind.

"Ok. That's all it was. Just checking into something. Thanks, Meredith."

And, with that, Shelly turned and left. An hour later, Dawn tried to reach Shelly by phone, to check some detail. However, Shelly's phone was switched off. No matter, it would wait until tomorrow.

Meredith wasn't seen again by the police team, that day. She remained in her home. The range of cameras that she controlled offered a limited surveillance view today. Watching the monitor at Crawley's, Dave Perryman had an all-day view of the outside of the front door, the side of the house, and the panoramic view across the rear garden, down to the orchard.

Meredith called Dave on the phone at nine-thirty in the evening; just to let him know that all was well, and she would be going to bed early. Although she didn't talk for long, she did mention to him that she would be nipping out again the next day; just into Lymm to visit her shop. No, she didn't want an escort. Dave reported it in to his boss.

"We'll post somebody in sight of her shop tomorrow." Grunted DI Williams. "Just to see whether she goes where she tells us."

293

Chapter 50

The following morning was damp and dull, and a little cooler than it had been of late. Overnight wind and rain had aged the trees in Meredith's garden, and they were now distinctly autumnal; shedding leaves over the lawn in an occasional brown and yellow carpet.

Watching on the monitor, Dave Perryman saw Meredith's front door swing open, just after nine. She stepped out, brushed a couple of wet leaves from the windscreen of her car, and got into it. In contact with his colleague, Tom, Dave announced:

"She's on her way."

Tom had already reached Lymm, and was about to park his car in a small car park on the edge of the historic village, close to the main shopping street. As was common with pretty villages in middle England, the roads around and through the middle of the place had not been designed for the quantity of traffic that now sought to use them.

"I'll keep the shop in sight, Dave. She should be here within half an hour. Any more, and she's taken another detour."

Sure enough, around nine-thirty, Meredith appeared among a handful of shoppers, walking down the street towards her own shop. She was carrying a leather bag, slung over her shoulder. Tom remained out of sight, further down the street, on the other side. Glancing around, as if nervous, Meredith disappeared from his view, as she went inside. It struck Tom as odd that, although there was a parking space available right outside the florist's, Meredith had obviously parked elsewhere. Her car was nowhere to be seen.

After only five minutes, Meredith emerged from the shop, and strode off back in the direction from which she had first appeared. Tom followed her, on the opposite side of the street.

She passed a rare traditional high street butcher's shop, a book-maker's, and a small Victorian-themed café. At the end of the block, she turned and cut through an alley-way; briefly disappearing from Tom's view. Tom

294

picked up the pace, just in time to see her climb a couple of steps, into a small, almost hidden car park. He realised that it probably belonged to the shop-keepers, and was reserved for their use. Her car was there, squeezed in between a white van and an old and dirty hatchback, that looked like it had been there for some considerable time.

Tom spoke into his phone:

"She's back at her car, Dawn. She's... she's off now. I won't be back at my car in time to keep her in view. Shall I get on the road?"

"We've got Graeme ready to pick her up on the M6, and follow her back. Yes, take the route you think she'll use."

Meredith drove back home, today taking no unexpected or unaccountable detours. Arriving at *Freelands*, she swept into her drive, watched on the monitor by Dave Perryman; and pulled up in front of her garage. She waited, as the automatic white door crept into action, and raised itself up to its full height, to enable access. Meredith drove the car inside, and the white door began to glide down into the closed position, taking her from Dave's view. The garage had an inside door, providing direct access to the house. It struck Dave as unusual that Meredith had taken her car straight into the garage. He had never known her do that, before.

Back at base, Williams and Frank Burnley had spoken by phone to the team at York, again; interested in whether there was any progress in regard to the report of their missing person, Lee Dann. There was no conclusive connection to their own case, of course. However, the apparent disappearance of a person who had a slight connection to Meredith seemed like an odd coincidence. DI Williams didn't believe in coincidences.

"What can you tell us about him, his background?" Frank asked DS Martha Wade, at York.

"He's lived in the York area for most of his life. Married to Samantha. They have one child, aged five. He has one sister. Brought up his mum... dad died when he was very young. He and Samantha run BS Alarms, based locally. Seems to be a reputable business; they have contracts all over the north, installing and maintaining alarm systems."

"Uh huh." Frank was listening.

"And, any suspicions yet as to where or why he's gone? Any known domestic problems?"

DS Wade had nothing:

"We're not getting any indications of trouble at home. The wife seems genuine. We've checked into his business affairs; it's ticking over. They're in the black; no major debts. We're looking out for his company van. ANPR haven't picked anything up on the major routes, yet."

"Do you know how long Meredith Wilde has been a customer of his?" Asked Frank.

"According to the records, about three years. She has a regular service of her alarm system. This was carried out by Lee's employee, Trevor Neesley. He's away on holiday, at the moment, in Corfu; but we've spoken to him by phone. He confirms he did the call, and spoke to Lee by phone while he was on site. Some technical stuff about the job he was doing. He hasn't had any contact with Lee, since then."

After their call, Williams and Frank conferred.

"Do you think there's a connection, Boss?"

"If there is, I can't figure what it is. But, there's just something fishy about it."

DI Williams rubbed his head, thoughtfully.

"Meredith's not being straight with us, we know that. But whether she has some connection to him... Even if she does, it's possibly nothing at all to do with our case. Purely personal. I tell you what: do a search back, Frank. See if you can find any connection between her and Lee Dann. He's in security, so maybe he has a forces background. Some history between them? An old boyfriend, even?"

"Will do."

Frank set to work; but, when he reported back, later that day, there was nothing to show.

"Can't find anything at all, Boss. He's not ex-services. The only connection is that she's a customer. Of course, it's possible that they've struck up some sort of relationship through that. No evidence of it, though. What do you think?"

Williams pondered.

"I wonder if their working records will show any sign of him spending time over here, maybe visiting Meredith. His wife may not know, but... See whether York can find anything."

"Ok."

The cops at York were unable to offer anything that seemed to be relevant. They had checked with Samantha Dann, who was able to tell them that, based on their business records, Lee did travel extensively around the north west. Furthermore, he did stay away from home overnight, on occasion; to minimise the driving. But, there was nothing to suggest that he frequented the area of Lymm, any more than all the other places where business took him.

Frustrated, weary of what might be merely a distraction from their main focus of attention, the one that had taken all their energies for over two months now, DI Williams reluctantly decided to park the issue of the missing person, for now. Briefing Dawn and Shelly on his thinking, he sounded unusually tired and fractious:

"Keep trying to stay close to her, Shelly. I know she doesn't want us around as much as she did, but we can't take our eye off the ball. Whatever else may or may not be going on in Meredith's life, our mission is to protect her, and catch a cold-blooded murderer and rapist. There's a prison cell with his name on."

Shelly grunted:

"Prison's too good for him."

Williams turned on her, sharply:

"That might be your opinion, but you need to keep focused. We have one aim; to catch him and bring him to justice. Do you understand that?"

297

Shelly nodded:

"Course, Boss."

Before Shelly took up her position at Crawley's that evening, she called Meredith.

"Hi, Shelly."

There was no warmth or interest in Meredith's voice; as if she was picking up the phone to an unwanted cold-caller, determined to sell her something she had no desire to own.

"Meredith, can I call in on you for a few minutes, before I go to Crawley's?"

There was a very brief pause. Just sufficient to show that her response was neither spontaneous nor enthusiastic.

"Yes, if you need to."

Shelly noted the word that Meredith used: 'need', not 'want'. However, no longer seeking or expecting enthusiasm, Shelly simply continued:

"I'll see you about six. Bye."

When six o'clock arrived, Shelly duly pulled into Meredith's drive. There was no sign of the Range Rover. Shelly was at first surprised; then remembered that Dave had mentioned Meredith had taken it into her garage. She parked, close to the garage, and went to the front door. Before she could even ring the bell, the door opened. Meredith had been looking out for her.

"Come in."

Meredith led her guest directly to the kitchen; where a pan was on the stove, bubbling away, and plates already on the breakfast bar. A radio on the worktop was playing music; louder than Shelly would have expected.

"I won't keep you."

Shelly could see immediately that she wasn't about to be invited to stay long, as Meredith was clearly preparing her evening meal. She had tried to

298

think of something important and urgent, to justify her call. However, she hadn't really come up with anything:

"The boss asked me to be sure and check in with you today; give you an update, and see if there's anything we need to know."

Meredith merely nodded slightly, and proceeded to give the simmering pan a stir, without inviting Shelly to sit down.

Shelly continued: "Police in York are still looking for a missing man; he owns the security company that looks after your alarm."

"I believe so." Commented Meredith, drily.

"As I already said, it wasn't him who came here, it was one of his workers."

Shelly hesitated; the sound of music from the radio filling the gap.

"Yes, a Trevor Neesley. He didn't say anything to you I suppose? Didn't mention his boss, at all?"

"No. He barely spoke. Just did his job. Why don't you ask him?"

There seemed to be a glint in Meredith's eye, and an icy edge to her voice. This, thought Shelly, hardly seems like the same woman that I met, barely five weeks ago.

"He's away on holiday. Left the country the day after he came here." Answered Shelly. "Otherwise I would ask him."

Meredith placed a lid on the hot pan.

"Anything else?"

Shelly looked at the radio, wishing Meredith might turn it down; but she showed no sign of doing so. Then, next to the radio, and almost obscured by it, something caught Shelly's eye. It was a child's toy. A small, doll-type figure. Colourful, a bright orange, with long, soft, flowing hair. A troll, perhaps, or an animal figure. Her eyes lingered on it for a moment; and she half opened her mouth to make a comment. Then, realising that Meredith had no need to account to her for the presence of toys or anything else in her home, she bit her tongue. Meredith appeared to

299

notice that her attention had been drawn to something, but said nothing about it.

"Any progress in the search for Gabriel?" She suddenly demanded.

She knew already that, for reasons that she accepted, the search was being kept very low profile.

Shelly shook her head, apologetically: "Nothing. But, as you know, we're not able to make too much noise right now. We want the killer to come here, so we can apprehend him. We don't want to scare him off. It's what we agreed, isn't it?"

Meredith shrugged, and appeared to cast an involuntary glance towards the kitchen door. Perhaps a sign that she wanted Shelly to leave.

Shelly turned, and stepped towards the door, then paused:

"If there's anything you want to talk about, Meredith... anything at all... I'm here to support you. Yes?"

Meredith appeared to shake off her mask of distance and coolness:

"Of course. I appreciate it." She rewarded her guest with a smile that was faint, courteous, and soon gone.

Shelly glanced out of the kitchen window, at the garden. A few leaves blew across, away from a tree.

"I haven't seen your gardener for a while. Reggie, isn't it?"

Meredith stood with her arms folded across her chest.

"He's taking a week or two off."

Shelly left, and was just opening her car door, when a van pulled into the drive. It was the building contractor, Brian Flannery; whom she immediately recognised.

"Hi there." Brian raised a hand to hail Shelly, cheerfully, in his unmistakeably Irish accent.

Looking around, he could see no sign of Meredith's car, which was inside the locked garage.

"Is Miss Wilde not in? I wanted to let her know I'll be getting started tomorrow."

Shelly was about to say 'yes, she's in'... but, instead chose to take the opportunity to pick up some information.

"What's the job that you're doing?"

Brian leaned on the door of his van.

"I'm digging out for the pond, down the back there."

He gestured with his eyes.

Shelly realised that she better let him know Meredith was at home:

"She's in. Her car's in the garage. Better ring the bell."

"Ah. Ok."

And Brian approached the door, as Shelly departed.

As she left the property, and drove the short journey to Crawley's, Shelly felt puzzled. Almost angry, that Meredith had become so cold and distant; when everything that Shelly had done, since first meeting her, was guided solely by the wish to keep her safe, and eliminate an appalling danger from her life, forever.

She thought again about the child's toy. She had been in that kitchen before, and never noticed the presence of anything remotely child-related. The house, she reflected, had always appeared to be one that was distinctly an 'adults only' dwelling. There was nothing 'child-friendly' or 'family-warm' about it. What, she wondered, caused Meredith to have what appeared to be child's toy there? Nephews or nieces visiting? She didn't know whether Meredith had any nephews or nieces. But, if that were the case, it would have been noted and recorded in the surveillance log. Perhaps a birthday present, bought and waiting for some young child? Shelly put it out of her mind, for now.

301

Chapter 51

Later that day, Shelly was sat at her desk, so deep in thought that it was almost a trance. She looked up in surprise, to see Dawn, who had just come into the office, stood in front of her.

"A lot to think about, eh?"

Dawn paused. She had been looking for Shelly earlier, but Shelly seemed to have disappeared for a while. She didn't mention that point, but continued:

"I'm bothered by things, too. Something's not right."

"You can say that again!" Exclaimed Shelly. "I'm just the same. It's driving me nuts. It's like something's going on right in front of our eyes, and we can't see it."

Dawn was relieved; she hadn't really wanted to raise her worries with Shelly, but felt the need to talk this over with someone. And, she never took her work home to her husband. Well, hardly ever.

Shelly made a suggestion: "Starbuck's?"

It was a place they occasionally went; only a few minutes from the office. Somewhere to chat. Semi-private, neutral territory, boss-free.

Half an hour later, they sat down, with coffee and the most indulgent cakes. They began to discuss what was on both of their minds. Why did things feel so odd? Meredith was under their protection. On the face of it, she was cooperating with them. And, yet...

Meredith seemed to have withdrawn into her own world. They knew that she had recently gone on a trip to Brent's garden centre, but had possibly deliberately thrown Tom off her track, so that she could disappear from their surveillance for a while. Why? They had no idea. Then, she had subsequently turned up at Brent's, and bought an insignificant pot-plant; despite having a florist's shop of her own.

302

Next, she had taken a trip to the shop at Lymm. Nothing wrong with that, of course. But, she had parked in an odd place, out of sight of anyone who might be watching the shop. Returning home, she had gone straight into the garage, and remotely closed the door behind her. Again, there was nothing wrong with this. No reason that she shouldn't... just that they had never seen her do that before.

Despite having been made welcome, initially, when calling on Meredith, Shelly now felt unwanted. She explained this to Dawn; not expecting sympathy – this wasn't about hurt feelings – it was just... a puzzle.

Also, there was the issue with Meredith's cameras. At first, she had seemed willing to allow the surveillance team to have almost unrestricted access to a visual cover of her property. Now, though, she was constantly switching the units off; taking complete control over what they could see, and when.

There was the unrelated matter – if it was unrelated – of the disappearance of a man who had some tenuous connection to Meredith. Lee Dann, from Yorkshire, was the proprietor of the company which maintained her alarm system. There was no real link established here, by anyone. Maybe he had left his wife. Maybe he had come to some harm. Either way, it was probably nothing at all to do with Meredith. But, it was just one more teasing puzzler. One more loose end.

Finally, Shelly remembered yet one more point that had caught her attention.

"I noticed today, that there was a child's toy, in Meredith's kitchen. I never noticed any sign of children visiting, before."

Dawn raised her eyes, puzzled: "Well, there are certainly no children visiting. Meredith doesn't seem to have any children in her life. What sort of toy?"

Shelly tried to describe it:

"A little princess, or 'my little pony' type thing. Girly."

Then, the thought struck them both, at the same time. Shelly spelt it out:

"Maybe Gabriel's... a gift for his daughter."

"Hmm... maybe."

Shelly added, partly in jest: "Even the gardener seems to have disappeared."

"Don't!" Exclaimed Dawn, with a grin.

"Something else came to my mind, Dawn." Shelly continued.

"We know he has threatened his victims with a knife. Some sort of nasty looking army knife; both in England and in Fuerteventura. Yes?"

Dawn nodded.

"But, how would he get a knife into Fuerteventura, through airport security? He couldn't could he?"

"Good point." Remarked Dawn.

"So, does that mean he has access to weapons when he's on the island?" Suggested Shelly.

Dawn shrugged: "I think it's more likely that he bought himself a knife while he was over there. Not sure where he would get one... but I suppose you can obtain a knife there, as easily as you can here."

"Hmm."

The two sat in silence, for a few moments, then attacked their cakes. Having digested a mouthful, Dawn asked: "What do you make of Meredith's father, the colonel?"

Shelly sipped her coffee, and thought hard:

"I should imagine he must have had a big influence over her, at one time. But, I think she outgrew that. Became very much her own woman. I don't know. Maybe he still has sway over her. I wonder what he thought when granny left an inheritance like that to Meredith."

Dawn's phone pinged to announce a message. She picked it up to look at it.

"The boss." She announced to Shelly.

Before Shelly could reply, her own phone bleeped, too. She grabbed it from her pocket, to read the same message that Dawn had received:

'Lee Danns van found 3 miles from Merediths Get in now'

"Shit!" They both exclaimed, jumping up.

Dawn called the office to let DI Williams know they were both heading back. As soon as they reached base, he filled them in on the details; which had been too much and too slow to put into an urgent text message.

Earlier that morning, a dog walker had reported seeing a vehicle, almost completely submerged in a lagoon, on the fringe of Denmoss quarry; which was barely three miles away from *Freelands,* in Lymm. Finally getting to investigate the call, which hadn't been seen as the highest priority, given the pressure on the emergency services; the van had been identified as the one registered to Lee Dann. There was nobody inside the vehicle. The position of it suggested that it had been deliberately dumped into the lagoon. It was a spot where other vehicles – stolen or unwanted – had been ditched in the past, or sometimes simply burned out and left in the nearby ditches.

"Any indication how long it's been there?" Asked Dawn.

DI Williams didn't have that information, yet: "No idea. But, let's work on the assumption that he's alive. The divers will be searching in that water soon; but it may not be until tomorrow morning. And he's very much a person of interest in our case. In the meantime, go see Meredith, and let her know. Frank's digging up everything he can on Lee Dann."

At that moment, Frank, who had been studying his screen, let out a gasp.

"Shelly! Look!"

Shelly hurried over to his desk, and her eyes followed his, to the screen in front of him. He was looking at the website of Lee Dann's company, BeSecure. Frank pointed at the company's logo; which was at the top of the page, and visible again on the image of a company van, and declared:

"Haven't we seen that before?"

Shelly looked at it. It did look familiar, but where from? Frank filled in the gaps:

"When we went out to Bernard Shay Tower, to see Bev Mitchell. There was a sign... we thought the BS referred to Bernard Shay..."

"Shit!" Shelly exclaimed. "You're right. It's him! That's how he got to Bev Mitchell. How he got through her front door. His company do the security for Bernard Shay Tower!"

On the other side of the Pennines, DS Martha Wade and her colleague DC David Drew were ringing the doorbell of Samantha and Lee Dann's house. When they were admitted, an anxious Samantha, bleary-eyed through lack of sleep and tearful days, sat down in a daze.

The officers gave Lee's wife the news, that his vehicle had been found. His vehicle, but not him. Those were the latest facts; anything more would be speculation. But, there was something else they had to speak about. A question they wanted to ask her. Something that their colleague in Manchester had asked them to raise. Had Lee ever been to Fuerteventura, or Lanzarote? Samantha was baffled by the question. At this time, when she was fearful for Lee's very life, the police wanted to ask about their holidays?

"Yes, we've been to Fuerteventura. We went there for our honeymoon."

"And, when was that?" Martha made a note in her pad.

"2008. And we've been back three times, since then."

"Uh-huh. What dates were you there in 2008?"

"July. The second and third weeks of July."

On further enquiry, Samantha Dann was able to give them some of the other dates on which she and Lee had been to the Canaries. The information was passed directly to DI Williams, who received the call, stony-faced, stood at his desk.

"Okay. Thanks for that."

306

He put the phone down, and turned to face his team, who were silent, almost holding their breath.

"The dates fit. It looks like he could be our man."

Dave was already at Crawley's, and Dawn was speeding over to join him. Williams turned to Shelly, who had not yet left the office.

"Get the picture that we have of him sent over to Fuerteventura. Ask your contact there to take it to…" He paused, trying to place the name.

"Adora Cranda." Filled in Shelly.

She sprang to her computer, and was about to start a communication, when she realised that she needed to get this to someone who would appreciate the urgency, and deal with it immediately. It was already late in the afternoon, and this wasn't something that wanted to sit on the shelf until tomorrow. So, instead, she picked her phone out of her pocket, and stepped out of the room, to call a private number. Listening to the rhythmic ringing at the other end of the line, Shelly muttered to herself:

"Come on! Pick up!"

Presently, her call was answered; and the voice of Millie Rodriguez greeted her. On hearing the latest developments, Millie was eager to help.

"Send it to me. I'll get in touch with her today."

"Thanks, Millie, I owe you one. Again."

Shelly stepped back into the office.

"She's on it, Boss. I'll call you as soon as she gets back to me."

"Okay, get on the phone to Meredith. Tell her about Lee Dann's van, but no more about him, and that we've increased the surveillance, then, get over there. Get inside the house if she'll let you, and keep your head down."

"Boss."

307

Driving over towards Meredith's house, Shelly called her on the phone, from her car.

"Hello? Oh, hello Shelly."

Meredith didn't seem too thrilled to receive the call. Ignoring her tone, Shelly began:

"Meredith, you remember the man we asked you about? The boss of the alarm company, who went missing recently? Well, his car has been found close to where you live."

She paused, to allow Meredith to take this in; and heard a muttered expletive at the other end of the line.

Shelly continued: "There's no need for you to worry. We've got extra officers nearby. Uniform have been alerted. Dawn and Dave are both at Crawley's. I'm heading over to your house now. I want to come and…"

Meredith interrupted:

"But, why do you think he's got anything to do with this? With Gabriel?"

Shelly hesitated:

"There are some things we don't know for sure, yet. But, he's looking like our prime suspect. So, we need to find him, and pick him up."

"You think he's still in the area?" Meredith's voice was calm.

"Well, we don't know. But, without his car… although, it's possible he's moved to another vehicle…"

"Ah, well." Meredith gave what sounded like a fairly relaxed sigh: "I can't see that he's got anything to do with this. I'm not worried."

Shelly tutted, to herself. Meredith wasn't making this easy. As she was trying to find the words to appeal again for an invitation to come and wait inside *Freelands*, just in case an unwanted visitor should turn up, Meredith went on:

"Of course, I've got my safe room. Nobody can get to me in there. I'll leave the cameras covering all the approaches. If he... if anyone should come near, you'll see him."

Then, abruptly, she added: "I'll have to go, I left a tap running. I'm not going anywhere tonight... speak to you later."

The phone went dead, to Shelly's frustration.

Chapter 52

As darkness approached, and rain began to fall outside, Mariana Navarro peered warily through the vertical venetian blinds, which were already in the closed position. She flicked on the light switch, and turned to see two ornate wall lights flash into action. The room was luxurious; higher quality than she herself could ever afford. Turning towards the wall-mounted television, which was playing the umpteenth episode of Pepper Pig, she sat down on the seductively soft couch, and stroked the hair of her daughter's head.

"You alright, Izzy?"

Izzy barely responded. Daddy Pig had just splashed into a muddy puddle, and she chuckled at his embarrassment.

Mariana looked across at the large double bed, on which her rucksack had been deposited; leaning against a construction of thick, soft pillows. Next to it, Izzy's small backpack was laying open, with some of her toys spilling out.

"Early night, tonight, darling." She whispered softly into her daughter's ear.

"Why are we here, Mummy?"

"I told you, sweetheart. Mummy has something to do, tonight. Then, we'll be going home, tomorrow. We'll be going on the train again. You like that, don't you?"

Izzy's expression betrayed no excitement about another train journey, but she resumed watching the antics of Pepper and her porcine family.

There was a gentle tap at the bedroom door, and it eased open, to reveal a calm and smiling face:

"Ready for something to eat?"

Mariana nodded, and looked at Izzy:

"I think this one is."

All the blinds at all the windows were now closed, and the heavy curtains drawn. The outside world would remain outside. Whatever might happen inside the house, was private, secret, and not to be shared with anyone.

In the kitchen, Izzy enjoyed a slice of garlic bread, a small bowl of pasta, and a selection of cheesy nibbles. Mariana had little appetite, but was glad to see her daughter relaxed, and eating her meal. Their host sat back in her chair, and smiled warmly at Izzy. Quiet, patient; conscious that there was something important to be done, this evening.

"What's Applejack doing here, sweetheart?" Asked Mariana.

She stepped to the worktop, and picked up the orange 'my little pony' character.

"Naughty pony."

She placed it on the table, in front of Izzy; who continued to munch on a cheesy breadstick, with Applejack perched on the edge of her plate.

"What time does Izzy go to bed?" Asked Meredith.

Mariana looked at her daughter.

"We'll be getting settled about seven."

Izzy followed up her savoury main course with fruit salad and cream. She certainly enjoyed her meal in this huge and impressive house. An hour later, and she was showing signs of tiredness. Her mother bathed her, dressed her for bed, and curled up with her to settle her down on the double bed that they were going to share. Listening to a story from her favourite book, it wasn't long before Izzy's eyes became heavy, and her grip on Applejack soon relaxed. Mariana recognised the weary sign in her little hands, and tucked them gently under the bedclothes. She turned down the lighting, leaving only a single wall light to provide some radiance for the sleeping Izzy. Mariana softly kissed her daughter's head, and left her alone; leaving the bedroom door slightly ajar, just like at home.

311

On the landing, Mariana saw a framed picture, glinting in the reflected light of a small chandelier, that hung at the head of the stairs. She had noticed the picture when Meredith had shown her to her bedroom, earlier; but had not paused to inspect it. Now, she studied the scene. Two soldiers in combat gear were sat astride a sandy-coloured jeep or troop carrier, which was festooned with leaves and branches. It looked like one of those occasions when serving soldiers needed a short break from the tension, or perhaps a relief from the tedium of an interminable stakeout. Either way, these warriors were taking a moment away from duty; having a laugh about something. Mariana recognised that one of them was Meredith; but, had no idea who the other shaven-headed young man might be.

A voice close by startled her.

"That was Greg and me, in Kabul." Meredith explained, joining Mariana to look at the picture.

She sighed wistfully.

"He didn't make it back. An IED." She added.

"I'm sorry." Murmured Mariana. "It killed him outright?"

"Oh, no. But, it took his leg clean off. Blasted a hole in him. He would never have walked again; been lucky to feed himself, or even stand up. I couldn't let him suffer. He was a good man. A good mate. He wouldn't have wanted to live like that."

She didn't conclude her account; leaving Mariana puzzled. As if sweeping the memory from her mind, and returning to duty, Meredith gently took hold of her guest's arm.

"Come."

She led Mariana along the landing, past the top of the stairs, and left; towards a darker passageway, with two doors on each side of it. Three of them were blank; but, on the fourth, a picture of a desk and computer introduced this as a study. Meredith opened the door, and flicked on a light, as the two entered. Mariana stopped, and caught her breath. Just a few metres away was the door of this house's innermost sanctuary, the safe room.

312

Although it was completely closed, something about the design, and the illuminated control indicators on it, made Mariana think of some futuristic space craft. She half expected it to glide open, and Captain Kirk, or other crew of the star-ship *Enterprise* to appear. They both stood, and eyed the door; then, Meredith stepped round to the control panel and monitor, on the other side of her desk. She pressed a couple of buttons, and looked at the screen, which was out of Mariana's view.

"Ready?" She asked; her voice calm, and reassuring.

Mariana hesitated, and nodded; with the words:

"You're sure it's safe?"

"Quite safe." Meredith assured her.

She pressed another button, and there was a little hiss, then a hint of a squeak, as the door began to glide smoothly open.

Unconsciously, Mariana grasped Meredith's arm, and stood slightly behind her, as if sheltering from some horrific danger.

"It's okay. He can't do anything." Meredith muttered, with a satisfied smirk.

The door was fully open, and Mariana, trembling slightly, gazed in wonder at what she had been invited to see.

Sat, slumped at a chair, with his arms handcuffed at his side, each separately manacled to a metal bracket, was a naked man. He half looked up to see his captor, then turned his face away, with what seemed to be a fierce scowl. It was hard to be sure, because his face was battered and bruised. Blood had streaked down from the top of his head, where he had clearly suffered a wound, part of a severe beating. His eyes were puffy and black; one of them nearly closed. His nose looked like it might be broken, and more blood had left him through his nostrils.

In addition to the manacles securing his arms, a leathery strap came firmly around his chest and back to the rear of the chair, holding him back in his seat. There was a plastic bucket on the floor in front of him; and metal shackles round each ankle made sure that he could barely move his feet. He wasn't going anywhere.

Mariana became aware of the stench that emanated from this pathetic creature; a mixture of sweat, body odour, and urine. As she sniffed, and put her hand to her face, Meredith recognised what she was thinking.

"Disgusting, isn't he? Why, I almost feel pity for him. Almost... but not quite."

She stepped closer, and picked up a can of air freshener. She held it up, and sprayed a sickly fragrance of lavender and summer flowers over him; as if she was using a fly spray to extinguish the life from an unwanted wasp. He turned his head away, but couldn't help choking and spluttering as he inhaled the heavy sweet scent. Meredith stopped spraying, and replaced the can on the shelf. The man continued to cough and splutter; gasping for breath.

Mariana looked on, as if observing an exhibit in a zoo; with interest and fascination, but no sympathy in her eyes.

"Not saying hello to your visitor?" Asked Meredith; approaching her captive, and lifting up his chin to look into his face.

"Where are your manners? You remember who this is, don't you?"

The wretch's sore eyes flicked from Meredith to Mariana, and he squinted, trying to focus on Mariana's face. He didn't appear to recognise her. She had never seen his face; but recognised him, the instant that he uttered his first words:

"Get off me!"

"Come on now, play nice. I think my friend may have a few questions for you."

Meredith sat back in a chair, regarding the prisoner, and turned to Mariana.

"I asked him some questions, yesterday. He didn't seem to want to talk to me. Not at first. But then we had some fun, didn't we, Lee Dann?"

Lee's body twitched, and he shuffled painfully in his chair, at the memory of what Meredith had done to him, the previous day.

Mariana stepped closer to him, more confident now; knowing that the man who had attacked her, seventeen months ago, could do her no harm today. Screwing her face up in disgust, she stood over him; and could see the bruising and abrasions on his bare flesh. His thighs were a purple and black colour, where Meredith had inflicted her violence upon him.

Seeing Mariana inspect him, Meredith chuckled:

"I learnt a few things in the army. Picked up a few skills. Not all good things. Not the skills they tell you about in the recruitment adverts. It's amazing what a man will do, when you handle him in a certain way, eh Lee?"

Barely acknowledging what Meredith was saying, and seemingly fascinated by the helpless creature in front of her, Mariana almost spat at him:

"Remember me, yet?!"

He cast a shifty look up at her, and squirmed. He said nothing.

"It's okay to tell him." Said Meredith, quietly. "He's not going to be making any complaints if you aren't polite to him. And, he'll need to know, so that he can answer the questions you want to ask him."

Mariana continued to glare at the man in the chair.

Meredith continued:

"He answered my questions. It came easily, didn't it, Lee. Once we got to know each other a little bit."

She paused, leaned forward, and picked up a solid wooden stick; as if it just happened to be there, close at hand. She stood up, and placed the stick gently on Lee's head, resting it there. A reminder, perhaps, of what she could use it for, if she chose. She smiled at him.

Then, in a flash, she swung the stick hard, bringing it crashing into the side of his face. The force of the blow would have knocked him from his chair, if he hadn't been strapped securely in. Blood spattered from his head, as he let out a yell. Meredith stood over him, continuing to look down on him, with an apparently kind smile.

Mariana jumped back, in shock. She watched him, spluttering and spitting out blood. She was as shocked by Meredith's action as by the violent impact on Lee's head.

Meredith, expressionless now, commented:

"I asked him where Gabriel was. At first, he didn't want to say. But then, when he began to talk, I could hardly stop him. So, when he's got his story straight about your husband, we can get ready do what he really loves to do."

The women looked at each other. Meredith explained:

"Make a movie. And this time, he'll be the star of it. Without a mask. We must send a copy to his wife, as well as to the police."

"Did you kill him?!" Shouted Mariana. "What did you do to him?"

Lee, still wheezing and spluttering blood, barely able to see straight, and with a throbbing head, moaned helplessly.

"You don't even know who I am, do you?" Mariana challenged him.

"Vito Navarro. My husband. He was found dead in a reservoir in Cumbria. How did he get there? Did you put him there? Did you kill him? Why?"

The torrent of questions may have come at him faster than he could have answered them, even if he had been fully composed. However, they did now make clear what this woman's interest might be in him... who she was. Through blood streaked eyes, he tried to look again at Mariana, more closely this time.

She cringed, feeling her skin crawl, as she imagined him recalling the night he had terrorised her, invaded her body, taken away her dignity, destroyed her whole life.

Almost hoarse, her vocal chords sore and spent, she pleaded once more:

"Why? Why Vito? Why me? What have we ever done to you?"

316

Mariana fell silent. Meredith's fingers closed around the wooden stick, again; as a warning to Lee that the time for him to provide some answers had arrived.

To Mariana's surprise, and Meredith's satisfaction, he spoke; in a raspy, wheezing tone:

"Because he was Spanish. I did you a favour."

The women stared at him.

Finally, Mariana demanded:

"What do you mean?"

He looked up at her, mournfully, through the saddest eyes. After a sideways glance at Meredith, he explained:

"A Spaniard ruined my life. Twenty-five years ago. Used me. Treated me like a dog. I was a child. If I could have caught up with him, I would have…"

He paused to gasp and splutter.

"But, I never caught him. So, his brothers, his cousins, his family… they've paid instead."

He turned to look at Meredith, who smirked at him, and said, with a chuckle:

"He has no idea how I came to be ready for him. Ready to welcome him to my humble home. Shall I tell him?"

Mariana didn't respond, so Meredith continued, anyway:

"The police realised that you've been killing Spanish men, on the twenty-third of July every year. And…"

She tailed off. Then, as a question had come to her:

"Why July twenty-third? Why that date?"

Surly, with a foul glare, but not wishing to court further treatment from Meredith, with her wooden stick, he replied:

"It was his birthday. Each year, on his birthday, he would celebrate, get drunk, and then…"

Meredith and Mariana watched him. His face was battered; he had black eyes and blood-stained cheeks. And yet… could it be that his eyes were glistening with fresh tears, at the memory of something, years ago?

"What?" Demanded Meredith, standing tall over him, and brandishing the stick threateningly. "Spit it out!"

She appeared to chuckle; realising that, with every word that he spoke, he was indeed spitting out blood and saliva.

"He abused me. He was a sick pervert. He abused me. He would have done it to my little sister, if I hadn't taken it…"

For a second, Mariana felt a flicker of sympathy for this wretch. She imagined the little boy inside him; cowering, terrified, screaming for mercy. She looked at Meredith; who, clearly, felt no such emotion, and simply lifted up the stick, again, to rest it on his head.

He grimaced, and tensed up; expecting the stick to come crashing down on him again. Instead, she asked, calmly:

"Is that what we should do to you again, Lee? The feelings that have been inside you, all these years, that motivated you to kill our men… should we remind you of them? Take you back to those days?"

She turned to Mariana, adding:

"Easily done. We can put him over that table, face down, and remind him what it was like to be taken from behind. What do you think?"

Mariana had turned pale, almost white. She couldn't decide which was the most horrific: this evil murderous rapist, or the side of Meredith that she was now witnessing. A woman… someone who could batter and terrorise a helpless human being… one who had been traumatised as a child… without even a hint of emotion or sympathy. Her feelings of hatred

318

towards the chained up snivelling wretch in front of her were gradually ebbing away. They were being replaced by revulsion, and fear, at what she was seeing in Meredith.

She sat down, slumping into her chair, and gasped: "I can't do this."

Meredith observed her, calmly.

"It's okay. I know you're not used to anything like this. But for the army, I wouldn't be either. We'll just get some answers for you... then you can leave the rest to me, if you want to. He's still yours, if you want him."

She turned to Lee.

"Well? What did you do to Mariana's husband? How did you kill him?"

She brandished her wooden weapon, again.

Lee flicked a glance at Mariana; realising, perhaps, that she was not going to be as hard on him as Meredith, and that he might do well not to antagonise her any more than was necessary.

"I drowned him. He was easy. It was quick."

Meredith commented:

"All good rehearsal, this; for when we make the video, and he confesses to all of them."

Mariana's face was still pale, and sickly. But, tears had begun to trickle down.

"Has he told you what he did to your Gabriel?"

Meredith nodded:

"Oh, yes. He's explained all that. And, we just need him to run through all the others, then this can soon be over. We won't need to put him through any more pain. All done. You'll be glad about that, won't you, Lee?"

He blinked at her, without a word.

Chapter 53

Stepping into Crawley's, Shelly was met by Dawn and Dave, who were studying the monitor. She put her white jacket down, on the back of a chair.

"Have you spoken to her?" Dawn asked.

Shelly grimaced.

"She's not really engaging with us, much. It's almost like she's gone into denial. She doesn't believe Lee Dann has anything to do with this."

At that moment, Shelly's phone rang, and she picked up.

"Millie, hi."

Dave and Dawn watched Shelly's response, as she listened to what her contact in Fuerteventura was telling her. The facial expressions made it pretty clear; but, after thanking Millie and concluding the call, Shelly faced them.

"It's him. Millie gave Adora a line-up of ten pictures to look at, and she picked him out instantly."

"Bingo!" Exclaimed Dawn. "Let the boss know."

DI Williams' relief at receiving the news was obvious:

"Right, at least we know who we are after. But this is far from over. Now, we have to find him. We'll arrange to show his picture to the other women; but, for now, go tell Meredith that we have a positive ID."

Shelly left immediately, not even pausing to collect her jacket; and drove round to Meredith's house. The autumnal evening had settled; and *Freelands* was now in darkness, as the lights of Shelly's car picked out the shadowy trees which stood to attention in the garden.

She decided that she wanted to speak to Meredith, face to face; so, instead of calling ahead, she went to the door, and rang the bell. Stood,

320

waiting on the step, Shelly looked up towards the camera, positioned over the door. She glanced round, at the bay window of the big lounge, with its curtains drawn, and no light emerging. A chink of light at an upstairs window caught her eye, and she looked up, to see the twitching of a curtain. About to mutter, under her breath: 'It's only me Meredith', she suddenly gasped.

Caught for a brief second in the light from inside the upper room, Shelly spotted the face of a child. A little girl. Stepping backwards, and almost stumbling over the step, which caused her to take her eyes off what she had seen; Shelly then looked up again. The curtain had closed.

At that moment, the front door opened, and Meredith looked out, with a calm look on her face.

"Hello Shelly. Come in."

Shelly's mouth dropped open, in astonishment. Had she really seen a child, up at that window? Or was the light playing tricks? No, she was sure she had seen a little girl.

Meredith stepped back, drawing Shelly inside. Shelly's voice was unsteady:

"Did I just see a little girl, upstairs? Who's that?"

Meredith's countenance barely changed, and she simply proceeded to close the door, gently. Shelly's mind was spinning. The little girl's face... was it someone she recognised? Only a brief glimpse; but, she had surely seen this little girl before. Shelly looked at the main staircase; feeling the impulse to rush headlong up those stairs, locate the right bedroom, and see for herself who Meredith's mysterious visitor might be. There was something incredibly strange about...

Crash!

"Ohhh!"

Shelly's body went reeling sideways; and she collided against the bannister, with a thud, before crumbling to the floor. Standing menacingly over her, with a stout wooden stick in her hand; Meredith inspected the damage, as Shelly, dazed and dizzy, slumped back against the wall. The

321

room swirled and faded from her focus, blurring into darkness, as Shelly lost consciousness.

Back in Crawley's, Dave had watched Shelly's car drive into *Freelands,* and park up close to Meredith's garage. He had seen her slim figure step out, and be admitted to the house. From the distance of the camera placement, he hadn't seen anything of Shelly's attention being taken towards the upstairs window.

Scratching his head, puzzled, Dave looked at Dawn:

"I can't understand why he would dump his van. Do you think he's got another car, that he left somewhere round here? And, if he has, why?"

"I don't know. But I know we need to pick him up. The boss wants us to maintain discreet observation, for now. Even though we know who he is, now; our best chance of apprehending him may still be if we can get him to approach her house. And that means us keeping out of sight."

Dave nodded, and looked back at the screen.

The images rotated round; the front view temporarily flicking off, to be replaced by a panoramic view of the dark garden. Then, the front view came back. After a few moments, he saw the front door of *Freelands* open, and watched the unmistakeable figure of Shelly come down the steps, get into her car, and turn on the lights. Then, it performed a careful manoeuvre to turn round, and drove out of the grounds of Meredith's house.

"Looks like she's on her way back." Commented Dave.

The screen image flickered again, and the lighting seemed to change. Probably the camera adjusting to a beam of light that Shelly's car had shot towards it, distorting the focus, he decided.

For a few minutes, Dawn and Dave watched the screen. It remained covering the front driveway, looking towards the house. At one point, it flickered, and the contrast level seemed to change, again; then it settled down, and appeared to give them a clear view of the house.

Dawn glanced at the time on her phone:

322

"I wonder how come she's not back, yet?"

Dave looked up.

"Hmm. Taking her time, isn't she? Has she taken the other direction, and gone back to the office?"

The drive from *Freelands* to Crawley's was a few short minutes, and yet, after ten, there was no sign of Shelly.

Dawn picked up her phone, and dialled. The call failed.

"That's strange. Her phone's off."

She called DI Williams, instead.

"Boss, have you told Shelly to come back in to base?"

"No." Replied Williams. "I wanted her to stay with Meredith, or come back to you."

"Ah, that's odd. She seems to have taken off somewhere. She went to speak to Meredith, then we saw her drive off; but she hasn't come back here."

Williams grunted:

"Have you called her?"

"Yes. Can't get through."

"Hum. Well, let me know when you find her. This isn't the time to go AWOL."

Chapter 54

Inside *Freelands*, Shelly groaned. She opened her eyes, and her head hurt, as if a metal spike was poking into the left side of her skull. She groaned again, and screwed up her face as the sickly taste of something that she must have drunk lingered on her palate. Shelly squinted as she started to focus on what was in front of her, and wondered how long she had been unconscious.

The room in which she was sat, she now recognised as Meredith's panic room. She became aware that her hands were tied firmly behind her back. As she tugged, the wire core of the ties dug into her wrists. She looked across the room; where, just a few feet away from her, sat a man, watching her. Naked, battered and bruised, tied up even more securely than her. She gasped, as, even through the bruising and blood stains, she recognised that this was the man that she had seen a picture of, Lee Dann.

"You…" She began. But then she stopped. There were so many questions, she didn't know where to start.

The two eyed each other. Finally, Lee Dann spoke.

"She's crazy." He rasped. "She's going to kill me. You too."

Shelly tried to make sense of what she was seeing and hearing. Just as she was opening her mouth to say something, the automatic door hissed, and slid open. They both turned, to see who or what was about to come in.

Meredith stood in the doorway, with a mobile phone in her hand. Shelly recognised it as her own phone. Meredith had removed the battery from it, and placed both phone and battery on a shelf.

"You won't be needing this." She commented.

"Meredith… what's going on?"

Meredith pressed the control button, and the door slid closed; leaving the three of them inside the room.

Meredith smiled, brightly:

324

"We got our man. Our little plan worked. In fact, it worked even better than you might have expected."

She looked at her male captive, and thumbed in his direction:

"Meet Lee Dann. Murderer, rapist, and all round typical man."

Shelly looked at him.

"I know who he is. We'd identified him, and we were ready to catch him, as soon as he came anywhere near here."

Meredith chuckled.

"Well, I've saved you the trouble, haven't I?"

Shelly tried to remain calm.

"Untie me, Meredith. I don't know why you've..."

Meredith interrupted:

"Untie you, and what? Let you arrest this pathetic creature, put him in handcuffs, march him off to court? Then, if you're lucky, get a conviction for multiple murder and rape?"

She gave a withering glance in his direction.

"And then what?" She stepped closer to Shelly, and brought her face up close in front of her. "Then what?"

Shelly saw a crazed expression on her face... the look of pure hatred in her eyes. She tried to give the sort of reply that she thought Meredith would want to hear:

"He'll go down for life. Spend the rest of his life behind bars. And, you helped to achieve that justice for all the men and women he's attacked. For Gabriel."

Meredith scoffed:

"Prison? You think he should be kept in prison, at our expense? A nice comfy cell? Reading books, watching television, looked after? You call that 'justice', do you?"

Shelly didn't reply.

Meredith continued:

"No, he's not going to enjoy the sort of justice that you would give him. He's going to die. Soon, but not quick."

She turned to him.

"We've already made our little movie, haven't we, Lee? While you were out... I gave you a little something to help you sleep for a couple of hours, Shelly."

Although it was still throbbing and muzzy, thoughts were starting to become clearer in Shelly's head. She realised now that the sickly taste in her mouth was the aftermath of some drug that she had been given.

"But, they know I'm here. My colleagues will be coming for me..."

She hesitated; wondering why, if she had been here for a couple of hours, as Meredith said, they hadn't already come to find her.

"Well, they saw you come here, Shelly. But, they also saw you leave."

She grinned. Shelly didn't understand; so, Meredith explained:

"Those cameras of mine, they are brilliant, don't you think? It took me a while to get used to them; but, after I mastered them, they've been fantastic."

Shelly still looked bemused, as Meredith laughed.

"You still don't get it, do you? You nearly caught me out, once. You told me my grandmother clock had stopped... then you were a bit surprised to find that it was ticking along perfectly well. That's because, whenever I want, I change the live video feed, that you've been watching, to a still frame. A shot of the bottom of my staircase looks just the same, whether it's live video, or a still shot."

She chuckled, again.

"So, whenever I want to do something without you seeing, I just show you a still frame, and you think you're watching live TV."

Shelly began to understand.

"The trickiest times are when it's getting dark. If I want to put on a still frame for a few minutes, to hide what I do, I have to get it back on quick, before the light deteriorates. Or you'll see that it got dark very suddenly."

A few things were starting to make sense. However, Shelly couldn't see how Meredith's camera tricks would have deceived Dawn and Dave into believing that she had left the house.

"I have quite a collection of little snippets, now, that I can play for your mates. So, after you came here tonight, while you were taking your little nap, I played a clip of you getting into your car, and driving away."

She continued:

"So, you see, they saw you drive off. And now they are probably wondering how you disappeared into thin air. You are currently absent without leave."

She chuckled.

Shelly looked at Lee Dann, who was watching, and listening.

"But, Meredith; they know that *he's* around here. They'll come and search your house for him. For me."

Meredith grinned.

"Well, they would, if his confession hadn't already been filmed and sent to them, to throw them off the scent. I sent it, in an email, through an anonymous route, of course, less than an hour ago. A copy to the police, and a copy to his wife."

Shelly challenged her:

"They will easily trace where an email came from. They'll be here any minute."

"Normally, yes. The source of an email can be traced. But, I learned a few things about communications in the army. And, with the help of an old colleague of my father's, I was able to route it through so many hoops that they'll never find the source."

Shelly thought quickly, and tried another approach:

"Why, Meredith? You might not think much of the justice system; but, why involve me in this? Kidnapping a police officer... and, if you've taped his confession, they'll be able to use that against him..."

Meredith shook her head, sadly.

"The film of his confession... he spills everything out. But, I know that wouldn't be admissible in evidence. I think there might just be some suggestion of coercion, don't you? No, that was just for information only. And, for the pleasure of seeing him squirm. Squirm, he did. And, apparently he likes to star in movies, doesn't he?"

Shelly was about to comment, but paused, as another memory was coming back to her... another question:

"The little girl! Who was the little girl? Why have you got a child here, Meredith?"

Meredith sighed.

"It's a pity you saw her, Shelly. If you hadn't seen her, I might have been able to get rid of you, without you getting involved in all this. But, you saw her."

She continued:

"She's Mariana's daughter, Izzy."

Shelly gasped. Of course! Only a brief glimpse, but that was why the little girl looked familiar.

"How do you know Mariana? No one has ever put you in contact with Mariana, or any of the other victims."

Meredith, smug, now:

"You came here one day, and you took a call on your phone from DS Pardell. Your speaker-phone was on. She said something about Mariana Navarro, and her husband Vito. Very Spanish names... it wasn't rocket science to figure out that they were victims. So I googled the names, and found the report of him going missing. Then, with the help of an old colleague, I was able to locate her."

Shelly cursed herself for being so unprofessional as to allow the name of somebody, in such a sensitive case, to reach the wrong ears.

Meredith was in full flow, and continued with her explanation:

"So, I went to visit Mariana. The day your colleague followed me to Brent's. You should have seen his face when I went twice round the roundabout! He was petrified that I might clock him. It's a short trip from Brent's to Tyldesley, where Mariana lives."

Shelly nodded, understanding more and more.

"And, today, Mariana came to Lymm, where I picked her up. I left a key to my car in a little spot where she could pick it up, while I was inside my shop. They tucked themselves in, out of sight, before I went back to the car, in case I was followed. Which I was, as I knew I would be. Izzy enjoyed playing the hiding game. Then, when we got back here, I put the car in the garage, and they came inside the house through the inner door."

Shelly was listening to all of this; feeling sick to the core.

"So, is Mariana here?"

"Oh, yes." Confirmed Meredith. "She's here. It was a pleasure to introduce her to our friend here, so that she could see how low he has sunk."

329

Shelly shivered, realising the vulnerability of her position. She had the protection of being a police officer. Yet... how much was that protection really worth? In a situation like this, did it even mean anything?

"Back to the 'why' question." Resumed Meredith.

"You remember looking at that picture upstairs... my grandfather, with Monsieur LeVelle, who saved him and his men at Dunkirk?"

Shelly nodded; with no idea what relevance that could have to what Meredith was up to.

"I tried to explain to you, then, what family honour means to this family. I told you that we always pay our dues... we don't sit back and wait for someone else to pay for us. Well, today you're seeing an example. That thing..." She gestured towards Lee...

"He incurred a debt by what he did to my Gabriel. What he would have done to me, given half a chance. So, what I intend to do, is pay him back what he deserves. With interest. That's what we do... we look after ourselves. Pay our way."

There was a glazed look in Meredith's eye, as if she was being drawn away by some memory... perhaps something that dwelt inside her and spoke into her ear with a deceptive voice, falsely pretending to be her friend.

"My car." Said Shelly. "They will see that my car is still here."

Meredith chuckled, softly.

"What they will see is that your car *isn't* here, Shelly. When I flicked the camera off, I moved your car out of sight into my garage. There's no reason for them to go searching in there. Their attention will be taken well away from that, so that I can get rid of your car, later."

She looked directly into Shelly's eyes.

"I'm sorry that I need to do this to you. But, you brought it on yourself. You are supposed to 'serve and protect'... that's your motto, isn't it?"

Shelly nodded.

"But, you didn't serve and protect all those innocent men and women, did you? You didn't protect Gabriel. You didn't protect Mariana."

She leaned forward, and stroked Shelly's head. Shelly recoiled, in disgust.

"Not just you, of course. But the police force, of which you are a part. So, you have to pay the price for all of them. They like you, don't they? You're one of the family... the police family. They will all feel the pain."

Trying to keep a clear head, and stay as calm as she could, drawing on all her experience, Shelly asked:

"Is Mariana okay? You haven't hurt Mariana, have you?"

"No, of course not. She's fine. She enjoyed listening to him make his confession. Enjoyed watching him squirm, I think. Well, who wouldn't? I did ask her if she wants to help dismember him, while he's still alive. Cut a little piece off him, as a souvenir. But, perhaps she's not quite up to that. Maybe just pull the trigger. She will feel the satisfaction, when she does that. For Vito."

Although Shelly couldn't see this, a blurred and painful memory caused the room to darken around Meredith, as she retreated into her past. Only the heat and the bright glow from a single lamp shone directly into her face. Her arms were tied up, over her head; the iron hook that was built into her cell bearing the weight of her body, as she hung, almost lifeless from the beating at the hands of three masked men, with her wrists strapped together.

This rancid, foul-smelling dungeon, stifling in the heat, and far from her real home – far from anywhere – in the heart of Afghanistan, was her present abode. She might as well call it home.

The top half of her army uniform had been sliced from her body with savage knives, and ripped open at the front, not caring where they had cut into her shoulders and arms. Her khaki vest was torn almost clean off, as her captors had invaded and tormented her body, taking away her dignity for their own entertainment. She wanted to cry, to call out for someone to come and help; someone to make it better. But, no; she wouldn't give her captors the satisfaction of seeing her beaten. There was nothing that she

331

couldn't endure. Nothing, short of death, that she would accept as a means to end her torture. What was death, anyway? Nothing to fear… simply release. Victory.

"Where is she?" Asked Shelly.

Startled back into the present… to the situation where *she* was the one in total control, Meredith answered:

"With her daughter. Maybe you'll see her soon. To say goodbye."

With that, she got up, and turned towards the door, then paused:

"Perhaps you're wondering how I got the better of our friend here?"

Shelly looked at Lee. Although at this moment he was weak and helpless, he must be a strong man; not that easy for her to overpower. Plus, how had she got him into the house, unseen? More camera tricks?

Meredith went on, apparently determined to tell Shelly, anyway; almost showing off at her cleverness.

"I've been on high alert for weeks, of course. But I had no idea who he was; until, one day, the other guy came to service my alarm. To make some change to the bell-box; which I was suspicious of, because I knew there was no need. He was working outside, and I heard him talking on his phone, as I was at my window."

Shelly was puzzled, but listening.

"The guy was asking his boss about something, asking him why he had to connect it up in a certain way. I smelt a rat there and then. And, when he was told that it would be over-ridden from the other end, I knew that couldn't be right. So, I watched, and I waited. I knew he was coming. I decided that, if it was me, I would get to this house from the bottom lane, across the stream, through the orchard, and in across the back lawn. So, I waited for him to come, and sure enough, he did."

She smiled sweetly at Lee.

"I had a welcome ready for you, didn't I?"

Lee looked away.

Having concluded her explanation, Meredith came back to the present:

"I'm sorry, Shelly. You're not the worst person, I know that. But... you took on the responsibility of being a police officer. I guess it goes with the job."

The door hissed, and swept open. Meredith stepped out, and the door moved back into place, locking shut with a click.

Chapter 55

In Crawley's Dawn picked up her phone to receive a call.

"Boss. Any news?"

"We've received an email. It contains a video; a filmed confession from Lee Dann."

"What!?"

"I'll forward it to you, now. Call me back when you've watched it."

He cut the line; but, after a few moments, Dawn's phone bleeped again, to announce the arrival of an email. Dawn opened it up, and took a deep breath, as she and Dave started to view the contents of the attached video.

Sat behind a table, wearing what seemed to be a somewhat tight-fitting white t-shirt, and in a poorly-lit room, Lee Dann was just about recognisable. He was looking at a sheet of paper which was placed on the table in front of him. This was apparently the script, from which he was going to read out what he had to say. The room – his makeshift studio – was shadowy; with a curtain behind him, in a slightly blue-green hue, as a backdrop. For a split second the lighting increased, causing him to screw up his eyes, momentarily; as a bright torch or perhaps an angle-poise lamp was turned in his direction. The colour of the turquoise curtain behind him caught the light, for a fraction of a second. Nobody else was visible in the range of the camera.

Lee looked directly into the camera, and prepared to speak. The lighting remained low; but his face was noticeably bruised, and stained. He gave a little cough, as a preliminary, and began to read from the paper.

"My name is Lee Dann. I wish to confess to the following crimes."

Dawn and Dave watched and listened, in silence, and astonishment.

Lee glanced up from the script, apparently catching the eye of somebody behind the camera; then continued:

"On the twenty-third of July 2008 I murdered a man in Fuerteventura. I buried him in the sand dunes on the edge of Corralejo. I don't know his name. In December 2008, I attacked and raped the man's widow, in her home, in Corralejo. She was called Adora, I think."

He continued to look down at the desk.

"On the twenty-third of July 2010, I killed a man in Blackpool. He was a Spaniard, but I don't know his name."

Dawn looked at Dave, with a raised eyebrow, muttering:

"We don't know anything about this one."

Lee Dann continued:

"In October 2010, round about the twenty-fifth, I attacked and raped his partner, in Blackpool. Her name was Sascha."

He paused, and cleared his throat.

"On July twenty-third 2011, I killed a man called Luca Mendez, in Fuerteventura. I attacked him at his boat, and drowned him near El Cotillo. In December 2011 I went back, and attacked his widow. I don't remember her name."

He lifted his left arm; showing, for the first time, that it was free, and rustled the paper. It became clear that there was more than a single sheet.

"On July twenty-third 2012, I drowned a man in Gouthwaite reservoir, North Yorkshire. His name was Tom. I went back and attacked ... raped his wife... partner, Maria, in December 2012."

He sighed, as if weary of reading, but continued:

"In 2013, I killed a man in Lanzarote. He was a coach driver. I went back at Christmas, and raped his wife. Then in July 2014 I murdered Vito Navarro, and later raped Mariana Navarro, on May twenty-eighth 2015. On July twenty-third 2015 I abducted and murdered a Spaniard from Rochdale. I dumped his body in a lake in Cumbria. I raped his wife later; in January this year."

335

Lee paused, and coughed. If a glass of water had been there in front of him, he would have taken a sip. But there was no water. He took a deep breath, and carried on:

"On July twenty-third this year, I murdered a Spaniard called Gabriel Tevitez, living in Lymm, Cheshire. I disposed of his body in a lake in Cumbria. I cannot continue to do these things."

He put down the paper, and looked directly into the camera, dropping his left arm back to his side. Then, as if continuing spontaneously, without any notes, he went on. This time, he seemed to be talking to one particular person:

"I'm sorry Sam. I can't go on like this. You don't know what he did to me, my step-father. He abused me for his own entertainment, every week, for years. And especially every twenty-third of July. He always threatened what he'd do to my little sister if I didn't let him... His 'birthday fun', he called it. And my mum knew about it, and did nothing. Nothing!"

He almost spat out the final word. Lee had reached, and passed, that point where it was clear whether he was reading what he had been told to read, or speaking from the heart. Then, as if composing himself, he lowered his voice, and went on:

"So, I'm going to join them. Cumbria is as good a place as any. Easier to get to than Fuerteventura."

There was a hint of dark humour in his voice, and a sinister glint in his eye; as he shot an involuntary peek to the left of the camera, where there might be someone else in the room. Looking immediately back into the lens, he went on:

"I've got pretty good at burying bodies. Now is my time."

There was, for the first time, the sign of a tear in his eye. It trickled down his cheek, and he brushed at it with his left hand.

"By the time you get this, I'll be dead. I'm sorry, Sam. I'm sorry, Lucy. Better that you never find me. The Lake District is a big place. This is the right way to go."

He thumbed at the papers on the desk, looked at the camera for a final time, and the screen went blank.

"Phew!!!" Dave exclaimed. "What do you make of that?"

Dawn was still looking at the screen. She flicked it off, and called DI Williams, as instructed.

"We've watched it, Boss. What now?"

Williams' voice was sombre:

"Where's Shelly?"

Dawn had no ready answer; but, she was puzzled, too.

"I don't know. I've tried to reach her, but…"

"So have I." Snapped Williams. "Not for the first time, in the last few days. Her phone is off. Why would she turn her phone off at a time like this?"

Without waiting for a reply, he went on:

"You saw her leave Meredith's, but she didn't come back to you, there. So, she can only have taken the other direction, and headed away from you. Why would she do that?"

He was thinking aloud, but would have been glad of any suggested answers. There was a silence. Then:

"Send Dave to drive the route, see if there's any sign of Shelly."

Hearing the order, Dave got up, and went out immediately.

"Do you want me to tell Meredith about the video?" Dawn changed the subject. "And, does this mean she's safe now?"

Williams was deep in thought.

"We can't assume she's safe; but, now we know who we're looking for, she's much safer than she was. He seems unhinged… he as good as said he's going to kill himself; but, we can't take anything at face value."

337

Dawn was thinking it all through:

"And, we need to stop him. Arrest him. Wherever he is."

Williams ignored her comment:

"Does Shelly know something we don't, Dawn? Is it possible that she's on to him, and trying to catch him, herself?"

Although she didn't want to admit it, this was a thought that had already occurred to Dawn.

"I can't see it, Boss."

Williams went on:

"Or, has he twigged that we are on to him, because of something Shelly has done; and this is why he's aborted any attack on Meredith?"

When Dave returned, without having seen any sign of Shelly, DI Williams instructed Dawn to go check Shelly's home address. It was getting late, now; and Dawn would check at her address before going home for the night.

Just before she left, Meredith called, on the video messenger.

"Hi, Dawn. No news? Nothing happening here."

Meredith looked relaxed, and casual, in her dressing gown.

DI Williams had authorised Dawn to pass on the news of the video that had arrived. She outlined the basics: that Lee Dann had been filmed making a full confession to multiple offences. Although unlikely to carry much weight in court, if he should ever submit a plea of 'not guilty'; it was certainly confirmation of what the police had come to suspect. She didn't mention the additional murder and rape, committed in Blackpool; of which the police previously had no knowledge.

"So, he's decided to run for it, then? Avoid capture?"

"It looks that way. But, we'll keep surveillance on your house, for now. Hopefully we'll pick him up, soon."

Dawn made sure not to mention anything of the puzzling absence of Shelly. Having already confirmed that she had left *Freelands*, and not said anything about where she was going, there was no need to concern Meredith any further.

Meredith appeared to give a sigh of relief:

"So, if he was planning to come for me, he's had a change of heart. Are you thinking he's gone up to the Lakes, then? To do away with himself?"

Dawn hadn't realised that she'd given quite so much away.

"It's certainly possible. We'll be looking out for him. We don't want him disappearing on us. He certainly can't go back home – we've got that covered. Now that we know who he is, we are going to bring him in, one way or another."

Chapter 56

The next day was Thursday the twentieth of October, and Alice Hawley was dispatched to staff the surveillance point at Crawley's. The rest of the team were in the office, for a meeting to review the position, and decide what to do next.

Alice had plenty of time to read the log, review all the recent camera footage as often as she liked, and generally muse about what might have become of Lee Dann. And Shelly. She played back the surveillance tapes of Shelly arriving at Meredith's, going inside. She could see that Shelly stepped back and seemed to look up at a window, before entering *Freelands*. But, this wasn't any great puzzle. She had just been waiting for Meredith to come and answer the door, probably.

In the office, Williams was grim-faced, as he faced his team, with DCI Floella York looking on.

"You called at Shelly's last night, Dawn?"

Dawn nodded:

"It was after ten. The place was in darkness; no sign of her. Her phone's been off since yesterday. I knocked on at her neighbour's; he hasn't seen anything of her."

"What about her car?" Pitched in Dave.

"No sightings of that?"

Graeme shook his head; he had been checking every traffic camera and ANPR point that he could find.

"Nothing."

DI Williams summarised the point that they all knew:

"Her last known movements were to go to Meredith's house yesterday evening; then, leave about half an hour later. We know she left; we saw her come out of the house, on her own, and drive away."

Dawn contributed:

"We assumed she would simply come back to Crawley's. But, after a few minutes, when she didn't turn up, we started to wonder where she'd gone. Dave went out to look for her, but there was no sign of her. So, we have to conclude that she took the lane in the other direction. Why? We don't know."

DCI York stood up:

"Okay. We have to face the possibility that Shelly's disappearance has something to do with Lee Dann. Could Lee Dann have abducted her? Or, and we can't rule this out: has Shelly abducted Lee Dann?"

There was a collective gasp in the room. York looked at Williams; who was perched on the edge of a desk. In a quiet voice, he addressed his team:

"In recent days, there have been a number of occasions when we've tried to reach Shelly, and her phone has been off. And at least one time when she's gone AWOL, only briefly. We just put it down to chance; thought nothing of it. But, she has also voiced an opinion. One that I had to pull her up on. She said that prison was too good for Lee Dann. Maybe just a chance remark; putting into words the sort of thing any of us might feel, when we know what damage he's inflicted on people. But... it's made me wonder."

There was a stony silence. Finally, Frank spoke:

"On the video confession, there's almost surely somebody else in the room with him."

Williams nodded.

"Somebody. No way of knowing who. But, what if it was Shelly? Has she captured him? Has she decided that she doesn't want him to grow old in a prison? Perhaps she has other plans for him."

Dawn tutted:

"Shelly's a good cop. She wouldn't do anything like that."

Williams turned to face her.

341

"I think that, too, Dawn. I want to believe it. Bottom line: we need to find Shelly, and we need to find Lee Dann. There's an APB out on both of them. Let's hope we find them both before this gets any worse."

The team sat, lost for words, feeling helpless. They wanted to race to the Lake District, and find Lee Dann... along with Shelly, if she was with him. But, the Lake District is a big place; they wouldn't know where to even start.

"Why now?" Asked Frank.

"Why would he stop on his mission now? Something's caused him to stop."

Dave Perryman was equally puzzled:

"And, so close to Meredith. His car was nearby. He must have been coming for Meredith. So, why stop now? Why not round this off with Meredith?"

Dave blushed slightly; realising that he sounded callous.

"I mean, he's so organised, got so much self-control that he can wait twelve months between strikes... he's not the impulsive type."

Chapter 57

Inside *Freelands*, Shelly squirmed with discomfort, in the chair to which she was fastened. She had no idea of how long she had been there; the artificial light inside the panic room was timeless, betraying neither day nor night. Her legs were sore, and her wrists raw from the effort of trying to wriggle from her bonds. She needed the bathroom.

Looking across, she saw that Lee was simply looking back at her. He gave a half smile:

"A great leveller, this." He said.

"A cop and a killer. Which of us is better off? Who's going to have the better end?"

Shelly was about to retort that he had picked on the wrong woman this time; but, instead, bit her tongue and ignored his comment. Just at that moment, a click and a hiss announced that they had company. The door slid open, and Meredith entered the room. She was dressed in combat gear.

"All right?" She asked, looking at Shelly.

Shelly grimaced.

"I need the bathroom."

"Ah." Meredith frowned. "Not much privacy, here, I'm afraid. Okay."

She stepped behind Shelly, and began to untie her legs. Shelly's wrists had been tied to the chair. But, deftly, she released one, then the other; almost as quickly fastening them together, behind her back. She tested the knots; giving a tug, to make sure that they were secure.

"Get up."

Shelly tried to stand. At first, her legs buckled under her, and she dropped back to the chair. At the second attempt, she managed to stand up. With Meredith behind her, she was guided towards the door, and ushered out, onto the landing. Meredith paused to close the door behind them, locking Lee inside. Then, they walked a few metres along the landing. The second door that they came to was a bathroom; and Meredith pushed her gently inside, following her in. There was a faint light coming in from the window; and Shelly deduced that it was early morning, perhaps sometime after seven.

Glad of the chance to speak to Meredith without Lee there, Shelly didn't want to waste this opportunity.

"We can fix this, Meredith. We both know that I'm not your enemy. It's understandable that the pressure of all this got to you... stopped you thinking straight. We can take him in, together. You know it's the right thing to do."

Ignoring her, Meredith said:

"I'm going to untie your hands. But, don't even think of trying anything. I'm afraid I'm not going to leave you alone."

For the first time, Meredith pulled out a gun from her pocket. It was a heavy looking revolver; no doubt army issue, thought Shelly, as she trembled to see it point in her direction. She had flirted with firearms training; but never had a loaded gun pointed directly at her. Not in the real world.

Trying not to focus on the gun, Shelly attempted again to engage Meredith in some discussion; hoping to make her at least reconsider what she was doing. But, Meredith was deaf and blind to her pleas. As soon as Shelly had used the toilet, and washed her hands, Meredith tied them again, behind her back; and frog-marched her back towards the safe room.

Just as she pressed the control, to open the door; Mariana appeared.

"Oh!" She exclaimed; seeing Shelly, dishevelled, and with her hands tied, and Meredith, dressed as a soldier in action.

"Mariana! Are you okay?" Gasped Shelly.

Before Mariana could respond, a second figure appeared. It was the figure of a little girl, behind her, wearing pyjamas. Pink, orange, adorned with princesses and ponies.

"Izzy!"

Shelly did her best to offer a smile; not easy as she was being shoved forward to return to her prison cell, aware that a gun was in Meredith's pocket.

"Go wait in the bedroom, darling." Mariana told her daughter, in a hushed tone; following the women into the safe room.

Meredith was about to lock the door; but paused, as she could see Mariana's backward glance to check that Izzy had returned to the bedroom.

"Are you ready to help me Mariana?"

Meredith smiled at her.

"Probably best to get this over with. The pit's been dug out ready for my pond, and the heavy moulded base will be coming in the next couple of days. The ground's soft, after this rain. It won't be too difficult to get them buried and out of sight, before the pond goes in. Don't worry, I'll do the digging. You'll be back home safe with Izzy by lunchtime."

Mariana shuddered, as Meredith sat Shelly back down at the chair, and secured her wrists, as before.

She continued:

"You know I did this for you, Mariana. You and Vito. And those other poor women."

She paused.

"And the men, of course." She added; an afterthought that suggested she regarded the men as less important than the women.

Meredith produced the gun from her pocket, and held it in her right hand. With her other hand, she pressed the control which closed the door of the room. The sound-proofing would contain the noise of the shots, keeping them away from Izzy's ears.

Mariana looked at the gun, in horror; but tried not to let Meredith see how alienated she had become from this 'mission'. Meredith's mission of justice... or retribution.

Steeling herself, drawing on reserves of courage that she didn't know she possessed; Shelly addressed Meredith, calmly:

"Mariana has nothing to do with this, Meredith. Mariana's a good woman. She respects the law. She's a victim, remember? She's not going to take the law into her own hands. This isn't the army, Meredith. This isn't the law of the jungle..."

Meredith's eyes seemed to glaze over, as she ignored Shelly's words, and stepped over to Lee Dann. He was still sat, slumped, exhausted, the beaten relic of a man. There was no life in his eyes. No hope; no expectation of mercy. Simply waiting for his fate to be confirmed.

Meredith hadn't even heard Shelly's words. She looked down on her helpless prisoner, like a cat that has trapped an injured mouse, and cowers over it; smelling the terror as it waits for its life to be extinguished. Hoping not for life, but for a swift death.

Chapter 58

At Crawley's, Alice looked up, as a car drew up outside. Dawn and Dave had arrived; after calling again at Shelly's flat, and drawing a blank. This time, they had forced entry, and checked around inside. They had found nothing out of the ordinary. Nothing that would suggest Shelly had been planning to be anywhere other than home.

They stepped into Crawley's, and Alice resumed looking at her screen. She was playing back footage of the last few days, and had a puzzled expression.

"Dawn, are you sure these are all live feeds? They couldn't have defaulted to still shots, could they?"

"What do you mean?"

Dawn and Dave crowded round the screen.

"Well, look at this."

Alice brought up a shot of the garden, from a few days ago, which flicked from one camera angle to another, then back again.

"What do you see?"

Dawn looked blank.

Dave said:

"The lighting."

"Yep. It seems to go light on the middle shot, from the camera on the garage, then darker again on the final angle. Like the middle one could be a still shot from a little earlier, before it was getting dark."

Dawn exclaimed:

"Alice – bring up that section where we see Shelly leaving Meredith's last night."

After a few moments, Alice had located it, and played it back.

Dave looked on, wanting to see something obvious about the light. Was it darker on screen than it should have been, or lighter?

"I'm not seeing anything…"

"Christ!" Suddenly shouted Dawn.

"The jacket! We recognised her by the jacket. But…"

She turned, and pointed to a chair in the corner:

"She left it here!"

Slung over the chair, almost covered by another coat, was Shelly's familiar white jacket. She had left it behind when leaving Crawley's to call round at Meredith's, and it had lain there ever since.

"Oh shit!" Exclaimed Dave. "Meredith's played us a previous recording. Shelly never left the house!"

"Played us!" Echoed Dawn. "You can say that again."

Within seconds, she was on the phone to the boss, as the pieces started to fall into place. All those strange behaviours of Meredith's, the unaccountable trips, the game-playing with the surveillance team, were starting to take on a new meaning.

"We've got to get round there!" Dave shouted, rushing out to his car.

"Stay here, Alice." Instructed Dawn, rushing after him.

As Dave drove, leaving a cloud of dust behind him in a squeal of tyres and with the engine roaring; Dawn began to realise something else.

"The video – the confession – I think I've spotted something else… Oh, God!"

"What?"

Dave kept his eyes on the road, as they raced past a quiet driveway from which a car was emerging; causing one of Meredith's neighbours to brake sharply to avoid a crash.

"The room where it's filmed... there's a dark curtain behind him. I'm sure I've seen a curtain like that... blue, turquoise, in Meredith's"

"Oh, great!"

Meredith, in Dawn's mind, had suddenly become a whole new person. One by one, the puzzles began to offer potential solutions. Dawn barely had time to convey her thoughts to the office, before they arrived at *Freelands*; and Dave screeched to a halt on the drive, scattering gravel far and wide.

"Armed response are on their way. Wait until they get there." Instructed DI Williams.

"Fuck that!" Muttered Dave, as he leapt out of the driver's door, and rushed around the other side of the car, towards the front door.

Dawn had the edge on him, getting out of the passenger side, and managed to grab his arm, before he could bang at the front door.

"Wait!"

She pointed up at a window, on the first floor. The face of a frightened little girl was looking out.

"Oh, Christ!" Dave exclaimed.

Staying calm, Dawn smiled up at the child; whom, to her shock, she immediately recognised as Izzy Navarro. With a combination of hand gestures, she beckoned to Izzy to come down, and open the door. To her relief, and hoping that the little girl would come down and open up, Izzy disappeared from the window.

Dave and Dawn waited, impatiently.

Dave muttered:

"We've got to get in. Shelly's in danger here, I know it!"

349

He was just about to throw himself at the door, to demand the Meredith let them in, when a quiet sound announced that there was somebody coming. There was a click, and the sound of a bolt scraping back. Then, the door opened, revealing the tiny figure of Izzy, still in her pyjamas.

Close up, she looked even more scared, and tearful.

"Where's your mummy?" Asked Dawn, stooping to give the little girl a hug.

"They're upstairs. That woman has got them all upstairs."

"Who else is there?" Asked Dawn, trying hard to remain calm, so as not to frighten the child any more.

"The lady who lives here. And there's another lady. And a man."

Dave pushed past Dawn, and made for the stairs.

"Careful, Dave." Whispered Dawn, as she followed him. "Meredith could be armed."

Dawn paused to look back at Izzy. They couldn't just leave her there. She would probably be safer out of the house. But, for all Dawn knew, Meredith could, by now, have gone outside *via* some other route. So, she made a quick decision to keep her inside.

"Come with me."

She ushered Izzy towards the stairs; as Dave looked back. He realised that, in a house of this size, they needed Izzy to help guide them to where Shelly, and the others, would be found.

As if understanding what was needed, the girl suddenly sprang forward, and began to run up the stairs; her little legs almost sprinting, as she passed Dave.

At the top, and without a sound, she pointed at a door, which was open.

Then, in a whisper:

"They're in there."

"Wait here, sweetheart."

Dawn pulled her to one side; and, looking into what appeared to be an empty bedroom, gently drew her inside. Putting her fingers to her lips, with a gesture that told Izzy to remain as quiet as possible, she half closed the bedroom door, and followed Dave to the open door that Izzy had indicated.

There was no sound coming from inside. Dawn saw the logo on the door, which told her that this was the study; and realised that, inside here, was the safe room. She remembered Shelly telling her about the sound-proofing, that she had reluctantly helped Meredith to test; and whispered to explain it to Dave.

He nodded, and peered round the study door. Sure enough, a second door was visible, inside. Shiny, on runners, and with a red light illuminated on a panel on the outside. On the study desk was a computer, lit up with a dashboard, that presumably contained the sequence of controls that would open the secure door.

Dawn and Dave looked at each other; unsure what to do next. They needed to keep the element of surprise; even if they could open the door, they didn't want to be confronted by Meredith, who might be armed. Suddenly, they both looked round in surprise, as Izzy appeared, and rushed over to the desk. Before they could stop her, she pressed a button on the control unit, and said:

"It's this one."

Chapter 59

Inside the safe room, Shelly and Mariana looked on, as Meredith placed her gun on the floor, close to Lee Dann's foot. He couldn't have reached it, to grab, or kick away, even if he wanted to. His feet were still securely shackled, as he knew only too well. She had placed it there just to torment him; to let him think about what he might like to do with the weapon if he could get his hands on it.

She sat down, and pulled her chair up close in front of him. She raised her nose in the air and sniffed; breathing in the stench of the unwashed, battered, soiled prisoner.

"You probably recognise that smell, ladies. That's fear. Or, perhaps you don't."

She leaned into his face, and, to the surprise of the others, muttered something, in a foreign language. Meredith's reality, as earlier, was becoming confused; as memories of the horrors that she had experienced in Afghanistan flooded back to her again. She drew back from him, with her head cocked to one side, as if waiting for a response. He looked at her, blankly.

"Well?" She demanded.

She spoke again in the foreign language, with a slightly raised voice, this time. He was unable to answer, because he couldn't understand; not even recognising the language. It was Pashto, a language of Afghanistan.

"They're all the same." She muttered, glancing round at Mariana. "They deserve to die."

She picked up the gun from the floor, and examined it.

"No!" Barked Shelly. "Don't do it, Meredith. You've scared him enough. Up to now all you've done is..."

She thought for a moment.

352

"False imprisonment. We can get you out of this. You're a hero. You caught him, when we couldn't. He picked on the wrong... the wrong soldier."

Meredith replied without taking her eyes off Lee.

"He has to die. I'd never be able to look my father in the eye again, if I didn't pay this family's dues."

Meredith raised the gun, with very slow deliberation, and pointed it at Lee Dann's head; slowly bringing it forward until it touched his temple.

"Let me!" Suddenly shrieked Mariana. "You promised me that I could do it, for Vito."

Meredith turned, and the fiercely grim expression on her face melted to something akin to a smile. A sickly, satisfied, smirk; that told Lee Dann she had won.

She drew away the gun, and passed it to Mariana; whose trembling fingers closed around it.

Shelly watched in horror, strapped to her chair. She had no way of knowing whether Mariana was actually about to do the deed; or whether this was a pretence, to take away the gun from Meredith's deranged hand.

Unable to intervene, and barely able to yell her final protest, Shelly gasped:

"No, Mariana. Don't do it!"

At that second, the click and hiss announced the opening of the door, and Dave Perryman's desperate countenance appeared, with Dawn a fraction behind him.

What met them was the sight of Mariana Navarro, gun in hand; while two captives were strapped to their chairs. Dave knew who they both were, but had no time to process the situation of either. He saw a soldier in combat gear, which he subsequently recognised as Meredith; squatting down, facing the man. Without a thought for his safety, Dave lunged at Mariana, to grab the gun. Simultaneously, Meredith sprang up, and tried, too, to snatch the gun from Mariana's grasp.

353

"No!" Screamed Shelly.

Mariana, pitched backwards by the momentum of two aggressors pouncing on her, crashed back against the wall.

Crack!

The ear-splitting sound of the gun echoed around the room, as it went off, out of Mariana's control, and was jerked from her hand by the shock of the firing. It bounced on the table, before crashing to the floor.

Lee Dann watched, immobile, helpless.

"Get the gun!" Screamed Shelly, seeing Dawn rush into the room.

Quick to react in the panic, Meredith dived across, over the desk; trying to grab at the gun, where it had come to rest on the ground.

Before she could get a proper grip on it, a thick wooden stick, the same one that she had used to beat Lee Dann with, came crashing down across the side of her head, and knocked her to the ground.

She groaned, as Dawn stood over her, gripping the weapon, ready to strike again, if necessary.

"The gun!" Wheezed Shelly.

"I've got it. Are you alright?"

Dawn jumped around the desk, and put an arm round Shelly.

She looked around at Mariana, as yet unsure whether she was a threat.

"Dave, make sure she doesn't go anywhere."

She looked back, and down.

"Dave? Oh, my God!"

Dave was lying awkwardly in the floor. His eyes were open, staring into the middle distance. Unblinking. Blood was trickling from the side of his head. He was still.

354

"Get me free!" Shelly begged.

Dawn, with one eye on Meredith, who was dazed, and wasn't ready for any further challenge just yet, knelt to take Dave's head in her lap.

"Dave? Dave, can you hear me?" She asked, weakly.

She knew the answer.

Bravely holding back tears, she softly placed his head to the floor, closed his eyes, and turned to release Shelly.

"Mariana, you stay there."

Dawn hadn't yet had chance to decide quite whose side Mariana was on. She'd had the gun in her hand, but...

A small voice came through the open door, followed by a small child.

"Mummy!"

Izzy rushed in, and threw herself into a hug. Mariana knelt with her, putting both arms round her daughter; smothering the throbbing tears that had started to flow.

"It's alright, darling. Everything's alright."

Within minutes, backup had arrived. Armed officers, too late to make any difference, swarmed over the property.

By the time DI Williams reached *Freelands*, Meredith had been escorted to a van, with her arms cuffed behind her back. Wrapped in a sheet, Lee Dann had finally been released from the heavy bonds, and was being put into another van, flanked by two officers. Mariana Navarro, with Izzy, was being detained in the back of a police car. A young WPC stood over them, to make sure they weren't about to leave.

Parked next to the garage, an ambulance, with lights flashing, and the back doors open, was being approached by two paramedics. They were pushing a trolley, which bore a body; completely covered and zipped up.

Shelly, with a blanket wrapped around to keep her warm, was sat sideways in the passenger seat of Dave's car, with the door open. Dawn was squatting next to her, with one hand on her shoulder.

DI Williams gave a heavy sigh, as he looked over the scene of desolation. He hurried over to Shelly and Dawn, and looked from one to the other.

"Are either of you injured?"

"No, Boss." Dawn shook her head. "But Shelly needs checking over. She's been through a lot."

Williams nodded, with a look at Shelly.

"You need to get to hospital."

Chapter 60

Twelve days later, a double line of officers formed a guard of honour, at a cemetery on the outskirts of Manchester. The Chief Constable, two local MPs, and the Mayor of Greater Manchester, all brought their presence to emphasise the gravitas of the occasion.

Stood together for mutual comfort and consolation, the team looked on; their eyes smarting in the biting rain on a cold and unforgiving day. Dawn stood next to Graeme French. At one point, she put a tissue to her eye. He squeezed her hand. Alice and Frank stood to attention next to them, with their colleagues, Tom, Carol, and Shirley close by. At the end of the line, DI Williams and Dr Sheen looked grimly forward, with DCI York just behind. In the second row, Shelly stood; her eyes glazed. Next to her, paying respects on behalf of their Spanish colleagues, Millie Rodriguez had made the journey. Opposite them, Dave's parents, flanked by the rest of his family and many friends, looked on. Occasional sniffs, sobs, and trembling shoulders, reinforced the gravity of the occasion.

The minister, an old man who had dispatched more than his fair share of good men and women; concluded his brief and traditional address. He invited the mourners to step forward, as the coffin was being lowered into its final resting place.

Taking a little earth from the box that was offered, one by one they scattered a few grains on top of the coffin as it descended to its full depth.

"Bye, Dave." Mouthed Shelly, as she took her turn.

Millie held her hand, as they stood towards the back of the crowd; watching the assembled gathering gradually start to fade away, back to their cars.

DI Williams appeared:

"Thank you, Officer Rodriguez. We appreciated your help. And, thank you for coming, today. It means a lot."

Millie nodded; swallowed hard, and blinked back a tear.

357

"Sir."

The rain had stopped. In the thinning crowd, Shelly suddenly spotted a face that she recognised. She murmured to Millie:

"I'll just be a moment."

Shelly walked across to where a woman was stood, with her face almost covered by a dark shawl.

"Mariana."

"Hello, Shelly."

"Thank you for coming."

Mariana looked uncomfortable, and shifted from one foot to the other.

"I didn't know whether I would be welcome."

Shelly knew to what she was referring. There had been some lengthy and heated discussions about that fateful moment when Mariana had taken the gun from Meredith's hand.

Of Meredith's intentions, there had been little doubt in Shelly's mind. For reasons best known to herself, perhaps suffering from PTSD, perhaps damaged by some other trauma from her past; she had made it her mission to capture and destroy the man who had invaded her life, taken away her man. Meredith was in custody, and would in due course be charged with multiple offences. She might not be given a life sentence, as Lee Dann would no doubt receive. But, she had committed a serious crime, and shown intent to do far worse.

No, Mariana's actions were open to question. Within the safe room, immediately prior to the entrance of Dave and Dawn; there were three possible witnesses to how Mariana had come to take hold of that gun. Two witnesses were Lee and Meredith. Therefore, the only one whose evidence was credible was Shelly. It had fallen to Shelly, therefore, to describe the moment when possession of the gun had passed from Meredith to Mariana.

Shelly had played over and over again in her mind the scenario. Lee Dann had been about to be shot between the eyes by Meredith. His life had, ultimately, been saved by the passing of that weapon out of Meredith's hands. What Mariana would have done if she hadn't been interrupted, nobody could say. But, in her report, Shelly had given her the benefit of the doubt. She had made the judgement that Mariana had accepted the gun so that Meredith wouldn't shoot him.

Was she right?

"I think you saved a man's life." Said Shelly, looking her in the eye.

Mariana looked to the ground.

"But it cost another man's life, didn't it? A good man. Maybe I should have just let her shoot him."

"No." Shelly shook her head. "You did the right thing. If she had shot Lee Dann, she would have probably..."

She tailed off, then:

"Probably shot me next."

Tears that Shelly had wanted to shed for twelve days finally started to flow, as she realised how close her life had come to being cut short. With a colleague dead, she hadn't permitted herself the luxury of such a selfish indulgence. She was still here. Dave was gone.

This time, it was Mariana's turn to console her, which she did; with an arm around her. She drew Shelly in, giving her a hug.

With Vito in her mind, Mariana said comfortingly:

"Life goes on."

The mourners had mostly dispersed, and Millie approached them. Shelly drew away from Mariana, wiping her eyes.

"Goodbye, Mariana. Take care. And, thanks."

She slipped her arm through Millie's; and, as the rain began to fall again, they walked away.

A message from the author...

Thank you for reading this story – I hope you enjoyed it. I would be very grateful for any feedback that you would like to give, so please submit it to wherever you obtained this book. I'd love to hear it.

My next book is in progress, and should be released early in 2019. That will also focus on the beautiful island of Fuerteventura; as it's the place I love to be. If you've never visited the island, you really should try to do so. If you already live there, or visit on holiday, maybe one day we'll meet up.

Take care, and thanks again for reading my book.

Kind regards,

Stevie Shaw

August 2018

Printed in Great Britain
by Amazon